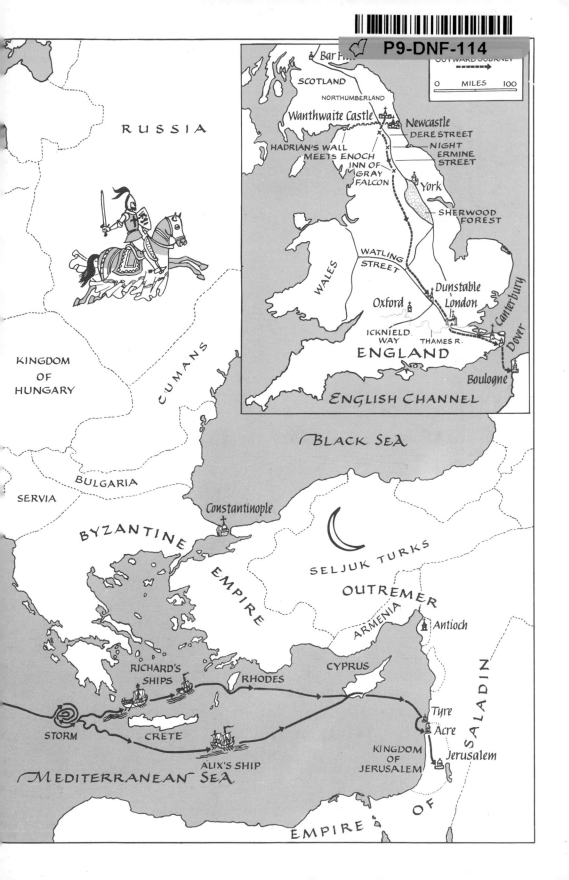

P9-DNF-114

OUTWARD JOURNEY

0   MILES   100

Bar Hill
SCOTLAND
NORTHUMBERLAND
Wanthwaite Castle
Newcastle
DERE STREET
NIGHT
ERMINE
STREET
HADRIAN'S WALL
MEETS ENOCH
INN OF
GRAY
FALCON
York
SHERWOOD
FOREST
WALES
WATLING
STREET
Dunstable
London
Oxford
Canterbury
Dover
ICKNIELD
WAY
THAMES R.
ENGLAND
Boulogne
ENGLISH CHANNEL

RUSSIA

KINGDOM
OF
HUNGARY

CUMANS

BULGARIA

SERVIA

BLACK SEA

Constantinople

BYZANTINE

EMPIRE

SELJUK TURKS

OUTREMER

ARMENIA

Antioch

CYPRUS

RICHARD'S
SHIPS

RHODES

Tyre
Acre

STORM

CRETE

ALIX'S SHIP

KINGDOM
OF
JERUSALEM

Jerusalem

SALADIN

MEDITERRANEAN SEA

EMPIRE
OF

SHIELD OF THREE LIONS

SHIELD OF THREE LIONS

PAMELA KAUFMAN

CROWN PUBLISHERS, INC.
NEW YORK

TO CHARLIE

The age of gold returns,
The world's reform is nigh;
The rich man now made low,
The pauper raised on high!

TWELFTH-CENTURY SONG

∴. . the man fulfilled vows made
when he was a girl.

OVID

1

CLATTERING RUMBLE SHATTERED MY SLEEP.

My pet wolf growled and I opened my eyes. *Benedicite*, dim stars still hung in the blue; owls hooted high in the oak. Tomorrow I would have to rise at this hour, but this morning let me sleep. I pulled my fur pelt over my head.

But the rumble persisted, closer this time, a heavy scaled dragon moving in fits and starts, echoing like rocks rolling on the moat bridge. Then I heard the crack of whips, angry shouts. When the ominous din seemed almost within my chamber, I threw off the pelt and rushed to my window.

Deus juva me!

Under the flickering orange flares of pine torches, half-clad sweating men whipped and cursed my father's best team of oxen, urging them to scrape our ancient catapult across the court on its rusted belly, the wheels having long since rotted away. Perplexed and frightened together, I watched until I saw my father come from behind. Quickly I slipped my chemise over my naked body and hurried to ask what all this might mean.

Followed by my wolf Lance, I ran barefoot down the stairs into the animal chamber where I slowed my pace to pick my way carefully across the soaked and besmottered rushes piled with night leavings, especially from our new litter of pointer pups. Our mastiff Courage almost knocked me off balance with his toothless greeting while the badger and weasel scurried under a bench and my mother's gaudy parrots screeched raucously. I continued to the courtyard.

There I stopped. The few shouting men had swollen in number in the brief period it had taken me to arrive, many of them huge, threatening knights mounted on snorting, pacing, wild-eyed war chargers. All were strangers, their greetings shouted in Saxon. Awed, I pulled Lance close against the arch and tried to see my father through the steaming breath and swaying horse bellies.

Instead, on the far side of the court, I glimpsed my mother Catherine as she scurried furtively along the wall on her way to chapel.

"Mother!" I called. "Wait!"

She couldn't hear, and I watched her enter the door where Father Michael stood. I was so intent upon her that I failed to see a broadsword which lifted one of my braids when a careless knight turned. *Deus juva me*, it could have been my eyes! I decided to go to the kitchen court where I would be safe. There I would ask Dame Margery what was happening, for she would know and she would talk.

As I sidled along the wall, I came upon our steward, John Leggy. Never had I seen him so distraught, his hair hanging in dank ropes, his eyes red-veined.

"Good morrow, John. Have you seen my father?"

He clutched my elbow hard. "Mercy on us, Lady Alix, how did you come here? Get back to your chamber at once."

"But I want to speak to my father . . ."

Abruptly he left me to answer a call from our horse keeper.

After a slow, cautious advance along the wall, I finally entered the gate to the kitchen court and paused in relief. Dame Margery and Maisry were stirring a large pot of stew over the firepit and didn't see me. I noted that Maisry now seemed more a woman than her own mother, for the wench's breasts strained against her brown homespun like ripe quinces, whereas Margery's dried cuds dangled near to her waist. Yet the dame had once been full, had fed both Maisry and me when we were babes, making us milk sisters. And I, eleven years old to the day same as Maisry, had the hollow chest-spoon of an eight-year-old boy, even though I drank gillyflower juice every night of my life. Maisry claimed archly that I wouldn't mature till I "became a woman in another way" but no amount of coaxing would make her say what that "way" might be. 'Twas all most mysterious.

I shouted above the din, "God's blessings, Dame Margery!"

She raised a worried face. "Alix, ye've no call to be out with all these soldiers. Go back at once before I rattle yer teeth."

"At least I have teeth to rattle," I replied, stung. "I must see my father."

Maisry smiled, her squirrel-eyes bright. "I believe Lord William is in the park. Leastways I saw him pass in that direction."

"And needs no pestering from his spoiled darling," Dame Margery continued. "Go to, My Lady. Lady Catherine will be worried."

"My mother sent me to find him," I lied. "She wants to know why these knights are assembled."

"I can tell ye well enow," the dame said darkly. "The Scots are coming."

"Scots!" I frowned uneasily. "Surely you're confused. My own father captured the Scottish king at Alnwick and there's been no trouble since."

Margery's eyes glittered and her nose turned bright red. "Confused, am I? When I seen many of these same knights here afore? Aye, much good did they do then, for my own sister Annie were marched away naked in the snow on the tenth of December 1174, fifteen long years ago and ne'er seen from that day to this, poor lass, and Scots swaling and murdering till blood soaked the swaths. It's the same feel in the air today. If not the Scots, then who?" She blew her nose on her stained apron.

Maisry and I stood dumb as dolls, unable to say who might want to attack Wanthwaite Castle, though soothly the Scots seemed part of a tale long past.

"I s'pose that means we can't see the pilgrimage either," Maisry said, crestfallen. "Archie Werwillie were here last night, Alix, and I wish ye could have heard him. They're going to show an Afercan snake big as a horse at the fair."

"*Deus juva me*, whatever for?"

"To tempt Adam and Eve in the play at the church."

We stared at one another, entranced by the wonders which lay ahead.

"Ye can forget about snakes, lessen they be Scots," Margery babbled, near to hysteria, I trowe. "Now get ye gone to yer chamber, Alix, and put on yer tunic and shoes when ye get there."

"I'll ask my father at dinner about the knights," I said haughtily.

"Do ask about the pilgrimage as well," Maisry entreated. "'Tis only a half day, and he did promise."

A nudge from Margery's wooden paddle stopped her, and I pulled Lance by his scruff to return to the courtyard. By now the sun was out full and our motte was milling with knights, more clopping over the bridge every moment. Aye, 'twas passing strange. Only last week Maisry and I had ridden the casting cradle of the old catapult, pretending it was a monster off the firth. Only yesterday my mother and I had raced barefoot across our empty court and leaped the privet hedge into the garden.

Yet I couldn't believe that the Scots were coming. Fiends and barbarians they might be, but they wouldn't ride without a king, so says my father who is never wrong.

IN THE DINING SALLE, my mother was almost hidden by a giant bouquet of geroldinga apple blossoms she held in her arms.

"Mary Alix, why weren't you at Mass, naughty wench?" she called from behind the trestle set for our meal. "Come, let's arrange these to make our table pretty for your father's last dinner."

I took an armful of branches. "Where's he going?"

She didn't answer.

"You said my father's last dinner. Is he riding forth?"

Her face turned pale against her low-cut ruby tunic. "I didn't mean last." Hastily she crossed herself. "That is, he's going to Tomlinson Manor but should be back by sundown."

I moved to the far end of the trestle, not knowing where to place the delicate blooms, and in so doing tripped over my new pointed shoes.

"Careful!" my father called from the door and I was swooped up from behind as blossoms fell in a shower. "That's what comes of wearing horse troughs on your feet. To get down, you must cry *mercy!*"

He tickled my ribs and I bent double with laughter.

"What about here?"

He touched my hipbone and I screamed, "Mercy! Mercy!"

"Still my silly Tickle-Bones, I'm relieved to see." He smiled, his tanned face so close that I could see the mix of gold and red hairs in his crescent waves, discern light and gray triangles like silver and pewter in his eyes, touch his high arched brow by leaning my forehead forward and breathe deeply of the sweet woodruff he wears on his skin. "Kiss me in our secret way."

I pressed my lips to his forehead, each cheek, chin and lips. Then he put me down.

My mother was on her hands and knees gathering the scattered blossoms.

"Leave them, Kate. They sweeten the rushes." He reached both hands to pull her upward and she leaned against him, her eyes glistening.

"Call the ewerer. I haven't much time." He kissed her, flicked a flower from her hair.

Mother summoned Joseph, our prayers were said and we began to dip our bread.

My father scanned my mother and me with bright gray eyes. "Am I under a spell, or do you both look especially beautiful today?"

I blushed, for indeed I had donned my new rose-colored tunic with a blue girtle, and braided cornflowers into my hair, the better to beguile him into letting Maisry and me go on the pilgrimage. I knew not my mother's purpose, but she, too, was dressed in her best scarlet finery and had woven gold threads in her dark flowing mane. However, she can never look anything but enchanting for she is a wild Celt, touched by magic.

"We always want to please you," my mother replied and pressed his hand.

"Besides, you're riding forth," I added boldly. "Are those knights going with you?"

He glanced at my mother who turned to feed the yammering pointer pups morsels of meat. "I'll take a few, but the greater number will stay here. Since you ask, please stay close to your mother and dress properly at all times. I believe I saw you this morning in most unseemly costume."

"Why are they here?" I asked, mortified at his reprimand but also resenting the presence which made me a prisoner in my own home.

"Tell her, Kate."

Mother raised her pale heart-shaped face and forced a false smile, which I can always tell is false because her dimples don't show. "Your father's called these men to guard us on a journey we're about to take, dear Alix. Finally you're going to see the country where I grew up, the magic circles, fells and hoary trees."

"*Benedicite!*" I clapped my hands in excitement. And Dame Margery thought the Scots were coming! Wait till she heard the truth. "When do we leave?"

"Day after tomorrow, after sundown. You'll ride at night," my father answered.

And my excitement diminished somewhat. How could we see fells and hoary trees in the dark? And why such a large guard?

"Is something amiss in your country?" I asked my mother straight out.

There was a long pause; then she deferred to my father.

"The west country is safe enough, but the road passes close to the border. Besides . . ." He looked again at my mother. ". . . We must protect you against abduction."

"Abduction! Who would want to abduct me?" I supposed it was a jape, though soothly I didn't think it very funny.

"Whoever covets Wanthwaite," my mother explained. "Now that you are of marriageable age, some landless knight could abduct you and gain your estate."

"Marriageable?"

She caught my rueful look downward to my flat chest and smiled, this time with dimples. "'Tis true that you're somewhat immature, but that will change. Your father's sisters both bloomed late and you seem closer to his family. Moreover, I was only twelve when I married your father."

They exchanged a long melting gaze of remembrance.

"And when you return," my father continued, "you, too, will be a bride and therefore safe."

I could hardly fathom his words. A simple journey had turned to a stealthy escape by night to avoid abductors and now changed again to a quest to get me married? I tried to absorb these rapid shifts.

"I'm not ready to marry, My Lord," I announced. "Nor do I care to journey if it be so perilous. I'll gladly stay here with you and my mother and spare you all this worry."

My mother raised wing-shaped brows. "Better to tell her, William."

He nodded curtly, rose from his bench and came to sit close to me. His eyes were crystal tunnels. "Alix, you're the usual mix of cleverness and silliness typical of your age, except that I claim you're cleverer than most. Therefore I'm going to confide in you. You already have a suitor, here, close to Wanthwaite, and we have refused his suit."

"Why?" I asked. "I would prefer someone close to you."

"At first we said he was too old—he's past sixty—and so he offered his foster son in his stead."

I gasped, much amazed. "Do they *both* love me?"

"They love Wanthwaite," my mother answered bitterly, her face lily-white, "and the older man is a raving madman."

"Kate!" my father warned.

"She has to know about the evil in the world sometime. Alix, heed me well, this suitor was married when he first proposed. Naturally we pointed out that this was an impediment to his suit, whereupon he murdered his wife and three children."

"No!" I cried.

"And impaled their heads on stakes outside his walls," she finished grimly.

I stared, aghast. "Why don't you tell our Lord Osbert of Northumberland? Let him punish the monster! At least then I wouldn't have to run away as if *I* were the criminal!"

'Twas a simple question and offered an easy solution. I couldn't understand the heavy silence that followed, nor my father's Viking look, as my mother calls it.

"Trust our judgment," he ordered. "Northumberland . . . can't help. You'll leave as planned."

I set my chin and thrust out my lip, but my mother tugged on my hair and I took her signal.

"For how long? Will I be home by autumn?"

Mother stroked my braids. "The journey is long, our purpose takes time. Even I do not expect to see Wanthwaite for two or three years."

"Two or three *years*! That's forever!" I pulled away. "Can Maisry come with me?"

"No one. We must keep the party small," my father replied.

Tears welled in my eyes. "But at least we can see the pilgrimage pass by tomorrow and the African snake."

"Pilgrimage? Snake?" He looked to my mother.

"Remember? You promised the lasses on their name day that they might see the next pilgrimage that passed through Dunsmere. They've set their hearts on one that rides close tomorrow."

My father tapped my chin tenderly. "Then unset your heart, Alix. You must stay inside, as I said. Do I have your word?"

"You *promised*!" I cried. "It's my last day with Maisry in my whole life!"

"Alix, that will be all. I'll not be crossed!" He rose and straightened the brown fustian he wears under his armor. "Kate, see to your daughter."

She, too, rose and took his arm. "She'll do your bidding."

He turned, put his palm on my head. "Alix?"

I stared upward through blurred points of light. "I'm sorry."

"And so am I, for this whole ugly business." He lifted me close again. "What will I do here without you or your mother? I love you better than life and already hate the husband who will steal you away. Come now, our kiss once more."

When I'd complied, he lowered me and turned to my mother who still held his arm. He clasped her close, whispered gravely as I strained to hear.

". . . led by Roland . . ."

She pulled back, shocked, then huddled to listen.

". . . men are utterly ruthless," he finished.

They both looked down at me.

"You'll be back by sundown?" she said in her normal voice.

"If there are sufficient knights at Tomlinson's. Otherwise I'll go on to Yarrow . . ."

"But I so want, so hope . . ."

"So do I." They kissed.

"If you can't, send a message."

"I promise." Gently he disengaged himself, then studied her face somberly.

And left.

We watched him speak to his squire, begin the difficult task of arming himself, mount his horse with assistance from the groom. Now he looked as great as King Arthur, tall, noble, his armor reflecting the sun like fire. He turned his courser thrice, raised his gauntlet in farewell, rode through the gate, across the bridge, and disappeared in the greenery of the park.

'TWAS A TORTUROUS AFTERNOON in the schoolroom, what with both Father Michael and Sister Eulalie much distracted by the army outside our window. I was relieved when my mother's shadow fell across my wax tablet.

"Come, Alix, walk with me in the garden."

"I'd best go with you, Lady Catherine," Father Michael offered eagerly, thus bearing out Maisry's belief that the priest loves my mother. "These knights may not be schooled in chivalry."

"Thank you, Father, I would appreciate your company as far as the orchard."

We said farewell to Sister Eulalie and crossed the court where the knights now stretched lazily, their armor piled in heaps beside them. All eyes followed my beautiful mother as she minced decorously before them, and I minced proudly in her wake, imitating her delicate gait. At the hawthorn bush, she dismissed the priest.

"That's a relief," she said impishly and took off her shoes.

Together we continued to the herb garden. She bent and broke off a sprig of celandine. "Take this with you, Alix, for freckles."

I clapped my face in alarm. "Do I have freckles?"

"Not now, but some jealous harlot may hex you. Or here, these starry leaves will keep your dreams honest."

I accepted them, wondering how she knew I'd dreamed about the pilgrimage.

"And the hemlock to keep your teats small," she teased, "though that seems less of a problem than freckles. However, it's also good against your husband's lechery—used in small amounts, of course."

I hung my head sullenly, still smarting at the slur to my breasts. She raised my chin to put a chaplet of hawthorn on my head. "There, Queen of the May, bride-to-be."

"I don't want to get married."

"But you will," she said gently. "And he'll adore you wildly or he won't get you at all, I promise. You are my pearl."

"Will he find me pretty?" I asked anxiously.

"Let's take inventory: high broad forehead, crowned by thick silver-gold hair like your father's. His eyes as well, delicate traceries and infinite depths. So far you'll do. However, you have my dark winged brows and my silly hollows in your cheeks. But soothly he'll have to take the bad with the good."

"I want to look like you!" I clasped her fiercely around the waist.

She pulled me away and we began to walk again.

"Most important is your mind, for a great man likes his wife to be good company. Suppose we test you. Here's a cherry tree and it has a secret. Do you remember what?"

I looked at the fuchsia-blossomed tree in triumph. "That's easy. The keys to our treasury are buried under the largest root."

"Brilliant," she said quietly. "Let's see you find them."

I dropped to my knees and reached around a black trunk oozing amber gum. "Ugh!" I flicked at ants that coursed up my arm, then dug for a time in the damp loose earth, and produced the metal box. "See?"

"Tell me how the keys are used."

"I could show you." I started toward the fruit cellar covered with grassy turf like a grave.

Her hand stopped me. "Best not, when so many people are here. Tell me the value of the coins in order."

They were buried in a locked box, I told her, and could be identified by their weight and feel: deniers, marcs, silver livres and gold coins from Byzantium.

"Excellent. Do you remember how to open the silver trove?"

I described the intricate pattern of stones to press and pry, and she was satisfied. I replaced the keys. Now as we strolled, her humor shifted to a brooding melancholy and I wondered if I dare broach my own question. We were rapidly approaching the hedge where Father Michael waited and I saw I must.

"Mother, it doesn't seem fair that Maisry and I should have to sacrifice our pilgrimage on our very last day together. We could leave before dawn and be back before Father returns from Tomlinson Manor."

She turned hollow inward eyes, the expression she assumes when she's having second sight. I didn't think she'd heard me, but she had.

"You'll obey your father, Alix. That's an order. Now let's see if he's returned, or if a messenger has come instead."

Again we strolled with dignified measure before the knights, but inwardly my fantastick cells were roiling. I loved my parents, aye, and had ever been a respectful daughter, but had never been so sorely tried. Formerly I'd found it easy to obey because they'd been fair. Now I saw that they weren't considering my wishes at all but were totally distracted by journeys and knights and mad old suitors and I know not what. Therefore, I began to plot.

MY FATHER'S MESSENGER was awaiting us at the hall entrance. He was very officious for one so young and his voice cracked when he spoke.

"Lord William sends word that he's bedding at Tomlinson Manor this night and will return by midday tomorrow. He says that all is well. You should prepare to leave as planned. Please sleep in peace and God's blessing."

"Very well bespoke," my mother said gently. "What's your name, lad?"

"Arthur, sir." He blushed deep red. "I mean, My Lady."

"Are you hungry, Arthur?"

"Yes, My Lady."

"Then go to the kitchen and tell Dame Margery that I said to feed you well. She'll show you where to sleep."

"I'll take him," I offered, for I needed to see Maisry immediately.

"Thank you, Mary Alix. I'll be strolling in the garden."

Dame Margery told me that Maisry could be found in the oats bin getting grain for the chickens. Knowing how chaff goes up her nose, I simply listened for sneezes and found her readily enough. I explained the disaster that had befallen us. She seemed to be as distraught as I was. However, when I presented my plan to go to the pilgrimage secretly, without escort—despite my father's orders—her response proved me wrong.

"I don't think you should go against Lord William's wishes, Lady Alix," she protested stubbornly. "There'll be other pilgrimages."

"No, there won't!" I shouted. "Haven't I just told you? You and I will never see one another more; we *deserve* this pilgrimage."

"Who's to say what we deserve?"

I invoked Dame Margery's formula. "God's will, the Divine Plan. I feel it, Maisry, we were meant to go."

Maisry still looked doubtful, but at least she listened. The pilgrimage was to pass nearby soon after dawn and would pause in Dunsmere at the hour of Haute Tierce. My father was due home at midday; we would simply watch the sun and make certain that we were back at Wanthwaite before he arrived. Maisry was terrified of his anger lest he find out, though I assured her I would take the blame and—more important—he would never find out.

"Someone will see us and report," she said.

Inspired, I began to improvise. "Not if I'm in disguise, no one will know."

"Disguised as what?"

"A villein, same as you. We'll be sisters."

"Not with your hair," she said unreasonably.

"*Benedicite*, Maisry, do you take me for a fool? I said *disguised*. I can't cut my hair square like yours but I can tie it in a band as some do."

Finally she agreed to find a brown spun tunic; one of Peg's old ones might do since Peg was big with child. But she was still full of concerns, now for what Lady Cathcrine would say.

"I rarely see her before Haute Tierce except at Mass which I miss half the time. We'll bribe old Robert to take a message that we're watching the duck eggs hatch and that the pecking has just begun. Before she can give it more thought, we'll be back."

'Twas a near perfect scheme with only two weak points that I could see: old Robert was somewhat dense and would need rehearsing, and the knights might want to stop us. Well, we'd just have to try. Maisry remained uneasy about the wickedness but I knew she'd forget that once we were on our way.

My mother and I supped together in silence, both of us deep in our own thoughts. In silence we again paced the garden paths, our heads bent low. Nearby we could hear the laughter of our visiting knights, vaguely see their lounging forms in the milky glow.

When the first star shone in the indigo blue, my mother stood like a statue, the only sign of life being deep moans emitting from her heart. I watched her carefully, fearful that her second sight was discovering my plans, but then she took my arm to walk again. Now the heavens grew black, the stars small and far away, a gibbous moon coasted slowly on the sky's steeps, and still we walked. I was yawning and bleary-eyed before my mother turned back to the castle, only to stop again at the entrance and sit looking upward as if reluctant to leave the velvet night. Finally she sighed and called for our tapers. Together we slowly ascended the twisting stair accompanied by eerie circles of light.

She stopped me at my chamber. "No, Alix, you mustn't sleep alone. Come to my bed."

Heart beating wildly, I protested, "I'm not alone, Mother, Lance is with me."

"Mary Alix!" Her eyes stared huge from their shadowed sockets. "This night you will stay with me."

"Of course, My Lady, as you wish." My mind raced forward to the dawn. Without doubt my mother suspected something for she never permitted me to sleep with her unless I was ill. *Benedicite*, I must get away without her knowledge and then hope that the rest of my plan would convince her.

We undressed by candlelight and when we stood naked, my mother Catherine drew me close to her body still smelling of blossoms. She kissed my lips gently.

"Sweet dreams, little Alix. This is the first of many nights we'll have together when we're on the road. We must learn to be each other's comfort and solace." She held my face and looked deeply. Two tiny flames burned in the centers of her lobelia eyes and the rays of color shot wildly inward. 'Twas an uncanny moment, entering the soul of my mother, and I knew I must confess my plans for the morrow. Then she blew out the tapers and sense returned.

Neither of us slept the entire night. I lay quietly while she walked to the window time and again. I saw her framed against the moonlight, peering outward at the dark. She also made sounds, spoke rapidly in the Celtic tongue, moaned. I watched her with an aching heart, feeling evermore guilty about my deception but at the same time afraid to speak lest I tell all and ruin my very last day. Finally she lay beside me, tossed fitfully a while, then seemed to rest.

I stared at the arched window and smiled to think of that African snake.

2

 Y MOTHER SLEPT.

The curve of her back glowed white as whalebone and her profile was etched against the dusky mantle of her hair. Silently I slipped from my side of the bed.

Like a wraith I floated down the stairs and into the whirling mists in the courtyard, for God had sent a fog to shield us. Lance was eerily quiet as well, as if he sensed my stealth. I could hear the movement of knights but the fog separated us. I almost fell over Maisry where she crouched in the gloom and soon we were giggling and whispering as I transformed myself into a villein. First I wound my long braids under a band.

"Take off your shoes," she ordered. "Those points betray you."

I obeyed.

"Where can you lock your beast? No villeins like us keep a pet 'less it's a cat."

I argued somewhat feebly, but at last shut my wolf in the cheese room that is rarely entered.

"Now are we ready?"

She gazed at me critically and smudged dirt on my face. "May do now."

Avoiding the main gate lest the donjon guard's sharp eyes spy us, we left by our usual path through the kitchen courtyard. No one was about, another good augur for the day. We had to feel our way along the damp outside wall, but by the time we reached the main moat bridge the mist broke somewhat and I saw to my surprise that the iron gate of the great door was down: we couldn't have used that exit if we'd tried. This must be a new edict of my father's to protect us while he was away.

Once across the moat, we entered the bailey where we picked our way through fowl, pigs, goats, sheep and milch-cows. The air was abuzz with pesty flies and we fought to keep them out of our eyes and mouths. Villeins were already feeding and milking the domestic animals, and were thus too busy to pay heed to us. We easily passed through the gate of wood palings enclosing the stock on our way to the dry moat. Now we ran down and up, over the earth-lip, and were in my beloved park. My hunter Justice whinnied when I passed; I scratched his nose and promised him a good run when I returned. We frisked among the trees on our way to the river, pulling at branches and swinging around trunks.

At the foot of the park we walked upstream and waded across a shallow ford. The water was icy from the winter runoff and the stones cut sharply. On the far side I paused guiltily; foam glittering over gray rocks reminded me oddly of my father's eyes. I shrugged off the reminder, for I knew his character too well to believe he would punish me for such a harmless adventure once 'twas done. Behind me the trees nodded gently in their spring-green leaves; ahead black fields glistened in curved swaths where they'd been freshly plowed. Without another backward glance I plunged after Maisry into the fields.

"Keep to the hillocks between furrows," she ordered, "or you'll sink to your knees."

I tried but there seemed to be a strong pull in the earth determined to draw me into the mire, and soon Peg's borrowed dress was gummy with mud at the hem and I'd begun to add my own store of sweat to the rancid supply she'd left. Maisry stepped forth like a square ox while I foundered like a newborn colt caught in a bog.

"Wait for me," I called piteously as I sloshed after her.

The mists were rising fast and the new sun turned the heavy sky to a bright clabbered yellow. Almost at once, we saw a huge company of monks thundering along the horizon like a flock of ravens. I stopped, wondering at their headlong flight. 'Twas Saturday, and Saturn is an evil god, yet monks are a good omen withal. I stumbled on.

"Maisry, wait!"

She turned and clasped her stomach in shrieks of laughter at my foundering. I filled my fist with mud and flung it straight into her rude mouth.

"Ugh!" She spat. Her round brown eyes bulged and before I knew what had happened she'd hurled as well as she got.

In a short while we were both besmottered and laughing and it looked as if the pilgrimage would be forgot, when Maisry raised a palm to stop me.

"Can you hear?"

In the distance, a muffled beat.

"Come or we'll miss them."

Hand in hand we pulled each other across the field, stopping only at the ditch to splash our faces, then through the hedgerow to the path.

"See there." Maisry pointed to a pile of steaming horse dung. "They must be around the next bend."

We sprinted ahead on new grass and, sure enough, there they were, a dozen or more. All were mounted and the harness bells made a pleasant jingle as they rode. We trotted beside them and gazed up shyly. At the back were two men together, experienced pilgrims, said Maisry, because they wore coarse cloaks and carried curved ashen staffs with waterbuckets dangling in the crooks. One was a palmer and the other wore the Canterbury flask.

In front of them were five women, all on little mares. Three had simple bands around their braids while the two older women wore wimples to conceal gray hair, I suspected, for they also painted their faces to hide wrinkles. Yet even the young ones were far from handsome for there didn't look to be one full set of teeth in the five mouths combined. I ran my tongue uneasily over my own and hoped I took after my parents in that respect, for both still had complete sets. Two of the younger pilgrims had had pox as well, yet taken all in all they were a handsome lot, for there were no cripples or wens to be seen.

We'd hardly joined them when the leader, a bishop, pulled his gelding to a halt and raised his hand for silence. In the distance bells rang, and his face grew puzzled. I knew immediately that this was my own chapel bell sounding from Wanthwaite and I, too, was surprised. I realized I'd heard naught at Prime when the sun rose, and surely 'twas too early for the third hour, Haute Tierce. Yet the bell was ringing, no doubt about that, and the bishop crossed the air and began to pray. All of us lowered our heads to receive blessing as I counted the strokes: fourteen, fifteen, sixteen. . . . They went on too long—Father Michael was too fat to pull the rope more than a dozen times ever. The unsettling suspicion crossed my mind that they'd discovered my absence and that this was my mother's way of summoning me home. Yet if I went back and were wrong, I would have given up the pilgrimage for nothing and I longed to see the play. When blessing was finished, I walked along with the others.

Dunsmere was a scattered collection of thatched wattle-and-daub huts stretched along the main path to the square where it met with a road from the opposite direction. As we marched under the broad oaks, the church bell rang and my stomach confirmed that this was indeed Haute Tierce. I'd carried two deniers in my sleeve with the thought of purchasing Maisry and me a treat for our dinner. However, there seemed nothing to buy, but fortunately Maisry had a trick up her sleeve as well, good dark bread and goat's cheese from the pantry. She pulled me to the edge of the square where some kine were munching grass and, when no one was looking, she yanked on the teats of a cow and we caught the foaming stream in our mouths. 'Twas the best dinner I ever remembered, even though 'twas without flesh. We then lolled and drowsed along with everyone else till the festivities began.

The piper began piping and the drummer beating as the square filled with an excited crowd. A few rustics swung their ladies to the beat and there was much laughter. On the outskirts were a knight and his squire on horseback.

"Look you," said Maisry, frowning. "Be those knights from your father?"

I studied the mounted knight and his red-haired squire and, although I couldn't see their features plainly, I knew they were strangers. Furthermore they wore different crests from Wanthwaite's: they were marked *N*. I reassured my friend and we moved with the people.

There was a stand with religious relics for sale and I begged Maisry to choose what she liked as a farewell present from me. I was disappointed when she selected a short red ribbon signifying nothing when there was a splinter of the True Cross to be had, but it was her present. Then I spotted an interesting metal vial and the friar told me I had a good eye, for it contained a drop of the Holy Virgin's own milk! I could hardly believe it cost only one denier and bought it before someone else should see it. I would give it to my mother Catherine as penance for disobeying.

"Stand behind the lines! Bear coming through!"

After the performing bear, there was another round of dancing and not a little tippling before we were told to get behind the marks again, for 'twas time for the Cumbrian wrestling.

"If we left now, we might get home before your father learns that we're gone," Maisry said.

"And not see the play? What are you thinking of?"

Staring over my head at the knight, she didn't answer.

A man stood in the center of the square (which he called a ring) and explained the complicated sport we were about to witness between the champion of the world and his challenger. They would do anything to get each other to the ground and ladies were warned to be of stout heart. The champion had a brown blob sewn to his chest which was a ram's head; the challenger had a four-leaf clover. Naturally I was for the challenger.

And he won! 'Twas a fearsome long battle with much bleeding of noses and groaning and grunting, but finally Green put Brown flat on the dirt and a new champion was born, as the referee said. Two farmers dragged a fine ram in full coat to the center as prize, as we all cheered lustily.

We were jumping up and down. "Who were you for, Maisry?"

She came suddenly to a standstill. "Let's move to the other side and to the front for the play," she said, and she elbowed her way forward.

For a moment her tone distressed me, but I soon forgot it as the crowd quieted for the play. A priest climbed up the steps to the platform to explain the great event.

"We're about to enact the creation of Adam and Eve here before you, the temptation of Adam, the temptation of Eve, and the expulsion from Paradise. Will you be quiet, please?"

He climbed down and the drum began a slow thump, like a heart beating. From a stairs behind the platform a man climbed to the center and raised his hands over us: he was all in white, wore a cross and a crown.

"That be God Hisself," I heard from behind me, and I went all gooseflesh.

Next God reached down the stairs and pulled up a second man, dressed in white socks and shirt much too tight.

"And that be Adam," continued the informative voice, "in his naked state."

God continued to make broad gestures and next produced Eve, a man dressed exactly like Adam except that quinces had been put under his shirt. Adam made much then of losing his rib, as if it hurt, and the crowd went wild with pleasure.

Suddenly a woman at the back of the square screamed. We turned around in time to see the Devil coming through, all in red he was, with a tail and loathsome mask with evil eyes and a long tongue, and we, too, shrieked in terror. He danced back and forth toward Adam and held out a round polished apple; Adam refused it. The Devil ran among us as we fell back screaming, then pointed to his head as a thought came, turned back to the platform and went up to Eve who accepted the apple.

"Where's the African snake?" I asked Maisry, disappointed.

"Now who's this bonny lass? Are you making merry, *p'tite*?" a man's voice said above me in French.

I glanced up, startled to see the knight looking down from his charger. How had he come on me so close and so quietly? Maisry squeezed my hand hard and I realized I should pretend not to understand French, so I stayed mute.

"Come now, your name, little rabbit. Such nice gray eyes and coins to spend too."

My mouth went dry, my stomach tight. He looked like a falcon with his black pouched eyes, deep frown and slick nose. His lips drew back in a sneering smile and two teeth were gone. I became aware of the heavy sweat on his horse, the sour stench from his oozing oily mail, his filthy hands holding his sword and reins and his hair chopped in uneven black patches. My knees trembled as he deliberately drew his sword and leaned toward me but, instead of stabbing me through, he used the point to raise the band from my hair. My heavy gold braids fell to my knees.

"So," he said mockingly, "the fledgling is found."

At that moment, God expelled Adam and Eve from Paradise and the crowd cheered. The unlucky couple dashed into the square and were surrounded by a whole army of demons in red, whacking this way and that, as everyone joined in the sport of hitting and yelling curses.

Instantly Maisry grabbed my hand and cried, "Follow me!"

She jerked me under two flailing sticks and I suffered a painful hit on my rump, then darted and angled back low into the screaming crowd! Behind us we heard shouts of protest as the knight tried to follow us on his horse.

"Out of my way! Give to!" the knight ordered.

We didn't look back to see his fate for Maisry had dropped on all fours and was crawling under the wooden platform with me close behind. We bunched our skirts to our waists and scooted like brown cats under the boards. Half mad with fear, I followed my friend blindly, having no idea where we were going or who was after us. We emerged at the back and far end of the stage.

"Should we seek sanctuary?" I asked, eying the church.

"No sanctuary from that devil," she replied grimly. "Come, and *stay low!*"

No need to tell me twice. I bent like a hunchback as she darted ahead, away from the church and behind a pigyard, then to a lilac bush, a cow-byre, a series of huts and trees till I was dizzy. Suddenly she pulled me inside a dark cot.

"I . . . see . . . some . . . body!" an ancient voice croaked from the floor. "I . . . see . . . some . . . body!"

"Aye, Gran, 'tis only me, Maisry. Here, dear, you've dropped your honey-teat."

Maisry thrust a small dirty bag between toothless gums. "My

grand-dam," she explained. "She's near blind, but a good soul withal. Get into the shadow."

She pulled me away from the door and stood to the side herself so she could see out.

"Is he there?" I asked piteously.

"I . . . see . . . some . . . body!" the crone whined shrilly.

"Go hold her hand, Alix, so she stays quiet."

I crawled on hands and knees across urine leets to where the old lady rested on her pallet under the eaves. Her hand was like bark.

The squire passed the door not five feet distant. Another horse rode close.

"Did you see them?" the knight asked.

"A boy said they came this way," the squire wheezed.

"Damn. The peasant girl may live nearby. Let's circle the village, you to the left, me to the right, and meet back here. And ask everyone."

We heard them ride away.

"We should run now," Maisry told me. "If they start searching the cots, we're lost."

"I'm afeared."

"Me too, but we must get back to the castle, Alix. Your father's there already, and 'tis our safest place."

I trusted her judgment more than my own. I'd never been away from the castle before, knew nothing of how to escape danger. Again we braved the dirt paths and soon arrived safely at the same wending way where we'd entered Dunsmere. We set ourselves as fast a pace as we could, close to a trot. Then, on the far side of a bend, we heard a horse neigh behind us. Maisry stopped and looked around desperately for cover. Nothing but bare fields, hedgerows, ditches. She pulled me through thick brambles bordering a ditch and again we bent low to run behind it.

The clop of hooves came closer.

At a corner, Maisry abruptly pulled me along the hedge of another field away from the path and away from Wanthwaite. For a while we thought we'd evaded him; then his horse neighed again. He was almost upon us.

Maisry whirled and spat through her teeth, "Do exactly as I say, Alix. Get into the ditch and find a spot where the hedge grows low to the water. Sink all the way in up to your nose—lean your head back so your hair doesn't show. Don't you dare move from there until I call you. Do you understand?"

"What are you going to do?" I faltered.

She gave me a rude shove and grunted, "Quick!" as she went back through the hedge and began to walk in the open. I plunged into the icy, muddy ditch and waded awkwardly toward a thornbush a few paces ahead where I stretched out on my side along the edge, allowing half my face to be exposed under the low cover.

Maisry had walked even with me when the knight reached her.

"Hooooa." He pulled his horse short. "All right, wench, where's your noble friend?"

Maisry truly didn't understand French and made no answer. The knight repeated the question in poor Saxon.

"Noble friend? I have no noble friend."

"Your noble mistress then," he said with heavy sarcasm, "the blond beauty in Dunsmere."

"Aye, yes, the blonde with braids. She stood beside me, I recall, but I don't know her."

I heard a jangle of coins. "These are all yours if you tell me where you hid the Lady Alix. Don't look so afrighted—I mean her no harm."

At the sound of my own name, I breathed in ditch water and almost choked. I put my hand over my nose to control myself and listened hard.

Clever Maisry assumed a wheedling whine. "Please, sir, I don't know no Lady Alix but I think I know what direction the blond doxy went, if you'll give me some coin. I'm only a poor girl and my mum gone with the falling sickness . . ."

He wasn't fooled.

"Yes, you know her well enough. You hid her in the village, then led me on this wild goose chase as decoy. I think you owe *me* coin for my trouble." He paused. "I'll take it in labor and save you embarrassment."

The word *labor* was filled with spite, as if 'twere a threat.

"Oh please, sir, no . . ." Maisry's voice was breathless with fear.

I heard the clank of his armor as he dismounted, then a scream from Maisry. Quickly I crawled up the muddy bank and peered through the bush. What I saw made my heart burst. Maisry had started to run when the knight reached the ground; she might have escaped too, for he was too weighted down to give chase, except that he caught her ankle with a chain and she fell. Then he lumbered over her, smashed her cheek with his metal knuckles so that she cried out again. As she lay there whimpering, he began to undress. He unfastened his scabbard and let it drop with a clatter; next came his tunic; then the long process of his hauberk and mail; then his blouse and he was down to his leggings and breeches. He untied the leggings and finally dropped his breeches to stand naked.

Deus juva me!

He was not a man—he was a monster! For no mortal ever looked so, never like this naked knight. Between his legs grew a horn, aye, a protruding red organ as long and as hard as a boar's tusk. 'Twas red in color and had a small head as if it might have a separate mind all its own.

Then it struck me what I was gazing on and I began to pray hard to overcome his evil. This was one of those monstrous offsprings born to a human woman and an incubus! In spite of his language, he must be a Scot for I'd heard all my life how the Scots mate with monsters, goblins, bears and boars.

Maisry gasped in horror and I thrust my fist to my mouth to keep my own cry in check. Should I go help her? *Could* I help?

The knight fondled his deformity and suddenly pushed Maisry to the ground. Then he was atop her and permitting his incubus-organ to bite her again and again as he pushed it against her. She turned away violently and our eyes met through the brambles! Instantly she mouthed "Get down! Hide!" and I withdrew into the stagnant water.

I seemed to be there forever. I knew the knight was dressing again, heard the clinking of his armor, then another hard thud, then the jingle of harness bells disappearing into the distance.

I waited for Maisry to call me. After all, someone else might be in sight.

My body was numb, the silence absolute.

Gradually and soundlessly I again rolled onto the bank and

looked through the bush: Maisry was still lying on her back, un-moved as far as I could see.

"Maisry," I whispered.

When she didn't answer, I rose to my knees and strained to see in the direction the knight had ridden. No one in sight. Shakily, I stood all the way. The faint throb of the drum still sounded from Dunsmere and invisible crows cawed from above but otherwise there was no sound or movement. The fields lay black and empty, the sky was a lowering gray.

I pushed through the hedge and looked down. *Benedicite*, what was this? Maisry was twisted in a strange position, her legs splayed apart. Then I saw blood gushing from her wounded crotch and her stomach streaked red!

"Maisry, what happened?" I cried.

I dropped to my knees to pull her dress down. Who would have dreamed that the horn was so sharp? That it could cut Maisry's skin to ribbons? Awful! Awful!

"Oh, Maisry, sweet Jesus save you! Do you think you can walk?"

I took her hand and looked into her face. 'Twas lying in the dirt in a position that never was, for her head was cut neatly off her shoulders!

The last thud! While I'd waited, he'd drawn his sword across her throat! Or mayhap his sharp incubus! Everything blood. Maisry's blood!

"Aaaaaauuuuu!" 'Twas an inhuman howl and had come from my heart, for *I had done this!* I had forced Maisry to come on this pilgrimage! She hadn't wanted to, had tried to dissuade me but I wouldn't listen. Oh, my God, how can I bear it!

I fell atop her mutilated body, still warm, the blood still warm. I would have kissed her dead face only it was detached, not there. Oh, surely 'tis a nightmare! This cannot be real! This blood, these tears, oh, God!

No nightmare.

I lay on her, my breath shallow. How can I face Dame Margery? How can I live with my guilt? How can I live without Maisry?

Should I have come out when he said my name? Could I have

saved her? Another guilt: aye, I could have offered myself for it was I he sought.

With harsh sobs, I hugged her close, my smiling curly-mouthed Maisry gone forever. I prayed for her, talked to her, hoping her soul was still near. Gradually we grew cold together, she in her thickening blood, I in my ditch water. My teeth chattered and I listened to the heavy stillness around me.

There above, the screech of a kite come to peck at Maisry, and I spread myself protectively over her. Then more silence.

The drum in Dunsmere—when had it stopped? Where was the sun in its run? Had I been here long?

I thought of the incubus-knight. He would have had time to get back to Dunsmere by now, to search for me, to ask people if they'd seen me with Maisry. Surely someone had and someone would talk when they heard that silver jingle. I sat up, my brown garb sticky with blood.

The fields seemed different, ominous, evil. I *should* have saved Maisry, but soothly she had died to save me. Was I going to betray her sacrifice by becoming still another victim? Methought I heard hoofbeats though it could have been my own heart, but I knew I must get back to Wanthwaite.

Quickly I bent over the dear tangled body to give it its last rites and ministrations. I said a fast prayer and blessed her on her journey, crossed her arms, arranged her head so it seemed to be part of her again, closed her eyes, weighted her kerchief across her face with a stone. From her clenched fist, I took the red ribbon for remembrance.

Then I stood and got my bearings. Wanthwaite's towers were visible to my left though a heavy cloud had settled on them while the sun, now small and pale as a sparrow's egg, hung timelessly above. Grimly I picked a course along hedgerows in case I was forced to hide again.

I wanted my mother.

3

 HE CLOUD OVER WANTHWAITE WAS SMOKE.

Dazed, I stood on the far side of the river and tried to understand. Flames still rose from the swaled bailey, but what was the damage behind?

Heavy chains squeezed my heart so that each beat was painful, but I fought to keep a clear head. Surely the iron gate had held, surely my father had long since returned and raised the moat bridge, surely all within were safe.

Still, best be cautious.

I dipped my headband in the water and tied it across my nose and mouth against the smoke, then began my slow ascent. No worm in the ground ever moved more invisibly than I did as I climbed through the hanger, flattening myself against one tree trunk after another, ever alert to human sounds or movements.

My horse Justice was gone, and I trembled with fear. As I neared the palings, I relaxed my vigilance somewhat for the flames were still flickering and there was so much burning stuff on the ground that I had to keep my eyes low. Moreover I didn't imagine anyone was lurking in the midst of the fire.

At last I reached the moat, prepared to turn into the kitchen courtyard gate on the other side of the bridge, but instinctively first sought the donjon where my father might be stationed.

There was no one at the window.

And the iron gate was open.

As I took in the awful significance of those facts, an iron gate inside my own head clanged shut: *Don't look ahead, take each revelation as it comes.* For I had to proceed.

The bailey smoke was cast behind me now so I could remove my kerchief. The acrid smell was stifling and there was a constant crackle of timber burning; otherwise 'twas eerily still. No humans, no animals; even the flies had departed.

After many tentative starts, I rested my weight on the plank bridge across the moat and began to cross, picking my footings with care. Even so, one board squeaked and sounded to my ears like a tree crashing! I paused a long moment, waiting for a response which didn't come. I continued.

Rather than go through the main gate, I again turned to the kitchen courtyard. Inside I saw a stew still bubbling, and in spite of myself felt a surge of hope. Then I went through the second gate to the main courtyard.

I leaned weakly against the wall, not understanding the grisly sight before me. All the flies in the world had descended upon Wanthwaite and formed a living buzzing mountain in our court. The enthusiasm of the beasts sickened me as I gazed at their blue-black bodies.

One round whitish object lying apart took my attention and I stepped forward to study it. 'Twas a bald human head, its open eyes crawling with flies—Sister Eulalie!

I clapped my hand to my mouth to hold back my scream.

The whole mountain—aye, *all* of it—my friends and servants, the knights, hacked, chopped to bits.

And my family?

I began my awful search. John Leggy, Father Michael, old Robert and young Arthur in loose embrace, all, all.

All but my mother and father.

When I was sure, I entered the castle.

I gazed in disbelief at the animal hall where the bloody pulps of pointer pups lay mixed with brilliant parrot feathers. At least the parrots weren't there. Could they survive naked in these northern forests? Our poor old mastiff Courage, his toothless gums bared in a feckless effort to guard our home.

Slowly, in a trance, I walked up the steps.

No one in my chamber.

I paused. Not a sound.

I stood in the arched doorway of my mother's chamber and gazed inside. The first thing I saw was her torn ruby tunic lying in a heap on the floor.

Her beautiful white body lay almost as I'd last seen it and I thought for a moment that she slept. Then I saw the deep gash across her throat where the murderer had drawn his sword, not deep enough to sever but deep enough to kill. And her legs splayed obscenely.

And her skin, scratched and imprinted by the mail of the in-cubus-knight, plain as a signature that she'd died in Maisry's man-ner. Still, she might have been alive except for her eyes, bluer in death than in life but the rays no longer leading inward, for the soul was departed. I reeled and pitched forward.

The chamber faded into oblivion.

I woke, hours or days later, I didn't know.

My mother?

I may have screamed though I heard naught. I wanted to die. To die and be with my mother. How could I live without my mother? Mother!

I huddled into the wall and prayed for God to take me and I cared not how so long as it was soon. Every moment in this wretched world was now torture. Then I heard footsteps and my heart leaped—my prayer was about to be answered!

"God help us!" Dame Margery filled the archway. "Catherine!"

Then she saw me. "Alix? So it was ye! *Deo gratias*! He's wait-ing—in such pain."

I looked at her dully, was folded into her bony arms.

"Your father is under the moat. We heard ye cross."

I came back from a long distance. "My father?"

"Hurry, he's in a very bad way."

My father alive? I could hardly believe it.

"Wait."

I pulled the stopper from the Virgin's vial to shake out the milk, but the bottle was empty. Quickly I squeezed a few drops of my mother's blood into the vial, took a lock of her hair. 'Twas all I would ever have of my mother.

"I'm ready."

Dame Margery made the sign of the cross and we left.

Speaking brokenly and with many omissions, the dame tried to tell me what had transpired after Maisry and I were discovered to be missing. Both she and my mother had guessed early where Maisry and I had gone and Dame Margery had been sent to fetch us home. She'd met that same company of monks I had seen, but they'd stopped her and asked courteously if they could find succor at the castle. She'd assured them that Lady Catherine was ever a devout lady. Later she'd heard the bell, and unlike me, had understood it as a call for help. Immediately she'd turned back and had seen my father with his small band approaching the castle. By the time she'd arrived, the battle was raging. It was then that she'd deduced how the Scots had made their entrance. The Scots? I asked in disbelief. Aye, they'd worn the monks' robes, then discarded them inside for Scottish war dress, thus taking our unarmed knights unaware. Dame Margery had hidden under the moat and been able to pull my father to the bank when he'd fallen into the water, mortally wounded.

When we reached the far side of the moat-bridge, she pointed down a steep embankment where a shallow earth-lip extended into the ditch.

"There." But she held my arm tight so I couldn't yet move, then asked the dreaded question. "Where's Maisry, Lady Alix? With my mother in Dunsmere?"

Horrified, I looked up into her blinking red eyes. "I—I—" and I swore I'd never tell her the worst. "She's dead. Killed by one of the knights," I sobbed. "I'm so sorry, so sorry . . ."

She weaved unsteadily. "Not Maisry. Why? . . ."

"She's dead," I repeated. "I saw him kill her—I don't know why."

But I did: because she wouldn't tell him where I was.

The dame fell awkwardly to the ground, then threw her apron over her head and huddled in a shaking heap. I patted her and tried to embrace her again, but she waved me toward the moat.

I slipped down the rocky embankment to a narrow ledge by the water where my father lay like a pile of discarded armor, his legs extended into the water. He heard me coming and turned his head. For a short moment we gazed at each other: I saw his left hand kneading his stomach, the trickle of red between his fingers. He lifted his right hand in horror and pointed to my stained tunic.

"You're not . . ." he gasped.

"No, no, I'm all right, Father. 'Tis someone else's blood," I said hastily and knelt beside him. "Can you walk?"

His breathing was labored but his eyes were clear. "I'm dying, Alix. I waited for you."

I couldn't bear his words and started to deny them heatedly, but his eyes stopped me.

"Don't waste time," he said with difficulty. "I must instruct you . . . try to raise . . ."

"Aye! Don't talk."

I slipped behind him and tugged on his torso, using my body as counterweight. He moved but cried out with pain, and I stopped. I slipped his shield under his head which gave him some relief. But the blood from his wound had now increased, pooling the moat water red.

He waved me closer, and whispered, "List to me well, Alix."

"Yes, Father."

"We were . . . sacked by Osbert, Lord of Northumberland. *Northumberland.*"

Surely he was in a delirium.

"Northumberland? Osbert? Our liege lord?"

His lips made a bitter line.

"And your suitor. He . . . wants . . . Wanthwaite."

I was horrified. I recalled a sour-breathed, croaking warrior, the dreadful things my mother had told me.

His eyes twitched impatiently and I realized that we hadn't time to discuss my feelings.

"He and his foster son, Roland de Roncechaux . . ."

I waited.

". . . want to make Northumberland a palatinate, their own kingdom."

I didn't understand *palatinate.*

"Want our land," he said.

"Did Northumberland lead the Scots then?"

"No, Roland . . . brigand knight . . . beast."

The knight at the fair with *N* on his shield. *Roland de Roncechaux.* Aye, it must be. And he killed Maisry, my mother. I tried not to weep before my father.

"And you knew that they were going to attack?"

He turned his eyes to mine. "Too late."

I pressed his hand.

"But you can still . . . go to King Henry . . ." and his whisper became so low that I could barely hear it. Yet he went on and on, remembering every detail.

"Repeat," he ordered.

I tried. King Henry was our friend and the only lord great enough to o'errule Northumberland, would give me a royal writ . . . would assign me to a good husband . . . send an army back with me if need be. There was a law in England against the sacking of castles and Northumberland would be punished, only . . . only . . .

"Don't go to the Assize Court," my father completed.

"Not to the Assize Court. But why?" I'd forgotten already.

"Osbert of Northumberland is the judge."

But I hardly heard him. All I could think of was that crimson flow from his wound.

". . . as a boy."

"What?"

"*Go as a boy*. Crucial . . . life depends on it. Boy, Alix . . ."

"Aye, Father, I will. Dress, name, everything."

"Find . . . companion. Never alone. Look . . . fier. And *boy*. They'll ride Scots to border . . . back soon. Hurry . . . boy."

"I'm to go as a boy." He seemed obsessed by my disguise. "Or I might be abducted."

"Or worse."

Maisry, my mother. Aye, I would go as a boy.

"And tell *no one but the king* who you are. Don't be beguiled . . ."

"No one but the king," I assured him.

Now he seemed to have difficulty with his thoughts as well as his words. His brow twisted with effort and he tried to lick his dry lips. I cupped my hand and dipped for moat water; he drank and the liquid spilled red down his chin.

"Even as a boy . . . not safe alone. Always . . . on road . . . travel with a companion. Seek a strong man, armed . . . feed you, help you . . ." he repeated himself.

"Aye, Father, I can do it. Only, please, rest now, you're wasting your strength."

He was still struggling to remember everything. "Take my commendation . . . King Henry . . ."

"Don't, I understand. Take the commendation for capturing the Scottish king to prove who I am."

His eyes approved. "And your grandfather . . ."

"Who fought with King Henry against the Scots. I'll remember, I promise."

"Sharp wench." He tried to smile. "Fortunately they don't know you escaped, won't be looking for you. Otherwise you'd have no chance . . . would be dead by sundown."

I couldn't tell him that I'd been seen. Let him die in peace.

Red spittle bubbled in the corner of his mouth. Quickly I wiped it away, but it came back, more and darker in hue. I stroked his sticky hair. He looked at me with glazed eyes.

"Kate?"

Did he think I was my mother? No, and I must answer, the biggest lie I'd ever told.

"An arrow struck her while she was at prayer. She felt no pain."

I was vindicated for my falsehood by his relief.

"Go to the king, Tickle-Bones. Kate and I cannot enter Heaven till you return . . . wait in Purgatory."

"I'll be back," I vowed, letting my tears come now, for I knew he could no longer see.

"Only then can we go to Heaven. Kiss me . . ."

I did, in our secret way, forehead . . . by the time I reached his lips he was dead.

NO TIME.

I took my vial, combined a drop of his blood with my mother's, a lock of his hair, took his engraved sword to bury.

But I kept his dagger for myself.

"Dame Margery! Help me!"

She half-slid, half-tumbled down the bank.

"They're coming back. Hurry, slide him into the water."

He didn't slide easily. I sloshed into the stagnant moat, ooze to my hips, and tugged his legs till he was submerged. We made the sign of the Cross and pulled each other back to the bridge above.

I looked into the park—no one yet.

"I have to find food! Hurry!" We ran across the bridge to the kitchen.

We were both weeping but it didn't matter. "I mun lead ye to Dere Street close on Hadrian's Wall," Margery said shrilly. "He told me as I must. Will ye eat turnips, My Lady?"

"Anything! Hurry!"

We both made bundles of our skirts, threw in bread, meat, onions, beans, everything mixed.

"Let's go, dearie," the dame said.

"No, not yet." I thought I heard a voice from above, mayhap in my own head, but 'twas my mother nonetheless. "I'll be right back, Margery."

And I ran away before she could protest, past the smoldering bodies, over the privet hedge, past the leek garden, the pot-herbs, the medicinal plants—where I neatly swooped up a handful of hemlock—past the hawthorn into the orchard. 'Twas like a dream, the blossoms still falling, my mother's voice still echoing from only yesterday.

"Mother?" I said in a wavery thick voice. "Mother?"

The blossoms swirled in an updraft and I saw her form bending and swaying.

"Mother!" I ran to her but she was far ahead and I kept running in and out of the trees, sobbing. Then I saw her direction: 'twas toward our fruit cellar, and it came to me what she wanted. The deep fuchsia cherry tree shivered by the path as memory flooded back.

"Yes!" I panted, "I understand."

Soon the treasure was up and I reached inside the box, grateful that I'd had to weigh and feel the coins for their value. I took silver livres, then fished for the gold coins from Byzantium and found twenty, tossed in a few deniers and marcs for immediate expenses. I carefully replaced the box.

"Don't leave yet," my mother ordered. "Put your father's sword with the silver and bury it with my vial and blood when you return."

"Yes, yes I will."

I pressed the wall to the right as I'd been instructed and a door swung open. Quickly I thrust my father's sword into the small room with our other silver objects and pushed the stone façade back in place.

"Will you talk to me again?" I asked the empty air, but there was no answer.

I retraced my steps toward the hall where I took the scroll, then to the kitchen. As I passed the hellish pile, my father's whisper now entered my brain: "Go as a boy. . . . Tell *no one* your true identity until you reach the king."

Holding my breath, I circled the human butchery to find someone near to my size. My father's young messenger Arthur was closest and his clothes appeared unharmed. Gulping back nausea, I began slowly to disrobe his stiff cold body. With my arms near full, I still must find weapons: I settled on a hunting bow and arrows carried by our archer, Gerald, for those with my father's dagger were all I could handle. I loaded Arthur's hat with my coins, threw his fur over my shoulder and walked awkwardly back to the kitchen.

Dame Margery stood in the yard, quivering with fear for she thought I'd been caught at last.

"There's some of them Scots hid in the cheese room to trap us," she wept. "I heard them scuffling around."

"Lance!" I cried, wondering how I could have forgotten. "*Deo juvante*, he's alive!"

The wolf leaped again and again to mouth my face in his great jaws, saying in his way that he understood the horror as well as I did.

"Hush!" Dame Margery clutched my shoulder. "Listen!"

In the distance we heard men laughing and shouting.

"They'll catch us sure!" Dame Margery's gaunt face showed every bone, and tears ran.

"The labyrinth!" I cried. "Maisry and I used to hide there!"

We ran awkwardly to the horse stalls, counted three from the door, knocked aside a stack of bales and pushed together with all our might. Behind us the laughter grew louder. Hooves on the bridge!

And the ancient door swung open. For an instant we saw the outline of a stone-hewn tunnel big enough for a horse, then pushed the door back and stood in darkness.

"I dropped our food," Dame Margery whispered.

"Then we must gather it. They can't hear us now."

We groped on the passage floor, now more aware of a close sound: rats. Lance growled and snapped at the vermin as we began to feel our way along the walls. 'Twas a long downward passage, a half mile or more of descent, hot and airless, straight into Hell. Then a cool breeze hit and we heard water running.

"We're at a cave by the river," I whispered, Maisry's and my secret chapel.

More and more knights at the ford, splashing back and forth, shouting out in thick drunken voices. Lance growled—I clenched his muzzle.

Then Dame Margery and I settled ourselves close against a wall for a long grim night.

4

HE COMING OF DAWN UNNERVED ME. THE FIRST day that my mother and father were not alive and I could not bear it. I began to tremble violently and my breath failed so I choked, waking Dame Margery from her groggy sleep. With face still puffed from constant tears, she comforted me like a babe, crooning and stroking me.

We then began our careful preparation for my escape. Arthur's clothes were too big for me but would do. First I slipped on his leggings made of coarse linen and none too clean and tied them at my waist with the braiel which was studded with metal disks. Dame Margery suggested we should slit the crotch so I could relieve myself with ease. Next I drew the socks of itchy dark green wool over my legs and tied them firmly by bands above my knees. His yellow linen shirt hung like a tent and the green tunic fell almost to my ankles. Dame Margery had her sewing bag at her waist and hemmed the tunic so it reached just below my knees, then punched the leather belt to fasten over it.

Finally she tore Peg's bloodstained brown dress into neat strips and stuffed some of them in the toes of the huge yellow boots. Others she stitched inside the yellow felt hat so it sat firm. The hardest part was cutting my hair, for it seemed so final. The braids came off to just below my ears and Margery hacked a fringe across my forehead so I could see. Without the weight, my hair curled against my head and the dame said the effect was not too bad.

I then had her construct a harness of the strips to wear as a money belt between my legs. She made individual divisions so that the coins wouldn't slide to one place to jingle and make an uncomfortable lump; I added my precious tiny vial, red ribbon and scroll to the treasure and we flattened the whole against my buttocks and inner thighs. She then devised a small bundle to carry at my leather belt with a few deniers and food; there were still strips left over to pack in my drafsack for emergencies.

Over and over our activities came to a breathless standstill when we heard lewd shouts and rioting from the castle. We clutched each other in terrified embrace and waited for the shouts to cease. Once a knight scared us most senseless when he appeared through the mist on the far side of the river, but he was stopped from crossing by the weir.

By late afternoon we were ready. I was dressed, had my dagger in my belt, my bundle on the other side, my bow and arrows slung on one shoulder, and a fur pelisse fastened on the other for warmth and sleeping. I'd been sorely tempted in my choice of fur to take my father's fine vair, but 'twas wiser to stay with Arthur's humble goatskin I now wore. Dame Margery said I looked like any common boy on the road, albeit a little small to be on my own.

"Best say ye're eight, if anyone asks," she advised. "Ye're short even for a girl. Also, not so much is expected of an eight-year-old."

"When should we start?" I asked.

"Not until dark." I could hear the fear in her voice. "I promised Lord William to guide you and certes I remember the way to

Hadrian's Wall. But London—well, we can ask a traveler which way it lies.

"Surely to the south. North leads to Scotland."

"Aye, of course," she said, relieved. "What will ye do in such a wicked city?"

"I'll go directly to King Henry for help. I promise we'll be back in Wanthwaite within the week."

"King Henry? There was a King Henry in these parts many years past who fought the Scots."

"'Tis the very same and my grandfather fought with him," I said boldly as any boy. "He knows my family, you see, and will be glad to aid me."

"I wish I could go with you."

"No," I said bravely. "Your family needs you here."

She broke into sobs anew to think of our fate.

THE MOON WAS FULL, the gloaming white as daylight, but we dared not wait longer. Depending on drifting cloud shadows for cover, we crossed the Wanthwaite River on a fallen oak far from the natural fording. On the other side we found a cow path which led through the wood to a pasture enclosed by a drywall. We climbed over the wall and walked close to it, prepared to stoop low if we heard anyone. The turf was spongy and uneven, my burdens heavy, and I turned my ankles constantly in my oversized boots. Soon my heels were bloody and I winced at each step but dared not ease my pace.

When the wall ended, Dame Margery became confused and only my own intervention kept her from leading us right back to Wanthwaite. At last she decided that a distant clump of trees concealed our next path. We made a harrowing way across open ground, but she was right: the copse had been mère saplings when she'd gone this way before. Cart-ruts marked our road but we still walked behind the hedge: though footing was firmer, the grade was upward and my flopping boots were torture chambers. Therefore I agreed to pause at the top for Dame Margery to rest.

The westerly wind blew strong on the hilltop, carrying with it a putrid odor of rotten flesh burning. Turning my head, I saw a red glow in the center of Wanthwaite's turrets, a flaming funeral pyre where the pile of carnage had lain. Now I could hear faint shouts as well, knights celebrating their foul deeds. No wonder they hadn't seen us with such bloody distraction! I cast one last grim look at my desecrated home and ran into the next valley.

WE REACHED the ancient Roman Dere Street at dawn. Standing on the bank, I observed that the road was rough, with many missing stones, and thought of my blistered feet. I prayed fervently to the Holy Virgin to send me a company of nuns with a little donkey to spare. We then settled to wait for a suitable companion.

The sun was risen to warm our backs when the first prospect appeared. Dame Margery squeezed my arm in possible farewell as we listened to harness bells and the unsteady clop of a horse on the treacherous stones. Shortly our candidate came in view; just as shortly we dismissed him. He was a fat churl with rolls upon rolls of lard giving his dappled steed a deep sway. His blouse was a filthy blue, his skin boiled, his eyes bright in their folds. Something bothered his breathing, for he snorted, sniffed, cleared his throat and spat, picked at his nose and ate the findings. We let out a sigh of relief when he disappeared on our right.

Our next man, a leather-garbed shepherd, was traveling toward Scotland. Lance growled at the unruly sheep, but a sharp rap on his nose quieted him.

'Twas a bothersome long time before we saw man or beast after that. My worry grew greater and greater, for we'd eaten all our bread and I was getting hungry, not to mention my numbing weariness from lack of sleep or the paralysis of my vital faculties. 'Twas crucial that I find a charitable wight who would share victuals and even a horse, but the outlook was discouraging.

My eyes had grown heavy when Dame Margery again grabbed my arm, digging her nails deep with panic. I listened and heard what alarmed her: the Scottish pipe. My skin prickled at the heavy deep drone dinning in time like steady groans from the earth's womb, and I felt hot and cold together. Dame Margery was trembling so that she could hardly stand and I was no better. We leaned into each other to steady ourselves, fearing to betray our presence by so much as a shaking twig.

All my life I've heard tales of the fiendish butcherers of the north, but nothing had prepared me for the apparition which now rode into sight. Mounted on a monstrous plodding white mule, he looked to be a bull more than a man, for he was covered with dark reddish hair and grew curved horns low on his forehead; furthermore his broad knarry shoulders bent to his pipe like a bull's hump. Yet he was a man withal, for he wore a strange garb of gaudy wool woven in cross-colors of scarlet, blue and purple; a cape pinned on one shoulder, a skirt on a thick leather band at his waist; dark red coarse socks tied below his knees with straw garters, soft elk boots laced high. As he drew closer I saw that the horns were attached to a bearskin hat and that a squirrel vest also contributed to the animal effect. The most chilling evidence that he was human, however, was the armory bristling on his person: keen daggers at belt and sock, broadsword on his right, the two-sided Lochinvar ax for which the Scots are famous on his left, hunting bow with arrows, a tall pointed pike resting in a thong under one arm. 'Twas hard to estimate his age as his face was hidden by his elflock beard and the mouthpiece of his bagpipe was on the far side from us, but his formidable bulging muscles appeared young and supple: he was a beast in his prime. Awed, we watched him draw closer and closer.

He was now almost parallel and we saw that he pulled a small white ass behind him, loaded with pelts, pans and household goods of all kinds. Closer and closer he loomed, a huge menacing form emitting deafening shrieks and harsh guttural drones in a relentless throbbing skirl which pained my fantastick cells to an agony I couldn't bear!

"Stop!" I screamed, full out of my wits, and clapped my hands to my ears.

In a flash, Lance leaped free and attacked. Just as quickly the Scot whirled with pike in hand to kill.

"Don't slay my wolf!" I flew from my bush and landed atop my snarling beast. "Please! Kill me first!"

I looked up the long deadly spike to his bulging wild blue eyes. He pricked me slightly on my neck to hold me in place as his eyes rolled that way and this to see if I were alone. There was a movement on the bank and he raised his weapon to hurl.

"Stop, 'tis my mother!" I screamed again, beginning to sob as well.

His flicking eyes fastened on the bush where Dame Margery hid.

"Quha gang ther? Fra quhair commit?"

She didn't answer.

"Can you speak Saxon, sir?" I asked faintly.

He leaned down and roared, "Quhat be ich spakin yif nocht Saxon?"

I understood that all right but was too weak with terror to reply.

"Gie me yer nam."

I was near fainting and could hardly stutter, "Alix Want—" before I stopped myself, appalled. My very first test on the road and I'd failed, after I'd rehearsed "Tom" for hours! I said a quick prayer to myself in case this was the end; then, when he didn't move to slay me, tried to read any flicker of recognition at the name in his face.

"Alexander Want," he repeated slowly. He worked his mouth to speak and finally managed a few words I could understand.

"In quhat direction do ye travel, boy?"

"Toward York," I said quickly, getting it right.

"And ye war waitin' to luik fier."

"Look fier? Oh, aye, you mean someone to travel with. Aye, I'm waiting." I stood again. "I'm sorry about my wolf—'twas the music that hurt his ears, I think. Come, Lance." Cautiously I prepared myself to get away and hoped he would leave me without harm.

"Wolf?" He looked at Lance. To my amazement, the wolf was now licking the white ass's nose and the ass seemed to like it. The Scot bared square white teeth in a hideous leer, which I saw belatedly was a smile.

"*Domes forte deme.*"

"Aye," I said, not understanding but trying to answer his smile as I edged to pull Lance away.

To my horror, the Scot bent down and seized my shoulder.

"What do you want?" I attempted to stay calm. He didn't appear belligerent after all.

Again he worked his lips and this time spoke English, albeit with a horse's tongue. "'Tis an omen, a sign fra God and the folets whan animals decide. Ich quoted ye a saugh! Fate must be. Which manes, laddie, that ye and me air doomed to ride togeddir. Gie me both yer hands."

Again his dreadful grimacing face bent near as I stood like a piece of stone.

Dame Margery slid down the bank on her buttocks and clasped me close.

"Oh no ye don't! I'll not have the boy stolen! Not after what ye did to my sister, ye murdering savage!"

The Scot gazed coldly and without surprise into her contorted grieving face. "I niver did nothing to yer sister. Niver murthered anyone that didna deserve it, and I'll not be stealin' bairns. I have a strang mule, plenty to eat, and I be headin' a' the way to London and beyond. Yif ye want protection on the way and no nonsense, Alexander, then I'd be happy fer yer company. Yif nocht, farewell."

For a long period, we seemed frozen in tableau. The sky was a cobalt steep behind dippling limbs, the road alive with leaf shadows, the sun alarmingly high in its run. I thought of the animal omen—a strong one, I felt—of my father's moldering body in its watery grave, his orders, of Northumberland. Time was passing fast and the Scot had not seemed to recognize my name. I must risk it—and change companions later.

"'Tis best I go," I said to the dame. "Thank you, sir, for your offer."

She knelt beside me, weeping. "Ye must decide, My Lady," she whispered, "and may God forgive me if I do wrong."

"Thank you for everything. Remember, 'tis only for a week."

This time I accepted the Scot's hand. "Enoch Angus Boggs at yer service, of the clan MacPherson."

And I was lying like a sack of meal across the mule's neck, then was set properly astride. Lance trotted in the ass's shadow. At the next bend, I was able to look back where Dame Margery still stood, her face pale as a winter moon, her mouth turned down in despair. I knew by her melancholy wave that she never expected to see me alive again.

5

HO WERE THAT BLUBBERIN' HAG, ALEX?"

"My—my mother." I considered. "No, not exactly my mother. My foster mother."

"Waesucks, bairn, make up yer mind. Ye shuld know yer ane mother even yif ye don't know yer father."

"My foster mother," I said firmly.

"Hmm."

We jogged on at a steady clop as I worried about whether I'd done the right thing. I didn't discount the possibility—more, the probability, considering where I'd met him—that Enoch Angus Boggs had been one of the marauding party. My head was much muddled with weariness and pain, but I tried to sort it out. The Scots had joined the foray for hard cash but took no share in the land spoils; that was what I'd understood. Therefore they might not be aware of my existence, either as a boy or a girl, nor care, which would explain why Enoch hadn't reacted to my name. However, I wasn't safe with such a cold-blooded killer and could well end up slaughtered in the bushes for kites to pick at, especially if he guessed that I carried gold. No, I was running from one enemy in the company of another. I tried to sit straight so I didn't have to touch him.

"Ye mun tell me, Alex, when I speak too broad. I'm talented wi' tongues but ne'er heard an Englishman talk with that newefangeled French mix."

"Norman mix," I corrected him. "You seem to be doing better already."

The swaying sun and shadow, the rhythm of the mule and the soft jingle of harness bells were quick hypnotizing me to a stupor. I fought to stay awake, to avoid that broad chest at my back, but 'twas hard.

43

"Be York yer home?"

I woke with a start. "No. Yes. That is, it will be from now on."

"Why do ye gang there?"

I breathed deep, tried to recall my tale. "I'm going to 'prentice with my uncle, my mother's brother. Aye, that's the plan."

"'Prentice in what trade?"

Trade? Something of which I had knowledge in case he pursued his questioning. "I'm going to 'prentice in Latin."

"In *Latin*?"

"Aye, the Latin tongue." Such an ignorant barbarian might not understand. "'Tis the language of the Romans spoke in Julius Caesar's day, now the tongue of the Holy Church."

"Thank ye fair informing," he said dryly and I flushed, remembering belatedly that he'd claimed he was good in tongues, which must include Latin. "Yer wolf seems a friendly beast. How did ye come by such a strange pet?"

I grew wary, remembering Maisry's warning that common boys don't keep wolves. "Actually he's not mine. He belonged to a little girl at the manor where my father was steward, and she lent him to me."

"Yer father *was* steward. Be he dead then?"

My breath grew short. "Yes, he died of the pox some months ago."

"And now ye air gang to York to 'prentice in Latin."

He began whistling again and I went over our conversation, satisfied that I'd done well. If he didn't already know my identity, he'd not guess from my words. Meantime, the relief I'd felt to be off my feet was offset by the agony of straddling that hard neckbone.

As if he read my thought, Enoch pulled the mule to a halt and dismounted.

"Come, bairn, let's piss." He lifted me down.

"I don't have to." I fought to keep from crossing my legs.

"Come now, force a drap if ye can, for it may be some time afore we stop again."

He reached casually under his plaid as I went stiff. I didn't think I could bear to see another pink tusk, the likes of which killed Maisry and my mother. Sweating hard and with pounding heart, I leaned against the mule.

Releasing a hard stream from a perfectly ordinary organ such as the villeins at Wanthwaite had, the Scot watched me curiously.

"Ye act like ye've ne'er seen a Scottish terse before." He gazed at his member. "I admit it mun put English parts to shame, for I've heard as how ye Englishmen dinna have pricks nor balls. Be it sooth then?"

"Nonsense," I snapped. "Every Englishman has one prick and six balls."

He tossed his head and bellowed to rent the sky. "Well bespoke, bairn—do what ye can for yer sorry race. But if ye're thralled with my horn now, wait till ye see it stretch to pull a finch."

He shook his organ dry and we climbed back onto the mule to continue our miserable ride. Enoch chatted on about his animals, how the mule was Twixt because it was neither male nor female, how the ass was Tippet because he carried so much. Meanwhile the pains of my bladder abated only to be replaced by the roiling and grucching of my stomach, for I was weak with hunger. At last I heard a faraway chapel ring Haute Tierce.

"There be a likely spot to dine," Enoch said, "with water for the beasts."

He headed to a flat vale where a stream shone under the trees. Too late we saw the rumps of horses and two men leaning over a pot of stew. Instantly my hunger was replaced by panic.

Enoch continued straight toward the water, but he slowed Twixt's gait and I felt his hand reach toward the thwitel in his sock. Now the wights heard us and looked upward. One was a pocked skeleton with a red cross sewn on his clerk's habit, but 'twas the other that had me in thrall: 'twas Sir Roland's squire. Aye, I'd seen him only from a distance but there could be no mistaking his thatch of red hair, his sunburnt freckled face. As we drew closer, I could make out the telltale *N* on his purple tunic. I swayed and had to grasp Twixt's mane to stay steady.

The squire lumbered to his feet. His mouth hung open in the midst of chewing; his small green eyes gleamed under pale bushy brows, and he, too, reached for a dagger.

"We don't want any Scots here," he wheezed. "Just move on and there'll be no trouble." He raised his dagger as if to throw.

"Our beasts need water."

The squire hurled his weapon, but was no match for the Scot. I saw one dagger lying at Twixt's feet while the red-haired wight clutched his bleeding hand and howled in anguish.

Enoch leveled his pike and pushed on the *N*. "'Tis anely a scratch and I mean no harm. But I want water."

"So take it," the squire mumbled, "and then be on with ye."

Enoch dismounted, picked up his thwitel, glared at the choleric squire, then lifted me to the ground. The pathetic clerk smiled with boiled gums. "You're a pretty child. Would you care to share our mess?"

I shook my head fearfully.

The squire, who'd paid me no heed till now, turned with sudden interest. "A *pretty* child *indeed*. Who are you, boy? What's your name?"

"T—Tom," I said quickly before Enoch could give my true name.

The Scot stared, as intrigued as the squire.

"Tom." The squire weighed the name as if 'twere a bag of oats. "Glad to meet ye, *Tom*. I'm Magnus Barefoot, squire to Sir Roland de Roncechaux. And this is my coz, Clerk Walter Pafey, who just returned from the Holy Land."

I said naught.

"Where are you from, Tom?" he persisted, leaning ominously.

"From—from Scotland," I said.

Enoch's face was a study in speculation and I prayed he wouldn't betray me.

By now the squire knelt so his eyes were level with mine. A brown speck like a grape-seed rode in one green iris. "Strange, you don't look or sound like a Scot."

I felt strong hands pull me back and Enoch answered. "This be Tom, my wee brother what's riding with me to Paris. He doesna speak as broad as me because he's 'prenticing for the Church and uses the Latin tongue. Say somewhat in Latin, brother."

"*Gallia est omnis divisa in partes tres*," I bleated.

Magnus Barefoot rose and faced Enoch. "Common Scots don't have wolves as pets," he said coldly.

"Namore do we," Enoch agreed. "This beast war a gift from the laird where I be steward. The wolf bit his young daughter. Now pardee, we mun take our water."

Balked, Magnus stepped away as I stared at the Scot, astonished at his fast wit. He pulled me to the edge of the stream where we stood with our backs to Magnus Barefoot. I dared not look at the Scot, grateful as I was, for I was also fearful. What was his motive?

When we turned to leave, we faced the squire again. He now smiled unctuously at Enoch.

"Forgive me, Scot, for my former harsh words. Wanthwaite Castle was sacked by Scots two days ago and all of Northumberland's men be alerted to suspicious characters."

"Scots doona attack across the border and ride south," Enoch replied.

I waited for my doom to fall at the word *Wanthwaite*, for soothly the treacherous wight meant to confront me now.

"I admire you Scottish wizards," Magnus continued in that same oily wheeze, "and especially in your art of physic."

Enoch raised his brows and waited. I, too, was much perplexed.

"You must have noted how my poor coz suffers from every sickness known to the Infidel, a heavy price for Crusading. I've often heard that the piss of a young boy can cure blisters. Do you think your brother would oblige by giving his water?"

"No, I won't!" I cried, seeing his purpose. He might not want to fight Enoch in direct combat but if he could expose me, I was lost.

Both men looked down on me, Magnus with triumph.

"That's no' Christian, bairn," Enoch scolded. "Take us to the sick man, Squire Barefoot."

The Scot's heavy hand led me back to the clerk. The poor fellow looked so grateful and beseeching together that for one wild moment I wondered if I could be wrong.

Enoch leaned close to the patient. "Ah, the worms hae delved deep. 'Twill take careful application, but may do."

"Strip off your habit," Magnus ordered Brother Walter.

The clerk obliged and soon knelt at my feet, his rump covered with angry whelks.

Magnus grinned fiendishly. "Go on, Tom, pull out your cock and do God's work."

My breath grew shallow, the scene pooled in my eyes, my heart raced. Then, as from a great distance, I heard the Scot's voice.

"Nay, Squire Barefoot, I sayed *careful application*, quhich means in two stages. Yif the boy spurts, we waste precious elixir. Here, Tom, use this bowl and see ye doona drip."

And I saw a possible reprieve. Smiling brazenly at Magnus Barefoot, I took the dish and lifted it up under my tunic to my crotch, using great care that my linen still dangled in front of the operation and concealed all. I spraddled my legs, bent a bit, and let go through the breach in my braies. I then lowered the brimming bowl to the grass close to the clerk, stood again, reached back to my crotch, took a thumb between the other thumb and forefinger, gave my invisible "member" a brisk shake as I'd seen Enoch do.

Squire Barefoot stared with narrow eyes, not totally convinced but not totally suspicious either. In any case, there was naught more he could ask.

"Yer bladder be big as a horse's, Tom," Enoch said admiringly. "Now, Squire, watch how I pour the ferst half."

We all watched my clear liquid spread over the angry whelks.

"There, let it soak in, so, fer an hour. Then rub it with a rough stone and give the second ministration."

"An hour?" Magnus protested, suspicious again.

"Either that or ye mun use goat dung and honey, and three days later ox piss."

"An hour, Magnus," Walter pleaded. "We're in no hurry."

Magnus smiled grudgingly at the wretch. "Nowhere that I can't make up the time. Be at ease, coz."

By now we were mounted again. "God's grace!" Enoch called in farewell.

The Scot slapped Twixt with a thong to make him trot up the rising road and I clung to the mule's mane again to stay astride. I didn't dare ask questions, nor did the Scot volunteer his intentions. At the sound of the next distant bell, he slowed our pace and without warning turned off the street, climbed up a shallow bank and sought cover in a rough thicket.

"Hssst!"

I heard a beat of hooves and saw a flash of purple and steel briefly through the brush. Magnus Barefoot riding alone.

"Ye might thank me fer giving us an hour's start on thc varlct," Enoch said dryly.

I gazed on him fearfully, not knowing how to answer. "Er— thank you. Only why is he following us?"

"Ye, bairn, he's following anely ye." He gave an evil smirk. "Ye can tell me why later."

I stared into those blue-pool eyes. He urged Twixt forth once more as I bumped on the neckbone in a daze. Aye, I would have to think up some plausible reason why I was being pursued, but my fantastick cells seemed in a trance. What could I say?

THE DAY GREW BITTER and chill, our road became steep as we started over the Pennine mountains, and my powers of invention dulled. Never had I dreamed of such outlandish country, naught but rocks, parched fern and straggly gnarled trees. Twixt's neck-bone fair cut me in two at each step, my stomach howled interminably, but most of all I was marrow weary. More than fear, my exhaustion o'erwhelmed me. With weariness came woe as I sank in a stupor of pain and grief. O'er and o'er my head jerked back, sinking against Enoch in spite of my efforts, then visions rose to make me sob, my own sobs woke me and the cycle began again.

I was wakened thoroughly only once through the long after-noon, when Lance attacked some sheep on the road before us. The shepherd waxed furious and we had to dismount and help him gather his flock.

"Whcn are we going to eat?" I whined, beyond shame.

"We mun find a shepherd's croft first, for it promises a foul night."

But the higher we climbed, the more the wind howled and the fewer the chances for shelter. At last the Scot gave up searching and' followed a twisty ridge downhill above a rushing stream. Occasion-ally I could glimpse valleys far below and thought the moon must ride at eye level tonight. Round and round we wound in the thicket, till at last Enoch dismounted and continued on foot, leaving me shivering alone under the shrill sough of a northerly wind.

"Cum, bairn, I've found as good as I can." He pulled Twixt forward. "Knarry knotty trees give little shelter, but 'twill do."

His camp was a narrow dry area under a rock ledge with two strong pines before it. Sleet now hit our faces and I huddled as close as I could to the wall.

The Scot regarded me with unfriendly eyes. "What do ye think ye're doin'?"

"I'm cold and hungry," I whimpered, "and tired."

"Ye'll be a good deal worse off if ye don't help, fer I'm not feeding no sluggards. If ye want to eat or sleep with shelter, ye'll move yer arse. Gather firewood in the wald by the gorge, and take the animals for water."

Gruffly he handed me the mule's bridle and I stumbled down a bank of hideous stubs to the raging water. When I returned, I had to rub the beasts, find fodder, then help tie furs to the trees for windbreaks. The skin on my hands broke into blisters.

"Ye're muckle soft for a steward's son," Enoch observed, "or did yer foster mother make a milksop of ye?"

I looked the murder I dared not express, for I'd never worked so hard. He didn't even notice.

Kneeling by the pile of wood I'd collected, he fanned twigs with a pan of charred tow and started a blaze. He arranged several pans of food on top, plus a kettle of water with birds in it, then liberally salted the lot.

"Cum, let's wash."

He dragged me to the stream again where we splashed our faces and hands. By the time we sat by the fire, I hardly cared whether I ate or not. He poured a horn of hot ale.

"Here's yer methier," he said. "Wassail."

I savored the warm drink and quickly took another. The food that followed was passing strange, but food nonetheless: we ate raw pressed venison, cocky-leeky, eel porridge, red cole-wart and cabbage and finally our last course, haggis. Haggis was the worst of the lot, being a sheep's stomach filled with oatmeal, liver and lights, but I choked down every crumb. I knew Enoch had a speculative look, but I didn't care.

At last I settled back, groggy with warmth and the hot food in my stomach, secure behind our fur curtain from the driven drench of fine sleet.

"Now what do ye think it would be worth for Magnus Barefoot to know yer whereabouts?" Enoch asked softly.

And I turned chill as a corpse. "I don't know what you mean."

"I think ye do, *Tom.* Mayhap there's a reward on yer head, mayhap ye've run away from yer rightful owner. Suppose ye tell me sooth why a lad called Alexander what speaks Latin pretends to be plain Tom, the steward's son."

"My master—er—William by name, was the oldest of three brothers," I said feverishly, then stopped.

"Aye, gae on," the Scot prodded. "I want no invention."

"And he had a son named Tom who was milk-brother to me; our nurse was that same Dame Margery you saw with me today. And our kind master, William that is—"

"I can remember a name fer two heartbeats. Get on wi' yer tale."

". . . educated us as if we were real brothers. Then when my own father died—of the pox, as I told you—Master William adopted me. Then his own son Tom caught the pox as well and I was made heir by the father, William. Then William himself was struck down." I paused, wondering if so many people would die of the pox.

"How big an estate? Where?"

I became confused. "Well, I believe it has—er—twenty good fields."

"Fiefdoms?"

"Aye, yes, that's what you call them."

"A good halding. Where?"

I racked my brain. "Close to—Newcastle." I had no notion where Newcastle might be, but Father Michael had gone there once so I knew it existed.

Enoch pursed pleased lips. "Newcastle. That be rich lond, on the right side of the oatline."

"Yes but—you recall that Master William has two brothers?"

"Do ye think I be an ass? Of course."

"The one in York, where I'm headed now, and his name be George and he's the youngest, well, he wants to support me in my inheritance. But the middle one whose name be George—"

"Ye just sayed the youngest was George."

"Aye, you're making me befuddled. The middle one is Gregory. Gregory is challenging my claim and wants me dead."

"I see. And where do Magnus Barefoot fit this muddle?"

"Magnus Barefoot?" I'd forgotten him entirely.

"Aye, ye mun know the squire since he's giving chase. He claims he serves a knight called Roland."

"I know naught of any Roland, but I've heard of Magnus," I prattled. "He works for George."

"George?"

"I mean, Gregory. Aye, for Gregory. He's a—a—I'm not sure what you call such wights, but he's been offered reward to kill me."

There was a long silence as Enoch stirred the coals.

He laughed then, a harsh dry hack. "I, too, be the youngest of three brothers. And I war steward at one time."

I didn't comment, not certain whether that meant he believed me or no.

"Tell me true, Alex-Tom-Want, how much do ye think Magnus would pay fer yer hide in one piece? Mar or less than George?"

I was shocked out of my wits by his black crass soul, though it confirmed what I knew of Scots. I sought desperately to find good reason he should spare me. "George—is—has—money, methinks. He's something to do with York Cathedral. Also—he says we can win in Assize."

"Assize?" There was an unexpected interest here.

"Aye, that's what he said." I couldn't recall exactly where I'd heard the word *Assize*, but my father's spirit must have supplied it to me.

"A decision by court. Aye, that's where the future points, mind me, Alex."

"Aye."

"And Gregory?"

I thought of my father's description of Roland de Roncechaux. "He claims to be a knight but is a common brigand. He has no money, I know."

"Wal, Alex, ye hae struck a dale. I'll git ye to George in York, and ye'll git me reward, or the Devil take thee."

A log broke on the fire, shooting sparks upward so that the Scot's eyes glinted red.

"Aye," I whispered.

He squeezed my shoulder hard. "Swear."

"I swear."

At last I was permitted to squirm deep in furs with my wolf's warm body next to mine. One day and a night since my parents had died and I was in the clutches of a thieving, murdering Scot, but he was dense as well, *Deo gratias.*

And I was still alive.

Before I could think of my situation more, I fell asleep.

6

 WAS WAKENED BY A RUDE SHOVE FROM A BOOT.

"Get up, dawdle-bones, before the craws pick at ye."

At first I knew not where I was but then it came back, how he'd been willing to trade my life for gold. Bile rose in my mouth, which I swallowed: he was a giant, I was a dwarf. Sulkily I staggered to my feet. An iron-gray lid hugged the earth tight and 'twas hard to say if the sun had risen or no.

"Take the animals to drink," the Scot ordered, "and see ye make haste. Ye've held us up long enow as it is."

Stop grucching, I thought, as I dragged the animals with me, for we'll part this day as soon as possible and you can fly straight as a warlock to Hell. I bent over the stream and splashed the sleep from my face.

Then I sought a private bush and squatted. Much refreshed after a time, I reached for a handful of soft young oak leaves to wipe. When I tossed them aside, I noticed that their green had turned red. I'd stood and begun pulling up my tights before the meaning struck me!

Again I squatted and wiped; again I saw red. Red blood? Holy

Mother of Christ, I'm bleeding! From my crotch, aye, where
Maisry got it, aye, and my mother, too, though she didn't bleed. *O
Deus, juva me*! Am I going to die then?

Almost quelling terror was a rage as big and black as the glowering heaven, for the Scot had done this to me. Yes, in the night when
I'd been heavy with sleep. No, more than sleep, drugged! No wonder that haggis had tasted so foul. Come at me with the serpent
under his plaid, out in the dark to attack while I slept, pricked at my
crotch to kill!

But why wasn't I dead?

I touched my wound tentatively and it didn't even hurt. Was it
possible he'd missed his aim somewhat? Or was his power less than
Sir Roland's? Or maybe it was a slow spell that would drag my life
from me drop by drop so I hardly noticed, so that he could deliver
me to Northumberland or, worse, marry me himself! That must be
it, for he could have sliced my throat with his organ in the manner
Maisry suffered.

"Alex, what's holding ye?" he bawled from above.

"I'm coming!"

Hastily I took the stuffing from my toes and placed the rags
inside my harness to catch the dripping. *Reward*, he'd asked for.
Aye, I'd reward him, and I clutched the handful of hemlock hidden
with my treasure.

Keeping my eyes averted, I helped him break camp. When it
came time to mount, however, I looked at him with all the gall I
could muster and said with heavy significance: "I can't ride on that
bone, tender as I am. You'll have to give me a pelt."

"Dynts yer balls, do it? Sure, lad, that be better now," and with
brazen smiles, he piled on a sheepskin.

We didn't speak again till we stopped to dine on the edge of a
bleak moor.

"Tell me, Alex, when did yer mother die?"

"Three days ago." I was so intent on keeping my tone cold that I
forgot I'd said naught about my mother's being dead.

"And ye're how old?"

"Eight." At least I got that right.

"That's what I thought, a wee babe of a bairn. No wonder that
ye called me mother in the nicht and huddled close."

"Yes, and I remember what you did," I said with the same heavy significance, but he merely leaned over and patted my knee. I threw my gruel into the fire to show my disgust, but the gesture was wasted on such a monster.

All day long the countryside grew ever more desolate as one gray heathery curve gave way to another and it looked as if I'd be with Enoch Angus Boggs forever. My only ray of hope was that far from feeling weaker, I seemed to wax stronger as the afternoon wore on. I might survive this yet.

We muddled ahead for long aching hours until we were in deep twilight and the wind rose to a harsh freezing gale, blinding our eyes and chilling our very marrow. Our situation looked hopeless, for the Roman Street stretched to eternity without so much as an ant hill to protect us. Then suddenly Enoch pointed and shouted: "We're in muckle luck, Alex. On the horizon there, an inn."

He urged our weary beasts to hurry but it was near dark when we halted before a rude leaning timber hut with half its thatch missing and a banging shingle with the legend: Inn of the Gray Falcon. The Scot hesitated.

"Ye knaw, bairn, that the chancit be that Magnus Barefoot is here. We havena passed him."

"Let's go on," I begged.

Enoch shook his shaggy head. "Nay, e'en the clattering streams will freeze this nicht. Best have shelter, come what may."

Soothly the wind stung my face like nettles and brought tears to my eyes. Yet I was so o'ercome by fear that my knees collapsed and I fell to the ground when I dismounted.

"Ho there, take heart. I'll protect my inwestment."

He knocked and the inn door flew open; a scrawny boy staggered toward our beasts. To my horror, Lance growled ferociously and would have sprung if I hadn't clutched his neck.

"I'm Jimmy," the boy piped weakly, "come to help ye with yer horses."

"Looks like our wolf prefers my brother Tom," Enoch said as he stepped between Jimmy and Lance. "Tom, ye see to Tippet and Twixt whilst I talk to Jimmy aboot his other guests."

Gratefully I grabbed Lance's scruff and pulled him along with our animals to the stable behind the inn. Once inside, I lost no time.

I dropped my braies, removed my rags and held them up in the dim light. They were dry! Baffled, I turned them this way and that, able to discern only a few rusted spots from this morning. I touched myself and verified that I had no injury. Before I could think more, Enoch bawled my name from outside.

"Coming!"

"Magnus and George be nocht here yet," Enoch informed me.

"George?" I caught his sharp look. "Oh, yes, George."

We followed Jimmy into a tiny, dark room. There were a host and hostess, two nuns huddled like blackbirds around the firepit, and these few people took all the space. Smoldering embers under a pot gave forth billows of acrid smoke but little heat or light; two rush lamps in the far corners completed our illumination. Meantime the gale was hardly impeded by the crude log walls. Animal pelts had been hung for warmth and now swayed til and fro as if the whole structure were breathing.

Enoch stepped to the center and took a menacing stance.

"Yif ye do exactly as I say, ye have nothing to fear." But his low threatening voice said otherwise and I could sense the panic around us.

"Jesus, help us!" screamed the older nun.

The sickly host reached a trembling hand. "Please, Sire, take whatever you like and leave us in peace. We have no valuables here."

"I be no brigand!" His blue eyes blazed. "I need to hide my wee brother. Now ye show me whar he'll be safe."

Everyone looked at me uncertainly while Enoch quickly searched the room. There wasn't even a fur large enough to cover me and my case looked hopeless. Just as the Scot turned back to the quaking host, he stopped suddenly.

"Quhat's that?"

We all followed his pointing finger upward.

"A shelf where I store a few personals," our hostess said.

"Would it take Tom's weight?"

"I don't know. No one's ever . . ."

Enoch was already lifting down bundles of rags to reveal a shaky perch made of a few rough boards laid across portruding logs. It had nothing to recommend it except that it was hard to see: it jutted just above a man's eye level in the very darkest part of the room.

"Well, Tom, looks like an unblythe bird hae found his nest. Up ye go."

He swung me so high that my head hit the thatch and knocked several chunks of dirt to the floor; then he eased me cautiously onto the shelf, releasing his hold slowly as the boards took my weight.

"There." He removed his hands. "Lay yerself as flat as ye can."

Hardly daring to draw breath, I extended first one leg, then another, and stretched out on my stomach. I squinted my eyes against the acrid layers of smoke and looked down at the folk below, their chins lit by the fire and their eyes in blackness.

"Waesucks, he's as wisible as a peacock on a thornbush."

"Put this over him," the younger nun suggested, offering her black cape.

Enoch took the garment and tucked it around me, even over my head. Apparently the effect was satisfactory, for there was a general sigh of relief. The cape didn't impede my own vision, however; I could see everything through the spaces between the boards.

Once I was hidden, an uneasy silence fell upon the group. Again Enoch took his threatening position, and now his dhwitel was in his hand.

"Everyone, list to me guid. Thar be no time to explain our situation, but one, mayhap two, scoundrels want my brother's life. I canna tell when they'll cum—boot I think 'twill be soon—and when they do, ye're to lat me do the talkin' and agree wi' whate'er I say. Yif anyone spakes otherwise, 'twill be his last word on this earth."

He tossed his gleaming dagger so that it twirled three times and fell on his open palm. All eyes followed the blade.

The hostess rubbed her hands on her hips. "We might as well be good fellows while we wait. I be Betty, Scot, and this be Bibs, my husband, and our boy Jimmy. Our guests are—er—"

"Sister Petronilla," said the younger in low dulcet tones, "novice in St. Anne's Abbey to the north. And this is my mentor, Sister Ursula."

"Herbalist at St. Anne's," added the toothless older nun in a quavering voice.

Before Enoch could say his name, a horse whinnied outside. The company froze. I panicked so that the whole room swayed and I thought that I would surely fall.

"Remember, nocht a worrrrrd," Enoch said. "Gae take their horses, Jimmy." And he whispered into the boy's ear.

Jimmy nodded and darted into the dark when the door opened and Magnus Barefoot entered.

"He's here!" he shouted exultantly over his shoulder.

"Where?"

Sir Roland de Roncechaux! My senses went tinty as the Norman knight stood there in a circle of light. All other figures receded into whirling darkness.

"Where's the boy?" he asked in that deep accented voice I remembered so well.

"Be ye referrin' to my brother Tom?" Enoch asked. "How be the spotted clerk, Master Barefoot?"

Neither man answered. Instead they began a grim search of the inn, much as Enoch had done but in ruder manner. They kicked at the frail walls, ripped furs from their hooks, opened Sister Ursula's traveling chest and spilled her contents onto the floor. Sister Petronilla knelt to replace them. Then Sir Roland looked upward.

"Tom be an angel boot he canna fly yet," Enoch said sarcastically.

His words had little effect, but a chunk of dirt did: it fell from where my head had touched and made Sir Roland dig at his eyes.

"The boy be nocht here," Enoch added. "He's laid up wi' a bad leg wi' a shepherd a half day's ride back."

"Search the stable," Roland ordered Magnus curtly.

Magnus pushed Betty aside to go out the door. Sir Roland stood slouched on one leg and regarded the company, each in turn; he settled on Bibs.

"I'm Lord Roland de Roncechaux, baron in your county," he said loftily to the host. "You know your duty and you know the punishment if you disobey your lord. I seek a runaway boy and am willing to offer ample reward for any knowledge of his whereabouts."

He lifted a bag of coins from his pocket and jingled them.

Bibs reacted to the title and money in equal parts, I trowe. His mouth began to work and he made little stuttering gasps.

"My brother be no runaway," Enoch interjected strongly. He too reached to his belt; very deliberately he removed his thwitel and began picking his teeth.

Magnus returned. "The boy's not in the stable."

Roland looked at Enoch. "You say he's at a shepherd's croft?"

"Aye, *George*." Enoch waited for a response from Roland, then continued. "My mule stepped into a hole on the street and threw Tom. His leg is broken, mayhap his hip as well. I found a shepherd to leave him with while I rode on to find help. Bibs here be gang with me ferst thing in the morning."

"We'll ride with you as well," Roland said grimly, as he removed his sword. "Hostess, serve us some flesh."

As the company took places to eat, I thought on Roland's title: *Lord* Roland, a *baron*, and realized that he referred to Wanthwaite. Only my precarious life stood between him and the reality. How long could I live? I tried to breathe evenly and keep my wits.

It seemed to take an eternity for the company to finish the mutton stew. Everyone imbibed mightily of ale, especially Magnus, and the host brought a pail of brew to supply an evening's drinking. Only Enoch didn't partake; the Scot stretched casually across the door and watched Roland. The Norman knight sat close to Sister Petronilla; his predatory eyes made me realize that the young nun was soothly a beautiful damsel. Her dark eyes flashed and she had full sultry lips.

"Begging your pardon, Sister," he ventured politely, "but I'd like to hear how you came by your new vocation. You must be very happy."

The sister spoke in low distinct words. "I feel like a prisoner condemned to Hell."

Everyone gasped and Sister Ursula wiggled forward to Roland.

"You must forgive her, sir. She's much distraught, but will be happy once she reaches St. Anne's. Our abbey is a paradise."

"Paradise comes with a hefty price," added Petronilla.

"Paradise!" echoed Magnus Barefoot in a drunken rasp. "I can find paradise right here this very night. What say you, harlot?"

He lurched against our hostess and knocked her to the ground. Bibs stood close, but could do naught; he looked on helplessly as Betty rolled her eyes toward him. Magnus buried his head in her ample lap and bawled out a song:

> *"I put my pole in Eve's deep hole*
> *And that was Paradise, Sir;*
> *I dug all day, we both were gay*
> *At labor oh so nice, Sir;*
> *And a ding, dong, bell*
> *Merry dong*
> *Long dong*
> *Ding!"*

He forgot to add that he murdered Eve with his long pole, I thought. Aye, that was Roland and Magnus's view of paradise: to slaughter innocent maids as they walked along the paths, to kill my mother who never hurt anyone. I pressed my lips to hold back tears.

Meantime Roland still pursued Sister Petronilla.

"You intrigue me, Sister. Surely you're fulfilled by being the Bride of Christ. Or aren't you?"

She understood his insinuation.

"Better Him than you," spoke the wimple. "At least He's dead and will leave me alone."

Roland leered at the challenge and deliberately touched her full lips with his finger. "Of course we've never met, but I'm willing to covet you, if that's what you expect."

She slapped his hand away.

"You or someone like you, what does it matter? In any case, a landless knight picked by King Henry."

Sir Roland rubbed his offended hand. "I'm far from landless, and let's not hear treason against King Henry."

"Is the bare truth treason? He wed me to a brute!"

"With your disposition, Sister, I think you should give thanks that he married you to anyone."

"I give thanks," she blazed, "right up King Henry's haunchbones."

Magnus yexxed loudly and tugged at Betty's skirts.

"I give thanks up Betty's haunchbones!

"At Vesper's chime we still beat time
And worked hard all the night, Sir;
The moon did climb, we heard the Prime
And fucked till it were light, Sir;
And a ding, dong, bell
Merry dong
Long dong
Ding!"

I could hardly wait for him to finish his obscene verse, for I must hear more about King Henry. I prayed that Sister Petronilla continue.

Sister Ursula again interceded.

"Please pardon her, Lord Roland, and be not offended. She's still in mourning for her departed husband and in no mood to marry so soon, that's all."

"My first husband was almost dead when I married him," Sister Petronilla said with heat. "At least he was kindly and left me a rich woman. That's when my difficulties with your Norman king began. First Henry wanted me to turn over my hard-won estate to the Saladin Tithe so he could reap glory in Jerusalem. When I demurred, he took his share anyway and awarded me and mine to a charming brute called Sir Denys. Sir Denys promptly beat me about the face and cast me into the dungeon because I refused to give up my treasure."

Her mellow voice had risen to a shout by the finish, and I was horrified by her words. King Henry had stolen her estate? Had assigned a husband who beat her? *Could my father have been wrong?*

Sir Roland answered me to some degree. He pulled away from the Sister angrily.

"By law King Henry could have confiscated your lands outright and thrust you directly into a nunnery. By law a husband has a perfect right to beat his wife unto unconsciousness. Only then must he stop lest her body give out a great fart and she die."

Sister Petronilla laughed nastily. "Would that I'd farted straight in his face."

The nun rose and walked to Enoch, a wise move. His thwitel was again in sight as he picked once more at his teeth.

Betty too was struggling and I hoped Enoch would rescue her as well by his presence.

"No, Sire, no more ale. We must to bed . . ."

"To bed," Magnus agreed as he pushed her roughly onto the floor.

Bibs cast an imploring glance at Enoch who shook his head almost imperceptibly.

Betty rose to her elbow, her sleeve pulled from her shoulder. She tried to crawl away and her skin shone like ruddy cream; the fire picked up small creatures moving in her mat of hair.

"No, I can't. You see . . ." She said something into Magnus's ear.

"That be wunnerful," he replied thickly. "I have a taste for doxies in their bleeding time. Aye, that slickery four days every month be best: sticky and soft as eels.

> *"I spilled my seed, Eve 'gan to bleed,*
> *Her queinte I longed to lick, Sir;*
> *It flowed much worse, for 'twas God's curse,*
> *And strengthened up my prick, Sir;*
> *And a ding, dong, bell*
> *Merry dong*
> *Long dong*
> *Ding!"*

The drama below blurred before my eyes as the meaning of his awful words penetrated my mind. *Women bled four days every month!* Then the Scot hadn't attacked me after all! *Didn't know I was female.* My relief was quickly followed by dismay. Every month? How could I conceal my sex then? And wait, Maisry had said I would grow breasts *when I became a woman in a different way. Benedicite!* Without thinking, I reached toward my chest and thereby released a rain of dust. It sounded like hail to my sensitive ears and I realized that conversation had ceased.

Magnus lay in a drunken stupor; Roland was curled on his side in the choice position close to the fire; the two nuns now huddled as one; the host and his family must be directly under me as I couldn't see them; Enoch still sat with his back to the door, quiet but with open eyes. The fire slowly turned to gray ash; the rush lamps went out altogether. Now the wind filled the void, a mean icy breath blowing viciously. I knew not what to do. Did Enoch mean to lead Sir Roland away in the morn so that I might escape alone?

Then the Scot slowly rose. He crossed the room like a black cat, reached toward me. First, though, he must take away the sister's cape. He lifted. It was caught under my body. He gave a few short sharp tugs and dirt rattled ominously. He made a gesture that I should try to rise slightly. Cautiously, I put my elbows into position and tried. A board groaned, creaked, splintered! The whole shelf crashed in a deafening explosion!

Everyone woke!

"The child! Stop!" Roland cried.

Enoch leaped like a bull with me on his shoulder. I saw Petronilla throw her cape over Roland's head as we ran headlong out into the wind. Enoch opened the stable doors and slapped Roland and Magnus's horses on the rumps to make them move.

"Hayt there! Go! Go!"

The startled beasts neighed and galloped across the wastes. We mounted the mule and rode toward the street, but Roland was waiting. Enoch raised his pike and thrust into the knight's chest-spoon. Roland gasped and fell, though I didn't think he was dead.

We rode as fast as we could by the side of the street to avoid its holes as the shouts grew fainter behind us. Into a black howl we rode, saying nothing, feeling nothing except exultation to be alive. At dawn, Enoch veered off Dere Street into the welcome forests on the far side of the Pennines. We followed the path of a raging stream for many miles before we halted by a quiet back eddy, under a grove of ash. Enoch lifted me to the ground.

"Oh, Enoch, you saved my life!" I cried. "How can I ever thank you?"

"I'm aboot to tell ye how ye can thank me." He leered, his teeth red in the rising sun. "Alix Wanthwaite."

GAZED UP AT HIS SAVAGE FACE COVERED WITH wild bronze elflocks, into those shrewd hard-sky eyes, those square grinning teeth that sensed a victory.

"Aye, Alexander Wanthwaite, new baron of Wanthwaite. Ye're a crafty lad, I'll give ye that."

And I took heart—I'd misheard that "Alix"; my secret was safe. "How did you find out?"

"Magnus Barefoot couldna keep it to hisself, but would be ever blatherin' in a loud whisper to that Sir Roland. 'Alex Wanthwaite,' he sayed, and it didna take long to see that Alex Want and Alex Wanthwaite had a passin' acquaintance."

"Very shrewd," I said.

"Aye, but I need to know more. What be their interest in ye? Why do they want ye dead?"

"Because they sacked my castle," I answered in an even hollow voice. "Sir Roland personally slew my own mother."

The words echoed in the sylvan glade, mocking its beauty. Even Enoch sensed their horror. He put his hand roughly on my shoulder.

"I'm sorry, bairn. No wonder ye cry for her."

I said nothing about the Scottish accomplices.

After a pause he continued. "And I take it they fear ye'll find means of gettin' Wanthwaite back, so they're out to kill ye fast."

I nodded. "I'm sole heir, but too young to claim it alone. My Uncle Frank who lives in London is my guardian. When I reach him, he'll take the legal moves to reinstate me. If you help me, I can assure you he'll give you proper reward."

He whistled his bagpipe tune and watched me with unseeing eyes as he thought. "Look ye, Alex, what will ye give to be deliv-

ered safe in London-town to yer uncle? Think now, for as I see it ye
canna git there without my help."

"You'll have to talk to him, but I'm sure he'll be generous."

"No," he said sharply, "with ye, richt now. Ye be the Baron of
Wanthwaite, the richest wight in Northumberland except for yer
earl. Ye tell me, and think what it means."

I considered. I probably couldn't get to London without him,
for I dare not return to Dere Street with an army at my heels.

"I personally will guarantee that when I take possession of
Wanthwaite again, I'll give you one hundred silver livres."

'Twas a generous sum, I thought, even for a greedy Scot, so I
was taken aback at his scornful bray.

"One hundred livres *fer yer life*? E'en a Scot values his breath
more than that. Mayhap ye're too young to deal, sae I'll gae back to
my original statement: *I'll tell ye* what to do. Now, Alex, lad, as a
youngest son, my drive is fer land and only land. I'll get ye to yer
Uncle Frank; aye, I'll do more if need be and chancit what e'er
comes our way, but in return ye'll promise me half of yer lands here
and now. Half of yer lands, nae more, nae less. There'll be no quib-
blin' or dealin' further. That's my terms."

He fair knocked my breath away. *Give up half of Wanthwaite?*
After what my father had said about his and my mother's souls
resting there? Never, never would I part with a mudball of Wanthwaite, not a twig from the park, not a stone from a drywall. I gazed
into that tough Scottish craw and smiled sweetly:

"Aye, Enoch, I see your point. Half my land is a small price for
my very life and the other half be plenty for me. The risk is great for
both of us. Why shouldn't the stakes be equal?"

He grinned back in broad triumph. "Ye're a smart lad and yer
good blood shows. Let me have yer hand."

I thrust my right hand forward into his grasp. No sooner had we
completed our shake than we heard a chapel bell in the distance;
instantly the Scot's gloating changed to caution.

"A clinkumbell jowin' Prime," he said. "Best be fleeing, bairn,
while we may. Here, take a few farls to stay yer hunger."

He lifted me atop Twixt again and handed me hard pellets
which had the feel and taste of dried mud balls. We shared

nappy from a leather flask to wash them down, but I was too panicked to care whether I ate and wished only that Enoch would push
his mule faster. He sought silent footings and took many pauses to
test the wind so that we seemed to creep. Usually any rustlings
turned out to be animals or birds, but once we heard human voices
and Enoch cursed softly that we'd drifted too close to Dere Street.

After a few false stops, Enoch was satisfied by a domed willow
whose tendrils created a room. Huddled behind its swaying circle of
fronds, we felt safe from view, though the spongy ground was criss-
crossed with streamlets and we had to cut faggots to make dry pal-
lets for ourselves and our beasts. We all bedded close, warm in our
mutual body heat and steamy breaths. Enoch and I spoke no more
that day of Wanthwaite.

The next day was the same, and the next: silent and tense. By
the third night out we were both hungry and cold for we dared
not build a fire or take game. Enoch explained that the punishment
for hunting in the king's park was death. Only Lance could take
his fill.

Indeed, the next day I became aware that prime game roamed as
pets around us. Only the king and his men could hunt here, but
they rarely did. Twice we came across ancient deserted villages
where people had been deprived of their farms to make way for the
king's sport. There we found roofs for our heads, wells for water,
good forage for Twixt and Tippet. And at the second village, Enoch
again brought up Wanthwaite.

"Where exactly be this Wanthwaite castle? Close to where we
met?"

His half-closed eyes glinted like sunstruck water and his voice
was deceptively friendly, but I instantly sensed a sinister purpose.

"Nowhere near there. Dame Margery had led me for the better
part of a week, I believe. I told you—Newcastle."

"Should be easy to find."

"Aye." I tried not to show my fear. "Speaking of distance, how
long do you think it will be before we get to London?"

"Twa weeks, more or less."

Two weeks! And I'd promised Dame Margery I would be back
in a week. Briefly I wondered if Enoch was deliberately stretching
our journey but decided he had no cause. No, I'd just have to suffer

through this period and get to the king as soon as possible once in London. The king would deal with the Scot.

From that night Enoch plied me with questions about my castle as I invented one "fact" after another. 'Twas deliberate on my part, but forsooth I couldn't have answered him honestly if I'd wanted to, for I discovered that I knew little about the husbandry of my estate. Yet 'twas better to make up answers than to admit my ignorance, for that might also admit my true sex, and I recalled what my father had warned: that a man could get Wanthwaite by marrying me. To be wed to a Scot!

However, Enoch accepted me completely as a boy which both heartened and surprised me. Certes I was feminine in my own eyes and gave myself away a hundred times daily. I finally concluded that for Enoch—and I hoped for everybody—once the sex of a person is established, that's the end of the matter. He seemed not to notice that I always sought privacy to relieve myself. Nevertheless, when Enoch wasn't looking I studied his person and habits, learning how to be manly and oafish together. If he'd turned suddenly, he would have found me strutting cockily in his shadow, my chin up, my feet pounding the ground as a woodman hits with his ax. When I spoke with him, I thrust out a belligerent lip, gazed coldly into his eyes, cracked my words like nuts. Sitting over odious cocky-leeky, I plunged my whole hand into the slops, chewed voraciously with open mouth as the fat dripped down my chin, then belched to make the leaves tremble. I blew my nose into my palm or directly onto the ground instead of using my sleeve as I'd been taught.

I didn't consciously try to imitate his Scottish way of speaking but certes one of us was changing, for his speech now sounded normal to my ear. On the one hand I wasn't eager to assume his guttural grunts and stops, but on the other 'twould be a good disguise if we were to pass as brothers. However, I would never master his savage vocabulary though I knew well what he meant most times by the way he said it. He was always positive no matter what: positively angry, positively hungry, positively calculating, positively suspicious. Not a subtle beast, a bull not a snake.

Enoch was particular about bathing and plunged into icy streams or weirs as joyfully as a salmon. Over and over, he invited me to join him though I demurred. On the day he announced that we were halfway to London, he said that we could be more relaxed and we lolled by a pretty pond after our midday nap. Suddenly he picked me up like a babe:

"Alex, no offense but ye stink like an otter that's been dead three weeks."

And he tossed me screaming through the air to the center of the water where I promptly sank to the bottom. I felt his hand grapple for my hair and pull upward.

"Waesucks, lad, why didn't ye say that ye couldna swim?"

I sputtered that I could, then fell silent. Best let him think as he list, for of course 'twas my treasure that pulled me down.

One night we lay gazing upward at the sky.

"See, Enoch, a shadow on the moon. Be that significant?" For he knew all omens.

"Ye've a keen eye. 'Tis the good folet Abunda, a witch that's guiding our steps."

"But I thought witches were bad."

"Who told ye that? Some witches be mischievous, but those take human form. Abúnda be a fine folet."

He then turned his back and snored as I continued to watch the drifting witch. By day I was too nervous to dwell on my grief but at night, alone under the stars, my loss made the cold earth seem a grave. Mayhap this witch could guide me back to my home and to life. I gazed and thought until the darkness dispersed her into the void.

THE NEXT DAY we met people. Enoch and Lance heard them before I did and took their familiar listening stance.

"Summun's callin' fer help," Enoch whispered. "Listen: 'Help! Help!' 'Tis a man callin' but there's also a woman—no, twa women."

Now I could hear them as well. "They're speaking some form of Saxon, not the Norman-French patois."

"Aye, they canna be Roncechaux. Well, bairn, what say ye? Shall we be chivalrous cnichts?"

"I think we should—you can't tell what may have happened." And again I saw Wanthwaite burning.

Warily Enoch prodded Twixt ahead while we both strained to see the distraught man. Well before he came in view, his voice was joined by a woman's howl of pain and a second woman's harangue of anger. We entered a clearing containing a mean hut of sticks and thatch whence came piercing screams, while before it knelt a scrawny churl crying for help and defending himself as best he could from the blows leveled with astounding force by a dark old crone.

"You feckless hog, you pig's arse, you timorous mite, get up and help!" she bellowed.

"I can't, Aggie, honest I can't," he whined. "The pope will come personally and kill me if I do and I'll ne'er get into Heaven."

"The pope's in Rome, God rot his soul, and I'm here! So consider that, you miserable turd."

She beat him with a handful of faggots to tear his skin in shreds and he took it meekly. 'Twas possible she was a witch in sooth for her brown face folded onto itself like saddle bags and her formidable arm had unnatural strength.

"Do you want the babe to lose its father?" he protested.

"Aye, that I do. Better that than father lose babe, that's *my* law which says you're hiding behind the canon law because you're a blubbering (*wham*), slobbering (*wham*), weak-gutted (*wham*), bitch-boned (*wham*), sour-breathed (*wham*), sticked swine what puts your popper in a pouch, then loses gullet when the seed comes back a babe. Get off your knees now and give help, for murder be a worse sin than witnessing a birth."

"Not for a man, Aggie, not for a man. Canon law says—"

"Get off your toute-ass and *help!*" she finished for him.

Enoch pushed Twixt a mite closer, then raised his horned hat and spoke politely. "Beggin' yer pardon, ma'am, be this man abusin' ye?"

There was a moment of startled silence while both the bleeding churl and the dame looked up with gaping jaws, nonplussed.

Her eyes, small and red as ladybugs, suddenly fastened on me and she jerked me rudely to the ground.

"Come on," she ordered. "You're a boy, not a man, so canon law doesn't apply. If I don't get help, Maud will die."

Now the screams from the hut took over to make my skin crawl. I cast a beseeching look at Enoch as Dame Aggie dragged me inside the shack. Neither of us could stand upright in the thick dark space and my ears split, my nose quivered and my stomach lurched at the sound and stench of the place. Gradually I saw a figure rolling on the floor at my feet, clutching a great mound on her belly.

"Oh, God help me!" the figure cried. "Where's Lucina? Lucina, come help me! Anybody, make the pain stop!"

"Don't worry, dear," Aggie soothed, "I've got help at last, a very experienced young leecher." Her tone was crisp. "You, boy, kneel down and take two corners of the blanket."

I knelt.

"Now lift when I say."

I got back to my feet, holding the corners. At her signal I tried to lift and nothing happened.

"Lift, you fool!"

Again I tugged along with the dame, but her side went up alone and Maud fell at my feet.

"Do you need a few lashes to give you strength? Up, I say!"

Terrified, I lifted with force I didn't know I had and Maud hung between us on a hammock, screaming ever louder in a series of spasms. We were killing her sure and my knees knocked in panic.

"Heave!" bawled the dame.

And I heaved as Maud flew high and fair broke my arms in her fall.

"Heave!"

Again we tossed her like a pulpy rock, up and down, up and down, while her stomach began strange gyrations.

"Now, lower her easy."

I did.

"Now sit on her stomach and get in rhythm."

"I'll hurt her," I whimpered.

"Sit on her stomach!"

I sat.

"*Up*! Lay on sore. *Up*! Lay on sore."

I felt the lump moving under me and closed my eyes.

"Stop, that's enough. Come help me here."

Too cowed to protest, I crawled to Maud's lower end and witnessed a huge dark mouth stretch wide, then spit a waxy bag in a torrent of slime and blood while Aggie pulled and pulled. The bag was fastened inside by a long piece of gut which Aggie snapped with her teeth.

"Lordy, Maud, it's twins born in their own caul. Was ever such a blessing? Look, darling, twins!"

Aggie ripped at the caul with a knife and lifted two wormy creatures as I leaned forward to see what they might be.

I gasped aloud.

"Get out of here!" Dame Aggie snarled viciously.

"But—" I said, too dazed to move.

"And not a word!"

"But—" I repeated in a stupor.

"Here's your payment. Don't let me see your silly face when I come out or you'll be sorry."

Still toty, I felt something thrust in my hand and was suddenly in bright light holding the bloody caul, which looked like a boar's liver.

"Augh!" I dropped it in disgust.

"Pick it up and let's go," Enoch commanded sharply.

Reluctantly I obeyed and soon we were riding rapidly away. When we were well beyond earshot, Enoch questioned me closely upon what had transpired for he'd never seen a baby be born. I described the revolting details as best I could and at last reached the terrifying mystery.

"And when I leaned to look closely, Enoch, one babe looked normal though hideous ugly, but the other had only two holes where his nose should have been."

I turned anxiously to see his reaction.

"That explains it, certes, for otherwise the old dame would never have give up the caul. She was buyin' yer silence."

"About the freak?"

"Aye, partly. Worse for Maud be the fact that her secret's out. When one twin shaws a marked difference fram the other, ye can be sure that twa sires bred the mare."

"What?"

"There's been two bittern booming in the mire. Adultery, my lad, simple adultery."

Adultery! One of the deadly sins, I knew, though I'd never been sure what it signified nor did I now. Yet I must have had some notion of it for I found myself surprised that a creature as low as Maud would be guilty. Somehow I thought only kings were adulterous. The sin went down somewhat in my estimation, like gluttony.

I held the purple-veined slime at arm's length. "Why is a caul so important?"

"A caul usually be destroyed by the babe at birth. When it comes whole, 'tis a token straight fram Heaven with strong magic powers. Niver let it gae, fer ye're the first wight I've known personally what received such a gift. It mun mean summit."

I was grateful to Enoch, for suppose I'd gotten such a loathsome innard without him to explain it? 'Twould have been flung in a ditch afore now. Then I had a further revelation: this caul was a sign from the good witch Abunda! Instantly I drew the flesh to my chest and hugged it tight. Never would I be separated from my caul until my mission was complete.

8

OOTHLY THE CAUL WROUGHT ITS MAGIC, FOR two weeks later we stood safely on a grassy verge overlooking a stream of people.

"We've changed to Watling," said Enoch, "where it joins Icknield Street nigh to Dunstable. Folk from the north and folk fram Oxenford march togeddir from this point on and we'll disappear in the crowd."

I looked at him in disbelief. Even after all this time, I thought him the wildest, woolliest creature ever born and he would disappear only in a crowd of Scots. Also, since Northumberland and Roncechaux now knew my disguise, I was as visible as Enoch. But apparently we'd have to take our chances, for Enoch assured me that the only alternative was to cut across open fields and I wanted no more of that ever again.

'Twas a wondrous crowd of people jostling along the way, but I was too anxious searching for my enemies to enjoy the sight. When we were sure all we saw were strangers, Enoch nudged Twixt down the slope onto the stones with Tippet trailing after and Lance a shadow under the ass's bulging belly.

My heart started and stopped in panic as the safety of the last two hazy green weeks was left behind. I tried to hide my face under my hat, peering from under the brim. Knights there were aplenty, such a ratty bunch of ruffians that they were more brigand than noble. Foot soldiers as well moved in the crowd, with bits of armor and an occasional helmet. Churchmen of all casts, friars, priests, monks, holy sisters, pardoners, even two hermits, but by far the largest group were buyers and sellers headed for the London market. There were physicians in purple robes and gray gloves, a sprinkling of strange folk with yellow circles on their sleeves and yellow pointed hats, rich landowners in coifs. Once we passed hand-carried litters of two noble young ladies, with heads held high on long necks, their expressions as regal and mean as swans'.

The din was fierce. Everyone talked or shouted in a babble of tongues while babes screamed from their cradle-boards and tore at their mothers' snoods and drivers flicked whips to clear the way for long lumbering carts crowded with ancients. Horses neighed and struck the stones smartly with their hooves while harness bells jingled and somewhere someone caught the rhythm and began to sing.

> "When misty clouds break to the sun,
> Then shall whistling soon be begun
> > Of May!
> > Of merriest May!
> Tunes to sing are delightful
> When they're made with fable full
> > Of May!
> > Of merriest May!
> No more have hearts to mourn in pain,
> No more let envy your lives stain;
> > Be gay! Be frivolous gay!"

'Twas a happy song joyously sung and I began to feel an excitement stir in spite of my fears, when of a sudden the Scot joined the chorus. What ailed the oaf? Had he forgotten utterly our need to be inconspicuous? Not only did he bray in his native tongue louder than anyone, he sang some toty tune up in the clouds known only to himself.

I tried to shrink wee as a fairy, but the horror was soon doubled when Twixt was jostled out of step by a fat horse, and a female voice called out, "Don't stop! Sing on and I'll join ye."

Enoch grinned and complied while I stared from under my hat at a plump partridge riding a white mare. She sang lustily loud, further off-key even than Enoch, her mouth stretching wide over her pointed gap-teeth. I had never seen such a bold wench, a chicken vendor to judge by the huge white hens caged on the rump of her mare, for her dress was cunningly contrived to show more than it concealed. Her egg-white wimple was starched stiff as parchment, but slipped back to display wiry red crinkled hair; her full freckled face was framed by heavy dangles in her ears; her pale brows were plucked above jade-green eyes threatened with sties; her bosom was covered to its cleavage—albeit with a transparent gauze; her kirtle was pulled tight at her waist so that both hips and breasts bulged like melons; her scarlet skirts were hiked to show a bold expanse of thick hairy legs above her brown boots. Yet no doubt she was a handsome dame in her coarse way, for she was spritely and friendly as a sparrow.

"Be gay! Be frivoli gay!" she bellowed a few beats after Enoch had finished, then laughed to make all heads turn for it sounded as if she were calling for cows: "Caaaa! Caaaaa! Caaaaa!" Whereupon her chickens cackled in loud chorus.

"That's good," said the Scot.

"Go on, ye're bletherin' me!" And she pushed him off balance so hard that Lance snarled upward. "Oh look ye, a wolf! Did ye ever see the menagerie King Stephen kept in the royal castle?"

"We've not been to London afore." Enoch doffed his hat. "Enoch Angus Boggs at yer service and my wee brother Alex."

I threw him a fierce look for not calling me Tom, but he was too dazzled to notice.

"Ye're a Scot then! La, I *love* Scots. O'course, that's why ye can sing so. Is that not called harmon-izement?"

"That it is, a Celtish gift. You English dynt on one note and think it music while we carol like birds in a tree, each to his own tune but working togeddir."

"'Tis a jolly dynt withal and you do it wondrous well, better than most men, I trowe. Caaaa! Caaaa! Caaaaa!" And off went the poultry again in a mad jabber.

Enoch laughed just as heartily though I failed to see the humor. Then the dame introduced herself as Mistress Gladys Stump on her way from Oxenford to Smithfield Market to sell her hens.

Her face grew solemn. "I have to support myself now that my dear husband is in his grave, alas, for I'm a poor widow." Her green eyes squinted and she added archly: "Well, not so poor, mayhap, if I had some strong smart wight to manage my property, for I was left with considerable."

"Ye're a brave lass and bonny. Certes ye'll nocht be alone long. I envy the lucky fellow what will take yer cue and gain him some fowls."

"Caaaa! Caaaa! Caaaa!"

Everyone stared as I winced and thought we might as well have carried a banner announcing our presence as to take up with such a brazen loud hussy. Enoch showed remarkably poor judgment after all his caution in the forest.

"So ye've ne'er been to London before. 'Tis a most 'wildering city withouten a guide to show ye the sights."

Enoch reached to pat the mare's neck and hit Gladys's flank by mistake. "I was hopin' I dared prevail on yer service, yif ye're nocht too busy sellin'."

"I don't sell all the time. Guidance I'll give away gladly." And once again came the long hawking laugh as I cringed and the fowl cackled.

And so they jangled through dinner and beyond, for we'd acquired a companion, that was sure. As the road became ever more crowded, she proved to know everybody and everything.

"See that haughty train there what deigns not to notice no one but itself? That be the Bishop of London on his way to his palace which be on this side of the old Bourn. He can keep an army of seven hundred under his roof."

We stared at a tall beefy prelate with a wispy goat beard.

"Or those knights, the ones with square helmets and cowls? They be Knights Templar goin' to their Temple which ye can just see beyond the next curve. They brought yellow stone all the way from Caen in Normandy to build it and 'tis said to be a fine place for pilgrims, but I think it monstrous ugly. Give me plain thatch and white walls and I'm happy."

"By what gate will we pass through the city wall, Gladys?" Enoch asked.

"The nearest be Ludgate."

"Be it a narrow way?"

"Aye, why do ye ask?"

"Well, let me confess a wee crime. Back a few nichts at the Sign of the White Swan, I had me a brawl with one of them nasty Border Englishmen who swore as how he'd wait for me here in London-town and git even. Now as I see it, his only chance of catching me be at a gate, for once in the town proper I'm like to pass through wi'out bein' noticed. Do ye ken my meaning?"

Her jade eyes widened within their red rims. "I'll bet he's e'en more afeard of ye, whoever he be." Her hand shot to his forearm and she also missed, touching his flank instead. "Ye just leave it to Dame Gladys Stump. I'll lead ye through Smithfield which be a broad way milling with folks coming to the horse fair."

I glanced slyly at Enoch's bland face, apologizing to him with my eyes for not kenning his purpose. I, too, had dreaded being caught at the gate, a natural checkpoint where we could easily be spotted and ambushed.

Mistress Stump continued an unbroken line of description as our road began to twist gradually downward, for now both sides of the street were lined with handsome palaces surrounded with wooded parks. Then we took a sharp turn to the left and suddenly the city of London lay magically at our feet. Enoch and I both gasped and pulled short, while Gladys turned her mare to stay with us. From this height, London lay in a round bowl surrounded by walls on three sides, a river on its fourth. The golden glow of the late-running sun caught hundreds of spires which grew like trees in the meadow of low houses. At that moment bells rang out Nones *cum multis aliis* in universal praise of God as the travelers bowed their heads in prayer. 'Twas all in miniature, clean and sweet as a confection. Then we began our descent again and lost it.

When we got close to our actual entrance, Dame Gladys suggested that I find some way to control Lance, for dangerous packs of curs roamed the London streets. I persuaded the wolf to jump on Tippet's back where I secured him with his harness.

Now the push behind us welled so we were forced to narrow our file in order to cross two bridges where rivers converged. Mill wheels roared around us while the sound of the city rose in awesome cacophony. The wall flanking Ludgate loomed eighteen feet above with guards poised to strike; mendicants lined the narrow passage with outstretched palms, and we gladly avoided its perilous way to follow Gladys to our left along the outside of the wall. I didn't breathe easy till we came to Smithfield, an enormous expanse teeming with horses and hawkers, so 'twas easy to get lost. To our surprise, Mistress Stump told us to wait till she sold her hens, for 'twas Friday, the day of the fair, and we would enter London at Newgate after dusk. 'Twas a good scheme withal, so we dismounted to see the sights.

Smithfield centered around a horsepool where all sorts of steeds were tethered for sale. Small boys rode bareback on huge war horses—called "destriers" here—for interested purchasers, and their skill was a marvel to behold as they dodged and turned in mock battle. The thought crossed my mind that I might do this if I were forced to stay in London long, for I was as good as they were, I trowe. Circling the horses were craftsmen making intricate harnesses and armor for the beasts, such fine leather and metalwork as I had never imagined. The outskirts of the field were filled with people like Gladys Stump, hawkers of every stripe selling their wares.

Enoch and I watched with interest as Gladys unfolded a neat contraption which turned out to be a platform, then set up broad swinging fans made of chicken feathers. Even before she was ready to sell, her stand was surrounded, for she was well known. When all was in place, three men helped her up, two on her arms and one pushing behind.

She spread her arms and shouted over the din with the blast of a hunting horn. "Come one, come all! Fat hens for sale! Stump broadies, none like them. Steady supply of eggs guaranteed or put them in the pot!"

"Heigh Gladys, how 'bout the red squawker afore me? I hear she be the best layer of all."

The dame flashed a grin. "The cock that claims that be a liar!"

"Never cry 'foul' to a crowin' cock, Mistress Stump."

"Then tell him not to crow before he sees dawn."

"Why not? A cock can hope, can't he?"

"'Tis a dumb cock that hopes for an early rising!" cried the dame.

Delighted laughter everywhere. Her method worked, for in no time her hens were gone and she was ready to show us the sights. I trailed behind her and Enoch as we watched the dancing bear, the quoit throwing, the javelin hurling. However, such wonders had lost their savor since Dunsmere. I hung my head low, remembering.

When the shadows grew long, harps and pipes began to throb a ditty and Enoch asked Gladys to jig. Sitting on the damp grass watching the Morris dancers, I tried to shut out the sights and sounds and concentrate on a plan of action. I touched my caul and wished for my father's whisper. How would I find the king? My mind stopped and listened but inside my head all was silence. Finally Enoch and Gladys returned and said 'twas now dusky enough to go to the Inn of the Red Fox, run by her friend Jasper Peterfee.

We were swept through Newgate and found ourselves on a main thoroughfare in twilight. Soon we were fighting off hawkers who fanned wares on the ends of long poles in our faces or used hooks on Twixt's bridle to pull us to their shops as they shouted and sang:

"Green rushes to sweeten your path!"

"Pewter pots, bright as silver! Look ye! Look ye!"

"Hot peascods! Hot peascods!"

"Hot pig's-feet straight from Paris!"

"Ripe strawberries picked only this morning!"

"Golden pears firm and juicy!"

When I could see beyond the vendors, I marveled anew at the beauty of the town for the houses built in rows were neatly whitewashed and timbered, with shops below and family quarters above in the gabled salles that hung over the street. Flowers abounded in little gardens and baskets: blue periwinkle and iris, orpine live-forever, red and white roses everywhere.

Looking down revealed a less attractive London, for the road was awash with an open gutter filled with piles of garbage and or-dure, which in turn drew flies, maggots, curs, kites and crows. Wandering kine, sheep, goats and fowl added to the general filth.

Worst of all was the smell of smoke hanging over all. Again the acrid fumes triggered memory and my heart pounded as I sought the cause. 'Twas not hard to find, for three houses in a row burned unchecked on my left, then another in a lane on my right, and still another a little way on. People wept and wrung their hands around these disasters, but I saw only four men actively hurling water. 'Twas a miracle the whole city wasn't in flames.

Cripples and freaks diverted small crowds who tossed coins to them. One freakish fellow pushed himself ingeniously by his teeth on a wooden plank with wheels, for he had neither arms nor legs; a feeble-minded wretch in rags danced frantically as stones were hurled at her legs.

I didn't notice when we turned off the main way into a narrow lane slanting downward, but I had to shade my eyes at the wide plain of shimmering gold before me, the Thames River which caught the afterglow of the setting sun. 'Twas broad as a lake with its soft green banks barely visible on the other side. The flood was low-tide, said Gladys, and as we drew nearer we could see the sandy bottom lying in shoals. We went all the way to the edge be-fore we turned left along the Strand. Our inn was not far away then, on a lane just two doors off the river.

Gladys jumped down before a double stone house with hand-some wood gables above as Enoch and I waited.

"Well, lad, I'm as good as my word for I've got ye safe and sound to London," he said while the dame went to make arrangements. "Tomorrow we'll gae to yer uncle Frank and mayhap by Sunday we can be on our way agin north."

"Yes, but—" I stuttered. "Uncle Frank knows naught of what transpired and we've never even met and . . ."

The Scot made me turn my face to his. "Dinna tell me that he'll nocht support ye, Alex."

His tone chilled me through.

"Not at all. Only he's not of this world."

"He's dead?"

"Of course not. I only meant—he's in the Church!"

To my great relief, Gladys then came out the door followed by a hobbling man on a peg leg. She introduced him as Jasper Peterfee.

Enoch and I dismounted to follow the host inside where we ducked our heads to avoid ropes stretched and hanging at all angles from the wooden beams to aid our crippled innkeeper.

As Enoch haggled with Peterfee about money, I squeezed my thighs against my treasure and guiltily considered offering my share to the Scot, but decided against it when I remembered the percentage he'd wanted of Wanthwaite. Let him invest in me, take his risk like any gambler. Finally we went up to our rooms to drop our packets and I found to my relief that the host had put me in a tiny annex off Enoch's chamber to accommodate Lance—for I'd been much vexed at the problem of sleeping in a room with the Scot and removing my clothes. 'Twas easy under the stars for we never changed so much as a sock. Now we turned around to join Mistress Stump in the salle for our supper.

A boy had already delivered cold pork pie, ale and cherry tarts when we got there, fare much to my liking. We sat with Gladys facing the Thames through an open window and 'twas a beauteous view indeed.

"What be that tall spire on our left, mistress?" I asked.

"St. Paul's Cathedral in the new Gothic style. 'Twas only just completed and is the greatest cathedral in all Europe."

"And that pile beyond?" Enoch inquired. "The massy battlement tinted pink."

"Westminster, where the king holds court when he's in London."

"*When* he's in London?" I cried shrilly. "Where would he be if not London?"

"Caaaa! Caaaaa! Caaaa!" hooted the silly hussy, only she had no chickens to take up the chorus. "'Where would he be?' asks the pretty little boy. Why lad, he could be a thousand miles distant in

Aquitaine, or across the Channel in Normandy, or in Anjou and he'd still be in his kingdom. King Henry rules the world, that he does. Would he could rule his family as well. Caaaa! Caaaa!"

"Do he still keep his queen in prison then?" Enoch asked, much amused.

"In *prison*!" I gasped, horrified. "King Henry has put his own wife in *prison*?" 'Twould make him hardly better than Northumberland! Were all such great lords so cruel and heartless? My heart tumbled to my yellow boots.

Dame Gladys leaned forward and patted my hand kindly. "Don't be so stricken, laddie. Queen Eleanor be not in a dungeon, such as the likes of us would be if jailed. She's kept in a tower, I believe, and probably comfortable enough."

"And she be lucky not to be hanged," Enoch added. "She gaddered her sons into an army against their father, and they all rode against the king. Yet he forgave them—at least to the point of sparing their lives."

"But he put his queen in *prison*," I repeated. "How long has she been there?"

"Hmmm, my Harry died in . . ." Dame Gladys counted on her fingers. "It be fourteen years now."

"Fourteen years!" Longer than I'd been alive. Such dreadful information on the king's character must bode evil for my chances of a happy marriage if he chose my husband.

"Sae lang as ye're askin' all these questions, Alex, come to the mast important one. Where be yer uncle?"

Gladys turned, smiling. "I don't know everybody in London, but I do know how to contact most everybody one way or t'other. What's his name and what's he do?"

I bit my lip and stared as my mind raced. "His name was Frank from Denoigh but I know not what name he took in the Church."

"Be he a clerk? Or a priest?"

"No." Then I was inspired. "He's of the Carthusian Order."

"That's part of the Benedictine," said Enoch, frowning.

"Aye, it means he's taken a vow of silence." I lifted my eyes innocently to the Scot.

"Then how—?" He stopped himself in deference to Gladys and studied me speculatively.

"La, a vow of silence, how miserable. I'd never make such a vow, might as well be dead as not talk. Well, now let me think. Carthusian? There be a man from Oxenford I used to play with—when we were children, of course—that became a priest at St. Paul's and listens to confessions on Sundays. Mayhap he could tell us where the order can be found in London."

I thanked her and asked to be excused. She and Enoch wanted to walk out until curfew but I was too tired and too fearful of being seen. Even Enoch donned a blue chape as disguise.

Left alone in my annex, I lay on my stomach before the low window and gazed out on the tiled and thatched roofs of London where they stretched under the tapered heaven. Somewhere in the maze Roland de Roncechaux, his knights and his men awaited me. I shuddered though the air was warm. The king's court at Westminster—I would question Jasper Peterfee about it tomorrow, how it could be reached and what days 'twas open.

Meantime, there was the immediate problem of Enoch. Our relationship was fast coming to an end for, as he'd said, he'd gotten me to London safe and sound. 'Twould be easy to disappear in this vast city but less easy to discover exactly where I should go and how subsist.

Until I saw the king.

9

Y ANNEX COULD BE ENTERED ONLY THROUGH A low chute hardly big enough for a rat. The next morning I was wakened by a cursing and grunting from the hole as Enoch tried to reach me.

"Waesucks! 'Twas made fer rigwoodie hags, methinks."

Finally he sat under the eave and glared down at me.

"Now, young fellow, ye and me mun talk a bit. Tell me agin

about the uncle what won't say a word. How can he help ye?"

"Mayhap he can write," I said. "Leastways my father was certain he could restore Wanthwaite or he wouldn't have said so. Father knew he was Carthusian."

"Or mayhap he has connections in court," Enoch mused. "Aye, 'tis possible. But let me speak a few words, for I've taken no vow—and list to me good. If by chancit this uncle turns out not to be able to help, or—and this be worse—if by chancit I learn that ye've told me another lie, then ye and me be gang to settle in our own way. Do ye ken?"

I understood his hot blue eyes all right, but not that word "settle."

"Not exactly. Only I'm not lying."

"I mean twa things: yif ye're lying, ye'll be whipped; yif the uncle cannot help, then ye still owe me half yer estate and we'll work out another way to get it. Now am I clear?"

"Aye," I whispered.

He backed out the hole and left me to my thoughts.

Mistress Stump had prepared to take us over all of London that Saturday. Enoch accepted her invitation but I declined, for I was too fearful of being seen to enjoy a holiday. In fact I would have preferred that Enoch stay inside also, for Roncechaux would follow the Scot as quickly as he would me, but there were greater advantages in letting him go. I *could* have escaped in his absence except that as yet I had nowhere to go that was nearly as safe. As it was, I sent for some hot water and washed both my person and my clothes in the wooden tub put in Enoch's chamber. The hot sun dried my clothes and hair quickly at the window and I then sauntered downstairs to seek Jasper Peterfee.

The crippled host proved most helpful. Westminster was close to our inn in the hamlet of Charing. He didn't know if King Henry was in London, but the chancellor listened to grievances every day except Saturday and Sunday and I could learn from the courtiers what the king's schedule was. For a silver livre, Peterfee agreed to remain silent about my activities.

On Sunday Fortune's Wheel turned against me, for Mistress Stump postponed her homecoming another day. Enoch insisted I attend Mass at St. Paul's in order to meet Gladys's friend, the priest from Oxenford. I balked and argued against it for I feared Sir Roland would go to St. Paul's if he went anywhere, but in the end I lost because Enoch claimed that if I refused 'twould mean I'd been lying.

Gladys led us directly to a confession box after Mass and called for Father Lucas. The holy father was a lusty-looking man who seemed disappointed that Gladys wasn't alone. When she told him our problem, however, he was most sympathetic. He turned soft lickerous eyes down on me and clucked his tongue.

"The Carthusian Order. Frankly 'tis not a popular order and I'm not sure they still have quarters in London. If you'll let me speak with some of my superiors, I'm sure I could give you directions this time tomorrow."

"That will be fine," Enoch answered for me, and we left.

Dame Gladys and Enoch escorted me back to the inn and left me there alone again. This day was less pleasant than yesterday, however, partly because I'd made what arrangements I could, thought of every conceivable variation on what might happen, and had naught to do now except worry. Gradually my gloom centered on Enoch. If he was as late returning this night as last, I'd already said goodbye to him. I couldn't wait to be free of him, yet he'd saved my life. Aye, more than once, for I pictured Sir Roland searching for me in the inn, the chase through the forest. I didn't want him to think me a deceitful, ungrateful boy who took what I list but would not honor my word.

I dined alone in the salle, peering all the while from the window for sight of the Scot and his dame but they didn't come. Finally I crawled into my hole and made ready to sleep, for I must be up well before dawn to make my escape. Enoch would just have to hate me if that's what he wanted. I twisted and turned in the mildewed room, vaguely disturbed by scratching inside the walls.

Curfew bells woke me and I heard Enoch moving in his quarters. Good, I could still say goodbye—without doing so openly, of course—and let him remember me sympathetically after I'd gone. Happily I crawled through the passage toward a flickering candle at the other end.

Enoch was naked on his pad when I arrived and I stood uncertainly a moment, for he was twisting so that I thought him in pain. His buttocks rose and fell as he groaned and grunted.

"Enoch?" I said softly. "Are you all right?"

"Aye, now, now, oh, careful . . ."

With disbelief I heard the voice of Gladys Stump coming from under Enoch and by leaning close I saw that she was there indeed, held by her wrists and crying out . . .

And I was seized by a manic disposition—head pounded—eyes saw red—I lost all reason! Horror o'erwhelmed me and I once again heard my own voice screaming over the inert body of my mother as my throat tore:

"No! No! No! No!"

I saw Maisry bleeding, saw my own blood dripping after my first night with Enoch and knew the truth at last! He *was* a demon-killer! *Did* have a serpentine tool to murder by night! I flung myself on his bare back snarling and scratching to slay him dead!

Up and down I rode, as I had on Maud's swelling stomach, only this was to the death instead of the birth and nothing would stop me till I had the Scot's blood!

"Don't worry, Gladys, I'll save you!" I shouted.

"What? What the—"

"My God, 'tis a bogle on my back!" cried Enoch, rolling over suddenly and throwing me on the floor. I was on my feet again when he rose and I saw my enemy clear by candle glow, a writhing, rising snake glistening purple. I lunged at the monster to twist its head off!

"Eeeeoooo! He's attackin' my terse! Quhat ails ye? Hae ye gan woodly?"

Whereupon his fist struck my jaw like a Lochinvar ax and I fell hard against the wall!

"Yow! Eeow! Oh, I'm gelded sure! I'll kill ye, ye blitherin' toad! Eeeeeooooow!"

"What happed? Oh Lordy, be ye sliced off? Who did the deed?" cried Gladys Stump as she leaned to look at Enoch where he clutched himself.

"Alex, that heilie fiend that I befriended! He's the Devil hisself!"

I'd tied Lance before I came, but now the wolf dashed from the hole and leaped on Enoch knocking him to the floor. I heard the beast growl and heard the Scot cry out as his hand groped for his dagger.

"Let me at the beast! I'll kill him. Ow, he's after my hurdies!"

Aching in every joint, I fell upon Lance and stopped him by taking his jaws. "Stop, boy, no. It's all right." For the Scot would slay him sure.

"Help! Help! Wolf!" Gladys flung the door open and rushed naked into the corridor.

Soon Jasper Peterfee was there, without his wooden leg, followed by servants and gaping guests.

"Let *me* at him!" a voice bellowed drunkenly. "I've killed many a wolf in my day, aye and fox too."

"What happened?" Peterfee asked the groaning Scot. "Are you bad bit?"

"Go to," Enoch grunted. "I'm all richt. The wolf went woodly."

Peterfee closed the door leaving Gladys, Enoch and me alone.

"I'd whup the lad till he couldn't walk, brother or no," said Gladys. "Are ye all right, dear?"

"Aye, by mornin' I'll prove it, only first I mun deal with this wallydrag." The Scot managed to stand straight and I noted with satisfaction that I'd gotten rid of the incubus monster. "Now, ye, Alex, ye mun have tint yer reason to carry on so, but that be no excuse. Because of our bargain, I'll let ye off easy this time, but ye mun apologize to Gladys here."

Outraged, I stared at the naked doxy. "I saved your life," I mumbled through a mouthful of blood. "You should thank me."

"Have ye gone daft? If this be dyin', then give me death say I. I invited him to my party. Aye, ye must be toty, or mayhap a Bulgar. Saved my life!" And the lady hooted with laughter. "Caaaa! Caaaa!"

"He was killing you!" I shouted. "I can prove it. Didn't I see the same thing happen twice before?"

"Quhat a ligging scoundrel!" Enoch bellowed. "Let me at ye! Easy, did I say? I'll beft ye to schit! Tie ye up in jackis and stryppis fer the wild beast that ye air!"

He lunged at me with his fist raised, but was held round the waist by his naked dame. "Oh no ye don't! Well do I know men's tricks, for ye'd punch him into a stupor so he couldn't tell me the truth! *Killed* other women, have ye? Blathered with honey, cracked boast 'bout your bodkin when all the time ye're full of hoker and pissmar for the fair sex! Take that! And that!"

And she too went for the monster as Enoch screamed like a Scottish banshee!

"Thank ye, Alex. I misjudged ye true!" And the naked lady flounced out trailing her tunic behind her.

"Gladys, wait!" Enoch started after her, then turned and hissed. "Ye stay here. When I finish wi' thee, yer buck's horn will ne'er make a toot. I swear ye'll kick a new moon before ye swonk any dame's hole!" And he was gone.

I slumped against the wall, completely worn out. Then I felt my jaw and wiggled it tentatively: not broken. The blood came from my bitten tongue and I ran that injured member over my teeth to be sure they were all there. Even if they hadn't been 'twould have been worth it to have thwarted the murderous Scot. And yet—she'd claimed she'd wanted him. The pounding subsided in my head as reason returned. Perhaps I should leave before Enoch returned . . . just in case I'd erred a bit. I crept to my annex and gathered my goatskin and bundle, then took Lance to spend the night in the stable with Twixt.

Snuggled in the dry straw, I thought on my farewell to Enoch. What a gullible fool I'd been to think I should try to ease the wrench from such a criminal oaf. For he was greedy and lickerous, no matter what. I hated him, hated him.

10

 WAS A BLUSTERY NIGHT OF WIND AND RAIN, BUT the straw was sweet and dry. As my shock wore off, I became more and more aware of my injuries: a badly bruised shoulder, a sprained neck, and a head that ached in every bone. I tried to remember every dreadful curse I'd ever heard to lay on the Scot and might he hang by his beloved killer-organ for striking me.

The rain and dark abated around Matins to be replaced by such a fog as I'd never seen. 'Twas dense silvery swirls of some stuff such as damp dandelion fluff, insubstantial yet engulfing as a shroud, for when I stretched my arm forth my hand disappeared, likewise my body from the waist down. When I was ready to leave, I hardly knew which way to step for all was without center, sounds which might be fore or aft or far or near, shapes which might be real or illusion. At least the mist gave me the cover I needed.

Walking my fingers like a crab along the wall, I turned left at the corner of the inn to go to the Strand. Once there, I again turned left toward Westminster. I could hear the wash of barges slapping against the shore on my river side while more and more hurrying shapes loomed in the street. After a long, slow meander, I reached out blindly and caught the garment of one.

"Please, sir, be this the way to the hamlet of Charing?"

"Let go your manhandling," snarled a woman's voice.

"You're entering Charing now," said someone else.

Jasper Peterfee had said it was half an hour's walk from the inn to the north gate of Westminster, but I felt I'd been on the road a week by the time I arrived. The swirls of fog were now separated by clear spots and I stood before a high stone wall with a double-doored wooden gate which was open to traffic but carefully guarded by four sergeants-at-arms who checked every person at entry. I leaned against a tree and watched for a time to discover a strategy. Fortunately 'twas easy, for one kind of person came and went without question, young boys carrying pies and ale. When two came out together who'd been frequent porters I followed them down the street. They led me to a large kitchen on the Strand crowded with merchants and sailors. Taking their lead, I stood in line for fresh capon pies and bought three. Quickly I gulped down one for strength, then carried the others aloft as I ran after my guides back through the gates.

Inside, all was confusion and I lost them. At first I thought some catastrophe had befallen to judge by the bustle and stir of the place. Valets were polishing spears and armor, grooms were brushing magnificent coursers royally caparisoned, huntsmen were exercising wolfhounds, coursing dogs and vulperets while serious soldiers hurried til and fro on urgent business. The court was big as a large park and I had no notion of which way to turn until an angry clerk pushed me to the right.

"Don't clutter the entry, boy. Make your delivery on the east and be gone."

I followed after him in what I supposed was an easterly direction through a second gate leading to a smaller court, then another gate beyond that and found myself in a spacious garden. The clerk's black robes were just disappearing down a graveled path and I ran after him. He went amazingly fast for a portly man and had already crossed the bridge over a rapid stream when I arrived on the near side, but after that there seemed only one way to go and I joined several others who were entering the portal of a square tower abutting a palace.

Inside, the vestibule was small and dark, the floors besmottered with muddy footprints, and the only way led up a steep stairs. I clung to a stone balustrade and followed hurrying men whose deep voices echoed hollowly. Once on the upper floor, I continued with the mob through a series of chambers that functioned as a hall leading after a great time into the very last, where once again I took a long winding stair into a chamber crowded with people.

The room must have been cheerful when unoccupied, for the ceilings were low and turret windows admitted much light (as well as rain), which illumined red canvas wall hangings emblazoned with the royal arms. There were no furnishings, however, no benches for sitting except in the deep recesses of the windows, and the rushes which looked fresh laid were nonetheless already soggy with water and animal messes, for dogs abounded underfoot and there must have been two falcons for every man there. I sought a window corner where I could observe and survey the area, and finally squeezed beside an ancient man in the habit of a canon who was gazing at the wherries and barges now visible on the river below.

At first the babbling crowd was a single blur, but gradually some distinctions became possible. Aside from such differences as those who belonged to religious orders from those who were nobles or knights, there seemed two groups: those who were fixtures in the place and had set up small folding tables for chess or bones, and those who were constantly entering and leaving a small door on the opposite side for what was clearly immediate business. After a long period of waiting, a clerk emerged from the door and called a name. One of the regular fixtures detached himself from a game and answered the call.

"Did you bring those pies for Master Walter Map, boy?" the canon asked suddenly. "For I heard him order capon."

I gazed into piercing brown eyes under furrowed brows. "Aye, that I did, but I don't see him now."

"Nay, perhaps not from your low angle but you can surely hear him well enough, for that bitter voice is the most venomous in the court. Hear how he argues with my lord of Ely whom he hates worse than a Jew or Cistercian."

I listened but heard only blithering. "Would you like a pie? I have two, you see."

"Thank you." He accepted it gratefully but didn't offer to pay. "I'm known as Richard de Monte and work in the Treasury."

"Alexander Wanthwaite," I said. "You must know much about the court and its proceedings. Could you tell me, please, if—"

"Hush." He put up his hand as two courtiers dressed for travel brushed by, talking rapidly.

"Count Richard and King Philip are even now laying siege—"

"But the fog lies low there as well. Surely the king . . ." And they were gone.

The old man seemed despondent. "Count Richard. Henry mixes him too much with the Young King, but the men have different temperaments entirely. Richard cannot be manipulated by evasion."

"Aye," I said to give him comfort, for he was sore perplexed.

Another old man, but this one wiry and small with a lean face, came from the king's inner chamber and immediately men clustered around him nervously. Richard de Monte and I strained to hear what was said but could catch only a few words.

"—will burn all in his path."

"Count Richard is a traitor . . ."

"King of England—"

"Barons are departing, especially those of Maine . . ."

"Tours! They wouldn't dare."

If the conversation was unclear, the anxiety wasn't, for it swirled thick as the morning's fog. All the men looked near breaking, their eyes sleepless.

"That was Ranulf de Glanville," my companion said when the lean man went back inside the chamber. "All the news must come to him."

"Why not the king?" I asked.

Before he could answer, one dog in the center of the room attacked another and soon the courtiers crushed back to allow a wide circle, for the curs meant to kill. The growls and barks, blood and bone-crunching made such a distraction that 'twas impossible to think. As I watched the owners try to control their beasts, I happened to raise my eyes to the door just as Magnus Barefoot walked in!

Magnus Barefoot? He must be a vision made from one part fog and one part my own obsessive dread! But no, neither fog nor fear nor the Devil's dead could be as real as this. As I moved behind Richard de Monte and peered at my enemy round the old man's sleeve, I saw that he was followed by Sir Roland de Roncechaux.

My skin became damp and my bones went to rope so that I thought I might faint. Roncechaux was no longer in his rusty mail, but elegantly turned out to meet the king. He wore a deep cherry robe edged in vair and dashing green boots, but nothing could change his saturnine face with its heavy hooded eyes and cynical mouth. Confidently he strode to the door of the antechamber and spoke with the sergeant. *Benedicite*, I *must* see the king before him or I would find that my estate had already been given away.

Desperately I turned to the old man. "Excuse me, Sire, do you know any way I might see King Henry right away?"

His lips spread over his yellow snag teeth. "Aye, lad, if you're a good swimmer." And he laughed at his own wit.

"What mean you?"

"I mean that the king's across the Channel where he's been since November last. Know ye not that the Angevins think more of their European possessions than they do of England? Though this Henry is better than most."

"Please, Sire, 'tis of utmost importance. Where is this Channel? Can it be forded?"

"What an ignorant boy you are! Where have you lived that you don't know about the English Channel, such a treacherous sea-path that even strong sailors dread for its sudden squalls? On the far side lies a series of domains, Normandy, Anjou, Maine, Brittany, Poitou, Aquitaine, all ruled by our king but with homage to the King of France. You heard the courtiers just now. My guess is that King Henry is in Le Mans fighting King Philip of France and his own devil-son, Richard."

He rose abruptly and walked away without another word, leaving me exposed to the room just as Magnus and Roncechaux who had not gained entry to the inner chamber were turning around. At that moment the contentious wight called Walter Map approached, deep in argument with another courtier, and I joined them as they strode, almost creeping between Walter Map's legs in my fear.

"Good Lord, who's there?" he cried. "Do you want to trip me up?"

I shifted my position, so that I was hidden by the courtier's cape. However, 'twas necessary to constantly adjust as they turned at corners or stopped to make a point.

Then, to my horror, I suddenly missed a turn and was left stranded in the center of the room. Instinctively I looked at my enemies and, as if fated, Magnus Barefoot looked at the same time.

"Alix!" I heard as his finger pointed.

I rushed out the door like one possessed. Coming up the stairs was a bearded personage whom I recognized as the Bishop of London. He went through the door and blocked the way of my pursuers for a critical moment as I flew through one chamber after another, knocking people this way and that, ducking under legs and robes.

Outside, I dashed into the wooded park, for the cover was better there than in the open courts. I could see the Thames glinting faintly through the trees but when I reached bottom I was confronted with a high wall again. I ran along it seeking a gate, found one that was closed, continued running as my lungs burst. Finally I saw the outline of an ancient Saxon abbey and ran through a low doorway into a dark hole. I groped my way through a passage and found myself inside a hall where Mass was being conducted. I edged my way to a far door on the other side where I glanced over my shoulder in time to see Roland de Roncechaux topple two kneeling priests in his haste to get to me. A high arched way offered an exit from the room and when I reached the other side, I was on a London street again and the fog was gone.

Before me stretched the Thames and a busy loading dock. Sailors sang chanties in a strange tongue while wharfmen pulled on ropes and pushed heavy carts loaded with fish. The waterside was too open; I turned the other direction into the city. Breathing hard, I ran up a sharp incline onto higher ground where commerce of all kinds crowded the way. I dared not look behind me for I knew that Roncechaux must be close and I couldn't spare an instant from my pell-mell thrust forward. In and out I went, into a smithy's shop with bellows heaving and out the other side, into a copper-pot shop with hammers ringing and through it, into an inn and out behind its stables. People started and tried to grab me, but on I went.

I sobbed with the pain in my ribs and still ran on. My mouth was dry as parchment and I passed wells without stopping. I knew not where I went nor cared, so long as I got away from the sure death behind me. Once I made the mistake of entering the open court of a palace and was almost caught, for Roncechaux saw me and shouted, whereupon he was joined by Magnus, and they tried to stay my exit by going to different gates. I fooled them by entering the palace—flying by the astonished guards—running to the roof, out to a balustrade and over the wall, dropping ten feet or more onto soft grass. And on I ran.

Then the fog returned. Slowly at first, then closing in rapidly. In one sense I'd lost them, but in another I'd lost myself even more, for at any moment I might run directly into their arms. Surrounded once again by ogre shapes and echoing voices, I groped my way along wet store fronts, touching stone, plants, horses' muzzles and people alike. My breathing and heart subsided in speed, but I was frightened more than ever and would have preferred to see where I was though the knowledge be useless. The one thing I was sure of was that I heard footsteps close behind me. Incorporeal in an invisible world, I was suddenly again on the mist-swathed fields of Wanthwaite, watching a timeless sun hang over the horror of the blood-drenched soil. I seemed to run without moving, cry out without sound, reach without touching. With my parents, I moved through perpetual limbo.

I walked for hours, I trowe. Curfew had rung, then Compline, and 'twas pitch black and silent in the streets. I reached out my hand and crab-walked along a wall until I came to a door. I pushed and entered a small room with the embers of a fire burnt low in the chimney. Silhouetted against the fire was the large figure of a man.

"Sae ye decided to come back after all," said Enoch's voice.

"No!" I cried and turned to run out.

His hand held me in a steel grip. "Not sae fast, laddie, for we've many things to talk about. Now sit ye doon on the settle."

He pushed me roughly to the seat and stared down, his evil eyes burning red.

"You hurt me!" I said vehemently. "I'd rather die than spend another instant with you! How dare you strike me?"

"How—dare—I—strike—thee? Indeed! Strikin's too good fer a twa-faced castratin' scoundrel like ye. I'd give ye yer wish and make ye dead if ye didn't hold title to my land."

"*Your* land!" I imitated his lady-love. "Caaaa! Caaaa! Caaaa! Did you really think I'd let a slimy snake like you take Wanthwaite? And a Scot at that!"

He sat beside me and squeezed my sore shoulder till I cried out in pain. "Listen to me, little high-and-mighty Baron," he said in his hoarse voice, "for as a baron ye're a beggar as long as yer land be held by an appointed noble of the king's court. Ye can neither give it or keep it, fer it's not yours to dispose of until ye've got it back. Do ye understand what I'm saying?"

"Of course. Do you understand that I *will* get it back? And that when I do you'll get nothing? I'll not ask that it be granted to me and a demon-Scot!"

"And exactly whom air ye gang to ask, Master Alex?"

"I know who."

"Aye, sae do I. King Henry what's in France somewhere. See, I know more than ye think. Ye always pay too little fer services rendered. Peterfee couldn't wait to collect from me as well. When do ye take the boat to France?"

I said nothing till he shook me hard by my sore shoulder, then I started to blubber.

"How do you expect me to go to France? Roncechaux's in London. And Magnus Barefoot too. They've been chasing me all day and . . ."

And I couldn't talk for weeping. Enoch offered no comfort, but waited for me to get a grip on myself.

"Where did ye see them?"

I told him what had transpired.

He let go of me and when I looked up again he was studying his dagger held in his palm.

"I've told ye twice now and I'll say it once again: I need land for I'm a younger brother. And I'll have land, no matter who pays. I prefer good Scottish soil such as Wanthwaite be—nay, let me finish—for all of Northumberland be rightfully Scotland. And ye be Scottish too since ye were born there. Now ye air the means of my getting what's mine by rights, and ye have proved yerself to be a skittery wretch what cannot be trusted because ye were brought up in the English manner. Before I can help ye or trust ye, we mun have a new footing. Give me yer arm."

"What for?"

He grabbed my hand and jerked my arm out straight, then quickly sliced my skin with his dagger and before I could feel the pain, bent and drank my blood. Helplessly I squirmed to get away.

Just as quickly, he cut his own forearm and thrust the bleeding hairy shank under my neck.

"Drink or ye're a dead bairn."

When put so immediately, I found I didn't want to die after all and sucked.

"Ugh! Let me up. I'm going to be sick."

"No, ye're not. Repeat after me: From this day forward, Enoch Angus Boggs and me be blud brothers. And I recognize that brotherhood and loyalty to the clan be the most sacred tie in the whole wide world. By bogle and houlets sent by Nick, by gannets from witches in the west, by the soul in my body, by the ghosts of my parents, by the Holy God and His Son, I swear that Enoch be my brother and I'll ne'er deceive him by word or by deed on pain of death. Amen."

Still choking, I gasped out the words.

"Wait, there's more. We shall e'er be together unto death and— list to this well—we shall ne'er hinder each other in love. But we *will* help each other advance, and in our case that means land. Sae let's hear namore of yer land or my land: it's *our* land. And let's hear namore of the demon Scots since one drop of Scottish blood makes ye as Scottish as me. We be brothers in all things. Now let me tell ye exactly quhat my plan be, fer I've had the long day to work out details."

He then proposed a most astonishing course. He would keep to his original plan of going to Paris to study law, only now I, too, would go to study with him, leaving my wolf with Jasper Peterfee. Together we would explore every legal means of recovering "our land" at the same time that we learned King Henry's whereabouts and made arrangements to meet with him. Once the land was ours, by whichever means came first, we would hurry back to claim it, share and share alike. The one wrinkle he hadn't anticipated was that Roncechaux would have seen me.

"'Twill take some schemin', sure enow, fer we canno' use the Thames to git to Dover. If 'tis foggy tomorrow, I'll venture out to find some other way."

By this time my eyes were gritty with sleep, but I couldn't let Enoch off yet. "Where is Dame Gladys?"

"Alive," he said tersely. "And satisfied as well, I believe, in spite of yer efforts. What dames have ye seen killt so?"

"A friend—" For the first time I uttered the awful truth. "My mother. 'Twas Sir Roland."

The Scot sighed deeply. "Aye, I thocht as much. My heart belches for thee, bairn. What he did was rape and it looks the same only it isn't. What I did with Gladys be, well, more like breeding."

My mind returned from that awful scene and I grew doubtful again. "You're lying. I know all about breeding of animals. The male mounts on the back when the female lets him."

"'Tis the same, only men mount on the front. Look ye, 'tis a deep topic and best needs plumbing when we're both more awake. Come, brother, for I have a token for ye."

Together we climbed up to his room where he lighted a candle and rummaged in his bag. He pulled out a piece of plaid wool.

"'Tis the breacan feile of our clan and here's a brooch to pin it to yer shoulder."

Shivering with disgust, I had to let him hang the gaudy chape over me and dub me a Boggs of the MacPherson clan.

"Remember, break oath and ye fall doon dead," were his parting words.

Snuggled in my breacan wool as the fog again turned to a driving rain, I thought of the terrible events of the day. The very worst was drinking Scottish blood, for while I knew the vow of brotherhood didn't hold since I wasn't a boy and could be no one's brother, I wasn't sure that I wasn't a Scot. A fate worse than death.

11

 URING A HEAVY RAIN ON THE TWENTY-FOURTH of June 1189, Enoch and I reached the outskirts of Paris, having escaped London disguised as cowled monks. Heads now covered by leather skins to hold off the downpour, we guided Twixt in the line of voyagers slopping along the unpaved road of Causée de Saint-Lazare. 'Twas impossible to see if dwellings lined the road as they had coming into London, but every inch of land was cultivated with fruit orchards.

Our trip had gone well insofar as we'd slipped out of Roncechaux's noose, but I was sore bothered by a lack of news about King Henry. Everywhere along the road I asked Englishmen and Frenchmen alike where I could find him, only to be answered by evasive eyes and fumbling rumors. Soothly, no one seemed to know.

Moving like slugs, we didn't reach the Chastelet Tower which marked the entrance over the Seine River till 'twas almost dark. There we had to dismount and exchange English silver for parisis, a process which held us long after our fellow travelers had departed in order for Enoch to find the best possible bargain among the many changers whose booths lined the stone bridge. Satisfied at last, he beckoned me from under the tile roof where I waited and said we'd go now to seek lodging.

"You're much too late," said the exchanger with malice. "All doors on the Île de la Cité close promptly at sundown from fear of brigands and roving students."

Enoch looked down from Twixt contemptuously. "Ye dinna need instruct us aboot inns."

"Nevertheless, if you should have trouble you might want to remember the name Madame Annette, a hostess on the left bank beyond the Petit Pont where many students live. Continue on the main road off the Pont counting streets on your left up to five, turn left and count to the sixth dwelling on the left. Knock on the door three times long, three times short, and say Jean-David sent you. We're cousins." He banged down his shutter.

"Aye, and partners in business as well, or I be a Roosian," muttered Enoch.

Soon we were circling on narrow murky streets under the sinister lean of houses which met five stories over our heads.

"Keep yer eyes open for a sign or shaft of light, laddie."

I kept my eyes open, though closed would have served as well. Rain torrented off gutters and Twixt's hooves sank ever deeper in sucking mud.

"Gar l'eau!"

The screech overhead was accompanied by a potful of liquid flung directly on our heads.

With dazed disbelief, we both wiped off the more solid parts of the offensive drench. Then Enoch let flee a howl of rage sure to freeze any heart within earshot.

"Let me in!" he cried, pounding on the door of the guilty house. "Let me in noo or ye're dead. In, I say!"

The French were deaf to Scottish wrath and finally Enoch admitted defeat, turned back to Twixt and led the mule along the curves till he found an open square. There we sat in puddles and let the rain wash us clean. There, too, Enoch saw a light bobbing in the distance and ran for it. When he returned, he knew how to find the way to the quarters of Madame Annette.

Yet it felt like the middle of the night before we finally knocked out the code to our hostess. Enoch then called "Madame Annette!" and was answered only by the roar of the rain. Again he shouted.

"For God's sake, madame, let us in, for yer own cousin Jean-

David said as how ye'd not allow strangers to chill to death in yer fair country."

This time after we'd waited hopelessly, I suddenly yelled the same message in French.

A black hole in the door instantly snapped open. "Six parisis for six months, payable in advance."

"We need a room for one night only for two people," Enoch said in rough French.

"For two, twelve parisis for six months, take it or begone," and the peephole snapped shut.

In vain did Enoch pound, plead, persuade, threaten, cajole, appeal to all the saints in Heaven; and in the end he gave in. Money for naught, for I'd be back in England within a month if I had to swim. We stabled our beasts in the back and waded to a narrow crack of light.

Inside a pitch vestibule, a white claw reached in feeble tallow-light for our money, then put the coin to a gaping black hole to bite. We glimpsed a round white skull striped with a few black strands of hair, bulging eyes looking in opposite directions like a spider's. Without a word, Madame Annette hoisted her skirts above her pipe legs and led us up a narrow twist of stairs to a small chamber where a young man huddled close to a parchment page laid on a table.

"This is your common room for repast and study," the dame chirped in a high nasal tone, "and your bedroom is through this door. You'll find bedsteads, a chamberpot and a pole for clothing behind the drape. The pot's emptied only once a week so you'd be well advised to use the garde-pit in the closet, two parisis extra. Food provided on the premises or wrapped for carrying if you have classes, wine extra." And she left.

"That was the Queen of France," said our new companion, sniggering. "And my name is Dagobert du Près, student of the physic from fair Poitiers."

He rose to extend his hand, but when we reached to take it, he jerked it back, then thrust it out again; again we reached, and again he withdrew. He might have been japing except that his whole body twisted and jerked in a most alarming way, and his face had a peculiar set smile. He was a queer fellow withal for his hair stood in spikes like tree branches, he seemed to have no eyebrows at all above deep currant eyes and his lips were thick and purple.

Enoch spoke in careful French. "A student of the medical arts, are you? We're going to study the law ourselves. With Magister Malcolm dou Petit Pont, mayhap ye've heard his name."

Dagobert whinnied and twirled, then choked till we had to pound his back. "Magister Malcolm is the most sought-after master since Abélard. But he takes only the finest—not Russian wolf-hounds."

Enoch drew himself up icily. "Exactly so, that's my understanding as well. This be Alex Wanthwaite, by the by, my wee brother what's studying to be steward to my estate, and I be Lord Enoch Angus, Baron of Wanthwaite."

I was stunned as a bird that's flown into a wall, then recovered and bellowed forth with all my strength, "That's a lie! You're naught but a thieving knot-headed Scot, a rascal, a . . ."

And I was hurled into the dark bedchamber where I fell to the floor. By the time the Scot followed, I was to my feet again and pummeling him with my fists. "I'll kill you, you snake! Baron of Wanthwaite, are you! I'll . . ."

He clapped a hand over my mouth. "Hush, dinna make such a blather. Where hae ye been that ye don't know that the first-born takes all? 'Twould make no sense at all for ye to be baron and me to be landless older brother but I'll share and share alike, which be more than generous. Meantime ye can be my 'prentice and serve me."

My eyes fair popped from my head above his palm, but he held me steady till I stopped struggling.

"I'll kill you dead before you take my title and lands," I spat when he released me.

His grinning teeth shone in the faint light. "In twa years I'll begin to worry."

He pulled folded bedsteads from behind the drapes and rolled our mats out upon them, then climbed into his and was soon snoring. I retired behind the curtain to change my wet clerk's robe for a dry plaid cape and shirt, then lay down, seething.

My patience was fast running out. All right, I was in France and apparently I knew as much as anyone as to the king's whereabouts. I needs must go on the road and find him myself. As for Enoch, let him drop into the garde-pit where he belonged.

And when I woke, Enoch was gone.

12

ANICKED, I RAN DOWN THE STAIRS TO FIND HIM. He wasn't in the hall, so I turned to the cellar. There I found Madame Annette creeping on spidery legs around a wine vat in her half-buried kitchen.

"Have you seen Enoch?"

She poured out a whine of Parisian French which was hard to follow, but I gathered that Dagobert was waiting for me in the street. As I left, she pushed two packets into my hands.

"For Haute Tierce," she said brusquely.

Heart pounding painfully, I climbed the stairs and stood dazed in the bright sunlight. All I could think of was Enoch.

"Ho, Alex, here!" Dagobert appeared from behind a cart on the road and walked up the muddy pathway. "Ah, I see that the queen has baked you a tart. May I?" He sniffed our packets of food and gave a fastidious shudder of disgust. "*Merde.*"

"Have you seen my brother, Dagobert?"

"He was eager to get to the Petit Pont to find Magister Malcolm, but said that you needed to sleep and that I was to bring you to him when you woke."

"Thank you," I said shyly. Much relieved, I noticed now that the air was fresh after the rain, sweetened by honeyed flowers, the rising sun shining through new grape leaves turned the world a bright green-gold.

"'Tis my pleasure, since I have a class in the healing arts at the same time that Magister Malcolm meets."

"What healing arts are you learning?" I asked politely as we strolled.

His brown eyes shot me a suspicious look from under his plucked brows. "Are you planning on practicing physic?"

"Not at all," I answered, surprised at his belligerent tone.

"Ah, then. Forgive me, but I had to ask. So many false practitioners, you know. We who are working for our ecclesiastical license cannot be too careful. Just now, we're studying the innards of the body. Do you know, for example, how you digest your food?"

I didn't forsooth.

"The stomach is normally cold, but when we eat, the liver turns on like a flame and heats the stomach from below, whereupon our food is cooked. You see? When the flame is too low, so to speak, the patient takes hot foods and herbs to ignite the liver."

He was so delighted by his knowledge that his pasty face flushed a lively purple, almost obliterating his many blackheads. Encouraged by his friendliness, I asked my usual question.

"It must be wonderful to study in Paris, but my real reason for being here is to find the King of England. Do you know where he is at present?"

Dagobert halted.

"No, I don't know where he is." He began to walk again, his head drooping low.

I followed, thwarted once more.

"But I know someone who could tell you if anyone could," he added. "She's known as Fat Giselle. Have you heard of her?"

I shook my head.

"Ah, well, perhaps her fame hasn't spread to England, but all the students here know her. Yes, Fat Giselle has a far reach." He smiled suddenly, displaying an expanse of pale gum. "I'll take you to meet her."

"Please don't concern yourself. If you just tell me where she lives—"

"No, no bother at all, and you're very young."

I didn't see what that had to do with it, but before I could ask we saw Enoch.

"Oh, Dagobert, please do me a favor: don't tell Enoch about Fat Giselle. I'd like to surprise him."

"My oath on St. Martin," and he squeezed my hand.

Enoch hurried toward us.

"You two are slow as bears in January. Alex, are you feeling better? You were overweary last night."

He was speaking Parisian French but was the same old Enoch e'en so. Now I wished that he *had* disappeared. Why had I been so frightened? He fell in stride with us along the grassy ridge at the center of the lane.

Dagobert breathed deeply. "Ah, Paris! The jewel of the universe! Except of course fair Poitiers."

"And Edinburgh," Enoch agreed, "the grandest pearl e'er made."

"Edinburgh? Is that in England?"

"Scotland, land of the Scots, the Picts and the Caledonians."

"Yes, but you *are* English nonetheless."

"Never!" Enoch shouted, turning beet-colored.

Dagobert instantly apologized, for he meant no slight; it was simply that all students belonged to one of four nations, English, Norman, Picard or French. Personally I thought the Scots belonged with the French as the lowest of humankind but apparently every nation had its own vermin and the Scots were ours. 'Twas important to understand about nations, Dagobert continued, for the city had no power over us; we were under the king's governance which is to say we were lawless, for both Philip and his father Louis before him were most tolerant of students. However, if we had a grievance our own nation might help us.

"Are there no laws at all then?" Enoch asked, nonplussed.

Dagobert nudged the Scot slyly. "Indeed there's one, *very* important: make your sexual preference known at once!"

"Preference?" Enoch was bewildered. "For one doxy?"

"If you like doxies," Dagobert replied. "About half the students have other tastes. 'Tis said that even the ducks are not safe in Paris."

Enoch stopped dead, his face blank. Then they both rent the sky with their guffaws; I laughed too, though I saw nothing funny in harming ducks.

"However," Dagobert gasped, "make certain that King Philip

doesn't hear of your deviations, for he permits Stewes in Paris just to be sure that no one sins. That puts *him* in a stew!"

Again I laughed along with them so they shouldn't know my ignorance. Just then we reached the noisy rue de St. Jacques and Dagobert shouted information about our fellow-students. There were about seven thousand in Paris, half of them serious, the other half roisterers; they ranged in age from twelve to eighty, in class from shepherd to count, in origin from the four corners of the world. We found ourselves almost trampled by lines of arm-linked men crying out ribald japes in Latin, laughing and tippling, openly kissing buxom wenches that I doubted were students at all.

We all crowded onto a narrow bridge along with hawkers and talemeliers where vintners beat drums to offer free wine to eager samplers; screaming students crowded round baskets of roasted eels, pork flanks and capons; everyone ate and shouted. In the midst of this chaos, teachers stood on platforms lecturing to small groups on the street, in narrow alleyways between houses, on stairways between floors, inside rooms, everywhere.

"Exedrae!" Dagobert yelled, pointing to the narrow alleys. "Magister Malcolm in number three after Haute Tierce!"

And we lost sight of him.

Holding my arm in a firm grip, Enoch got us into the relative calm of an exedra and led us to a bench by the Seine where we could watch small boys diving naked into the current to find coins. No sooner had we settled than the heavens pealed in a cacophony of bells to sink the small isle, for it seemed that all of Paris was made up of bell towers ringing the hours of prayer. We bent our heads, then raised them to silence. The bells had stopped, even the pounding on the new Cathedral of Notre Dame. Everyone was eating.

"Well, bairn, this be our first dinner in Paris," Enoch said cheerily.

We carefully removed the coarse gray linen from our packets to find a pot of pudding and a pot of stewed fruit. Eagerly I bent to my pudding, prepared to suck it direct from the pot as I, too, was hungry. Just as my lips touched the rim, a piece of pudding quivered in the center, rose in a shape like my finger and wove back and forth before my crossed eyes. It climbed from its nest and crept over my hand, leaving a wet trail.

"Enoch," I gulped. "Look you."

"Hmmm?"

His mouth dripping yellow slime, he gazed uncomprehendingly at where I pointed, then exploded onto the ground where his own spittle came alive.

"That cheap slut-daw!" he cried. "Givin' us slops fram a midding! I'll kill the hud-pykis, see yif I don't!"

And I began to laugh. I howled till my eyes streamed, clutched my aching ribs.

He gagged, choked, slobbered and glared at me. "Aye, laugh and make gekkis at me. At least it's better than a face sour as a slaeberry. I thought ye didna know how to crack smile."

"Certes I can laugh," I gasped when I could. "Jump in the river, *Lord Enoch*, and I'll die laughing." And I was off again.

At first he glowered at this new peal, then shook his head and took my shoulder gruffly. "Come, lad, no more harsh words. Ye're my brother and ye've a bonny face when ye smile. Come, I'll buy ye a pigeon pie to prove my good will."

I followed him back to the main street and grabbed a pie, a spitted pork, a ham turnover, a sweet pastry and canestel, taking a fast bite from each so they couldn't be turned back.

"Traitor!" he howled. "Whale-belly! Do ye think I'm made of silver?"

Again I smiled, though 'twas hard with my mouth so full, and noted that Enoch ate near as much as I did, lacking only the ham turnover. Satiated at last, we walked to the third exedra which was still empty of students.

Belching in the noonday sun, I stretched along a bench and dozed a bit as students drifted in. Most of them were clerics, although Enoch had said we were to study civil law, not canon, and most appeared older than average. Those who weren't clerics wore a student's uniform garb, so couldn't be distinguished by nation.

They stood to respectful attention when Magister Malcolm arrived. He was a wizened old man, slightly bent in the shoulder, shuffling of foot, and his hair blinded me with its whiteness. He was richly dressed, however, in a heavy scarlet cappa lined in miniver in spite of the heat, and a curious four-sided board with a gold tassel atop his thick locks. Two students helped him to his platform where he made the sign of the Cross as he reached for some parchment pages with the other hand, then muttered a fast prayer ending *"Ego sum alpha et omega, Amen,"* and looked up.

His eyes met Enoch's and suddenly his old face was radiant.

"My Lord!" he cried in a strong youthful voice. "Lord Enoch!"

He leaped from his platform like a roe and hurried toward us. Everyone was astounded but no one more than I. *Lord* Enoch? *Lord* Enoch? Then I felt a tree fall on my head: *Enoch had managed to send Malcolm a message about Wanthwaite!* What else could it be? I watched the ancient master embrace the churl, tears freely flowing, and knew he must be privy to the scheme to steal my estate.

The two men were muttering to each other in a strange tongue when the students began to stamp impatiently and Magister Malcolm tore himself away, his hand lingering on Enoch's hairy arm. Enoch looked different than I'd ever seen him, exalted and ecstatic as if he'd beheld a saint. Forsooth I, too, felt as if a miracle had taken place, though I wasn't sure exactly what it was.

Now the exedra fell quiet: Magister Malcolm began to speak, this time in the rolling thunder of an organ. In spite of myself, I was hypnotized by his words, then appalled as I began to translate.

"Raptus mulieris ne fiat defendit tam lex humana quam divina."

He was lecturing on the laws concerning the rape of women: *Rape of women is forbidden by human laws as well as divine.* Rape? The same act as Enoch's with Gladys but done with different intent. With the intent to kill. I forgot "Lord" Enoch and my own full gullet as I strained to understand.

The magister quoted the authority of antiquity, *"Et sic fuit antiquitus observatum, quod si quis obiaverit muliere vel alicubi invenerit, si sola vel socios habuerit . . ."* I didn't catch every word, but the gist was that the practice in former times was that if a man met a woman or happened upon her, whether alone or with companions (as I had been with Maisry), he must let her go in peace.

Here a student interrupted and asked what was meant by "in peace." Master Malcolm answered that it was a euphemism for "not raped" which would not have the same interpretation if applied to a man.

"Si per inhonestatem tetigerit . . ." (If against her will he throws her

to the ground . . . and again I heard the thud when Maisry struck the earth, heard the hauberk falling.) *"Quod si impudice discooperuerit eam et se super eam posuerit, omnium possessionum suarum incurrit damnum . . ."* (If he impudently disrobes her and puts himself upon her, he incurs the loss of all his possessions . . .) *"Quod si concubuerit cum ea, de vita et membris suis incurrit damnum . . ."* (If he . . . with her, he incurs the loss of his life and members, and I supposed that word *concubuerit* must mean to let his incubus-organ bite her.) Aye, 'twas a good law of the ancients, I thought grimly, provided the lady lived to make her claims. A wave of despondency made me sink to a ledge so that I could no longer see the master, though I continued to listen.

The magister went from Roman law to that of the Franks who punished the offender's animals by cutting the scrotum and tail of the horse close to the buttocks, a most unjust and cruel act as a horse has never been known to rape. Dogs were treated in like manner and even a hawk was relieved of its beak, its claws and its tail which left it little reason to live at all. The second step of the punishment was that the rapist's lands and title were awarded to the woman, *even if she were a whore*, for if she'd cried out at the rape she was not a whore at the moment of attack. This was a point hotly argued by several students who could see women of ill-repute gaining great fortunes by invoking such a law. Magister Malcolm answered with a long involved story about a jongleur's wife and how this jongleur had died while entertaining a count, and then the count had raped the wife. I didn't know the meaning of "whore" and couldn't follow the tale for my mind was gripped again by the terrible events at Wanthwaite . . . my own mother.

I glanced around the exedra as Magister Malcolm paused for questions: all the students were men except for me, and most were clerics. What did they make of these awesome statements? Were they as impressed as I was? Enoch and Gladys Stump—aye, there was a difference, for certes the dame had wanted the Scot to do what he did.

Then the master began speaking again of the rape of virgins. Maisry. I closed my eyes; his Latin rumbling brought back the buttermilk sky, the caw of crows and a drum beating. *Et est raptus vir-*

ginum quoddam crimen quod femina imponit alicui, de quo se dicit esse violenter oppressam contra pacem domini regis, quod quidem contra pacem domini regis . . . ut sit membrum pro membro, quia virgo cum corrumpitur membrum amittit. By which I learned that the rape of a virgin is a particularly heinous crime for the rapist destroys her member, and therefore must lose his own.

I continued to follow, for it seemed that if my friend had lived she would have had recourse with the law. And I would have helped her. The dry lecture in law translated itself in my head as a joyous act of vengeance. I heard the words at the same time that I relived that awful day, only now I supplied a different ending. So much we might have done, if Maisry had lived. I was in such a trance that I hardly noted when the lecture was over.

Finally everyone was gone except for Magister Malcolm, Enoch and me. "This be my new brother, sir."

Seen close, Magister Malcolm's oak-leaf eyes were so keen that I felt he must be a sorcerer. He took a long time to study me as if searching my heart, then touched my cheek gently.

"He's all right, Enoch, all right. You're just sad, aren't you, lad? Ask Jesus to help; confess your despair and He'll ease your burden, for you know that your mother and father are in their heavenly home."

"Yes, sir, I know." In Purgatory, that is, until I could regain Wanthwaite. I glanced at Enoch. Had he revealed everything about my life?

"And they're happier there than they ever were on earth. You cannot imagine, Alex, the joy of the afterlife."

Soothly I couldn't, though I tried. Perhaps 'twas because my thoughts had been taking such a different direction since his lecture.

"And now you have a brother, a whole new clan who loves you."

"Aye," I said, unimpressed.

"Enoch tells me that you would like to accompany him to my lectures on the law. I'm afraid they'll be beyond you, but you're welcome to listen."

"I understood today's."

"Ah, on rape, hardly a fitting subject for an innocent child, but I'll do better from now on." He smiled so sweetly that I could have worshiped him on the spot if I hadn't known how he was abetting Enoch.

Enoch now spoke again in pure Scottish, what I think is called Gaelic, and Malcolm's eyes grew even softer.

"Poor bairn. Try not to dwell on such evil; put hatred and revenge out of your heart for it can only corrupt you. Already you see His goodness at work, for didn't He send you Enoch?"

"Yes, sir, I know, sir. Thank you." My eyes slid to *Lord Enoch* and my heart was instantly corrupted with all the hate and vengeance I could muster. Learn the law and retrieve Wanthwaite, would he? I'd see him in Hell first.

"Why did Magister Malcolm call you *Lord* Enoch?" I asked the churl as we walked home.

"Likely because that's my name."

"You're not a lord!" I cried. "*I'm* the baron! And therefore lord."

"I be the Lord of Dingle-Boggs," he said smugly.

I stopped where I stood. "You lie, and you know it. There's no such place as Dingle-Boggs."

"Aye, that there be. I be a Boggs of Dingle-Boggs, Lord of the whole estate."

"Do you think I don't remember that you're the youngest of three brothers?"

"That I be," he agreed, then amended, "or war. My twa older brothers died sum time ago."

"Died!"

"Aye,"—he leaned close, leering—"of the pox." And he laughed like a fiend at his own macabre jape.

"If that's true, you must have an estate!" I cried.

"Aye, a goodly portion."

"Then why do you claim you must have Wanthwaite? That you need land?"

His eyes glittered with heat. "Because Dingle-Boggs be fens, black moors, sea-lochs and crags. Every inch be bathed wi' my father's blood and be *my land*. But I need fertile acres below the oatline: Wanthwaite. And I'll have it sure!"

I made up my mind forthwith to have Dagobert take me to Fat Giselle. The sooner I reached King Henry, by whatever means, the better.

13

Y DETERMINATION TO SEE FAT GISELLE WAS NOT easy to bring about, for I could never get away from Enoch. Not only were the law lectures consuming (for we were supposed to memorize all we heard), but Enoch enrolled us in logic with a Master Roger who was pupil to a pupil of Abélard, a stimulating but heretical instructor, and Enoch studied the new Arabic mathematics as well. We were forever walking, listening, pricking on our tablets, examining each other, mostly on the difference between sin and crime.

Some crimes were not sins, for example coin-clipping, and some sins were not crimes, the most obvious example being heresy, but there were others. I was especially intrigued by a strange sin that seemed to pertain to shitting in bed, incredible though that seemed: "He who intentionally becomes polluted in his sleep shall get up and sing seven psalms and live on bread and water for that day; but if he does not do this he shall sing thirty psalms. But if he desired to sin in sleep but could not, fifteen psalms; if however he sinned but was not polluted, twenty-four; if he was unintentionally polluted, fifteen." After hearing this, I resolved never to sing psalms again lest people get the wrong idea.

At last, however, I had a hurried conference with Dagobert on the stair and he agreed to take me to Fat Giselle's on a day that Enoch had promised to spend with Malcolm to discuss Scottish matters.

So again Dagobert and I strolled down the lane alone and I felt the delicious frisson of both sin and crime that I was outwitting Enoch. However I was disturbed by Dabogert's bizarre behavior, for he jerked this way and that, began sentences and left them mid-air, looked everywhere but at me. 'Twas similar to his ordinary manner but more pronounced, and I feared an attack was coming on.

"We can postpone this meeting, Dagobert, if you're not feeling well," I said anxiously.

Instantly he became normal, his face stiff. "As a doctor of physic—almost—I assure you my vital spirits are in excellent condition. I assume that you were referring to my *arrogans* polish, which naturally a barbarian from Scotland wouldn't comprehend. 'Tis the height of fashion to behave so, I assure you, and I had thought to teach you and your brother a little grace so you be less conspicuous, but if you're honestly so savage in your sensibilities that you think I am ill, well then!"

Quickly I begged his pardon, assured him that both Enoch and I would be grateful to learn his tremors, and we continued on our way. When we came to the rue de St. Jacques, we were forced to halt before a parade of people marching toward the Petit Pont, screaming, singing, scuffling in frenzied joy. 'Twas three times its usual size and in hysterical mood. We both stared, puzzled. The only clue as to the meaning was a song sung over and over.

> *Redit aetus aurea*
> *Mundus renovatur*
> *Dives nunc deprimitur*
> *Pauper exultatur.*

As we walked on the grassy bank in the opposite direction from the students, I translated the ditty but was no further enlightened:

> *The age of gold returns*
> *The world's reform is nigh;*
> *The rich man now made low,*
> *The pauper raised on high!*

I supposed it was some new cause of the students who always needed more money.

We must have gone three miles or more and were in the thinning suburbs of Paris before Dagobert turned off St. Jacques to lead the way up an ancient Roman street surrounded by groves and crumbling villas. Finally we stopped before a villa placed at a crossroads marked with painted stones, one reading "Trousse-Puteyne," the other "Gratte-con." The walls of the villa were freshly whitewashed, and when we entered the gate I saw that the house itself had been well restored, albeit painted a garish rose color. The cobbled courtyard was filled with horses and snoozing grooms, while from within came a chorus of shouts and laughter, singing and piping, confirming that Fat Giselle was indeed popular. Accustomed as I was to the strident students, I hung back timidly from entering and Dagobert had to turn back to fetch me; I'd not faced such company before without Enoch.

When we entered the second gate, we were still outside in a second court, but one surrounded on its four sides by two stories of rooms, those above opening onto the court through balconies. There was a canopy rolled back onto the roof, and today the court was open to the sky. Though 'twas crowded with people, the first impression was of a garden with flowering vines climbing and tumbling everywhere, with blooms overflowing in pots as well.

Yet the people quickly dominated nature and a gaudy lot they were. Many were students of course, all shouting at the top of their lungs, and bold-faced women dressed in every shade of the rainbow. Then there were soldiers and—to my amazement—clerics, plus merchants and many more I couldn't recognize. The smell of sweat, burnt honey, roast capon, ale and sour wine permeated the air; huge frescoes covered every wall, so lascivious that I blushed and turned my eyes downward only to find the same tongues flicking genitalia in mosaics under my feet. Arrested by the cacophony and dazzle, I almost tumbled into a sunken tub of water wherein sat a naked pink lady with an equally naked tonsured cleric.

At last grasping the evil nature of the place, I tugged at Dagobert's tunic. "Please, Dagobert, I think I should go home . . ."

But he couldn't hear me, so he pulled me forward toward a huge corpulent woman dressed in black standing in a far corner. We had to struggle through the patrons and I lost count of the pinches I suffered on my buttocks, but there were at least twenty. Fat Giselle was arguing with a student who'd left his cloak as surety, then re-

fused to give it up when he lost at dicing. As the harangue promised
to be long, I turned my attention to a singer who appeared to be
marvelously skilled if I could have but heard her.

She was frail and almost as small as I, too pallid for prettiness
and with enormous bulging eyes, but her voice resonated throughout the court. The crowd confirmed my opinion by crying against
the din: "Berthe! Berthe! Let Berthe sing!"

She smiled graciously, raised her arms and invited the patrons to
join her:

> *"Redit aetus aurea*
> *Mundus renovatur*
> *Dives nunc deprimitur*
> *Pauper exultatur."*

Everyone went wild, cheering and tossing pieces of clothing,
clinking tankards. Dagobert and I watched, still perplexed, for the
frenzy went far beyond students' causes. Suddenly we were both
enclosed by two black-clad arms and hugged to Giselle's soft body.

"Isn't it wonderful?" she boomed.

"What's happened? What's all the excitement?" Dagobert asked.

"King Henry's dead! Richard is now King of England!"

And I fainted.

WHEN I REVIVED I was lying under a tree with my head in the lap of
the girl who'd been singing, Berthe. Behind her stood Fat Giselle
and Dagobert, the dappled sunlight swaying over their bodies and
making me feel sick so that I closed my eyes again. In the distance I
could still hear the roistering crowd and knew we were somewhere
in the villa. I wanted my mother.

"I think he's conscious," Berthe said. "Alex, can you hear me?"

She touched my cheek and I turned away fitfully, not wanting to
wake, not wanting those awful words to be repeated. Oh, what
would become of me? How would I ever retrieve Wanthwaite?

I knew that Giselle had knelt next to me, by the strong smell of
her rosewater.

"Come on, boy, you'll be all right. You're not hurt. Drink this."

My eyes closed, I sipped a burning liquid.

"Go back to your friends, Dagobert. Berthe and I can look after Alex."

There was no escape: I must wake. Berthe's lavender eyes protected me tenderly and she smiled. Fat Giselle, too, appeared much softer than she had when haggling with the student. It wasn't really fair to call her fat, though she was buxom, but she was also shapely and quite attractive. Her large brown eyes were friendly as a cow's, her skin dewy white, her mouth wide and turned down at the corners, her black tunic cut shamefully low to her nipples and her straight dark hair clipped at her neck.

"My, my, aren't you a luscious apricot," she crooned. "My, my, I've never seen a boy more beautiful. Berthe, look at that skin, the eyes. Do you have all your teeth, Alex?"

I nodded, feeling the blood flow back to my face.

Berthe smiled. "'Tis almost a shame to waste such glory on a boy."

"Boys have their uses too," Fat Giselle answered.

I sank dreamily into the warm liquid of memory: how nice to be with females, how sweet their voices, how kind their flesh. The courtyard cries faded into the distance; there were only the gold-edged elm against a cerulean sky and women doting on me.

Fat Giselle stroked my cheeks. "Roses are blooming again. You're feeling better, aren't you, honey-pot? Would you like to talk now? Dagobert said you came to learn about King Henry."

The elm blurred into puddles of green; I turned my face against her bosom.

The women were silent as I listened to the solid thump of Fat Giselle's heart; then Berthe asked me gently if I'd like to look at their menagerie: they had apes, a bear and a cat from Africa big as a dog. I nodded and struggled to my feet. Fat Giselle scrutinized me carefully from head to foot as if I were a prize horse; she turned my face this way and that, lifted my hair to see my ears, pulled my upper lip to count my teeth, ran her hands along my sides, e'en sniffed my skin. I was repelled but not offended by her odd inventory for it seemed so impersonal. Yet she lost her motherly kindness by her acts; I now noticed heavy bulges under her smudged eyes, hard lines around her mouth, a brisk professionalism in her hands. Berthe, however, remained the same.

She chatted as we began to move. "You're in Zizka's school for jongleurs, you know, and his animals are trained by Tue-Boeuf and his wife Pax."

She spoke as if I should know Zizka, but I couldn't recall him from the Petit Pont.

"Who's Zizka? What's a school for jongleurs?" I asked shyly.

Berthe explained that Zizka was a Bohemian, the topmost jongleur (that is, performer) in France, oft appearing before royalty. He was the first to receive love songs (*trouvères*) from the south writ by famous troubadours and he introduced them to cultivated people everywhere. Furthermore he knew all the heroic tales (*chansons de geste*), including the most recent rage, the stories of King Arthur and his Round Table. He had a legendary library of manuscripts. Would I like to see it? I nodded.

All the time Berthe talked, I was aware that Fat Giselle continued her appraisal of my person and I wondered—though without too much concern—if she'd discovered that I was a girl. I was also aware that King Henry had died, but I wasn't yet prepared to confront the hideous fact.

The library was housed in a large cottage, which also served as home for Zizka though he wasn't there at present. I'd never seen so many leather-bound volumes assembled in one place and wondered if this Zizka was a sorcerer. I doubted that even Magister Malcolm had such a collection.

Berthe pointed. "Those are the *chansons de geste*, but Zizka claims that their day is finished which I hope is true, for they inspire war. I much prefer the songs from the south; love is a sweeter subject than war, don't you think? My father was Papiol, you see."

Before I could inquire who Papiol was, Fat Giselle asked me abruptly if I could sing.

"Aye," I said uncertainly, not sure what the question imported. Certes I could sing Christian responses and the Celtic lays my mother had taught me. If she meant could I sing *well*, I would have had to confess that I was not so gifted as Berthe. Yes, I decided, not too well, but loud, forsooth.

We went back into the sunlight to look at a bear called Belle-Belle, a friendly beast but treacherous. Pax, the lady handler, was teaching it to appear more fierce than it was.

Although the menagerie was diverting, I was more intrigued by the human activities around me. A family of midgets was practicing a balancing act on a pile of straw and though they hadn't far to fall, being so small, 'twas a dangerous activity. More alarming was a woman dancing on a high rope with no straw below to protect her. She had the darkest skin I'd ever seen, a huge mane of crisp black curls and performed with an utter disdain for safety or modesty, for we could see straight up her flashing skirts.

"That's Dangereuse," said Fat Giselle.

"An appropriate name," I said wittily.

"So we thought when we gave it to her, though we'd not seen her on the ropes then, but it suits her in all ways. Her Gitano name is unpronounceable."

So far all I'd seen had charmed me, but now I noticed disturbing practices on my left, people twitching almost as Dagobert did.

Fat Giselle caught my frown. "Those are Jobelins. You remember Job, patron of thieves. Look you how cleverly they can dissemble. Those applying sores and tumors are Pietres; it takes years to learn to hobble convincingly. Behind them, the Sabouleux have soap in their mouths to simulate froth; the Francs-Mitoux are trying falls for they faint in public places. These profitable arts pass largely through families, but other deceits can be learned by any honest applicant, how to forge documents for example, or various hoaxes such as pretending to be robbed. The variations are as many as there are fools to believe them."

The offhand smugness of her words belied their evil and at first I heard them as from afar. Then suddenly my ears and my conscience came unplugged together, as if I were rising from water, and I recoiled in horror. *Benedicite*, I must leave at once!

"Where's Dagobert? I have to get back to my brother," I said.

Hands of iron gripped my arm. "Soon. Only first we must talk of why you came."

"There's really no need, now that—" and I managed the awful words—"King Henry's dead."

But I was forced to go to her upper chamber with her as Berthe stayed below, forced to say that I was carrying a message from my dead father—but if the king was dead, that was that. Naturally I didn't feel so resigned, but I was desperate to leave. It was time for Enoch to be home.

"Why King Henry?" Fat Giselle offered me a cup which I refused. "Why not King Richard?"

"I know naught of King Richard," I said uneasily. "Some of my family fought with King Henry, you see; he would have remembered us."

She raised skeptical brows. "Old Henry had many soldiers in his time. Surely Richard would appreciate the message just as much, perhaps more. He's a very noble person, Richard of Poitou, Eleanor's son through and through."

I stared at the black drapes swaying behind her in the faint breeze, trying to adjust to this new circumstance; my father's words had been so explicit, so positive about King Henry. I'd never dared tell Enoch that my own father had been with the expedition which had captured Scotland's king for Henry, the very day after Henry had done penance for killing Thomas à Becket. Feeling the victory was a sign of God's approval, the old king had been so jubilant that he'd declared a national holiday and sent commendations to each English nobleman personally who'd been in the field, the parchment I now carried. Surely Richard would be unimpressed by such news since he'd fought his own father. But personal considerations aside, would he honor England's law and restore Wanthwaite even so?

Giselle interrupted my reverie, almost as if she'd read my mind. "King Richard will be a most gracious monarch, you'll find. All new kings work to redress the wrongs of the old; it's to their advantage to appear beneficent in comparison to what went before." She stood and paced, paused to play with my hair. "Of course I know not your business with the king, but I can tell you this, Alex: *I can get you a private audience with him, that I promise!* Zizka will be sending a message to Ambroise soon; be sure you're ready if you want to be included. I'll take you to Zizka now if you like."

"Ambroise?" I hedged.

"Richard's official troubadour, Zizka's oldest friend."

"I—I'll have to think about it. There are—things," I trailed miserably.

Her eyes, cowlike no longer, burned into mine.

"Think it over, but don't take too long and don't deceive yourself that there's another way. No small boy with a message about Henry will reach King Richard, I can assure you, for the new king must get his kingdom settled and leave on his Crusade. Only those critical to his grand project will have audience. This is a rare turn in Fortune's Wheel for you, my pigeon."

She spoke with chilling authority and though I sensed both sin and crime in her person far beyond what I'd seen or learned of in Malcolm's class, I believed her.

"Thank you, you're—very kind. I'll let you know," I muttered. "Now, could you please take me to Dagobert?"

I thought on her words all the way home, sinking more and more into a melancholy slough that turned my liver cold. With Henry, all my hopes for recovering Wanthwaite had died as well. My mind ran through one dark labyrinth after another but found no exit. *Benedicite*, King Henry had been hard enough to chase, and now I was told that King Richard would be impossible, what with his Crusade to the Holy Land which might last years. And then what quality of king was he? Sister Petronilla hadn't liked Henry, of course, but my father had; I'd try to learn all I could of Richard, though I came back to the undeniable point that it would avail me nothing to know his character if I was never able to see him.

Of what might happen if I never returned to Wanthwaite, I dared not think.

14

T FIRST I DIDN'T CONSIDER ACCEPTING FAT Giselle's offer to help me. Soothly I didn't trust her kindness and wondered how such a fleshy trollop had gained access to a great king. Yet a strange thing happed: once I'd actually met with the hussy, I seemed to hear "Fat Giselle" on everyone's lips and all of it good. Of course most of the gossip came from students who were not famous for their fine moral discrimination, but anyway they thought she was Queen of the Universe because she'd formerly been a Goliard wandering from one master to another and had accumulated most of the knowledge of this world. In any case, she might have been a great Latin student once but she'd sunk into a sinful pit.

My resistance to Fat Giselle came to an abrupt end about a week later when the Scots talked openly about Wanthwaite. 'Twas right after a class on testing innocence by ordeal, a subject which stimulated Enoch and his master to a heinous plan. It concerned a single challenger to battle, *which was always on the issue of ownership of land*. Fought on foot or on horseback, the state paid the bill and decided on the methods, and winner take all.

"Do ye believe England would permit a Scot to challenge a Norman?" Enoch asked eagerly.

"Not Henry's England," Malcolm drawled. "But Richard's England will be a kingless England. While Richard is on the other edge of the world, who will go to the marches to adjudicate? Eleanor? Her worthless son, Count John? Many a northern English lord is loyal to Scotland, and this is our time to move."

Enoch showed surprising modesty. "Of course this Roland de Roncechaux appeared to be a fierce fellow. 'Twill nocht be easy . . ."

"In which case the clan moves. We're free now, free at last of the English yoke! By the time Richard returns—if he ever does—'twill be a completed fact."

Although Enoch glinted smiles in my direction, by and large I was as noticed during this treasonous blather as if I'd been a cur. But I heard and I decided: thief or no, Fat Giselle was my only chance and I needs must act *at once*. If Enoch won Wanthwaite by battle, then I was finished.

ENOCH DECIDED to sup that very afternoon with Magister Malcolm in order to continue their talk and sent me home to wait for him.

"Don't worry if I be late," he said.

But I was already on my way, praying that Dagobert would be in his quarters, and again Fortune smiled, for he was haggling with Madame Annette about a message he claimed had gone astray. Finally becoming impatient, I interrupted to ask him to lead me once again to Fat Giselle's.

The hour was still early but the air dark and sultry under a
sullen sky. Late-autumn flies bit us fiercely to alert us to the coming
storm and we hurried as fast as we could through the thick mantle of
fallen leaves. About halfway there, huge drops spattered on our
faces and we began to run. Treetops bent in a wind we could not yet
feel as the rain fell ever faster. Finally the storm grumbled loudly
and broke as we streaked across the cobbles of the pink villa.

Inside, servants scurried to pull food and tables under the balconies while men above unrolled the canopy. Guests japed in loud
tones about "getting cleaned" and seemed to enjoy the diversion. Fat
Giselle was nowhere to be seen, but a waiter told us she was in her
chamber.

"Do you want me to go with you?" Dagobert asked as he eyed
the dicing table.

"Of course not. Enjoy yourself—I'll be right back."

I spoke more bravely than I felt, but fear is a sharp spur and I
saw that Enoch and I were in a hot race back to Wanthwaite, "winner take all." On the stair up to Giselle's apartment, the sky forked
white and thunder shook the foundations, forcing me to huddle
against the balustrade before continuing. I knocked sharply on the
door, competing with thunder, then again.

There was no answer, but in the brief lull that followed I
thought I heard voices within. Shivering in the rain, I beat again,
only to have my effort drowned by another belch from the sky. I
must have repeated my pounding a half dozen times before I gave
up: either no one was there after all or I couldn't make myself heard.
Defeated, I looked up at the rolling heavens and huddled close to the
door.

Whereupon the door swung open and I fell flat on my back into
Fat Giselle's chamber!

Stunned, I gazed upward as three heads and six breasts dangled
over me! Three women, naked as jays!

Fat Giselle bent down and jerked me upward by my hair. "What
are you doing, sneaking into my private chamber? Who are you
anyway?"

"Oh! Oh!" I gasped. "I knocked, only . . ." And the pain was too
great to say more.

She eased her pull. "Wait a moment, aren't you the boy I picked for Zizka?"

"Aye, you told me to come back." Tears choked me.

She was mean as a bogle. "You took your time about it. I daresay he has someone else."

When she released me I felt like a discarded rag. I stood, weak and disconsolate, as the ladies considered me. Yet I was also intrigued by the variety of shapes in so small a number. Fat Giselle *was* fat after all, only her folds had an interesting contour, layered in great loops like a candle running down. The tall pretty one beside her was shiny gold all over, her curves elongated like melons, her muscles still supple. The last, a tiny shriveled dame, appeared well-used: her buttocks were flaccid bags, her breasts looked to have been chewed by wolves.

She was the first to speak. "Well, this is a real asses' bridge. What do we do with him?"

"He's a pretty child, and frightened," said the golden one, reaching a tender hand to my cheek.

Both deferred to Fat Giselle who was studying me with the same intensity as of yore. "I'm never wrong, that's the truth. I have an uncanny eye. Look you, is he not Love personified?"

The other two nodded in agreement.

Fat Giselle sighed. "I'll have to take him to Zizka, but since he's seen this much we might as well continue our business and swear him to secrecy. Better than turning him loose to gab to the wrong people. What say you, Margot?"

The small one said, "Aye, we can put the hook in him."

"Tullia?"

"Yes, let him swear."

Instantly I felt better. "I swear I won't . . ."

"You'll swear when and in the manner we tell you," Giselle snapped. "Meanwhile, sit and be quiet. Alexander, was it?"

"Aye, Alexander of Wanthwaite," I said in a small voice.

Fat Giselle shoved me into the chimney corner and placed a cup of hot wine in my cold hands. Trying to be quiet and invisible, I nevertheless coughed softly from a mixture of smoke, a sweet effulgence from their glistening bodies, and a third stench which was

familiar but hard to place. The ladies lolled informally on plump
cushions, Tullia with one knee drawn to her chin so that I couldn't
help gazing on her hole, Margot on her side so that her breasts now
seemed collapsed bellows. Fat Giselle presided from a straighter
position, but her fat naturally spread to make her seem a plump hen
brooding on chicks. Assured that I was going to see Zizka and no
longer affrighted, I gave myself up to the astonishment of the occasion. Never had I dreamed that women took their ease so, never
having seen more than one at a time naked. Perhaps they'd just risen
from naps and not had time yet to garb.

"Now I'm all addled," Fat Giselle began crossly. "Where was
I?" She thought a moment. "Ah yes, according to his figures, there
are now twelve thousand *poules* in Paris trying to catch lizards in
their holes and the competition is keen."

Which absolutely astounded me, for I could hardly recall ever
seeing any chickens wandering the Paris streets, nor could I recall
any chicken I'd known eating a lizard.

"Therefore we have security to offer, a steady supply of swords
for their sheaths."

Bewildered, I tried to see how I'd missed a leap in her terms,
moving from chickens to the military.

"Do you have any students in mind?" Margot asked in a slickery
voice which made Tullia glance up sharply.

"Well, yes. Brother Matthew, an advanced student in the Cathedral School. He has only two—and I like the small number—and
they seem of rather exceptional quality."

Tullia sat up straight. "Surely you don't mean Mathilde, that
greasy *cocotte*."

"What's wrong with Mathilde?" Margot asked angrily. "She has
good fleshy thighs and a high nasal voice."

"She's a fool," Tullia snapped. "Nothing above her eggy breasts.
She acts like a tipsy adolescent when a hound brushes her skirts."

Fat Giselle frowned. "Are you certain Brother Matthew can be
trusted, Margot? You know I don't like dealing with priests."

Margot flushed bright red. "I don't understand why you're
worried."

Tullia agreed. "Really, Giselle, the Church isn't demanding a
share."

"That's not what I'm referring to," Fat Giselle answered darkly, "and you know it. The pope's letter very specifically referred to the Crusade in the Holy Land to destroy heretics. But who knows where the Holy Church will look for heretics when the Infidel is conquered? I predict right here in Paris—and our priest could prove dangerous."

"I guarantee Brother Matthew's high character," Margot said stiffly.

"Tullia?" Fat Giselle asked. "Your opinion is more objective."

Tullia paused. "Aye, and less certain. You know how much I respect you, Giselle. I can't take your fears lightly. Perhaps we should accept Brother Matthew, since he's *intimately* known, but take no more clerics hereafter."

With that decision, their meeting was finished, leaving me both perplexed and humbled. I'd thought myself capable of following the most advanced lectures on the Pont, yet was unable to make any sense of their arguments or conclusions. Their terms shifted from husbandry to politics to the military and, finally, the Church, thus confusing their logic. I was awed by their erudition and understood for the first time Plato's distinction between appearances and reality, for certes they didn't look to be so deep.

Now they turned their attention on me, and it seemed that the storm intensified. Wind leaked in behind the black drapes making them billow; thunder growled round us like a mad dog. As the three naked women stood and gazed down, I subtly pressed my caul between my thighs.

"Is he for Ambroise?" Margot asked after a time.

Fat Giselle nodded.

"Isn't he too young?"

"Nonsense, Bernardo was only eight. How old are you, Alexander?"

"Eight, ma'am."

Tullia leaned forward and sprung one of my curls. "Alexander the Great, a fitting name. Isn't he adorable?"

Feeling like a haunch of mutton, I nonetheless basked in their approval.

"I'd like to take him to Zizka while there's still light," said Fat Giselle. "Let's make our ceremony short."

She disappeared behind a drape and came back with three black candles, put them on the trestle and disappeared again while the other two added powders to the hot wine. When Giselle returned, with the candles lighted, wine flagons in hand, they formed a tight circle with their backs to me and chanted:

> *"Euch'rist of bone and lapwing's blood,*
> *Union of woman and Holy Stud,*
> *Come, Spirit, to our feast,*
> *Come, Spirit, to your beast."*

Benedicite! Witches!

I dashed to the door and was caught again by the hair so that my neck near snapped.

"No, you don't, boy. You fell into more than you bargained for, didn't you? No harm will come to you if you do as we say, but you'll swear . . ."

"I swear! I swear! Only let me go!" I screamed, whereupon I was pushed to my knees, enclosed by a cage of female legs.

"You'll swear to the archfiend himself on forfeit of your immortal soul if you break faith."

The legs moved to the drape, the curtain opened and I gazed directly into the yellow slab-eyes of a nervously bleating goat. Aye, that was the rancid odor I hadn't been sure of. Using their feet, the witches turned the goat's face to the drape and fastened a black candle between his short horns, then fell to their hands and knees in front of the animal. Now I found myself staring into Fat Giselle's nether eye.

Margot, first in line, lowered her head three times to the ground.

"Praise Lucifer, Fallen Angel, friend to all women and the dispossessed, I do swear Thee everlasting obeisance. I pray that You fill Rafe's scrotum with fistulas, let maggots devour his eyeballs, stick Mercury's wand up his ass-hole and turn it slowly. In the name of the Archfiend Satan, I thank Thee."

Whereupon she raised the goat's tail and kissed his hole!

Deus juva me, Holy Mary, St. George, St. Martin, please, please, they don't expect *me* to do that! My heart shook my ribs so that I hoped to faint, only I didn't and I was afraid to pretend in this company.

Margot had risen and Tullia was speaking:

"God of the sublunary world, all hail! Make my progress invisible so that I may not lose income, my delivery easy, my body supple to return to its shape. I thank Thee."

She placed her lips firmly on the odious hole.

Giselle spoke all too quickly:

"My Lord, continue to keep me safe from the poisonous tentacles of the venal Roman Church. I thank Thee."

Now I was before Satan's knock-kneed besmottered back legs. My breath became shallow as bare feet nudged me and Fat Giselle hissed the words I must say.

"Take my immortal soul—to Hell—" I gasped, "if—I—ever—breatheawordofthis."

I tried to get up and was held by the feet.

"Go on, Alexander."

I tried to think of Wanthwaite; my throat grew tight, my head woodly.

I brushed my sleeve quickly over the area, held my nose and kissed the goat's fud.

Somehow it was over, the goat back behind his drape, the witches gone, Fat Giselle dressed again. My head was whipped by the icy drench outside; gratefully I lifted my open mouth to be cleansed of goat taste before Fat Giselle thrust me under her cope and hurried me across the court to Zizka's cottage.

We burst through the door without knocking and saw our host sitting at a desk, a second man behind him. Never had I seen so many candles used in such a small space, and each was backed with a circle of silver so that it glowed like the sun. Fat Giselle wrung water from her cloak, ruffled my plastered hair to make it stand up, then spoke unceremoniously.

"Here's the boy I told you about, Zizka. He was negligent about returning and you may have filled the position."

Position? *Another boy?* My gullet twisted in agony. I stared at Zizka as he reluctantly quit his study and stood to greet us. Tall and in monkish robes, he defied category, for he didn't fit into any of the four nations which I now easily recognized. His eyes were sunken tarpits, his hair equally inky and pointed upward in such disarray that it might have been struck by lightning, his skin pale, his spade-jaw twice too long for his face and off-center. A strange wight rose behind him as a shadow, cloven in two parts: one side bald, the other bristling with brown hair, one side of his face painted white, likewise his tunic and breeches, the other bright red. Yet if he'd been properly garbed he might have looked more weird yet, for his eyes were uncanny, huge and staring, and he wore a perpetual silly grin. Zizka gestured courteously to me.

"Come closer, boy; my eyes are weak. Giselle sang your praises for weeks and she's a difficult mistress."

Reassured by his deep kindly voice, I walked into the light. Zizka came around his desk and peered squint-eyed, then beckoned to the other wight.

"Brise-Tête, come see. Is this not a likely cherub? Quality here, true quality."

Brise-Tête nodded enthusiastically.

"Boy, what's your name and background? How came such an angelic countenance out of the Paris gutters?"

"I'm Alexander Wanthwaite, sir, and I'm only visiting Paris to study with my brother. We're from—"

"Aragon?" he guessed, rubbing my plaid.

I was thinking rapidly and decided it might be more prudent to withhold the truth. "No, from Scotland."

"Ah, no wonder I didn't recognize these weeds. I've always heard that Scotland was barbaric, inhabited by rough, hairy men wielding clubs. I see I'm wrong."

He was right but I didn't contradict him. He rose and drew me to his chair where he sat, putting an arm loosely around my waist.

"Tell me where you're studying, Alexander."

More and more at ease, I rattled on about the civil and canon law, the *sic et non* of the disputation in logic, universals and nominalism, adding even a few samples of medical knowledge gleaned from Dagobert. All the time, Zizka watched me closely.

"You were right, Giselle, better even than Bernardo. Nothing more exciting than the tight bud sleeping before dawn. The intellectual and spiritual glosses add piquancy.

"I told you," she said smugly.

"So, Alexander, you want to join my troupe?"

"Oh, no sir," I blurted. "I want to meet with King Richard. Fat

Giselle promised me that you could arrange it. I have business with the king."

Zizka raised heavy brows at Giselle.

"I hadn't had a chance to talk with him," she explained, then became angry toward me. "What did you expect? That we'd pass out audiences with the king like alms? Of course you have to earn your keep."

"No need to be nasty," Zizka said mildly. "I'm sure Alexander will be happy to conform. The situation is this: King Richard's court troubadour and historian, Ambroise, has commissioned me to bring my troupe to Chinon to perform for the king before he leaves on his Crusade. Some years ago Ambroise saw a particular act I devised requiring a small delicate boy of exceptional beauty, and requested especially that I include this act in my repertoire. Naturally I agreed, but unfortunately my former boy is now a man, so I need to train a new boy. If you can sing a little, I think you would be perfect. However I would want you to train with me personally, for we have our reputation to maintain. What say you? Will you join us?"

It sounded so simple—and so sure to get me an audience. "Aye, yes, soothly I will," I said eagerly.

Before he could answer, the cottage was struck by a force that tipped a few candles and made the desk jump. Then Enoch rammed in, bellowing like a bull!

"Where be the slummock what stole my brother?" He whirled on Giselle, his gaveloc raised to kill.

Just as fast his arms were pinioned by criminals and freaks who'd run after him. Dagobert slunk behind them and tried to signal me that he hadn't told, and I knew that Madame Annette had betrayed me.

Zizka put hands on hips and walked close to Enoch to study him.

"Now this is more in keeping with what I'd heard of the Scots. Yes, a true wildman. What cold gale blew you hither?"

"Stand back or I'll bite yer terse off! Alex, come here!"

I sidled next to him. "It *is* my brother Enoch, sir. You can tell your men to let him go—he's harmless."

"Harmless, am I? If these roughs be not bagits, their balls be dust. As fer ye, Master Sweettalk, ye with yer flower face, ye're the most ungrateful warlo of all! Ye'll learn how harmless I be."

By this time he was free and I smiled gratefully at Zizka. Not that I cared if they tossed Enoch into a bag of snakes and pulled the top tight, but I was glad to even the score somewhat: now I had saved *his* life.

"Come, we're gang home."

I didn't move.

"You're to be congratulated, Master Wanthwaite," Zizka said smoothly. "Your brother has just joined our troupe, the aristocrats of jongleurs we call ourselves."

Enoch stared down at me, his eyes fair jumping from their sockets. I couldn't contain my triumph. "I'm going to meet King Richard."

"King Richard, is it?" He whistled softly and turned to Zizka. "King Richard, very clever. He's the bait—where's the trap?"

"No trap, Enoch," Zizka answered, bemused. "Alex has told you the truth."

Enoch pointed to Fat Giselle. "And I hear that this slut-daw arranged his meeting with the king. Or mayhap some of these sticked swine around me be special friends with the king. Wake up, bairn, or a trompourer will rob ye blind. Aristocrats! Ye know that I bow to no man when it comes to despising English kings, but e'en I have to defend King Richard from such sludge-mates."

Zizka's jaw wiggled til and fro, which I guessed was a sign of anger, but he remained courteous.

"Unfortunately you're all too accurate, Enoch, in defending the king from such questionable taste in company, but King Richard does appreciate the arts of minstrelsy and verse-making. After all, he grew up in a different . . . clime? . . . from Scotland, an ambience of troubadour poetry, the Arts of Love. 'Tis one of history's temporary ironies that the purveyors of such elegant entertainments are outside the law. Here in Paris, we're required to live with the more disreputable elements who are also outlaws, but I assure you that we are a breed apart." Then he repeated what he'd told me about Ambroise.

"I'm going to see King Richard," I repeated firmly.

"Be quiet, Alex." Enoch looked long at Zizka, impressed I could see, then took in the books lining the wall, the fastidious desk and lights, all indeed a contradiction to the motley people in the room. I knew I'd won when he spoke in French.

"How much is this Ambroise going to pay you for Alex's presence?"

Zizka shrugged. "A small fee. Not enough to matter. It's the art which must be served."

"The art for you, money for Alex and me."

"You!" I exclaimed. "Who asked you to go?"

Zizka took a wary step closer to the Scot so he could see his expression.

"Naturally we'll feed and house the boy while we're on the road, provide costumes, at least the one for that particular act."

"All his expenses and a fee for each appearance," Enoch said adamantly. "What are his duties?"

Again the shrug. "Almost nothing. To sing, dance a little. He happens to be the physical type I'm seeking."

Now Enoch's eyes were narrow and his lips rolled tight. "Physical type for what?"

"Please, Monsieur Wanthwaite, you're embarrassing me. You can see for yourself, a sweet little boy. He's to play Cupid . . . I don't know . . . we might revive a number about Alexander. Two or three solos, playing the clappers with our instrumentalists if we're short, learning a few choruses."

"Write it out," Enoch ordered. "Be sure you include everything you want, for he'll not do one thing else. We'll want two parisis for each performance, room and board for both of us. I'll look after him."

"Robbery!" Fat Giselle called out. "Make the Scot wrestle with Belle-Belle the bear if he wants pay."

Zizka and Enoch were eye-locked like two male dogs meeting on the road. I hoped Zizka could outwit him but didn't think he could. As long as I had my audience with King Richard *alone* I supposed it didn't matter too much to me.

The haggle went on for some time with Enoch winning most points; then they came to the date of our departure.

"Ambroise writes sometime between April and June next year," Zizka said.

"*Next year!*" I bawled. "But I can't wait! You promised, take me now!"

Everyone except Enoch gazed, astonished.

"Great heavens, child," Zizka admonished mildly. "At your age, six months flies."

"Aye, ye'll wait, bairn, and ye'll learn the law like we intended, and logic as well. I'm thinking astronomy might be a good course too, for we'll come here to rehearse only on Saturdays."

"Oh no," I moaned.

The men shook hands, made arrangements for contracts. On the way out, I spoke to Fat Giselle.

"Thank you kindly for your help. I—I—"

"You'd better deliver, for that price," she said, boring into my eyes so I trembled. "And remember your oath."

Outside, Enoch, Dagobert and I made a human chain as we walked to the gate where Twixt was tied. Enoch was going to make Dagobert walk home in the knee-deep mud, but our shivering friend pled so pitifully that he was permitted to mount on the mule's rump and we began a long stumbling trek back to Madame Annette's. The crashing and sizzling on all sides couldn't keep Enoch quiet; he would harangue and scold if the world came to an end.

"One thing I promise is that ye'll stay innocent yif I have to chain yer ankle to mine."

"You're too late!" I shouted, exasperated beyond endurance. "I'm already not innocent!"

At my words the heavens split in two parts in a deafening crash and spat a maelstrom of fire! Twixt stumbled and stopped while I made a silent prayer to Satan that I hadn't meant it.

"That were some fireflash," said Enoch, awed. Then, as we continued, "How be ye not innocent?"

"I know as much as you," I improvised to cover my blunder. "We go to the same classes."

"Aye, as much aboot some things. Let me ask ye, ye've seen the stones by Fat Giselle's. What think ye means 'Trousse-Puteyne' and 'Gratte-con'?"

"Easy," I said. "Whore's-slit Street and Scratch—uh—cunt?"

"That's the English. Meanin'?"

"Whore—hoar, hoary trench. The ditch must get frosty."

"Aye, there be some such. Go on."

"Scratch—a cunt is a small furry animal. We have them in England but you may not have any in Scotland."

"I believe I've seen a few. Well, I admit ye've surprised me, bairn."

And that stopped his mouth, but it didn't stop my thoughts. One piece of secret information was a canker in my joy and I crossed my arms, pressing hard: still no breasts, nor had I bled again.

But six months from now?

Dry and snug in bed much later, I still fretted and turned, worrying and seeking. Then I sat bolt upright.

In all my concern about Enoch racing me back to claim Wanthwaite, I'd completely forgotten Roland de Roncechaux and Northumberland! Was it possible that they'd already sought audience and sealed Wanthwaite's fate? King Richard had gone to London for his coronation in August and this was November.

I lay back so hard that Enoch grunted from his mat. *Deus juva me*, I hoped King Richard was as fair and Christian as some people said, that he would honor my claim.

Otherwise I was lost.

BOOK TWO

KING RICHARD

~~~~~~~~~~~~~~~~~~~~~~~~~~~~~~~~~~~~~~~

The ripened maid delights to learn
In wanton Ionic dance to turn,
And fondly dreams, when still a child,
Of loves incestuous and wild.

HORACE

15

IZKA TURNED OUT TO BE RIGHT ABOUT ONE thing: the next six months did fly fast, though not because of my age forsooth. Enoch kept me so busy running from early morning to sundown from one class to the other, then sitting half the night by candlelight trying to absorb what we'd heard, that there was no time to reflect on the passage of time. The Scot, too, had predicted rightly when he'd said I'd never be free of him an instant. Zizka was more fortunate in his shadow, for Brise-Tête was a dumb mime, unable to speak because someone had relieved him of his tongue when he was young. Would that same wight had snipped Enoch's waggling member.

Nor did I mature in my body, *Deo gratias*. My breasts didn't appear; I didn't bleed again; I was still fitting easily into Arthur's rags. This kindly turn of Fortune's Wheel may have come because of some invocations I remembered my mother teaching me, but 'tis more likely that 'twas simply in my stars. I also recalled what she'd said about my aunts who were so late developing into women.

Yet I did go through an inner change which was dreadful worrisome though not even Enoch seemed to notice it. I think I caught a peculiar fever from Madame Annette's kitchen, or mayhap 'twas from that time I forgot and drank Paris water which everyone warns is poisonous. Whatever the source, the symptom was a fierce burning through my innards and straight to the fantastick cells in my head. Although my skin remained cool, my cheeks pale, my eyes clear, nonetheless I was racked day and night by a pounding heart, sudden gales of laughter and frantic joy over *nothing*, followed by such a melancholy humor that I sat for hours contemplating the icy

Seine, paradoxically enjoying my despondency. I finally concluded that my liver was enflamed, that the fire therein was stoked too high, and I asked Dagobert for an elixir. He was unsure what to prescribe so asked his master in turn who said 'twas impossible for the liver to cook too fast and that 'twas more likely I was possessed with a demon. He suggested I come and confess, then be exorcised, but since I didn't have anything to confess except my kissing Satan's toute-ass which I dare not tell on pain of losing my soul, I just accepted my condition.

When we finally left Paris in June, my pulsing liver almost exploded in a burst of joy and dread. The joy was easy to fathom, the dread more complex. Naturally I feared that Northumberland and Roncechaux had already succeeded in annexing my estate. If the whole country of Scotland could be bought, why not Wanthwaite? Well, I would soon find out. Then the thorny question rose: Could I persuade King Richard to reverse such a decision? I would have to try. A more murky dread lived like a snake hidden in the depths of my vital spirits: *I was afraid to become Alix again.* 'Twas passing strange, I knew, and I couldn't understand it but there it was. I couldn't go back to the girl I'd been because I hadn't her circumstances, and to be a girl in my present condition was fraught with dangers, both known and unknown, for I would now be a woman. And I thought of my mother and Maisry.

Yet the dice had been thrown at my birth and there was naught I could do.

BRISE-TÊTE tugged my leg and pointed to his shoulder, then shaded his eyes and turned his head from one side to the other as if scanning the horizon.

"He wants to show me something," I interpreted. "He wants me to get on his shoulders."

Enoch looked at Zizka's dumb mime with disbelief. "Is he woodly? Yer hurdies be not exactly feathers. And even Twixt is melting in this sun."

'Twas true. This central valley of France was a bowl of hot broth, resisting our forward movement, immersing us in our own drench. Furthermore we were presently atop a grotesque escarpment which grew in this flat bowl like a wart. Nonetheless, I slipped off Twixt onto Brise-Tête's muscular shoulders and he immediately trotted up a steep cliff on our left.

"Heigh, fool, where gang ye? Bring the boy back!"

"Fool, bring the boy back!" the dark-skinned performer Dangereuse echoed, for she was so enamored of Enoch that she repeated his words like a litany.

There was nothing wrong with Brise-Tête's hearing but he paid no heed to the cries for he was a headstrong fool. Leaning into the sharp angle, he climbed straight upward as I clung to his head. When he lifted me down I saw that we were on a narrow ledge overlooking the next steamy valley. He pointed eagerly, then turned an anxious face to watch my reaction.

"Be it Chinon?" I asked.

He nodded proudly.

On the far side of a hazy shallow kettle perched a long horizontal series of towers and rocky outcroppings, a jagged vision softened by its reversed reflection in the Vienne River below.

"Alex, air ye all right?" The Scot was streaming with sweat and had turned a dangerous red color.

"Look."

By this time Dangereuse and the singer, Berthe, had also crowded beside us.

"Is King Richard there yet?" I asked Berthe, for she is our authority on royal banners in this part of the world. I'd learned that her father Papiol was jongleur to the infamous Bertrand de Born, the troubadour who'd incited King Richard to rebel against his own father.

She squinted. "Champagne, and someone from the French court—the Princess Alais would be my guess. We may sing at a royal wedding if King Richard decides to consummate the affair at last."

"And the king?" I insisted.

"No, not yet."

Several of my organs went back to their proper places in relief. I'd become so nervous about the outcome of my interview that I almost wished I'd not come. A week from now I might be the most miserable creature alive, the assigned wife of some gross, brutal Norman knight, and I would look back on this free life with the jongleurs as a period of pure joy. If I'd had more talent, or if it hadn't been for my poor parents, I don't know if I would have pursued my goal further. But there it was: I had no choice.

A long twilight had given way to black velvet before we began our final climb to the castle gate of Chinon. Large twinkling stars seemed brightest close to the horizon as if Heaven had dropped her ripe fruit: campfires, Enoch explained, of new Crusaders awaiting King Richard. Sure enough, as our awkward two-wheeled long carts rumbled over cobbled paths, peasants and archers clustered about us to see if we were from the king. On we went, across the lowered bridge, past the guards at the gate, through torchlit courts stacked high with armor, around vassals rolled in blankets at our feet. Finally we reached the kitchen court where we swiftly created our own little fortress against the wilderness.

Only this was no wilderness: this was the castle of Chinon at last. The end of my journey, more than a year in the making but done at last. I lay with hot eyes gazing into the familiar mystery above and rehearsed in my head just what I would say and how I would phrase it. *Laudatur Maria* the king would prove kind! He *had* to be, must have sympathy for my youth and wretched state. Somewhere in the distance outside the wall men sang "The Crusader's Hymn"; inside other male voices rumbled pleasantly; from another direction the *Te Deum* in female voices.

All awaiting King Richard.

THE NEXT MORNING we learned that he would arrive this very day, albeit too late for us to perform for him. That would take place on the morrow. Nevertheless we rehearsed like demons, doing our best and worst together from our extreme excitement. Zizka was impossible to please: he acted as if he'd been given a group of imbeciles to whip into shape under threat of death. After a wearisome exasperating siege, I slipped away by myself to try to recover my equilibrium for the greater trial ahead, my interview with the king.

Carrying my lute under one arm, I fled toward the heart of the castle. Finally I stood in a maze of stone paths amidst greenery, surrounded by invisible laughter like birdsongs. Women! Ducking behind a clipped hedge, I looked through the leaves curiously but saw no one. Nevertheless I pushed on farther to find solitude, be-

yond a high wall of gaudy blossoms, down a slippery bank. At last it
was quiet. I found a moss-covered rock and sat basking in the dancing pattern of sun and shade, then plucked on my strings and prac-
ticed softly the song Zizka had criticized most:

> *"Now be done with drudging,*
>   *Life is sweet!*
> *Let's enjoy the juices*
>   *of youth's heat!*
> *Our springs too quick a-springing,*
>   *'Twill not repeat.*
> *We have brief time*
> *To quest for budding pleasure;*
> *Let's trip the lover's measure*
>   *While we be young!"*

As my voice trailed off I watched the closed green canopy expectantly, knowing my music must evoke enchantment on such a day.
And soothly a delicate white hand stole forth and moved a branch,
then another, then a face appeared and a body, and I gazed delighted upon the most beautiful young lady in all Christendom. She
stood with light brown hair curling around her petal face, wide eyes
the same color as her hair, pink lips parted in wonder, her exposed
throat heaving, her tiny waist enclosed in a green satin gown.

I was afraid to speak for fear she was an airy nothing from my
own head for she seemed my female self as I might be, or Maisry
come back in new guise but with the same merry eyes. Therefore
was I relieved when she sat next to me and spoke first.

"Hallo, you're a very pretty boy. Where did you come from?"

"Zizka," I answered, fearful that she'd despise my lowly station.
"Have you heard of him? He's very famous."

"Zizka? Of course I know him. My mistress, the Countess
Marie, has brought every great artist in Europe to our court in
Champagne. She sponsored Chrétien de Troyes. Have you heard of
him?"

Because of Zizka, I was happy to say I had.

"What's your name?"

"Alexander of Wanthwaite."

"I'm Lady Isabelle of Troyes. Well, you sing very sweetly, Alexander, though your voice still be soprano. I'm sure King Richard will be entranced. May I?" She reached for my lute.

"Please take it."

She plucked aimlessly for a few chords, humming to get the key she wanted, then slowly picked out a song with many false starts and stops:

> "*Gentle handsome friend.*
> *We sit here, the two of us;*
> *Where-e'er our fates may trend,*
> *Now have we cheer, the two of us;*
> *Beneath the sun, the boughs that bend,*
> *With naught to fear, the two of us;*
> *Yet soon I leave, my heart will rend*
> *When we're not near, the two of us;*
> *But let us kiss before I wend,*
> *And pledge our love, dear, the two of us.*"

She handed back my lute. "Well?"

" 'Twas wondrously well wrought. Did you compose it just now?"

"Aye, but it could use polish. The last line doesn't scan, though I'm getting better under Marie's tutelage. However, I meant the sentiment. Did you like it?"

"Oh, yes, yes I did," I said fervently.

"Then we'll be friends." She thrust her head forward, her eyes closed. "Sealed with a kiss."

Lightly I brushed her warm dry lips with mine.

Instantly she leaped to her feet. "Good, now let me help you, for friends must be ever alert for each other's interests. Come on, there's someone you must meet."

I took her hand and stumbled after her up the small bank, through the oleander and into the patterned garden again. We walked openly among languorous ladies taking the air, their bare tresses shining down their backs, their long trains hissing silkily across the gravel, through a clipped gateway into a tiny enclosed square where sat a lady alone, her brown hair topped by a narrow gold and diamond crown.

"Your Highness." Isabelle dropped to her knees and I did likewise. "I'd like to present my good friend Alexander who sings with Zizka. Alexander, Princess Alais Capet of France, sister to King Philip."

" 'Tis a great honor, Your Highness," I said, taking her hand.

This was King Richard's betrothed? A drab dun-colored dame well past her prime with sagging skin, lined eyes, even a touch of gray in her dull locks, and the expression of a cowed child. I looked into hazel eyes which accepted the world without wonder, curiosity or resistance.

"Please take your ease," the princess said tonelessly.

"Wouldn't it be wonderful if Alexander could sing at your wedding festivities?" cried Isabelle. "His voice is surpassing sweet."

Princess Alais livened a little. "Indeed, I would like that. When think you that the wedding will take place, Lady Isabelle?"

I could hardly countenance her humility, that a princess would consult a lesser lady on such a great matter.

"Oh, I'm sure 'twill be soon, even here at Chinon. Countess Marie says King Richard will never leave on Crusade without trying to have issue before. 'Tis essential for the kingdom, is't not?"

Princess Alais nodded and repeated. "I hope 'twill be soon for both of us, Isabelle."

"No! No!" My friend shook her head angrily, then sang out: "You marry a god/I marry a clod! Really, Alex, 'tis true. I'm betrothed to a cull from the German royal tree: his breath smells of dead rats, his feet of old cheese, and his parts of what you'd expect. Furthermore he's a tyrant."

The princess smiled vacuously at this choleric outburst, though I thought I caught a shadow in her eyes at the words "a god."

"With your permission, I must take my leave," I said, nervous that Enoch would come crashing upon us and ruin my new friendship.

"I'll walk with you." Isabelle took my arm and we bade farewell to the numb princess.

"There," said my new friend when we were out of earshot, "I've given you entrée into the English court for when you grow to be troubadour. Alais is loyal for all she's a lifeless old bat. Didn't you find her a pathetic creature? I daresay Richard will have his share of

Rosamunds tucked away, for he's said to be as lusty as he is brave."

"Are all princesses so passive?"

Isabelle shouted with merry laughter. "*Benedicite*, no! Wait till you meet my Countess Marie, also a princess of France. She has her mother Eleanor's head, some say her balls as well. She and the queen wrote a book called *Tractus de Amore et de Amoris Remedia* which came near to making that old fool Pope Clement excommunicate them, and he would have too, except they were clever enough to have it penned by a cleric called Andreas Capellanus so that it seemed religious."

"What sort of a book? Poetry?" For I was thinking of Isabelle's learning the art from Marie.

"Not a bit. 'Tis more a legal tract on the rules of love. There are thirty-one articles in which women teach men how to behave through love."

I stopped short and looked at her with new interest.

"What mean you by *love*, Lady Isabelle? And how may a *woman* teach a *man*?"

"Ah, you see?" She waggled her finger archly. "No woman would ask that question. We are endowed with a superior nature and know from our birth about love, while all that you men ken is lust. Therefore do you fight and pillage, rape when you list."

I felt I was on the edge of a cataclysmic discovery and stuttered in my urgency. "No, w-wait, don't walk on, I must know."

"Of course you must," she agreed, "if you're ever to make your lover happy, or become a *galiol*."

"Aye, please instruct me so that when I marry . . ."

She brushed me aside with an impatient hand. "Who speaks of marriage? Marriages have naught to do with love. Love is based on the heart's choice and therefore must be adulterous."

I was shocked speechless. The only adulterer I'd known was the unfortunate Maud whose midwife had given me my caul, and she didn't seem an ideal lover. Of course I'd seen her under trying circumstances.

"Men naturally feel lust, as you may already know"—her eyes slid toward me—"but lust alone is abominable, a sin against nature. That's why the Church prohibits lust in marriage and passes laws against pleasure, such as the *chemise cajoule*, a nightshirt with a padded hole placed so that it stops joy in the act. We women on the other hand feel that simple lust should be transformed to transcendent love, an ecstasy beyond belief, for 'tis worship plus passion, soothly a religion of love."

Utterly confused, I tried to sort out her words but 'twas made difficult by my unruly liver. I groped toward what for me was the central issue. "You say that your Countess Marie and her mother Queen Eleanor wrote this tome. Tell me then, does King Richard adhere to its rules? Does he believe in the importance of love?"

"King Richard? Who can say? Of course he believes in chivalry, which is related to the rules, and courtesy."

"Yes, but I mean in marriage, when he assigns marriages."

"I don't know. Besides, it doesn't apply."

I thought of my father and mother, for one transfixed moment thought I heard one of their voices, then lost it.

I was sore perplexed. "I don't understand. Can't man and wife be lovers? Must marriage always be—brutal?"

She laughed scornfully. "You must have been born in a bluebell. Why do you think Eleanor and Marie devised the rules? Certes they'd both like happy marriages, but their experiences have taught them the odds. 'Tis too unequal—the man rules his chattel while love *must be free*. Hear me, Alex, I'm to be wed to a smelly old man, Count Conrad. Think you that I love him? But I want to love . . ."

She looked at me with burning eyes. "Alex, have you passed rule six yet?"

"What is rule six?"

"'A boy cannot love until he's reached maturity.'"

My mouth went dry. "I believe not."

"Oh, well, it doesn't matter. We can still be friends."

She turned and ran, her green train slithering at her heels like a snake. I returned to the camp where I could see Enoch pacing in front of our tent and impulsively I, too, ran toward a small copse of poplars where I threw myself on the new grass to think.

My senses were much addled by Isabelle's odd information: I was excited and depressed together. Sap ran in my veins akin to the whispering silver leaves above me and I near swooned at the power of my natural spirits. My boiling liver was all ablaze and if Isabelle hadn't told me 'twas impossible I would have said that I felt desire. Not love, for there was no one to love; not lust, for I hated the impulse which had brought about my mother's and Maisry's rapes; but *something*. And that *something* demanded that I not be assigned to some dreadful revolting Conrad of my own. I pressed my hot forehead deeply into the cool grass and prayed to the Blessed Virgin to help me, to influence King Richard's heart.

Everything depended upon the king.

NOT MORE than an hour later, Lady Isabelle shouted from the step, "Alex, he's coming! Follow me to the wall!" Then she turned and ran. I dropped the gold sandals I was polishing and dashed after her.

"Alex, where gang ye? Wait!"

Carrying her train high, Isabelle dodged among flowers all the way to the women's court, then straight to a high wall and a narrow stair which led to a walkway. Enoch and I followed her upward.

"You can't really see him yet because he's beyond that crest, but his fanfare was heard." She looked at Enoch. "Who are you?"

"I'm yer friend's brother," he said dryly, "what tries to look after him."

Then we all noticed a fourth person: Princess Alais stood quietly staring into the distance just a few feet from us.

"Your Highness." Isabelle bowed, as did Enoch and I.

"Please, Lady Isabelle, take your ease with your friends. 'Tis a great occasion, is it not?"

Her expression belied her words but I knew 'twas a great occasion, one that would decide my fate.

"I think I hear a trumpet!" Isabelle cried.

"No," I said, "'tis a bee on the yellow bloom."

Enoch shaded his eyes. "No, methinks the Lady Isabelle be right, for I can see dust directly in line with that bit of tile roof in the treetops, there."

We all strained to see where he pointed and, aye, one of the dark cloud-shadows hanging over the valley seemed to have direction in its movement, then glints of light coruscating in its center: reflections on shields! My liver blazed and my hands shook so that I had to press them hard on the stone. At last, oh, my God, at last! Oh, surely he would grant me Wanthwaite! Surely assign me a fine knight!

"There, I *was* right!" Isabelle laughed over her shoulder as we all heard a faint silvery snarl from the cloud.

At the sound, the slumbering fields below suddenly shook themselves awake as people burst from the turf and ran in circles like ants.

"The king is coming! Get a place on the road!"

"Where? Where? Let me see!"

"The cross, put on your cross!"

"Move those cows!"

Behind us we heard the heavy groan of the castle doors swinging open, then the echoing clatter of hooves as a host crossed the moat to meet the king. They rode below us, archbishops and their companies, Countess Marie in green and gold and her son Count Henry with a hundred barons in their train, each with colorful banners flying. Foot soldiers lined the roadway with archers behind as the men and young boys who'd been waiting in the fields crowded to get a glimpse of Richard. All were united in that they wore bright crosses on their shields or shirts. Yet none, I trowe, was as excited as I was!

Now the cloud became a sinuous, undulating line creeping over the edge of the world and we could distinguish tiny horses bouncing brightly in the fore. And finally the sound! A slow rumbling roar, a catapult spewing stone from the earth's stomach, as the beat of hooves, the thin whine of horns combined with the deafening shout from the common human voice: "Richard! Richard! Hail to the king!"

Trumpets blasted nearby as Marie answered her brother's fanfare, then a choir of men's voices chanted the *Te Deum*, and holy tapers were lit to give God's welcome.

"I can see him! I can see him! Is that not the king, Princess? Under the canopy!" Isabelle jumped up and down.

"Yes, 'twas his father's," Princess Alais answered, "the silken canopy of Plantagenet scarlet and gold." A faint pink flushed in her cheeks.

"They're takin' it away so he can be seen by the crowds," Enoch said. "Look ye, Alex, the one in the center on the big cream destrier. That be yer king."

Now they were approaching rapidly, the king clearly visible on his Spanish stallion, his red cross set with jewels so that it sparkled like diamonds in the sun, his long crimson shield emblazoned with three golden lions. He was surrounded by magnificent coursers rid by the highest dukes and bishops in the kingdom, but all paled in his roseate light. Closer, closer, borne on a wave of shouted love, answering with a gracious wave of hand, his face turning this way and that, his narrow ruby crown sitting like a halo on his golden hair.

"Hail to King Richard! Hail to the king!" I heard myself scream.

Then for a short time only, just as he reached our side of the Vienne, I was able to see him clearly albeit still somewhat far away. He *was* a god, nothing more nor less, taller, more beautiful, more touched with glory than any mere mortal could be. Like the stone carvings on the cathedrals, he showed his greatness first in size, for he was the largest man I ever remembered, dwarfing all those around him, yet was he well proportioned. His face was oval, his cheekbones high, his chin chiseled, and his wavy hair deeply burnished in the troughs, gold in the crests. But most of all his manner marked him: imperious, strong and gentle together with the confidence of one who knows his infinite power. Then he disappeared in a copse, to reappear directly below us where we could see only the top of his head and his horse.

"Hail, King Richard!" I screamed again, but he didn't look upward.

"Come!" Isabelle cried. "Let's see him in the courtyard!"

She and Enoch ran ahead and somehow I became tangled in Princess Alais's train.

"Oh, I'm sorry, Your Highness. There now, you're free."

"Free?"

Our eyes met and held. For the first time, I was aware of an intelligence working. Somber, cold, desperate. Then the moment passed.

" 'Tis a glorious occasion," she said dryly.

"Aye, glorious."

And I hurried down the stair to find Brise-Tête awaiting us. We were to return at once to begin preparations for the great feast tomorrow. At last my moment had come.

AT DAWN the next day a large wooden tub was placed in our tent by Zizka and Pax, the animal trainer, who was to help me dress.

"I'll bathe myself, if you please," I said firmly.

'Twas the first time Pax had applied my make-up and she was obviously confused at this strange request till Zizka whispered into her ear that I was unduly modest because of my youth, and they both withdrew. Carefully I tied the tent-flap behind them, put a long blanket over my shoulders and disrobed beneath it. Still holding the blanket like a cocoon, I slipped my treasure belt into a declivity I'd dug beneath my pallet. Poor Enoch! If he knew of my riches! He kept an accounting of all he spent on me and someday I planned to repay him, but not from this hoard which represented my only security. Quickly I jumped into the tub with a toss of the blanket, then sank completely under to get my hair clean. After much soaping and rinsing, I dried under the blanket and pulled on the undergarment of my Cupid costume, flesh-colored tights which barely spanned the distance from waist to top of legs and made me appear naked, as Zizka wished. I put aside the rest of the costume to don after I was painted, and slipped on a splattered smock.

"Did you remember your teeth?" Pax asked critically when I emerged.

Soothly I'd forgot and pulled hazel shoots and wool between them, then dipped pumice in a mix of barley flour, powdered alum and salt mixed with honey for a thorough polishing. When I'd finished, we sat on opposite sides of a plank loaded with exotic paints and powders.

She cupped my chin in her hand, her eyes narrowed. "Can't improve on this much. Yah, to be young again. E'en so, such delicacy fades in artificial light so we'll enhance nature just a little, sugar-lips. Bah, alabaster powder's too white—you're not Brise-Tête. Wait here."

In a short time she returned with a basket filled with various items and whipped up a concoction of powdered chickpeas, egg white and lukewarm rosewater which she spread evenly over my face, neck and shoulders and the side of my chest that would be exposed.

"Good," she muttered, "just a touch of sandalwood for the cheeks, turnsole to the lips—press together tight and hold—enough. Now close your eyes: heliotrope on the lids. Wait, I'll take some off, too blue. We'll leave your brows and lashes as is. Now I think we're ready for the hair. Still damp? Good."

She mixed olive oil, alum and honey in equal parts to quicksilver, combed it through my locks, then turned them around a warm poker to make ringlets in the Greek manner.

"Want to see?" she asked, handing me her precious sliver of mirror, a rare French glass backed with silver.

Moving it from one side of my face to the other, I saw that my skin glowed a pearly pink, my lips a parted rose. Then I saw that my shadowed eyes were my own father's luminous gray irises staring back and I almost dropped the glass! Gazing into one probing orb after the other, I silently promised him that I *would* succeed, I *would*!

Alone in my tent again, I slipped on a tiny bit of gauze fastened on one shoulder, a shameless garment but what Zizka claims Cupid really wore. Then a narrow gold belt, gold sandals laced up my smooth legs, my bow and quiver of arrows, my mask and my wings.

"Zizka!" I screamed. "Come here!"

After a long time he appeared, his black brows drawn down. "Alex, you're not the only one who has to get ready. What's the matter?"

"These wings," I said angrily. "They stink."

He sniffed, bellowed, "Tue-Boeuf!" Then, when Pax's husband came, "Tell that imbecile cook Julian that this flesh has turned rank and maggoty. He'll have to kill another swan. And at once!"

When Tue-Boeuf had trotted off, the jongleur examined me carefully, turning me all around. "Well, I must say that Pax has excelled herself. As pretty a morsel as will be served this night."

"When will I have my audience?" I asked anxiously. "Have you arranged it yet?"

"Audience?" He laughed grimly. "Not I. That will depend on how much the king likes your performance."

I looked up, both appalled and disbelieving. "My performance?

What has that to do with my interview? I'm not auditioning to be the king's troubadour; I have important business to discuss."

"That's your affair," he drawled, "if he chooses to see you. So take care that you sing sweetly and true; watch your high tones which tend to go flat."

"You promised in Paris. Fat Giselle said absolutely that she could get me an audience, that she was the only one, that . . ."

"Complain to Fat Giselle, then. I said I would bring you to Chinon and I have."

"But your friend Ambroise?" I would have wept except that I was afraid of smearing the heliotrope.

"Of course, but Ambroise is a troubadour, not a sorcerer. He can hardly persuade the king to see you if you don't impress him, can he? Perform as splendidly as you look and you'll have no worries."

"But I *can't*," I wailed. "You say yourself that I'm no singer. You promised!"

"I said I'd get you to the king and that I *thought* Ambroise could arrange an interview, but there's nothing in your contract. Come on, let's go for those wings ourselves."

"I don't believe you," I insisted as he wrapped me in his cape. "Enoch said he would put everything in writing: he must have told you that I should have audience with the king and you cheated him."

Zizka looked at me, bemused. "You overestimate my abilities and perhaps Enoch's intentions. I remember distinctly what he said: 'I will then be able to meet with the king,' and that's all. I supposed he was representing your interests. But come, you'll do well and get your precious interview, and such talk now will only upset you."

In that he was right, but he should have thought of it sooner. As I trotted beside him, I hardly knew whom to blame more, Enoch or myself. How could I have been so dim-witted? To have let him make the terms of the contract! And now, here I was, *auditioning* for my audience like a lowly jongleur—except that I had less talent than a croaking frog. 'Twas an ordeal of single combat which I'd entered with no arms. No wonder Zizka had rehearsed me so unmercifully—I'd *needed* it!

The kitchen looked like a battleground between men and beasts after the victorious army has departed. Everywhere were blood, innards, skins, horns, grease, eggshells, bones and feathers up to our knees, all o'erladen with flies and the sweet stench of blood. Cooks like inept surgeons screamed and waved dripping shanks at one another while a few silent boys carefully replaced feathers in the cooked pimply skin of fowls.

"Wait here," Zizka ordered, "while I find Julian and see about your wings."

Picking his way on high spots in the detritus, he crossed the kitchen and disappeared through an arch. Almost immediately he was back and held up fresh wings for me to see.

"They're still bloody," he said. "You might as well stay here while I have Pax clean them and attach them to your harness. Here, sit on this stool and keep the cape closed. We don't want a blood-stained Cupid."

Which unfortunately reminded me once again that I was soon to be a girl and I panicked. I cursed my fate, cursed the Scot, cursed Zizka for being so nasty, until I'd worked myself into such a state that I thought to make myself sick. I tried to observe what was going on around me to distract myself.

Under the surface chaos I could now discern an emerging order: on the far side of the kitchen the largest meat dishes were being decorated. The dead head of a stag was being sewn to his kneeling cooked body which was artfully painted with blood to match the real fur. The eyes had been replaced with carbuncles which wouldn't attract flies. Less successful was a standing bear, for the cooked body looked flayed compared to the head, a problem the decorators were trying to solve by replacing the real fur pelt. Unfortunately the fur piece hadn't had time to cure and the strong rancid odor of putrid bear-fat dominated the room.

Then my eyes fell on a pastry carving of King Richard and my liver was aflame again.

Quickly I turned to the fish courses for solace. Saffron-gold turbot, thornback and sturgeon floated on berry seas; at the other end of the table monsters of the deep wallowed in hoof-jelly water. A little man called Antoine identified them as dolphin, swordfish, seals and whales. They rivaled the bearskin for stench.

I liked the birds the best. Peacocks, swans and eagles had been brought back to life and sat on nests of partridges, sparrows, larks and sucking rabbits. Still, such game brought memories of Wanthwaite and more and more I felt I was being readied for a public execution.

Antoine had been called away, so now I studied his masterpieces lying before me, the dainties: pig-stomach stuffed with ginger and stuck with nuts, spices and almonds as spines; whale and dolphin livers smelling like violets; deer testicles floating in sweet and sour sauce; ling tails, eels in saffron sauce, salmon belly and baked herring in sugar. Carefully, so I wouldn't drip or smear my make-up, I dipped a ling tail in alaying juice and ate it. Immediately I felt better.

'Twas almost an hour before Antoine returned and discovered his table bare.

"Some thief stole my dainties!" he howled. "'Twas Raoul I wager, that jealous rat! Julian, come here!"

Julian waddled across the kitchen at the call and gazed with disbelief at the empty trays, as did I.

"Boy," said Antoine, "you've been here all the time. Did you see a small weasel of a man hovering near?"

"I believe I did," I lied, trying not to belch. "What color was his hair?"

"A piled head with a fringe of gray."

I was just nodding sagely when Zizka returned to rescue me.

"Sorry I took so long. Pax was in the middle of doing Dangereuse's pigeon dress," he said, holding up my wings. "Julian, can we take Alex to his ropes?"

Aye, take condemned Alex to the execution. "May I have something to drink first?" I asked.

Julian handed me a flagon of spiced wine which I gulped greedily.

"Take care, Alex, you have a long wait." Zizka took it from me. "And you can't leave your perch, once there."

"Perch?" Eyes swimming, I followed him and Julian across the kitchen into the dining hall.

Marshals, squires, ushers, and sergeants-at-arms, all dressed in Plantagenet red and gold, lined the walls which themselves had gone through a marvelous transformation since last night. Garlands of flowers hung over the tapestries while carpets of blooms under-foot made the salle a bower of sweetness. Tiers of tables had been added, each richly set with plates of gold. Julian walked rapidly to the top tier where the king would sit in solitary greatness. At his place was a huge iron pan lined with a thick pastry; it had three handles tied with heavy ropes wound with flowers reaching up-ward. Beside the pan sat a skillful pastry rendition of the Holy City of Jerusalem complete with Calvary and Richard holding his cross on high.

"Why did they put it here so soon?" I asked Zizka. "I thought I was last on the menu. Shouldn't I be brought in on a cart?"

He pointed to the ropes. "We're going to fly you, from there."

I looked upward a hundred feet or more to a pulley attached to the vaulted ceiling.

"I won't do it!" I cried. "That's dangerous! Besides, you never told me."

"Because I wasn't sure in Paris that the machine was in good order, but Julian assures me it is."

Julian nodded impatiently. "Only one accident in five years. Please get in, time's flying."

Time mayhap, not Alex. "It's not in my contract!" I yelled.

"Of course it is. Shall I call Enoch?"

I stared speechless into his malicious eyes and allowed myself to be lifted to the center of the pie where Zizka attached my wings, put a wreath of fresh red roses on my hair and tied my mask in place, for of course Cupid is blind.

"Don't worry so, boy. After all, you sing only a few lines and you look like a god, I assure you."

"Put your head at this end or you'll suffocate," Julian instructed. "There's a breathing hole in the tabernacle. Now stay perfectly still while we put the boiling sugar on the edge to make it stick, then the top."

I laid my face on my hands, rump high, as my saffron eels swam from my stomach back to my mouth. Then the air became hot and my lid was on. Shortly my pan moved, swung free, began a slow squeaky ascent. Once in midair it moved til and fro in sickening arcs till I thought I must vomit and swallowed all those dainties twice again to keep them down, though they'd lost their savor second time round. Finally I was lodged next to my pulley, quiet at last, *Deo gratias.*

But so hot! No air, my nose stuffed with wheat flour; an iron bubble in my stomach near blew me away. At least I couldn't be heard. I belched like a braying jackass but made air faster than I could discharge it. I couldn't e'en think of my song: my griping stomach was my lord this day and I must find ways of appeasing it.

Then through my own belching I heard fanfare and the banquet had begun. I tried to imagine the king walking to his table, Marie and Isabelle. But no, a baked herring begged for attention and I let it return to be rechewed, then a whale liver now smelling more of cowpat than violets.

Either the banquet was taking months or they'd forgotten me. Tears of self-pity welled in my hot eyes as I thought of myself withering up here to a mere skeleton. Mayhap someone would find me hundreds of years from now and think me a saint, make my bones into holy relics to be displayed in some cathedral. Pilgrims would gaze on my fiendish smile and wonder how I'd flown so high with such small wings. Or mayhap something was askew with the ropes and I would suddenly plummet like a stone from a mangonel, killing myself and Richard in one blow. Wouldn't Enoch bray with glee! No Alex and no English king to thwart his devilish schemes! I willed myself to survive just to cross him: I *would* descend, *would* sing, *would* get Wanthwaite.

And it worked! Slowly I felt that sickening swing and in stomach-lurching drops I began to descend. I tried to flex and unflex my muscles for they were cramped and I'd need them, tried to ignore my hanging pouch under my gauze. Now I could hear Zizka's voice and knew I was level with the balcony.

> *"From Greece's sea a goddess came*
> *With beauty rarely wrought;*
> *Aphrodite was her name*
> *And love her only thought."*

The pan bumped onto the table; I lowered my elbows to prepare for my shove on cue. Shouts of aproval at the pie and loud applause almost drowned out Zizka:

"O'er earth and water she did roam
Spreading love, yet all alone;
Weeping for her empty womb,
She languished for a son."

I licked my lips, tasting the bitter turnsole. My heart bounded with panic: my moment had come!

"Black Mars thundered in a cloud
And struck with lightning's fire;
Shrieked the goddess all aloud,
'I have my heart's desire!'"

Now! I took a deep breath and stood. Only I didn't stand! My back hit the top with a dull thud, not making a dent. How odd, I must be weak from being in a cramped position so long. I bumped again and again, forgetting anything but getting out of here. The top would not budge! I banged as if it were a kettle but I might be buried six feet underground for all the difference I made.

Dimly I heard Zizka continue through the part where I was supposed to take bows.

"Born is Amor,
Beauteous boy!
Love is Amor,
Desire's joy!"

Frantically I beat like a chicken in a stone egg. Perspiration coursed down my arms and thighs as I pushed and pushed and pushed. No one would ever believe that I was so weak that I couldn't break through sugar!

"Now is Cupid here on wing,
Brought by England's fame!
Filled with love for England's king,
Richard is his name!"

Unless it wasn't sugar at all! And my mind chilled. This was mortar I was fighting. The Scot's macabre plot—to bury me alive in a pie! By the time they finally opened Jerusalem, I would have expired. Call that scabrous, filthy goat a devil? Enoch was old Clootie himself!

"NOW IS CUPID HERE ON WING . . ."

Zizka bellowed out the verse thinking I hadn't heard. May Enoch burn in damnation! I drew myself taut as a catapult, then released myself with all my might. And I was out.

"Oh, look you! 'Tis Cupid himself!"

"Who would have thought!"

Delighted applause and calls surrounded me as I groggily dropped Jerusalem off my back and stood on weak legs. Blinded by my mask, I fumbled for my bow and arrow and tried to perch on one toe as Zizka had instructed me. The music thrummed, I sneezed out a few crumbs, remembering to smile:

> *"King of love and right,*
> *Valiant warrior true,*
> *Peer exceeding bright,*
> *How I love . . .*
> *Love you!"*

And I let my little straw arrow fly toward his broad chest.

"Ahooooo!" a dog howled in pain.

Benedicite! I ripped off my mask, my back to the king, leaned forward to see if I'd killed the poor beast, saw a limp-eyed hound scratching its ear—

And suddenly let flee a fart from my backside that could be heard in Paris! "*Rrrrrrgg*!"

Stricken, I whirled to face the king.

One royal hand was at his nose, the other fanned the air.

"God's feet!" he cried for all to hear. "Cupid's shot me with Greek fire!"

The whole hall roared approval for his wit, as I died.

"I'm sorry, sorry, forgive me," I whimpered. Wanthwaite lost! Zizka struck my chord again and I sang, facing King Richard this time though all I could see were halos of light from the torches surrounding him. But he could see me: desperately I looked at him with my father's gray eyes, smiled with my mother's dimples, evoking their doomed spirits to save us all.

"King of love and right,
Valiant warrior true,
Peer exceeding bright,
How I love . . .
Love you!"

Then I repeated the words in my normal voice, hoping he heard through all the jangling, trying to reach his heart as Cupid would do.

Then I bowed deeply—this time holding my wind—and sank on a little stool by the king's feet for the rest of the program. I couldn't have borne my failure through the dreary hours ahead except for the hot bile that coursed through my veins at the thought of Enoch. How cunning he was, a Scottish viper with fangs of honeyeyed poison, always pretending to help me when all along he was plotting an ignominious end to my quest! *Benedicite*, signing a contract with no guarantee of a royal audience, sealing me in a confection, pulling me in a sickening crate to the sky, mayhap e'en planting those dainties to make me sick, for I'd oft told him my weakness for deer testicles. No point looking ahead now for I had no future, or back because I couldn't bear it. I existed only because I wanted to murder Enoch.

After an interlude of troubadour songs, Brise-Tête came forward on the platform to do his ass act. He was the head of the donkey, a wight called Chebo the hind part. Atop Brise-Tête's half sat a droll effigy of an old man controlled by strings in the mime's hands. The substance of the pantomime was simple but the execution cunning to the extreme. In essence the old man couldn't get the ass to move, no matter how he tried. "Hin! Han! Hin! Han!" Chebo brayed from beneath his skin as the ass planted his feet firm. The old man insisted; from the balcony, a horn blasted in a good imitation of breaking wind and the audience howled. Now the old man beat the ass with faggots, whereupon the ass raised its tail and three turds fell as the kettle beat time. I listened gloomily to the hysterical audience and wished I'd been assigned Chebo's part. That's where my talent lay.

Again the music sounded and I became hypnotized by King Richard's feet. They were big as eelboats and richly dressed in red velvet, their long stuffed pointed toes drooping over the edge of the platform. As I watched they jigged with the music. Then I felt a tapping on my skull: the king's forefinger rapped the measure on my head. I sat still as a stone, enthralled by that steady tap. Was it a sign? Should I turn and smile? More songs followed, each with a different rhythm, and the king altered his beat. My neck grew stiff but I didn't care: I wished my head would resound like a kettle for the king's pleasure.

Then the clappers ran in circles making a terrible din to announce the final number and the piper sounded the dove theme. Dangereuse mounted the platform, her elbows bent to simulate wings, her feathery costume shining silver in torchlight. Two viols soared together as she dipped and swayed in her graceful dance and the audience fell silent, for Dangereuse is an impressive performer. Then she bent to the ground and leaped forward as if she would truly take wing, thus releasing a hundred white doves hidden in her dress.

Instantly all the falcons in the room climbed above the fluttering doves to make their dives. Soon the doves turned to thousands of drifting feathers and dripping blood as the talons took their prey! The entire audience was on its feet cheering the climax to our program: everyone but the king and me.

King Richard was brushing crumbs from my curls with his long fingers. With pounding heart I watched bits of Jerusalem fall to my feet as his busy hand ruffled my Greek ringlets. I should respond— but how?

The king's fanfare snarled and it was almost too late. The hand stopped as he rose to his feet. Desperately I turned and gazed upward. His glowing face was remote and distant as a December moon atop a tall pine, but he smiled at me.

"What is your name, boy?" he asked, as other dignitaries rose as well.

"Alexander of Wanthwaite," I answered.

"Ah, Alexander." He seemed to nod significantly, then was gone.

His feet were veiled by a band of gold orphrey as he marched slowly away. Vaguely I saw glittering groups fall into his train and follow as our band played lustily, but I was too entranced to move myself. Instead I turned to gaze on the throne so recently occupied by his greatness, the red cushion still showing the imprint of his royal person.

I reached forward and touched the crimson hollow. Still warm. I edged my stool close and lay my throbbing head on the velvet: so close, so close, and yet so far because of the Scot's perfidy. Never would the king deign to give me an audience now.

Then suddenly I forgot the king. I sniffed the cushion feverishly and looked upward. 'Twas my father's own scent, the sweet woodruff he wore.

Was he near to me now? What did it bode? Aye, he'd come from his Limbo to console me for my failure. Or was it to chide? Again I buried my face in the cushion, this time to hide my tears.

MY HEMLOCK had dried to powder and I couldn't decide on what other method I should use to murder Enoch. We sat outside our tent staring at each other in the darkness, for I refused to go within.

"Dinna be sae blethered, bairn, fer 'tis no disgrace to fart. Ye mun learn to accept yer fate, to lean with the wind. Oh, no offense, I mean flow wi' the current."

"Now I'll never see the king. Why didn't you require it in my contract? You knew 'twas my whole purpose in coming. You betrayed me!"

"No point demandin' what can't be delivered. Richard mun decide such matters, but we were guaranteed access which ye have had."

"Thanks to my own strong back, for you told Julian to seal me into that pie forever. You wanted to kill me as well as cheat me. You hoped I'd die, didn't you?"

"*Me?*" He pretended outrage. "Why would I hope a woodly thing like that? I had naught to do with the pie."

"So you could steal Wanthwaite, that's why. And in case that failed, you dangled me up in the sky hoping I'd drop like a stone and be splattered right before the king. You hate me! Want me dead!"

We both sprang to our feet.

"Now, Alex, ye be in one of yer tinty moods again like that time ye tried to twist off my terse. Yif I remember rightly, on that occasion a small blow knocked sense into yer head. I'm sorry fer ye, aye, that I am, but not sorry enow to take yer wild insults. Do ye apologize or do I persuade ye?"

Even in the darkness I could see his raised arm. I'd had all the blows I could stand for one evening and dashed into the tent, pulling the flap behind me.

The next morn Enoch tried to cheer me with chilling talk about arranging his own audience with Richard through William du Hommet, constable to the king. It seemed Richard had made Earl David, brother to the Scottish king, to be Earl of Huntingdon in England which Enoch took as a sign that Richard would be willing for a Scot to own Wanthwaite.

"I promise ye, Alex, that Wanthwaite will be in our hands by tomorrow. Wait here now."

After he'd left, I finally discarded my Cupid garb, replaced my treasure and tunic, then sat to think seriously about my next move. Though Zizka might not want me at this point, my only alternative was to stay with the jongleurs. As if on cue, Zizka called my name from outside.

"Alex, put on the heather tunic Pax made for you. We have an appointment with Ambroise."

"Go without me," I managed to say thickly.

The flap opened. "Nonsense. Yesterday you spoke of nothing else and the meeting's called specifically for you. Holy St. Martin, boy, wipe that woeful look from off your face and get dressed."

He stepped out as I obeyed, now washing the stale egg white from my face as well.

"That's better," Zizka approved when I emerged. "You may snatch success from failure yet, though it wasn't entirely your fault. Julian was so afraid of his towers toppling that he used burnt sugar which is hard as mortar when he should have used egg white."

We walked to the far end of the castle where the king had his apartments. Zizka cleared us with the guard, whereafter we climbed the stair to a small airy chamber. A rotund man stood against the window with his back to us as he studied a manuscript in the light.

"God's blessing, Ambroise, I've brought our protégé, Alexander of Wanthwaite."

"You're up early, old friend, for a performing man, but I appreciate your punctuality. So much to be done in only two days!"

Ambroise skimmed toward us, airy as a bubble, and took my hands in his small moist palms. The sunlight caught the fur on his bald pate like new asparagus, and his watery blue eyes beamed welcome. I thought him kindly, crafty, curious. 'Twas hard to fix his age for his plumpness hid wrinkles, as his genial mask hid his character.

"Well, boy, I hear you have unique talents, not the least of which I witnessed last night when you showed yourself to be an angel-clown."

I winced at the jape.

"Are you soothly literate?"

Only long apprenticeship of Enoch's arrogance made it possible to reply, for I boldly claimed that I was highly educated for my age.

He smiled at my manner. "Tell me of your languages, how rapidly you can write, everything."

I couldn't imagine how this information would get me an audience with Richard but I took no chances, listing languages, travel, study of law and logic, even the smattering of medicine I'd learned from Dagobert. Ambroise nodded and glanced at Zizka.

"Come to the window seat, boy, so I may see you better." He stared in the same friendly fashion, but I felt uneasy beyond my shame for last night. Something was askew: 'twas as if nothing that was said or done was exactly what was meant. "Well, Zizka, you didn't exaggerate."

"Aye, he's a comely lad," Zizka said dryly.

Ambroise continued to study me, his genial mask dropped for a more calculating expression: no doubt about it, he was weighing me as carefully as a gold-changer.

"Alex, I'm told you want to meet the king," he said at last.

"Aye, oh yes, more than anything. 'Tis why I'm here."

The troubadour nodded. "Just so, just so. Well, you're fortunate. King Richard has a little time available this evening in his chamber after he has met with the Archbishop of Canterbury."

I gaped upward, not comprehending.

"Well, Alex, aren't you going to thank Ambroise?" Zizka prodded rudely. "After all, 'tis not every day . . ."

"Thank you! Oh, thank you, Sire! 'Tis my dream, my hope, I mean I'll ne'er forget your kindness. Are you certain? What hour should I come? Should I—"

Zizka covered my mouth. "Don't overdo it, boy. I told you, didn't I?"

Ambroise chuckled. "A fortuitous choice, Zizka. I like his enthusiasm. Yes, all will go well."

Zizka stayed with the troubadour as I wandered in the courtyard, dazed. Despite my freakish performance, despite Enoch's tricks, I was to see the king after all! I gazed at diagonal cloud streaks behind the round tower, listened to the persistent barking of a dog, breathed deep of horseflesh and leather, for I must remember this moment forever and ever, when my Fortune turned me back to Wanthwaite.

And I ran to the chapel to thank my father and mother.

After I'd finished praying, I met Zizka as he was leaving Ambroise.

"Alex." He put an arm o'er my shoulder and drew me to a stone bench behind a pile of saddles. "Alex."

I waited. Zizka had ne'er been tentative before.

"Alex," he said a third time, "I hope you get whatever you want from the king, but you're very young, more innocent than most. A spoiled pet in our group."

Puzzled, I still waited for the point. What had any of this to do with my success?

"The king is . . ." Again he foundered. "Well, he's beautiful as you can see, chivalrous, courteous, elegant and talented in the arts as well as in arms, but . . . You must remember at all times that he's the king."

I was getting frightened. "What are you trying to say, Zizka?"

"I'm trying to warn you for your own good. Let the king decide whatever issues come between you; don't argue."

"Why would I argue?"

He shrugged but wouldn't meet my eyes. "Because you don't know any better. You haven't been schooled as the rest of us have, I see that now. No king will be crossed or tolerate what he perceives as lying, breaking one's oath, and other things. All I'm saying is that you should approach Richard as the most kingly of kings; he's been known to be harsh."

After he left, I sat considering his words. If I hadn't known him so well, I would have sworn that Zizka felt guilty about something and was trying to make amends. Let him worry if it pleased him. As for me, I was going to see the king!

COMPLINE HAD RUNG hours ago and still I'd not been admitted to the king's chambers, after I'd rushed there directly in my new Alexander the Great costume from tonight's performance. I was the only person still awake in the antechamber: the king's secretary slept across his desk, knights slouched on the floor and Enoch snored beside me. Outside, summer lightning flashed through the arrow slits and in the far distance the faint rumble of thunder sounded. I gazed around the dozing company with a sense of superiority: every heartbeat brought me closer to the transformation from Alex to Alix and not one of these oafs realized the momentous occasion at hand. Most important, I was beating Enoch to the king; by the time the Scot met with him tomorrow, I would be firmly reinstated.

A crash and blast of air startled everyone upright as Baldwin, the Archbishop of Canterbury, hurtled forth from the king's door like a great black raven. Just as quickly he feinted, turned and vaulted to the desk where the secretary, Sir Roger, sat up groggily.

"Send in the next applicant," the archbishop snapped.

Sir Roger bent a bleary eye to his book and ran his finger down the page. Enoch stepped forward as I sidled around the archbishop who hadn't moved, noting the black hairs in his nostrils, the putrid stench of his robe.

"Alexander of Wanthwaite be next," Enoch informed Sir Roger.

"Ah, yes, Ambroise's boy, I had forgot. Come, child, I'll announce you."

Enoch squeezed my shoulder hard and I glanced up, trying to control my trembling lips, then followed the secretary's thick short legs into the arched dimness beyond.

I was alone with King Richard.

He stood on the far side of the vaulted chamber gazing through a dormered window into the humid night. A rising breeze bent flickering flames of tapers and torches, fluttered his white silk robes around his powerful figure. He turned finally and approached, the aroma of sweet woodruff numbing what little sense I still had so that I barely remembered to bow.

"Stand, boy, so we may see you."

I tried to obey but was suddenly hurled to the left and struck the sharp corner of a chest with my elbow so that I almost swooned. Clinging to the wood and choking back nausea, I saw that I'd been pushed aside by the Archbishop of Canterbury who had returned and now stood in my place, trembling with fury.

"My Liege, you cannot do this rash act, cannot, I say. Think of the consequences, I beg you: of the Crusade, if not yourself. The greatest enterprise since the world began, ruined for cheap vengeance!"

Richard's white figure burned like fire and his voice thundered. "How dare you question my act or my motive? I was the first monarch to take the Cross, the only one who has the acumen to defeat Saladin, and it has nothing to do with Princess Alais. Apologize at once for your presumption; for your stupidity there can be no amends, but my patience with your arrogance runs short, Sire. Remember Becket."

Archbishop Baldwin seemed querulous and weak before King Richard's awesome authority, but he didn't back away. "Indeed I remember Becket, and I hope you do as well, for his sainthood triumphed, did it not? As for my presumption, my first duty is to God: this Crusade *must not fail*, but surely it will if you insist upon insulting King Philip before you even start."

Richard smiled grimly. "Philip will contribute nothing to the Crusade, as you will see, so to insult him is to lose nothing. However, to protect Alais in Rouen's tower until we return to wed her is hardly insulting."

"You bandy words," Baldwin answered. "Call it what you will, the tower is prison."

I gasped at the word *prison* and their two heads turned.

"Who's there?" the archbishop demanded. "Stop skulking in the shadow and come forward like a man."

Trying to pretend I was Enoch, I stepped forth as boldly as I could.

"*Jesu*, what knavery is this?" the prelate asked scornfully, eying my scant costume as Alexander. "'Tis hardly appropriate, Your Highness, to permit cheap jongleurs in your chamber during state meetings."

"He might well ask what right you have to interrupt his appointed audience," King Richard replied icily. "He's here at my command, a protégé of Ambroise."

I hardly knew what to do, but King Richard took my arm and guided me to the chair behind his desk.

"Wait here, boy," he said kindly. "I'm nearly finished."

I sat obediently and tried not to succumb to terror. The vague confused dread I'd felt for months at becoming Alix now hardened into abject sniveling cowardice. Sister Petronilla's martyrdom, Queen Eleanor's imprisonment and now Princess Alais's future in the hands of my hoped-for benefactor all fused to a dire warning which I wanted desperately to heed. I sat in numb misery at my lot.

"*Caritas*, Richard, in the name of Our Lord who protected the weak, don't put Alais in Eleanor's care. King Philip will never forgive such an act. You know how he hates her."

"If he hates the Queen of England, he must learn to put policy before personal peevishness. Alais belongs to England and Eleanor *is* England during my absence."

"Rich—"

"Enough!" the king shouted. "God's feet, Baldwin, use what few wits God gave you!"

His face was now filled with choler and red whelks stood forth along his jaw. I began to shake so violently that my chair tapped the floor like a woodpecker. Was I about to witness another murder of an Archbishop of Canterbury such as King Henry had done to Thomas à Becket?

But no, the archbishop capitulated. "We'll speak of this again in Vézelay, My Liege."

"The subject is closed," the king answered grimly, "*nunc et semper.*"

The archbishop bowed, flourished and left.

Again the king and I were alone. My breath was short, I couldn't speak. He turned and went to his wine table, then approached me with two goblets of frothing red wine.

He handed me one, smiling, and held his own to toast. "To solitude and quiet. 'Twould be better if he were dead, but to have him gone is some reprieve." He drained his goblet. "Ahhh. Tell me, boy, does the priesthood attract pretentious windbags of little intellect, or is there something in the profession that dulls the reason? Yet you would think even fools could tell the truth. Above all things, I hate a liar."

I still couldn't speak. My heart fluttered high in my chest most alarmingly, and on top of my terror toward Richard was added an equal fear that I wouldn't be able to make my plea, after all this waiting. I began to breathe deeply and to count my heartbeats in a stern effort to get control. Then I thought of Wanthwaite.

Meantime the king had gone back to refill his cup and now approached a second time. "Well, I believe I had asked you to rise so I could see you."

I stood stiffly as he took a candle and bent near. We appraised each other. The flames of a hundred candles danced in night-dark eyes, now blue, now gray, now layered in turbid depths, subaqueous creatures hidden there; a high arched brow, firm pearcheeks, a long chin with a small squared beard and a thrusting lower lip, mouth now pursed in a quizzical smile. A face, I thought, capable of any expression except humility.

He tapped my nose playfully. "Cupid-Alexander, I think you'll do, you'll do."

The words—my mother's when she'd said I was pretty.

"You mean—" I started to say as I'd answered her, then stopped myself.

"I mean that you're the prettiest child I can recall, and I've seen many. Now, let's get acquainted, shall we? Come, you'll sing to me."

He took my hand but I held back.

"What's this? You're frightened; your hands are trembling." He frowned and I willed myself not to sway.

"Aye, Your Highness," I gasped. "I—I've ne'er met a king afore."

"Would that my presence had such an effect on bishops and kings," he remarked, grinning. "But come, Alex, you have nothing to fear. You are tense and I am tense, so let's relax together. I'll recline on my bed, so, and you stand here, so, and sing me the Alexander song from this evening's performance, for I liked the sentiment."

He'd led me to his bed and sat at its' head. I stood near, somewhat tangled in the fringe from the Persian covers.

"Now?"

"Of course, don't be shy."

Very nervous, I began feebly, then stopped because I was pitched too high, and started again.

> *"On Macedonia's rocky shore*
> *I strum my golden lyre*
> *To sing of conquest, searing war,*
> *A world on fire."*

"Know you of Greek fire?" he interrupted. "No? A good image. Go on."

> *"Wise Aristotle well does know*
> *Where to seek the prize*
> *In lands where Nile and Ganges flow;*
> *There my fame will rise."*

"You should have included the Euphrates. Also, there's some question about the extent of Aristotle's influence on Alexander's strategy, but you're permitted poetic license."

I waited to be sure he was finished, then continued, as he hummed in a deep mellow baritone and conducted with his hand.

> *"For God has made me Persia's foe,*
> *For God is filled with wrath*
> *That Pagans in His cities go*
> *Along Our Lord's sweet path.*
>
> *"Yet God withholds the Persian crown*
> *From my deserving head,*
> *To wait a Christian king renowned*
> *When I'm long dead.*
>
> *"Now is King Richard here,*
> *The proper king at last!*
> *King Richard is without peer*
> *And Persia's thralldom past!"*

I stood waiting for his comment, but for a long moment he just twirled his goblet and stared at me with glowing lambent eyes.

"A pleasing prophecy," he said at last. "God make it true." Then almost as an afterthought, "And nicely rendered. Very nicely. Well now, Ambroise tells me that you're an educated lad as well as being musical. You read and write Latin?"

"Yes, Your Highness, and French and English as well."

His high arched brows shot up. "Trained by Zizka?"

"Partly."

"He's outdone himself, I must say. Unusual to find a Parisian boy of the streets with such erudition."

I recognized my cue as surely as if Zizka had given it.

"Except—except—I'm not a Parisian boy of the streets."

"Really?"

He reached toward me with a huge hand and what breath I still had stopped. But he merely placed a forefinger on my cheek and traced my chin, so I forced myself to continue.

"No, I'm not from Paris at all. And I studied law and languages on the Petit Pont, not from Zizka."

"Ah, a student." He smiled knowingly. "But you're too young. How old are you?"

"Nine," I said promptly, then tried to take it back for I was soothly twelve, a fact he would soon know. "Nine," I repeated weakly, then frowned in vexation at myself. I seemed not to control my own resolve.

"Very young indeed," he mused. "Let's see if you're old enough to serve us another glass of wine." He handed me his goblet.

I was old enough forsooth but not too steady as I poured. Again I faced him.

"And I'm not from Paris, Your Highness. I'm from—England."

Something squeezed my heart hard: again I stood on a hill looking back on my flaming castle in the moonlight. A dormer window behind me blew shut, then banged open, and I felt a fresh breeze at my back. It seemed to whisper, whisper . . .

"Good." He laughed. "For I'll tell you a secret, just between us two. I hate the French! And naturally I love the English, for they are my subjects."

Is that why you're discarding the French princess, I thought wildly, and putting her in prison for no reason? I pushed the thought away and listened to the wind's sough, the words buried in its sigh.

"So you are a student of the English nation and you are learning the jongleur's trade. I—"

"No!" I interrupted. Then, seeing the shadow across his face, "I'm sorry, Your Highness, please continue."

"I will, but tell me first how I've erred."

He was leaning on his elbow now, perfect teeth glinting, his finger again reaching. I breathed deeply and prepared to be Alix.

"I'm Alexander of Wanthwaite, baron in your own country."

Appalled, my mouth hung open like a fish's. *Baron? Baron?* What was wrong with me? Again the shutter banged, the room darkened as several candles blew out. The wind said *Why not? How will he ever know the difference?* Aye, my anguished mind replied, but how then can I get my castle? For the whole purpose was to throw myself on his mercy so that he could find a husband to recover my estate. *You'll find a way, and he'll be gone on the Crusade*, the wind counseled.

The king's finger had stopped midair. "Baron of Wanthwaite?" He frowned. "From the north, close to Scotland?" He sat on the edge of the bed.

"Aye, in Northumberland," I said rapidly. "The largest land-owner outside of the earl, and loyal to the English kings forever. Both my grandfather and father . . ." and I rushed on about the siege of 'sixty-five, the taking of King William at Alnwick when my father had been there. From a packet at my waist, I took out the commendation from King Henry.

The king studied it. "Why have you kept this a secret? Zizka and Ambroise don't know, do they?"

"No, Your Majesty, but 'twas necessary because our castle was sacked and I fled for my life."

"Sacked? In England? I thought the Scots were tamed."

By now the wind behind me was a howl which entered the back of my head and came out of my mouth. I hardly knew what I said, but I spoke firmly and boldly.

"Aye, so they are. 'Twas our own earl who turned on us, greedy to control all of Northumberland. Osbert, Earl of Northumberland, sent his army disguised as monks; once inside our gates, they

stripped to Scottish plaids and proceeded to kill every living creature. Then the knights were sent forth again on the pretext of
searching for the Scottish marauders. 'Twas a heinous plan, brutally
executed."

"Preposterous! Northumberland has ever been a chivalrous lord.
And you, young lord, are a talented storyteller. In short, you lie."

I looked up at his enormous height, twice as tall as I at least,
thought of Princess Alais, and said coldly, "I never lie. Osbert,
Lord of Northumberland, and his foster son Roland de Roncechaux
followed me to London and would surely have killed me to prevent
my reaching you, except for the efforts of a friendly Scot I met on
the road."

"But Northumberland, Northumberland, he . . ." and he sank
back onto the bed. "Why didn't you go at once to the Assize?"

I trowe I know not whence my words came, from my father or
from the months of study with Malcolm. "As you know, Northumberland is virtually a country to itself, a palatinate, and the king's
men ne'er come so far north. Therefore Lord Osbert is the judge of
the Northumberland Assize Court. How could I complain to the
perpetrator of the crime?"

"But *Northumberland* . . ." He shook his head. "When did this
happen?"

"The twenty-second of May, 1189," I answered easily enow.

"Ah, that explains . . ." And he actually smiled.

I was horrified. "Why do you ask, My Liege? I mean, 'tis my
greatest dread that mayhap Northumberland or Roncechaux may
have reached you first. During your coronation? I know they were
in London."

He seemed to think. "Osbert, you say? What sort of man is he?
Describe him."

My voice lost its assurance as I tried to recall all the diabolic
things my father had told me. *Deo gratias* the king couldn't make me
this monster's wife.

"Get me another cup while I think," he ordered. Then, when I
handed it to him: "No, my little lord, I assure you I ne'er met your
Osbert. No claim has been registered with us. However, I also assure you that if it had, I would not hesitate to seize the castle and
punish the criminals, so you have nothing to fear."

For the first time I tasted my own wine, then went on to my second stage.

"Therefore, Your Highness, I've come this far to ask you for a writ of ownership, stamped by your seal, which I can then take to your justicier in London. Certes Northumberland would have to honor such a direct order."

He studied his wine, licked his upper lip, then smiled radiantly. "Nothing easier. A *fait accompli*. As of this moment, your estate is restored and all privileges thereof, *teste me ipso*. This has indeed been a refreshing interview, a rare opportunity to please."

Tears had welled in my eyes and I forgot the king. I felt I'd been carrying a huge rock for a long distance and now I'd dropped it at the crest of a hill, watched it roll away from me forever. The concomitant lightness made me airy as a bubble. I was floating in ether, delirious.

"However . . ."

I remembered protocol and dropped to my knees. "Thank you, how can I ever thank you?"

"However, as I assume you have no guardian to help you till you are of age, the actual possession of Wanthwaite must await more propitious times."

I looked up. "I need no guardian, My Lord. I can . . ."

"Lead your knights to keep the peace? Husband your lands and adjudicate your villeins? At nine years old?" He laughed in kindly fashion. "I fear your knowledge of language and music would not take you far. You needs must become a squire, earn your spurs, and in general be trained for your position. Did your father tell you how to achieve the proper skills?"

My father had treated me as a boy in many ways, but I'd learned from Enoch's questions how little I really knew. I gazed upward and waited.

"No, I thought not. Of course you would have been only seven or eight at the time, too young, I fear. No, child, look not so woebegone. What is a king for if not to protect his wards? As it happens, it fits well with my plans."

Belatedly I recalled that he had called this meeting, not I.

"How so, Your Highness?"

"Well, you know surely that Zizka was answering a summons

from Ambroise when you were sought. A talented young jongleur who was also literate. Could you not guess why?"

I shook my head. "It didn't occur . . ."

"No, perhaps not, for 'tis an honor rarely offered to street gamins, which we thought you were. You were going to apprentice with Ambroise in his great epic poem, become a scribe and troubadour together."

"A great honor," I agreed humbly.

"Yes. *Ars longa, vita brevis.* And you may still dally a bit, for such skills are most refining in *preux chevaliers.*"

Like the Rules of Love, I thought, hardly following what he said. I was determined to get my writ, and then let Richard speak of learning verse if he wist.

"But now that I know those arts which you must learn, I think that working in my own household would be appropriate."

And Fortune's Wheel inched in my favor at last! If I could learn how to manage Wanthwaite alone! And from the king!

"I can take a personal interest in your welfare." Once again his powerful hand fell on my curls, stroking.

Better and better. A terrible enemy, this king, but perhaps a fierce monarch would be best for retrieving my home from the equally fierce Northumberland.

"Therefore I will make you my personal page until you reach your majority."

I knew not what "majority" signified, but I kenned well what an honor had been bestowed and what it could mean to my future. Part of the royal household!

"Oh thank you, Your Majesty, I don't know how to show my gratitude. How may I serve? What should I do?"

He smiled at my delight. "Well, first you must prepare yourself. Get properly outfitted, then a horse."

A horse? To be a page? Mayhap I didn't ken the assignment after all.

"What should I do with a horse?"

"God's feet, child, you will ride your horse unless you want to walk."

"Ride it where?" I asked, cautiously this time.

He laughed aloud. "Where do you think, boy? I'm taking you with us to Jerusalem!"

"*Jerusalem!*" I howled with the wind and would have fallen in a heap if the king hadn't swept me up in his arms.

"I thought you would be pleased." He pressed my head into his muscular shoulder where I whiffed deeply of sweet woodruff. "'Tis the most glorious quest of all time, better than the search for the Grail, for it affects all living Christians."

I shuddered and he held me tighter, one hand under my hips, one on my back as if I were a babe. Then he gently leaned me away from him, but our faces were still close.

"Sealed with a kiss," he said, and his features approached, the eyes like blue pearls, his breath smelling of wine and fresh mint. "I look forward to hearing the details of your romantic odyssey in our leisure."

His lips pressed mine in the courteous kiss of peace but they were surprisingly warm and tender so that my mindless liver leaped in pleasure.

"You have little time to prepare. Go to Sir Roger tomorrow and he will assign you your vestments, then to my page Sir Gilbert for further instructions."

Somehow I went through a ritual of thanks which must have satisfied, for as I bowed my way out, he stood with a secret smile, pleased as a graymalkin watching a fallen bird.

I SHOUTED out my tale of woe to Enoch in competition with the rain which beat our leather tent like a drum. His black hump didn't move, his mouth was dumb.

"Aren't you going to say anything?" I beseeched, hoping for some miracle to reprieve me from my fate.

"Jerusalem," he said in disbelief. "Bairn, I canna say nothing. I'm dungin' as a serpent without his stang. Jerusalem!"

I huddled miserably in the dank air which had suddenly turned cool.

"Do I have to go, think you? Suppose I told him I was sick?"
He didn't reply.

Suppose I told him I was a girl, was what I was really thinking and another sort of shudder shook me. *Laudatur, Maria* that I'd heard about Alais and her prison, also that Zizka had warned me unequivocally about the king's attitudes, for I saw clearly that I couldn't admit that I'd lied and still hope mercy from Richard. Furthermore, 'twas no doubt easier to survive or escape the Crusade than it would be to escape a bad marriage. Ee'n so, how could a female child travel with such an army?

"Puts my teeth on-char," Enoch said morosely. "Jerusalem, a pot of hell fer a wee bairn." Then he requested that I repeat the interview again which I did, word for word.

"Air ye certain ye've told all?"

"Aye, every word."

"Then I con assume that ye didna mention that we war brothers."

"I said we traveled together."

"That we war brothers!" he roared. "That we share Wanthwaite!"

"There wasn't time," I whimpered.

He grabbed my shoulders. "Aye, there war time to sing about Alexander, but none to protect our estate. Ye canna fool me for all ye tried to make a beard. The king may think ye're a sweet pig's-eye but I know ye for a scorpion. Only this time ye've stung yerself with yer own tail. Jerusalem! Tell me, who owns Wanthwaite?"

"I do. I'm the heir," I said more bravely than I felt.

"Wrang. Try again: Who owns Wanthwaite?"

"You want me to say that we own it together but I won't. Never! Never!"

"Niver?" His laugh was a hollow bray. "I dinna want nothing but the truth. And ye canna tell me because ye don't know."

There was something beyond threat in his statement that made me pause.

"All right, *you* tell *me*. Who owns Wanthwaite?"

"King Richard the Ferst of England, that's who. I mun learn ye the law, I see. Yif ye present yerself as sole heir, the estate goes to the king automatically."

I yelled before I thought. "Aye, *if* I were a female!"

"Sex makes no difference when ye're only nine years old. Ye're under age and Wanthwaite is therefore Richard's fief. He can do as he likes with it. Mayhap he'll give it to ye; most likely ye'll fall in the field or from his grace long before that. Kings air known to turn surly when heirs come of age."

"But my father said. . . . My father thought . . ."

"That King Henry were alive and would recall ye. Mayhap. I believe most men found it otherwise with Henry, but it doesna signify that Richard will do likewise in any case. Yif I were presented as yer brother with just claims, then a writ could be used. Aye, Alex, yer greed hae doon ye in."

And he released me.

The truth of his accusation cut deep, for I now remembered King Richard saying, "I don't suppose you have a guardian." If I'd claimed that Enoch was my blood brother, I would at least have gotten half a loaf instead of no loaf at all. And I'd forgotten that I was a child as well as a female. Since boys don't have to be assigned wives when they're so young, and in any case wives could hardly abuse them, to pass as a boy had seemed such a triumph.

But what guarantee was there that Enoch would share? Hadn't he already claimed my title? No doubt I would dwindle to a landless younger brother in his hands and be no better off than I was now. If he permitted me to live at all.

With these heavy thoughts, I slept fitfully.

After Haute Tierce the next morning Enoch went to keep his own appointment with the king, his face the most serious I'd e'er seen it. No sooner had he gone than Zizka called me to the main tent. Grimly I went to confront him for his perfidy. The hot words died on my tongue, however, when I saw that Ambroise and Zizka stood together. Zizka appeared piqued, Ambroise amused.

"Well, Lord Alex, you certainly fooled us all!" said Richard's troubadour. "What a clever boy you are truly, what a loss to the troubadour world. However, I'm hoping that I may have the pleasure of coaching you a little in the craft, for certes the arts of music and poetry befit your station. Knew you that King Richard was a master in the new harmonics? Aye, he can sing the Gregorian chants as well, but then can counterpoint to make an organist envy. Furthermore, he composes poetry in both French and Provençal."

"I ken that he's a talented lord," I said, glaring at Zizka. "I had no idea that I would be so honored as to accompany him on his Crusade."

Zizka glared back, his spade jaw waggling furiously. "Nor would you have if I'd known from the first that you were a lord. You deceived me!"

Ambroise glanced sharply at Zizka, then me.

"But surely you're pleased to be going," he protested. "Rarely does King Richard take young boys into his care, though I believe King Henry raised several. The old king was fond of children."

Knowing that this exchange might be reported to the king, I forced myself to pretend eagerness until Ambroise seemed convinced. He then patted my shoulder and went to make his own preparations for the long ride ahead.

"You're a fool, Alex," Zizka almost snarled. "'Twas foolish to dissemble, even more so to confess your identity. Ambroise would have taken care of you, trained you well, kept you out of battle, protected you! Knowing what I told you about Richard, you still put yourself at his mercy! Frankly I doubt you can survive! Do you have any knowledge of fighting? Of what Richard expects?"

"You dare speak to me of dissembling?" I shot back. "Or of the dangers of the Crusade? You who cold-bloodedly committed me without a word! And you too knew the king—you could have warned me of his plans. If I die, 'twill be on your head. As for Richard, he will be fascinated at your treasonous remarks!"

And I ran from the tent. Knowing I must go to Sir Roger, I nonetheless dashed first to seek Isabelle, for I had to see her at least once more, my only friend. We almost collided at the gate to the women's court for she was coming in equal haste to find me.

"Oh, Alex, have you heard about Princess Alais? Is not the king a monster? She may be an old sop, but prison! My lady Marie is fair besotted with anger, for you know they're half-sisters."

"I heard it first." And I told her about my interview. She sank to a bench and gazed at me with eyes wide, flatteringly impressed.

"You are a *baron*?"

"Aye." It was on the tip of my tongue to tell her I was a baroness, a twelve-year-old maiden the same as she was, but I refrained. *Not until I told the king*, my father's instructions recalled.

"Where is Wanthwaite? Is it a large holding?"

"The largest barony in Northumberland, soothly a wonderful estate. I wish I were returning right now." My voice shook a bit.

"Oh no, I'm sure you don't. To go on the Crusade in the king's personal service, why, 'tis an honor to dream upon."

"Do you know much about the Crusades then, Isabelle? Except that King Richard goes now and his mother went in her youth, I know naught of their purpose or how they're conducted."

Her pearly teeth took her lower lip as she thought. "'Tis not a subject that ladies speak much of, but I believe Jerusalem be fearsome far away, close to the original Paradise, I trowe. A priest once described the Holy Kingdom to us: 'tis on a verdant plain bright as emeralds, and trees bloom there with strange sweet fruits which grow as quickly as you pick them. Rivers flow with honey instead of water and cows give forth only the richest cream. The city itself can be seen from afar and you must remember to shade your eyes lest you be blinded with its splendor, for God makes it to shine like diamonds and the streets be paved with gold."

"In sooth?" I asked, awestruck.

"So said the priest and he would not lie."

We sat silently a short while more.

"In the king's personal service. La!" she said at last. "You'll be a great man someday."

"Aye. I really should go see to my outfitting."

"Wait, I have something for you." She held out a soft vellum book of a few pages. "*Tractus de Amore*, writ by my Countess Marie and her queen mother."

I took it, much awed. "Thank you, but it's so valuable."

"I hope you benefit from its instruction," she said archly.

She took me in her arms and kissed me, I think passionately for it hurt my teeth, though did nothing to my liver.

"God be with you," she whispered.

"And with you."

I left her finally to see Sir Roger about my appointment.

SIR ROGER kept me waiting a long time at his desk as he served several ahead of me. When he finally gave me his attention, 'twas in a surly manner.

"So you're to be a page. I wish the king would tell me when he takes someone new. Gilbert and the others are pages enough in my opinion, and Gilbert's served the king long. And at such short notice. There be no way to put you in his chamber before Vézelay; I can't train you nor can Gilbert. Get properly outfitted at once; go to the keeper of the horse where two mounts have been put aside and ride close to the household through Tours. I can't give you room there, for the city is tiny. You'll have to camp alone."

He waved me aside and I left with sinking heart. To ride alone with the rabble, to camp in the wilderness of tents. Where would I e'en get a tent? Was food provided or was that up to me? I went to collect Plantagenet garb and my steed.

Back in our leather tent, I donned the smaller of my two scarlet-and-gold outfits and rolled the other into a bundle. Later I planned to use the padded vests to make a new harness for my treasure. Then I went out to care for my sweet dappled stallion, giving him of Twixt's grain to eat. I would call him Thistle because of his gray color.

Enoch found me fast asleep when he returned in late afternoon. The tent was muggy hot and my head felt to be in a vise.

"Waesucks, bairn, come outside. There be not enough air in here for a flea."

Groggily I stumbled after him.

He put his hand to my forehead. "Be ye with fever? Or is't the tent? Be ye hungry?"

"Aye," I said, thinking I'd best gorge to prepare for the fast ahead.

"Haly St. George, whar cum that purple horse?"

"He's not purple," I cried, stung to anger. "He's dapple gray and his name is Thistle."

"Best call him Stem, for the prickly Thistle rides on top."

We both busied ourselves preparing our fowl while the Scot whistled cheerily. Aye, he was pleased to be rid of me, even if the price were foregoing Wanthwaite, I thought with a pang of self-pity. I wondered if anyone would ever like me just for myself again, or if my estate would always be the lure. Then I remembered that Enoch had just seen the king.

"What did you talk about?" I asked cautiously.

"The castles he returned to the Scottish king, somewhat of my family which he remembers."

That piqued my curiosity but I let it pass for the moment.

"Anything about me?"

He spat a bone into the fire. "Aye, I set the record straight about our bein' blood brothers."

My heart leaped in dismay. "What did he say? Did you mention Wanthwaite?"

Enoch belched from his heart, then held up a rolled parchment.

"Aye, he gave me yer writ fer safekeeping."

"My writ! Let me see!" I grabbed but he held his arm aloft.

"Not sae fast, bairn. Ye've shawn yerself to be a lump when it cums to protectin' our estate, sae I'll tak care of it."

"Can't I just see? What does it say?"

"I dictated the terms myself," he said coolly. "Ye can rest easy."

"As you dictated my contract with Zizka!" I cried bitterly. "I'll be lucky if I end with so much as a grave plot!"

"Nay, Alex, when have I e'er done ye wrong? 'Tis not perfect, but 'twill do. Remember: *Qui in uno gravator in alio debet relevari*."

"If I'm aggrieved on one point, I can't be relieved by having you steal what is mine!" I shouted in contradiction.

"Well, I tried to learn ye but ye be summit tinty. In short: I be appointed yer legal guardian and I will manage yer estate till ye be of age."

"*If* I become of age, you mean," I wailed close to tears. "For you know very well that I'm likely to die on this Crusade." Aye, the odious king had betrayed my hopes in two ways, by sending me on this woodly trek to the Holy Land and by placing the Scot in legal authority over me. Then I had a second thought. "If I perish, who takes over Wanthwaite? You or the king?"

The Scot picked at his teeth with his dagger. "Such a possibility ne'er came up in our discussion, but now that ye ask I believe the king would prefer that a trusty Scot be in command sae far north."

I was stunned at the possibility yawning before me: I would be sucked into the abyss of the Crusade, Enoch would hurry back to London and claim me dead, take Wanthwaite and that would be that. If I survived at all 'twould be much too late.

I turned my back on him, thanking God that at least this was our last night together, and said as coldly as I could, "I hope you enjoy your victory. I hate you and I hate the king, both of you. Taking advantage of my cruel loss to line your own pockets." I put my head to my knees. "And sending me on this journey to be sure I'm out of your way."

"Now, Alex." His hand shook my shoulder. "The king be not sae bad as ye think."

"Not to you!" I cried. "But ask Alais! Or me!"

"Nay, bairn, stop grucching and sniveling long enow to listen. The king be most particular that ye fare well on this Crusade. That's why he asked . . . turn around and see feor yerself."

He forced my head to turn and I gazed uncomprehendingly on his gaudy sark: over its plaid was sewn a crude jagged cross.

"Ye see, bairn? The king made me guardian on condition that I take good care of thee. I be gang with ye on yer Crusade!"

16

 WASN'T FOOLED BY THE KING OR ENOCH WHEN they said that they wanted me protected on the Crusade, for I kenned that the king needed the Scot's good will in the north and that Enoch needed the king's support to his claim for Wanthwaite: I was merely the expendable pawn in the middle. However, for the moment I didn't care. I was so relieved that Enoch and I could continue as before that I could have kissed him—but didn't. Already my mind was racing far ahead to the time when I would steal my writ while he slept, slip away alone now dressed as a girl so neither the Scot nor the king would know how to find me, go back to London and make my own deal with the justicier before anyone knew I was gone. Toty with optimism, I prepared to ride out on the morrow.

Enoch had already gone to the wardrobe and the keeper of the horse and had a fine Plantagenet uniform (which he refused to wear) and a horse named Firth. His assignment as I understood it was somewhat ambiguous: he was to ride with me, protect me on the road, supply himself with food whilst I would be fed by the king after Vézelay. He was also a mounted soldier, mayhap a knight though I didn't know if he'd won his spurs, and was supposed to aid the keeper of the horse in some way. His first task was to put in supplies for our journey to Vézelay and we worked together throughout the night to load Twixt down with staples of all sorts. I won't say we stole, but hens, eggs, loaves and cheese gravitated fatally to our tent that night.

The last thing I thought as I put my head on my goatskin was that the Scot had also relieved me of my immediate nightmare of discovery. Certes a girl in a rough army is not as safe as that same girl among jongleurs and I'd not given myself much more than a week in such company. But crawling into Enoch's tent was entering a lion's lair and I doubted that anyone would be tempted to follow.

Enoch was busy working with sticks, dried seeds and cords when I rose. Amazed, I asked him how he could play at games at such a time, to which he replied that this little instrument might be more important than a gaveloc, for 'twould keep us informed as to the numbers moving and their demands on the countryside.

"'Tis called an abacus," he explained, "a Chinese invention. Logistics be the problem, Alex; 'tis logistics what whipped the old Crusaders and 'twill be logistics again this time. But not fer us Scots."

By Matins we had mounted our steeds, with Twixt on a rope behind us, and edged as close to the royal quarters as we could get. A hundred lords or more were organizing their own companies of trained knights to follow the king; pennants of every color and design were held high to show the knights where their lords could be found, and the numbers spilled from one yard to another. High above us a fanfare sounded as a mighty cheer rose to the king, but we had only a glimpse of his scarlet cape and sun-struck crown as he waved from the tower, then lost him as he descended to take his place at the head. Horses pawed nervously and everyone asked everyone else what was delaying us. Suddenly we learned that the king had already departed, whereupon Enoch grabbed my bridle and guided our three animals forward to the gate.

As we crossed the moat—perilously close to the edge—we saw that the king was indeed far in front, his gold silk canopy bobbing in a sea of red as his guards fought back eager Crusaders from the fields who wanted to march close to him. Several knights rode back and forth along the lines—Brabantians, Enoch called them—and acted as ushers to keep order in the ranks. Once we were clear of the moat and had a place, we again came to a momentary halt and I looked back at Chinon. Several of the jongleurs had assembled on one of their carts by the roadside to view the departure, and Dangereuse broke free to run after us.

"Enoch! Enoch!" she wept, clutching at his knarry knees, then babbled on in her strange tongue that no one could understand.

"Why don't you stay with her?" I asked. "She *needs* a guardian."

"Aye, that she does, fer Gitanos be namore liked than the Jews, but she isn't of my blood as ye be." And he bent to pet her head kindly as if she were a dog, his farewell to a devoted lover, for I knew well he'd shared her pallet for months.

Zizka stood in a black cape, glowering like Mars, and beside him Brise-Tête. High above on the walkway I saw the small green figure of Isabelle waving with both arms, only this time there was no Princess Alais beside her.

As the ranks began to swell behind us, soldiers of the Cross chanted a marching rhythm, "St. George, *Aie*! St. George, *Aie*! St. George, *Aie*!" while others sang "Wood of the Cross" so that the air vibrated with the excitement of voices and pounding feet behind, golden fanfare and *Te Deum* before! Enoch took out his pipes and wheezed counterpoint. For the first time I sensed the awesome magnitude of the holy quest.

Yet by midday the voices had silenced under a hot vaporous sky and we heard complaints that we were moving too fast, that it was all very well for the quality on horseback but what about the poor foot? On a slight rise we looked back again and saw that the fore of the army was a sleek head while the rear fanned like the straggling tail of a molting peacock. Enoch shifted his beads til and fro, then announced that we were about seven thousand men, that the first would reach Tours before the last had left Chinon. Be as be may about Chinon, Enoch and I first saw Tours under a pale green sky with Venus hanging bright o'er the wall. As in Chinon, the fields were crowded with new Crusaders come to join the king.

Despite Sir Roger's order, Enoch squeezed us through the city gates before they closed, for he said he didn't want Twixt's store of food to be attacked. There was no place to camp inside, so we laid our mats out in the city square which turned out to be a fortunate choice, for we were directly in front of St. Martin's chapel, and therefore managed to witness the king officially begin his Crusade the following morning.

We were pressed against the back wall of the chapel and Enoch lifted me to his shoulders so I could see over the heads of the glittering assemblage of noblemen, knights and churchmen in full regalia to the altar with its large golden cross and relics of the blessed St. Martin. Finally the Gregorian chant was begun and the sonorous solemn sounds quieted the waiting audience. Archbishop Bartholomew, who had given Richard the cross three years ago, came and knelt before the altar, then rose, arms uplifted to welcome the king. We all turned to watch King Richard enter and walk slowly down the center aisle to the altar. He wore a heavy jeweled crown with raised points, a robe which glittered as it moved, but 'twas his face which outshone all, for 'twas afire with joy and inspiration.

"Why are ye tremblin'?" Enoch whispered.

"I'm not." And I marveled that he could e'en ask.

After the king had knelt, Archbishop Bartholomew started his Mass, beginning with "*Quasi sponsam decravit me corona, et quasi sponsam ornavit me monilibus.*" Richard was taking the Lord as his spouse and I thought bitterly of poor Alais in her tower. When would she become his spouse as well? The archbishop went on through the *Kyrie eleison*, the *Gloria Patri* which was sung, the *Gloria in Excelsis Deo*, the *Pater Noster*, and the king rose to face him.

The archbishop now spoke directly to Richard, naming him the first monarch to answer the pope's call when Saladin took the Kingdom of Jerusalem, the most blessed among kings for his valor and reverence, the hope of the Christian world. Then he presented the king with his official emblems of the Crusade, a pilgrim's scrip and a tall ashen staff.

The king faced his audience, his emblems held high for all to see, his face transfigured with holy zeal. "I herewith accept these insignia of God's blessing for our Crusade! And in His Name and for His Son, we shall succeed!"

The words rang like bells, his eyes flashed blue fire and he brought his staff to a thunderous crash to underscore his vow.

But the staff broke!

The audience gasped in horror. The king staggered as the staff gave way and would have fallen if two knights had not leaped forward to help. All saw alike what this must mean, and stifled moans swept the chapel. Before the panic could grow, Richard held up both pieces of the broken staff and smiled exultantly, his face glistening, his voice suddenly hoarse:

"Two staffs are better than one! God has blessed us with double strength!"

"God bless King Richard!" someone called and others took up the cry. "God bless King Richard!" The music started again and the king walked forward to the door, a staff in each hand, his smile still exultant. As he passed near us, however, I saw a small trickle of sweat flowing down his temple from his crown, a muscle jumping in his lower cheek which held the smile steady.

Outside the door, the king immediately mounted and our march to Vézelay continued via the city of Tours and out through the opposite gate from the one we'd entered. 'Twas hard to say whether we were suddenly joined by vast numbers of Crusaders or whether our camping army behind us now entered the city, but what started as an orderly line quickly became a mob. We were jammed two and three abreast into narrow streets with steep walls which made every horse's hoof sound like thunder, every voice like a hundred. Babies screamed in terror and angry crowds called to us to move. Yet 'twas impossible to round corners, to ride forward or back, and the inhabitants surrounded us in a diatribe of hatred. I could hardly believe my ears as I heard us cursed and reviled, called the filthy long-tailed English, murderers and thieves! Horses reared and a little boy was badly kicked by flying hooves.

The usher-knights continued to try to guide us, not hesitating to strike our beasts and push us rudely to keep us controlled. The one with a black fringe and wicked scar which pulled his lip upward, had the greatest authority: Captain Mercadier. I shrank as I passed, more afraid of his dagger than the mob's fists.

"Don't answer! Keep courteous! We're in King Philip's territory and must hold our tempers. The king's orders, keep calm there!"

"Aye, and King Philip be our partner. Think of what less friendly countries will be like," Enoch grunted, pulling Thistle's muzzle close.

Some people were less hostile but e'en more upsetting. They were the families come to say farewell to their loved ones and the rumor rippled through their ranks that the staff had turned into two serpents, that we were doomed men marching straight to our graves. They hugged pimply young boys and balding husbands with screams of anguish, prayers, sobs, desperate embraces and cries of "*Dix nous aide!*" By the time we went through the far gate, we all felt like marked men and wondered what insanity had led anyone to join such a cursed endeavor.

Fortunately reactions during the rest of our march to Vézelay were just the opposite. In Luti, Mount Richard, Celles, Chapelles and Dama we were the greatest heroes alive, holy men with magic in our touch. Well-wishers lined the roads and screamed their love and hospitality, offered us food and drink, as much as we wanted. Enoch quickly responded to their kind generosity and we picked up cheese, flour, bacon, smoked eel and wine to strap to Twixt. And in all those villages we gathered more men as well as supplies.

At Vézelay we halted outside the city walls to await the French king who would ride forth to welcome Richard. Mercadier and other captains organized the royal household into parallel lines facing one another along the road. Enoch and I were in the lower ranks, too far to get a good look at King Philip but with a fine view of Vézelay. 'Twas an ancient Roman city with a pagan white-and-gold basilica, now a Christian church, rising above gray stone houses. Then royal fanfares blared and the French royal party rode forth. Philip from this distance appeared to be a slight man, his hairline receding, his nose sharp, and he sat poorly on his horse. The barons around him, however, were a magnificent group, elegantly clad in very short tunics and tight hose, their beards trimmed

neat and square, some woven with gold threads. Enoch called them
all fops. We followed the *fleurs-de-lis* through the city gates. Here
Enoch sought Roger for decent quarters as he'd promised; here I
would first serve King Richard. We found Sir Roger rasping at the
stewards, but he took a moment to tell us where we might sleep, and
to order me to report for instructions from the head page, Gilbert,
tomorrow morning. All the time he talked, he stared at my Plantagenet uniform with distaste.

Before we could wander the streets to see the sights, Enoch
dragged me up the steps to the top of the wall to study our situation.
Truly 'twas an astounding panorama we saw stretched over the
country, men and horses as far as the eye could reach. Enoch began
muttering and pushing his seeds back and forth as I broke a stick
into parts to indicate how many thousands. After a time, he'd calcu-
lated that King Philip's army numbered about forty-three thousand,
which with what the English had accumulated brought the total
close to one hundred thousand.

"Impossible." He closed his eyes. "It canna be done."

"What can't, Enoch?"

"The country can't feed so many. There mun be pillaging and
fighting ahead, mark my words. Only about one-third appear to be
trained for the field—aye, 'tis a swart time ahead."

I could see his point but my mind had sunk to a lower level.
How could I possibly remain undiscovered in such company? How
could I perform my private necessities? None of my former ploys
would work in this great army. I was confounded by the awesome
logistics which no abacus could solve.

'Twas a vexing problem but one I would have to defer to another time, for now I must report to the abbey where the king
resided, there to receive my first instructions from Sir Gilbert and
the other pages. With considerable trepidation, I stood before the
low-built structure, told my name and business to the guard. Inside was a severe white chapel with a columned court beyond, and
beyond that the private chambers. Here I was ushered into a magnificent room hung with rich tapestries which I recognized from
the king's chamber at Chinon. Two young men stood working at
a long trestle.

"You must be Sir Alex," the shorter of the two said pleasantly. "My name is Sir Eduard, and this is Sir Gilbert."

I greeted each in turn and received opposite responses. Sir Eduard was a seductive fellow in his late teens with a delicate jaw, dark liquid eyes and a satin skin; I liked his gracious manner and low cultivated voice. Sir Gilbert, the undisputed authority, was so aggressively rude that I could hardly believe my senses: I thought I must be mistaken because of my own uncertainties. In my opinion, Sir Gilbert was odd-appearing though with his huge almond eyes and rosebud mouth he might be deemed handsome by some. He was quite tall, as tall as the king, but seemed not to know how to move his long, soft body which apparently lacked both muscles and joints, leaving only bones and flesh connected by tendons. His back humped slightly, his shoulders drooped, his feet turned inward toward his ankle-bones. I suspected that he'd been a beautiful child who'd grown up poorly. He tried to compensate for this lack of grace by elegant clothes, and both his subtle perfume and delicate gold laces bespoke great care in grooming. Therefore, while all of us wore the Plantagenet red and gold, Sir Gilbert was in a class alone, the king of pages. His face was smooth, slightly puffed with full jaws, his eyes saffron yellow, his mouth well curved over perfect teeth, his smile constant but never touching his eyes. He didn't greet me directly but made telling verbal blows in my direction which passed for instructions.

"So you're the new page, Alex, that we've heard so much about. Such a pity that you must begin tomorrow night with the king when this is obviously a meeting requiring the greatest finesse, the most delicate discrimination if the whole thing is not to collapse from blunders emanating from a crude mind. How old did you say you were?"

"Nine, sir." Though I hadn't said.

"Nine." He gave a faint frisson of disgust. "What can the king be thinking of, to bring his distinguished guests into a nursery? And not just *any* child but a wizened barbarian from the wilds of England. I wouldn't be surprised to see the entire Crusade fail before it can get started when such momentous conferences are attended by an idiot. What is your secret, Alex? Come, you can tell us. How did you worm your way into the king's good graces? You look like a weeper to me: yes, that must be it. Tears would do the trick where talent or intelligence be lacking. What sentimental tale of woe did you use, my dear? Come, don't be shy, repeat it to us. Don't expect us to cry, of course, but we do enjoy a good laugh."

All this was delivered in a jocular offhand manner as he moved busily setting up the trestle, as if the words were not downright insulting.

Sir Eduard put a hand on my shoulder. "Don't mind Sir Gilbert, Alex. He likes his bit of fun."

"*Au contraire*, Alex, you'd better mind Sir Gilbert for I won't let the king's household deteriorate, whatever his whims. Tell me what you know of serving wine, the king's favorite vintage, the protocol relating to great personages. Go on, share the wisdom that made you indispensable to His Majesty."

"I believe I am not indispensable," I said, trying to placate him. "I am his ward because of my parents' death, and this is simply his easiest way of caring for me. That's what he said."

Sir Gilbert put his hands to his hips in mock-amazement. "You are *not* indispensable! Did you hear that, Eduard? Note the humility, the implied ignorance of the boy. Well then, you'd better pay close attention, for what the king meant by 'easy care' was to thrust the unwanted burden upon me. Now, listen carefully, for I'll not repeat. The king will come to his chamber first to bathe and change his garment. You will have his water ready, his fresh tunic laid out, will help him disrobe, dry, take away his old clothes. Is that clear?"

"Yes. Well, not totally. What should I lay out? Where is the basin for water?"

"Come, Alex, let me show you." Sir Eduard shot Sir Gilbert a wasted disdainful look and carefully elaborated upon the instructions, opening the king's wardrobe, pointing to the basin, the basket for dirty linens, and explaining the process.

Sir Gilbert plunged ahead in his scornful diatribe of how to serve wine, how to keep it cool (water from a well below, surrounded by willows), the order of service according to the guests' ranks. My head swam and I almost wished myself sealed in a pastry again. Then Sir Eduard enunciated the rules of discretion, for I would be privy to state secrets. "To talk outside is treason," he finished. "Yet you must listen withal, for the king may test you afterward. We are his unwritten records of events."

"I understand."

"Don't worry, Alex. I'll come tomorrow before the meeting to be sure you're prepared," Sir Eduard comforted me.

We were then dismissed, except that Sir Gilbert suddenly held me back. "Stay a moment, Alex. I must speak with you privily."

I watched Sir Eduard go through the door, then turned back to Sir Gilbert who made no effort to smile now. His eyes were hard as agates, his full lips twisted in contempt.

"I have no idea what trumpery you used to fascinate the king, young faker, but I want certain things clear between us. First, your body odor is a disgrace. Do you have the flux?"

I was startled out of speech and just gasped. Actually I hadn't washed my treasure belt since Wanthwaite and there had been one small accident—two if you count the dysentery in Paris—and I knew I should clean it soon.

"I believe the king must have had a cold when he met you for I can't explain otherwise his tolerating such a foul stench. Then there is your appearance. Call you that mess a uniform?"

I looked down at my large drooping outfit; 'twas not my fault that I was too small for their issue.

"Fix it at once," Sir Gilbert continued in his icy tone. Then he moved closer. "And do not be presumptuous."

Before I knew to step back he reached down, grasped my treasure where it bulged in front and twisted it viciously. Of course it didn't hurt a twit but I recalled perfectly Enoch's howl of anguish when I'd pulled at his terse and I understood Sir Gilbert's intentions.

Tears filled my eyes and I jumped back. "Why did you do that?" I cried.

"To show you that you're not the man you think you are, little weasel. Try to insinuate yourself into our circle and you'll feel worse, I promise. Now get you gone and look to yourself."

He pushed me so that I almost fell.

Blinded by fright, I stumbled into the street. I was now supposed to go with Enoch to the basilica to see the kings together, but I detoured first to the wardrobe where I asked for shearers, needle and thread. I'd been meaning to replace my treasure belt for some time and knew now that I mustn't postpone it more.

Now late, I ran to the Basilica of Ste. Madeleine and found it already filled. My Plantagenet colors admitted me but I was then pressed by a crush of bodies into the wall and could see naught.

"Alex! Here! Come forward!" Enoch bellowed unceremoniously.

Excusing myself this way and that I edged to where the Scot had saved a narrow space for me on the bench beside him.

"Whar were ye?" he now whispered. "The kings will soon be here."

I squirmed and didn't answer. We were so close—did my stench bother him? Or the priest on my other side? I crossed my legs and hugged my arms tight, hoping to contain my own noxious emanations. The priest glanced at me once with a wrinkled nose which made me push harder against Enoch.

"Do ye need more room? Shall I hald ye?"

I shook my head dismally, glad he didn't seem offended by my person, but fearing to risk his lap.

My musings were cut short by a fanfare of trumpets: the kings had arrived. A procession of archbishops and bishops preceded the royal persons down the central aisle as the musicians played a solemn accompaniment to the chanting choir. First came King Philip of France and his train, then King Richard and his. The two monarchs turned to face the congregation before they sat on their thrones. Both were exceedingly grave, though it seemed to me that Richard's mien was exalted while King Philip's was plain dour. I studied the French king with great interest. He was a short slender man, youthful in body and face except for his crabbed posture and closed expression. His eyes were close black dots like a ferret's, albeit one appeared a bit milky, his nose long and pinched, his mouth a slash set close to his nostrils, his chin a spade. Not a handsome man nor a pleasing one, though in all fairness he might be more amiable somewhere apart from King Richard. Even from here I could see that Archbishop Baldwin had been right: King Philip was angry at Richard. If I gave forth foul gases, King Philip exuded rage. He sat listing slightly away from Richard, as if an invisible sword rested between them.

King Richard was lucent as a saint by comparison. He cast an enraptured gaze upward as if he had a private vision which led him forward. Yet I noted that he respected the invisible sword as well. Neither king looked at the other.

In full contradiction to what I observed, the Archbishop of Canterbury was at this moment reading the list of agreements reached here in Vézelay between the two "brother" kings. On the long journey ahead they promised on pain of excommunication to be loyal to each other, to be fierce in battle, to share and share alike all treasure won from the enemy. Their route had also been agreed upon: they would begin together as far as Lyons-sur-Rhône, and there separate into two armies. Philip would march to Genoa, thence to sail to Messina; Richard would meet his fleet in Marseilles and sail to meet him there. The next rendezvous was set for September, whence they would proceed to Acre together.

The points were simple but the spinning long and again my attention wandered. This time I was arrested by a page in King Philip's train who wore a most interesting costume. Unlike our English tunics which were cut midcalf, his reached only to the knee and was slit up both sides to the waist into gonnes to make riding easier. Naturally this would have exposed his braies in indecent manner but he'd o'ercome this problem by winding his braies to above the knees where they met with baggy pants. The more I studied, the more excited I became, for such an outfit would o'ercome a multitude of difficulties for me.

Finally the covenant had been read, the benediction said and we all trailed into the sunlight.

"Enoch, you go see the sights without me. Sir Gilbert has told me that I must alter my garb to the king's specifications."

He left without argument and I ran all the way to a well I'd spotted from our window where a clump of willows grew. Using my father's dagger, I cut off several stems of varying girths, went quickly to the scribner's and begged a sheet of parchment, then ran back to my room where I tossed the stems on the floor to sort according to size.

My plan was to make myself a prick.

Before I could proceed with the cutting of willow and parchment, however, I had to create a design which would fit snugly on my parts so that I could piss through it and fool anyone who watched. The problem rose when I tried to discover exactly whence my water dropped for I was amazed to find that I was a stranger to my own crotch. Did it flow from a sensitive piece of skin on my front? Or from the hole somewhat deeper that I could feel but not see? Or my anus? Promising myself to scrub well afterward, there was nothing to do but explore. After a few puddlings, I knew my source and it couldn't have been more difficult in terms of design. I would have to form an organ the span of a hand and a half with a wide slantwise opening against my body tapering to the tiniest hole at the tip. No one willow sufficed, so I set about whittling and joining till I worked up a sweat in the effort. Then none of the pieces was sufficiently flexible and I must choose between forever drooping downward or lifting upward. Knotting my thought, it seemed to me that 'twould be more convincing if it turned up so that I could arch my stream. I had to drink wine till I was toty to refill my bladder for trials, but finally 'twas done: adequate but unconvincing, e'en to my prejudiced eyes. Never had man nor beast been plumbed with such a skinny long pipe, but 'twould have to do.

I was able to compensate somewhat with the parchment which I oiled to make waterproof. I anchored the willow in a broad double pad and cushioned it gradually to shape like a member and began to feel pride in my work. Now I stitched the whole into the quilted money belt which I fit inside my thighs so it wouldn't bulge. This went smoothly, and soon the whole creation was in place.

Now there remained only the short tunic with its gonnes where I could slip my hands to hold my "prick" without exposing it, my baggy pants, and 'twas done. Quickly I bathed, threw away my old garments and dressed. The prick pushed against the tunic like a tent-peg, but after a few futile attempts to make it lie flat, I decided it didn't matter. From what I'd seen of men, a prick which was too long and erect would not be a handicap.

BY THE TIME I ran up the curving steps to the king's quarters the next afternoon, I was as carefully groomed as a French fop from my scented curls to my polished boots. Both Sir Gilbert and Sir Eduard awaited me and although Sir Gilbert took in my new appearance his manner was still waspish.

"Why are you late?"

"You're not late, Lord Alex," Sir Eduard interjected smoothly. "It's just that Sir Gilbert came especially to show you what to do."

Sir Gilbert pointed to a magenta-and-rose brocade robe stretched across the bed. "They must be put just so. These have been tested for freshness for the king is fastidious about cloth next to his person. Here is a basket for the robes he removes; put it under the table till later. The water has been poured into his basin, the soap—so—and the towel. You should have done this yourself."

Soon after, he took his leave while Sir Eduard remained to instruct me about the wine.

"Tonight you will use the gold goblets—placed here—the finest Jews' work, and keep the wine cool. You see how I've submerged the flask in cool water? If the guests are late, you may have to freshen the water."

He then pointed from the window to the well in the garden hid by my clump of willows.

"How many guests will there be?"

"We're told three, though one never knows. I've put out five goblets which should suffice."

I counted the goblets, a woodly thing to do.

"Most important is to serve according to rank. Do you understand?"

"The king first . . ."

He nodded, smiled and was gone.

Left to my nervous solitude, I gazed through open windows at a glorious sunset, somewhat marred in its effect by my compulsion to test the water. Three times I descended the steps and sloshed up with the heavy pail to keep the wine temperature perfect. The sky had deepened to a crystalline aqua with Venus again suspended like a sapphire. Suddenly I heard footsteps and voices. I shifted the goblets around, then put them on a round tray, but the tray was uneven so they didn't stand upright, and I took them off again.

The king shouted, "If King Philip wants to quit the Crusade, let him!"

Did that mean we weren't going to crusade after all? I strained to hear an answer, but the king strode in and I bowed and flourished.

". . . tenting with a crocodile." King Richard waved his hand at me.

Mercadier, Algais, Louvart—the king's mercenary captains—Ambroise and the king, five people exactly. I poured a heavy jeweled goblet full to the brim, then couldn't carry it so full, tried to pour a little wine back into the flask and spilled it into the water, glanced around furtively to be sure no one had noticed. Now the goblet was wet. I wiped it on my new tunic and carried it carefully to the king. *Benedicite.*

Now I poured a second goblet and looked around helplessly. Who was next of rank? Ambroise nodded subtly at Mercadier.

The captain took the drink and said, "If he stays in France, Philip will march through the Vexin straight to Normandy. The Vexin territory is essential for your defense."

"Do you think I don't know that?" The king's face was contorted with fury. "And despite Philip's claims, the Vexin is legally mine, a part of Princess Alais's dowry."

The flasks were not very large, so I put a second one to cool in the water, emptied the dregs of the first to make my third goblet. *Deus juva me*, the king was finished with his already. I must work faster. I took the royal cup, poured the third for Louvart and managed to carry two at once. I was getting better.

Except that the king had just taken off his crown and cape. I rushed to his side, getting there just in time. But where should I put them? As I stood, bewildered, Ambroise smoothly poured two more goblets of wine, one for himself, one for Algais, and smiled at me.

"His popper in his pouch would wither if you spat on it," the troubadour said dryly.

Did he mean my popper? It took all my will not to touch my new prick.

Then Richard answered, "Except that it's a long spit from Jerusalem."

I let out my breath in relief; they were still speaking of King Philip.

Then I lost all interest in their argument, for the king began to undress.

Horrified, I watched him unlace his long over-robe and let it drop at his feet. 'Twas not so much that I didn't know by now the anatomy of a male (better than a female as I'd recently discovered), but the king! He wore a sorcot, underpants and braies same as everyone else, yet I stood hypnotized as one by one he discarded each piece while his diatribe against the French king continued unabated.

I felt a slight shove. "Pick them up, Alex," Ambroise whispered, smiling, and I turned violent red for I'd been gazing on the king's parts which were as huge as the rest of him.

I scurried to scoop the clothing into a basket, then reached for the magenta robe. By now the king's milk-white body was bent over the basin where he scrubbed himself thoroughly and I stumbled over a trailing braie as I saw that his backside was covered with hard red whelks. Riding sores? I stood on tiptoe as he leaned down to slip into his fresh robe.

"—won't fight if I know the scoundrel, but will be on hand to collect the spoils," he said as his head came through. "Damn his greedy soul! He'll suck me to a husk."

And I let out a long breath of relief: the king was dressed.

I took the basket from under the table and stuffed the dirty robes into it. But I dared not put the basket back where it would be in full sight. I looked around for a likely spot and saw only one. Casually I dumped the robes back onto the floor close to the bed; then, pretending to straighten the cover, I kicked the offending garments under the bed. I stood, pleased with myself.

"Wait till Messina," Mercadier advised, "where you'll sap his will. Then you can deal with him as you like."

"Hush." Richard held up a warning hand. "I believe my guests arrive." He raised his voice in what was obviously mock rage. "How dare de Sabloil translate my orders to his own liking? I wrote the command and meant it to be taken literally: sailors who take knives to one another must be tied together and cast overboard. Send a runner and see that 'tis done, Captain Louvart."

"Yes, Your Majesty."

The three captains brushed close by the men who were entering, causing gracious apologies on both sides though the Archbishop of Canterbury held the same derisive expression at the company that he'd turned toward me at Chinon. I was most awed by his companion, Ranulf de Glanville, the author of England's book of common law which Malcolm had oft praised. Then I realized I'd seen him briefly before at Westminster, a slight man with a strong nose and chin and dark intelligent eyes. His nephew, Hubert Walter, showed a family resemblance but hadn't as yet developed as much authority in his face.

However, 'twas the king's face that made me forget my duty, for 'twas a reversal of the gruff, caustic soldier he'd been with the captains. Now he was again the lambent painted saint, glowing, courteous, almost unctuous. Zizka himself could not have changed so rapidly.

A nudge from Ambroise brought me out of my reverie; he nodded and frowned toward the dirty bath water. *Benedicite.* I must empty it of course. I picked up the basin and again looked around. Certainly this couldn't go under the bed. I considered the open window and dismissed it as too obvious. But if not there, where? There was only one possible place: I poured it into the wine water.

"My lords, welcome to our cramped quarters. Please take your ease and forget cold ceremony. Alex, the wine, please."

I jumped guiltily, fearful of the reprimand which might come later because of my laxity. Aye, 'twas easy to be king and snap your fingers, but I had no goblets! All had been used. Quickly I gathered the glasses and wondered if I dared serve from dirty cups, but no, one was the king's; he'd never forgive me. Now sweating, I looked to Ambroise but he was addressing Ranulf: "I say the king is not a bit too harsh." And I submerged the glasses into the wine water.

Then almost swooned! 'Twas floating with dirty suds from the king's own parts! What should I do? I turned my back, quickly dried them on my tunic which was getting quite damp by now.

Ambroise came close. "I'll help you serve. The archbishop after the king."

I smiled at him weakly, more grateful than he knew.

"A loyal subject should obey his king without question," Ranulf said, and took his wine.

Not so easy to do, I thought grimly.

Richard's eye sparked dangerously. "Except methinks when it applied to my late father. Becket dared disobey."

What did that mean? Then I had a brilliant thought: King Henry had made Ranulf Queen Eleanor's jailer—and he should have disobeyed. How I hoped the king would test me later so I could share this insight, with proper modesty of course.

"Vengeance for Eleanor is understandable but not good politics," Ranulf was saying and I'd missed something. I hoped it wasn't important.

"Alex, are you serving cakes tonight?" The king again!

"Yes, Your Highness. At once, My Liege." I blushed and stammered and fought tears. Would he tell that horrible Sir Gilbert?

There was a short silence as I refilled the cups and arranged the cakes on a platter. Then Hubert Walter changed the subject to the division of spoils. Here the issue was how to define the enemy, whether the Crusaders fought the Saracens only, or whether their mission included heretics. To my surprise, the archbishop considered anyone who wasn't a Roman Catholic a heretic. I knew that the Crusaders had been invited to Jerusalem by the bishops of the Greek Orthodox and Byzantine Churches, which I'd always thought were Christian. However, since I still couldn't tell one order from the other in the Church, I had no call to have an opinion. Then I was vindicated by Ranulf.

"I'm shocked! Are we going to destroy our sister Greek Church? Prey on it as the Infidel?"

"'Tis not my order," Archbishop Baldwin protested, "but comes from Pope Clement himself. There are former Crusaders in the Holy Land who have become corrupted by marriage to the Infidel, many of them accidie or pagan by now. Then certain Byzantine Christians choose to give aid to the Saracens."

"One can almost see why," Glanville commented dryly.

King Richard was amused by the interchange. "Well, Glanville, you're learning the difference between civil and canon law I believe. In England it is illegal to attack the rich; in God's domain it is legal to attack the rich, provided one proves heresy later."

"'Tis a most cynical view, My Lord. I'm surprised you go forward if you believe so."

"There are as many reasons to crusade as there are men to do it. The Church exports troublesome aggressors and beggars in exchange for wealth and power. I go for the simplest of reasons: for the glory of God."

"So do we all, so do we all," rasped the archbishop. "The king is a tease, Glanville, and means only half what he says."

By this time Glanville was openly staring at King Richard as if he saw him for the first time. I would have given much to read his mind.

Baldwin was now impatient to be gone and in a short time the interview was finished, much to my relief, for the wine was getting low and I knew not where the supply was kept. By the time the door was closed, I, too, was ready to depart.

The king caught my arm. "Not so fast, page. We are not done with you yet. 'Tis protocol to wait till you're dismissed."

"I'm sorry, Your Highness," I mumbled. The hot evening and my own nerves made me to sweat profusely, for I couldn't recall what Sir Gilbert had said I should do after the conference. I soon saw. King Richard lifted off his crown, unlaced his cape and tunic, held forth his arms to be disrobed.

"Ah, that's better," he groaned. "This is one of those insufferable southern summers. Is there any wine left? Baldwin soaks up the grape like sand. Good, pour one for each of us and let's see what you absorbed of the night's conversation."

He sprawled naked on his bed, half sitting, half lying, and gestured me to come close as I had that first night. I was not so shocked as before at seeing him naked, but still sufficiently disturbed to spill a red trail across his navel.

"I'm sorry, Your Highness," I said again, reached my hand to mop, then withdrew it, tried not to look below his waist.

He laughed softly. "Don't be sorry, it cools me. Well now, how do you fare? Which horse did you choose?"

I was concentrating so hard on what Mercadier had said, how Ambroise had responded, that for a moment I knew not what he meant. "Oh, the gray, aye, the gray. Thank you, Your Majesty."

"You're welcome." He bowed his head. "Does he have a name?"

"Thistle."

"This-tell?"

I had to explain, for it seemed the king knew not one word of English.

He rubbed my tunic between his thumb and forefinger. "And you have an adequate garb at last. Much better fit than that bulging tunic in Chinon."

My heart jumped and fell in a dead heap, then ran rapidly again. *He'd* noticed the bulge—had he also ordered Sir Gilbert to test me? I was suddenly so cold that my skin bumped. Surely he didn't guess that I was a girl! But no, or he'd not appear naked or take me on a Crusade. My heart became regular again.

"I thought—I thought that Ranulf de Glanville showed diplomatic skills," I began, to prove I'd been listening, then stopped when the king waved his hand and I fetched another glass of wine. When would he let me go? Soothly he seemed not to want to discuss the evening.

"I had a surprising interview with a Scot in Chinon, a young knight from a noble family in the highlands. Do you know whom I mean?"

I frowned. "Aye, Enoch Angus Boggs."

"Dubbed by the Scottish monarch, I believe, when he earned his spurs in some clan war. In any case, I was curious as to your relationship. What is he to you?"

Again my innards began leaping. I wanted to say "Nothing, an impostor after my land," but that would cross the king who'd already made the Scot my guardian. Best be tactful for now.

"He said you were brothers." The king nudged me.

Anger at the traitorous Scot gave me strength. "Not really brothers, My Liege. He protected me—I think I mentioned that I'd met a Scot—and he insisted upon going through a ritual. Sucking . . ."

"Sucking?" the king repeated with sudden interest. "What do you mean?"

Vastly ashamed, I described the whole odious business of becoming the Scot's blood brother.

"God's feet, I thought only the Saracens believed in such savage rites. What was the nature of your oath?"

Rapidly I rattled the terms, to be faithful till death, to help each other in all things, not to interfere in matters of love . . .

"Ah," the king interrupted me. "That's different from a knight's oath. And do you permit the Scot his lovers?"

I thought of my attack upon him and Gladys Stump and flushed.

"Not at first, but afterward, yes," I mumbled.

"Why not at first?" He lifted my chin.

I wondered at his examination of this dour topic, but must answer.

"I didn't understand what he was doing. I'd never . . . and I thought he was killing her."

The king choked on his wine, spilling more than I had across his chest and this time he gestured that I should clean him. I looked around helplessly, not wanting to use the soggy towel from earlier. Finally I put my hand delicately to his skin and rubbed so that the wine dribbled down his side to the floor.

"Again," he ordered.

'Twas most inefficient. The king guided my hand with his and I became hot with embarrassment though I tried to be casual. He released me, smiling.

"That will do. What about you, little Alex? Does he permit you your lovers?"

I caught the teasing note but had to answer. "Oh, I'm sure he would except that I'm . . . I can't . . . that is, I haven't yet passed rule six."

"Rule six?"

"The Rules of Love," I reminded him.

"Oh, of course, that a boy must be . . . Well, that applies to becoming a lover, but you can still be the beloved of course. How about it? Are you someone's beloved?"

I thought of Isabelle. "Possibly . . ."

"If the Scot permits you. Tell me, Alex, do you like the Scot's ministrations?"

Much as I detested Enoch, I dared not lie. "He takes good care of me, I believe. Fights, feeds me, keeps me innocent."

"How innocent? Didn't you just tell me you had a lover?"

I was finding his questions made me breathless and couldn't understand his fascination with my personal life. "A friend, which is not the same."

"No indeed. So you're still innocent."

I thought of Satan's toute-ass and flushed deeply, almost grateful that Fat Giselle had made me promise not to tell. "I believe so."

"Only believe?"

"If I knew, I wouldn't be innocent."

He burst into laughter. "Checkmate! Well, 'tis a relief, I can tell you, and I'll rest better knowing that you're *innocent*. Now the hour's late, time to kiss me good night and be on your way."

"Yes, Your Majesty."

I hesitated, waiting for him to rise, but he stayed supine. Balancing precariously, I leaned to peck his lips in the civil kiss, but he clasped me with his free arm and I fell heavily so that my lips pressed as hard as Isabelle's had pressed mine, both hurting my teeth and stimulating my liver to wild gyrations. When I stood, it was with pounding heart and I was almost too weak to move.

"Yes, the Scot will be kept busy." He smiled through bright half-closed eyes. "I was much pleased with your service tonight, Alex."

"Thank you." I flourished, bowed and somehow stumbled into the arched corridor where I leaned against the door and wondered what I'd done wrong that he hadn't tested me on policy.

Inside I could hear him laughing to himself.

17

 S IT HAPPENED, NO ONE PAID ME ANY HEED ON THE long ride to Lyon-sur-Rhône for each Crusader was concerned with his own problems. First there was the rain, for it poured each day as if preparing for the flood, cleared muggily by night so the mosquitoes could feast, then returned with another onslaught at daybreak to assure black sticky mud for men and beasts to slosh through. As for my finding privacy for my ministrations, I had a

much easier time than my suffering fellow soldiers who'd been tempted by fruit orchards along the way. Peaches, plums, apples and apricots dangled golden and red on the branches and I reached hungrily along with the rest. Enoch squeezed a peach, slapped my hand away, and pronounced the entire crop forbidden fruit.

The slow progress, the sickness and stench, the angry tempers confirmed what Enoch had predicted and the kings pushed hard to reach the point where they could separate their armies. On the seventh day we arrived at a bridge on the Rhône above Lyons and decided to camp until stragglers had caught up. The rain then stopped, but left us in a quaggy mire and the kings thought to cross the bridge to the higher meadows on the eastern bank. Philip went first, followed by his army above the churning waters of the flooded river. King Richard ordered that only his household should follow him until the French army had departed; the rest of the English would have to founder in the mud, which they were now used to. Enoch and I got into single file, for the bridge was narrow, Thistle in the lead. The rushing foaming water below made me toty but the fresh spray felt good.

"Where shall I go?" I called over my shoulder.

There was no answer. When I turned farther, I saw that I'd been the last to cross. Through some error several of the king's household had been held on the western side. Uncertainly, I guided Thistle along the bank and stared across the swirling mists from the rapids. Then I saw Enoch almost opposite. He cupped his hands and called but the roar was too great. Finally he waved encouragement and I waved back. Well, there was naught to be done. I turned Thistle to where the royal pavilions were being raised and watched the pattern of the encampment: long carts were being positioned like spokes of a wheel around the pavilion centers, each space between reserved for special lords and their men. Priests were setting up altars and everywhere food was beginning to cook. I sighed for Twixt more than Enoch; this was one night I would go hungry. At least I'd kept my goatskin from Wanthwaite and could sleep on that.

Then by good fortune Ambroise discovered me sitting alone and invited me to share his bowl which I gratefully accepted. Later I again missed my comfort. The stars and mosquitoes were both out in such droves during the night that I looked forward to sleeping in our little leather tent on the morrow.

The morning broke bright and warm with birds welcoming the change of weather in a bright scolding chatter. The French royal pavilion was struck, the French army made ready, and the two kings rode away together, for King Richard was to see Philip courteously on his way toward Genoa. Enoch and I again waved, again tried to shout, but 'twas hopeless over the churning waves. He pantomimed eating and I nodded, pointing to Ambroise. Then King Richard returned and gave the sign that the English should cross, for it seemed our road to Marseilles also lay somewhat to the east. Enoch was first in line, Firth and Twixt held firmly together. I squatted in the tall grass to watch them come.

The horses objected to the narrow pine planks, the swirling water below, but one by one they were forced and the slow progression began until there were a hundred mounted men on the span. Enoch was now close, his grin broad. Then I saw his expression change—both Twixt and Firth fell to their knees. I jumped up and ran forward. Enoch was now looking downward, his face frozen in horror as the first pine arch slowly splintered and gave way. Horses and men slid helplessly forward and sideward, Enoch the very first to go!

"Enoch!" I screamed.

Now everyone saw and the shouts and neighs echoed above the water's roar as the entire bridge collapsed. People on shore stood paralyzed until the king leaped forward.

"To the rescue!" he cried. "Ropes! Lances! Everyone *move!*"

He tore off his robes and dashed half-naked into the river sinking instantly to his armpits, then shouted for his lance.

"Grab hold!" he yelled to a floundering knight.

Soon everyone followed suit and the water was a melee of drowning and rescuing.

"Enoch!" I yelled and waded waist-deep with my saddle rope in hand. My scream was lost in the chorus of shouts, whinnies, cries! Knights were racing and yelling in utter confusion. Trumpets sounded for order but no one heeded. The fast current knocked me down and when I stumbled to my feet again I saw Enoch's hairy face bobbing fifty yards downstream, going fast as an arrow.

"Enoch!"

I scrambled up the slippery bank, clutching at grass, then ran along the river in the direction he was being carried. Beyond a turn the Rhône gained speed over a small weir and already a few heads floated in the backwash, but not Enoch's. I dashed on as rapidly as I could, trying to keep pace with the current by watching a tumbling branch, but it was so fast! Finally my breath gave out and I had to sit to let pains in my chest abate. The cries behind me sounded eerily in the calm day, as if the infernal pit had opened momentarily to swallow a few souls for breakfast.

Surely I'd missed him, for no one else had drifted this far. Surely he was safe on shore by now, looking for me. I trotted back, examining every snag and crest, for he might have struck his head. The river by the bridge was still pandemonium, but a few horses stood dazed on wobbly legs, a few men gasped in their own puddles. A quick survey showed that none was Enoch. Richard still worked hard with others to use stretched ropes, while hardy swimmers were diving below the surface to pull up half-drowned Crusaders. Enoch *couldn't* have swum back to this point; he must be somewhere downstream.

Again I ran down past the weir, beyond where I'd been, stopping and starting, determined not to turn back. The sun was low in the west before I gave up.

All the horses had been saved; only three men were unaccounted for. King Richard was elated and went from man to man, congratulating each on his survival or his help. The priests said a special Mass of gratitude for our escape from tragedy. 'Twas a good omen for God's soldiers.

When the moon rose full, I mounted Thistle and retraced my steps, for sometimes objects show more clearly in the water's afterglow. Several times I called his name, waded out to handle rocks or snags, all to no avail.

The next day the river disgorged two bodies, mangled and torn almost beyond recognition. Almost but not quite: neither was Enoch.

Now the king's only remaining problem was how to transport his army across the Rhône without a bridge. After a few fruitless scouting expeditions to discover another bridge, Richard devised an ingenious scheme of lashing fishing boats firmly together and thus constructing a floating bridge for the stranded men. 'Twas tedious labor, hazardous when done, but it worked. In two days we were ready to march again.

While all this was going on, I continued my search in desultory fashion. My reason told me 'twas futile but I was too stubborn to quit altogether until my body weakened for the task. Finally I sat on a mound apart from the camp and watched the knights and foot accomplish their slow exodus across the treacherous waters, Enoch's grave.

I was stunned to a stupor by grief. Still, I wondered at my woe. I'd *hated* Enoch, had often dreamed that he'd expire in some hideous way, and now I couldn't bear it. My depth of feeling was akin to the loss of Maisry whom I'd loved. Were love and hatred so close then? Aye, in that they gave reason to live. I saw clearly now how fortunate my meeting with Enoch had been on Dere Street, for my empty well of love had been instantly filled with hatred and I'd been sustained. Now I was empty again and felt I must collapse inward upon myself.

Without Enoch, the whole pattern of my quest was revealed as lunatic. I'd told Dame Margery I'd be back in a week and I was in my second year; I was supposed to travel north and I was going ever deeper to the south; I wanted to rescue Wanthwaite and I was committed to saving Jerusalem. Aye, 'twas as pointless as the wanderings of the Jew. Yet Enoch had given it reason, had pushed his abacus and come up with figures to account for the madness.

Well, Enoch was dead. And at last, so was I: killed at Wanthwaite, now ready to lie down.

I couldn't go on.

No one paid me any heed as the fanfare sounded and the slow march began. E'en so I took certain care to conceal myself behind a bush. I put Thistle to graze free, then curled tight to sleep.

"ALEX, WAKE UP. You'll be left behind."

Blearily I gazed upward at Ambroise's face, half-hid above his fat belly.

"Go on without me," I mumbled. "I'll catch up."

"I thought the Scot was looking after you."

I heard my own mad cackle. "Aye, at the bottom of the river. He's calling me to suck eels."

His footsteps retreated. Instantly I fell asleep again, vaguely feeling ants crawl over my ears; then hands wedged under me to lift.

"No!" I flailed weakly. "I want to stay here!"

I was tied onto Thistle's saddle, water forced down my throat, a honey-teat put in my mouth. Ambroise rode on one side of me, Sir Eduard on the other. As from a great distance I heard the creak of saddles, men's voices talking and laughing, felt the flick of Thistle's tail as he struck at flies. Still encapsulated by my stupor, I was beyond experience, beyond anguish.

Then drops plopped around us and I brushed my face irritably; there were more, and more. Our three-day respite of fair weather had ceased, rain had returned. But this was no ordinary rain. Lightning cracked on the gray horizon and thunder growled ominously above as a giant began to stir. Our army plodded forward, the men covering their valuables with blankets and leather as best they could. I tried not to think of the swollen river raging behind us with a torn body battered somewhere against its current. Steamy rain washed hot tears from my cheeks.

Ambroise leaned across Thistle and said something to Sir Eduard, then galloped forward alone. Another crack, closer this time, and the sky blanched a deadly silver-blue. Then another, another, and suddenly the drops turned to a tide and we were engulfed in a furious driving flood of water. Everyone was now pinned to wherever he stood as the elements flailed from all sides and volition ceased. I lay my head against Thistle's neck, breathed deep of his warm horsy smell, thought of Enoch. Enoch.

Then a hand pushed me back into sitting position and my reins were pulled forward. Thistle stumbled after our guide, a rounded shape which must be Ambroise. Like snails in ooze we inched forward until a shattering flash revealed a pile of high rocks by the roadway. Here I was lifted from my perch and passed from one set of hands to another, finally to be engulfed against a body smelling of sweet woodruff.

"Is he hurt?" I heard the king say.

"Only in his heart." There were mutterings. "He's dazed, which is just as well."

"He'll stay with me."

"I'll care for him, Your Highness. He is my charge."

"Thank you, Sir Gilbert, but I believe he is *my* charge first of all," the king answered.

And I was aware enough to feel gratitude.

Thereafter the king settled himself into a position that was somewhat dry, whether under a tent or a rock I didn't know, for I kept my eyes closed. I knew only that he leaned back against something solid with his knees bent and held me wrapped in his cloak against his half-bare chest as if I were a babe. He talked to people around him concerning our whereabouts as I lost all sense of time, and he occasionally patted or stroked me. I felt his warm sticky flesh against my cheek, listened to the strong thump and swish of his heart, felt his voice rumble both in my ear and in the resonance against my face. He was my sanctuary.

I may have slept. When the king stood, I woke and saw that it was dark. The rain had abated but still fell in a steady drizzle and the king's pavilion had been raised.

"Well, Alex, you had a good rest," he said as he placed me on my feet. "Come, you'll stay with us tonight."

He led me into the pavilion where Sir Gilbert and Sir Eduard were busy setting up the trestle and the king's bed. Sir Gilbert shot me a venomous look and I hid behind the king's tunic, but Sir Eduard came and asked how I fared. I tried to say all right but found I still couldn't speak.

"Lay a pallet for the boy at the far end," the king ordered.

Sir Gilbert moved to obey and, as he brushed by, bent and whispered, "Congratulations, you've outdone yourself. You're a weeper *par excellence* but I warn you, don't overplay your hand."

The tragedy of my loss was too great for me to respond.

Lanterns were lit; the king supped and drank wine; bishops and great lords gathered around the trestle to talk of strategy. How hard the king works, I thought, as I watched his serious eyes dart this way and that over a map, his underlit features softened in the waxy

light. He seemed the most intelligent, the quickest, the most ener-
getic of men. It seemed to me that he labored half the night, though
my own stricken senses were not reliable timekeepers.

Finally all lights except one were extinguished and even Sir
Gilbert had departed. Only then did the king turn to me again. His
huge white-robed form approached, knelt in the dimness, and he
wiped my forehead free of beaded sweat.

"Alex, I didn't know till this afternoon about your brother-Scot.
I'm very sorry, boy; I understand your loss."

Again my words of gratitude came out as a strangled sob.

"That's all right, child. There's no disgrace in honest grief. We
all feel it for departed brothers. At least he's assured of direct entry
into Heaven since he died for God's cause. The pope granted absolution for all martyrs to the Cross."

The comfort was lost in the chilling finality of his words: Enoch
was dead.

Richard leaned close to kiss me good night and felt the tears on
my cheeks. He sighed deeply and picked me up again.

"Come, Alex, this is no night to be alone."

He carried me over to his own large bed and placed me on it,
though my clothes were still damp. Then he dropped his robes and
climbed in beside me, put his arm across me and pulled me close.
'Twas strange, I knew, that a twelve-year-old girl should be sleeping with a naked king in his bed, but it didn't seem strange at all.
His kindness, his warmth and his marvelous strength made it the
rightest thing in the world.

When Sir Gilbert woke me in the morning, I was back on my
pad and the king was dipping his bread, already garbed for riding.

I WAS INSULATED by deep despair. Vaguely I saw we had entered a
part of the country where it looked as if it had not rained for a year.
Under a blazing sheet the earth parched and reflected upward so
that we were caught in a double anvil. Knights peeled to loincloths,
heaping armor, mail and winter clothes onto spare horses or their
squires. Less fortunate foot soldiers staggered under their own
heavy gear, many dropping to the ground and sitting sullenly as we
rode past. I saw men retching and squatting by turns as their cods

collapsed, some lying in their own filth. Two shook their fists at us and announced they were quitting this mad march into Hell.

Then my hand was lifted from my side. I looked up to see that King Richard rode beside me. He smiled, said nothing. So we rode for miles and miles. Then he put my hand back to my rein, squeezed it gently, and cantered ahead where an archer sat staring at his bleeding feet. By the time I was abreast of them, the king had poured water from a flagon on the feet, bound them with a silken sash torn into bandages. As he rose, the archer said something I couldn't hear but I could see the adoration in his face.

All day long I watched the king ride the lines til and fro, now leeching, now listening to plaints, now praying with some weeping Crusader. He loves them, I thought with wonder. In late afternoon, he returned to my side, edged his courser closer, placed his arm around my waist as we jogged. His presence made me break down again. I made no sound, kept my face forward as I wept and wept, unable to stop e'en though I knew he was watching.

That night as I placed my goatskin before Ambroise's tent, King Richard was suddenly before me, a huge nacreous shadow against the night.

"You'll sleep in my pavilion from now on."

Soon I lay in his silken tent as big as a hall, fenestrations admitting a slight breeze, and listened vaguely to the parley among the counselors about tactics in the Holy Land, how to reach there with all due haste. We must march to Marseilles within the week, the king said, for the fleet is waiting. March two hundred twenty-one miles in this heat? There won't be any army left, said someone else. And I dozed.

The next day I dined on beef broth and bitter brew of ox testicles to restore my strength. Again the king answered calls all along the line and gave freely of his ministrations, but 'twas late afternoon before he came to me.

"How do you fare, Alex? Are you stronger?"

"Yes, Your Majesty." I glanced shyly. "Thank you for everything."

A radiant smile and again he took my waist. After many miles he withdrew his arm, and I missed his touch.

"Alex, no one can or should replace your Scot, but I hope you will think of me as your protector from this point on. You are my ward, I am your king: that very fact makes us closer than brothers, believe me."

I knew not what he meant but believed him anyway. How could I not? His eyes, his smile, his touch all testified to his truth. And that night I was able to help the pages serve wine to his counselors when they came.

After they left, the king himself picked me up and cuddled me for one moment, then lay me gently on my mat.

"Good night," he whispered. When he kissed me, I responded to show my gratitude.

And I *was* grateful, e'en though I cried myself to sleep.

THE COUNTRYSIDE grew ever more fiendish, marked by grotesque rocks pushing upward, their sheer drops pocked by ancient cave-dwellings. The sun, too, continued its relentless glare, a topaz heat enclosing the ravines in eerie light. Occasionally the wilderness was broken by a sudden thrust of past splendor—Roman aqueducts, theaters, bridges—in startling contrast to the savagery. I was vaguely aware of passing through villages, some abandoned by their citizenry who fled our locust army, others white-baked hamlets lined with a blur of shouting people: Vicaina, Mount Galonte, St. Bernard, Valence, St. Paul of Provence. Then one day I heard someone say we were in Montelimar. The town was prettily planted with plane trees which cut the roadways with black shadows. Not till we'd entered did we see the populace lurking in the obscurity.

Then I saw a white arm, an object flying!

"King Richard! Careful!" I screamed.

He veered sharply and just missed being hit by a large rock.

"Antichrist! Killer King!" a woman shouted, and cast a rotten melon at him.

A whole crowd took up the chant as ugly missiles of all kinds filled the air. "Pope-lovers!" "Plunderers!" "Vatican wolves!" "Read your Bible!" "Turn your other cheek!"

And turn his other cheek Richard did, straight to the city square!

"To arms!" Richard cried to his dumbfounded knights. "The mayor!"

His mercenary captains sped after him, followed closely by his most prized knights as the Earl of Leicester took command of the army. We were formed into a close phalanx and marched to the center. All around us the ugly crowd grew and continued to hurl abuse and hatred, while a cordon of knights with raised lances held them at bay.

In a short time the king returned with his prisoner, an elderly, richly dressed gentleman. He was stumbling at the end of a rope and was followed by a lady and three half-grown children, all weeping loudly.

"What has he done?"

"For God's sake, show mercy."

"Who are you? Why have you taken him?"

The king paid them no heed but quickly conferred with his captains, who called on yeomen to build a gibbet. A few stout men stepped forth and the work began.

The mayor and his family continued to beg and plead for mercy, denying any guilt, but none of Richard's men responded to the hue and cry. The watching crowd fell to a grim silence.

Then the same men I'd served at Vézelay forced an aisle through the crowd and came to confer with Richard: the archbishop, the bishop and Ranulf de Glanville. They spoke earnestly, but Richard's face was carved in wrath.

The king ran up the steps and tested the hanging rope, came down and motioned that the mayor be brought forth. The trumpets sounded for attention.

"This is Richard Plantagenet, King of England, Count of Poitou, Duke of Normandy," he shouted. "I am told that you are Albigensians and Christians. Therefore shall I be clement, though you are also insurrectionists; only your mayor will die to serve as example."

Again the family sobbed and cried out with new energy while the mob knelt and prayed. Henry, Count of Champagne, and two other knights often in Richard's pavilion now joined the prelates in a close circle around the king to add to the argument. Richard's adamant graven face flushed red as he was forced to listen. The condemned man collapsed in the dry dust. His wife threw herself on top of him and screamed for them to take her instead.

Tears scalded my eyes and I dropped back into my slough of despair. So many dead—Wanthwaite, Enoch and now this.

Then the trumpet sounded once more. In the deathly silence, Richard spoke in a smothered voice: "Let the gibbet suffice as reminder of your guilt. But if we come this way again, beware of Richard."

He whirled his destrier, and dashed forward on our road. Quickly the rest of us formed a line and followed. The last thing I could see as I left was the mayor staring vacantly after us as his family stood like statues.

The king remained in a rage throughout the day and, at nightfall, I felt 'twas more prudent to stay away from his pavilion. Ambroise's tent was too small to house me, but 'twas a hot night and I didn't mind sleeping outside. I threw my goatskin a few yards distant from the troubadour's tent, though he was somewhere else at the time.

The sun was long setting, and the moon full when it rose, so 'twas too light to sleep. Or mayhap I was too disturbed. I longed for Enoch to explain what had happened today, missed him so that 'twas a physical pain.

All over the camp, men were shouting belligerently, their voices drunk and angry, and I knew that everyone was confused. Then a file of roisterers passed close to me and stopped in a small dark copse where they tippled and talked.

"What do you think the king should have doon, Pat?" a nasal-voiced wight asked.

Pat answered in a hoarse guttural rumble. "They be a filthy bunch of heretics. He shoulda killt them."

Was that true? I strained to hear.

"How be they filthy, Pat?" a boy asked with cracking tones.

The men sniggered. "They dig ore in black earth, Jack," said one.

"Wex but don't multiply," said another.

"Like priests?" Jack insisted.

The guttural Pat drawled, "Hell, boy, *priests* have children. These Albigensians turn the *other* cheek. Take my meaning?"

There was further talk.

"In the ass-hole, dolt!"

The boy said something I didn't hear, but it seemed to be a question.

"Seems that Jack wants to be showed, Pat," the second voice suggested. "C'mon Jack, drink up. Good French wine, sweet as vinegar, put you in slickery mood."

There was more mumbling, the guttural man upmost, and more laughter.

Pat then asked, "Jack, did you e'er hear of Buggers?"

"Aye," said Jack. "Buggers is men from Buggeria."

Hooting laughter.

"That's it! The boy kens! All right, Jack, these men from Buggeria crawls on all fours, see, like this. Now you do it."

Jack resisted. "Them Albigensians warn't on all fours."

"Not when we seen them, no, but that's the way they go to church."

I didn't believe it.

"Go on, Pat. He's ready as he's going to be."

"Aye. All right, Jack . . ."

The boy screamed! A throttled scream, as someone clamped his mouth! Then grunts and squeaks, muffled laughter, like pigs rooting.

My heart thumped in fear and I tried to pull a little closer to Ambroise's tent. Then suddenly the men fell silent. In the quiet— the sound of a horseman approaching.

King Richard.

He was about fifty feet away, apparently oblivious to his hidden audience. Then he reined his horse to a stop in the shadow of the giant aqueduct. He seemed a carving himself as he sat in silhouette, gazing upward.

He dismounted, tied his horse. Then he turned toward Ambroise's tent.

"Alex, are you there?"

"Yes, Your Highness."

I scrambled through the brush toward his outstretched hand, taking care to go round the patch of darkness where the soldiers were hidden by the copse.

"Let's climb down to the bank where we can get a better view," he said without preamble.

Infinitely grateful to be escaping the ruffians, I climbed down the slippery stones with his help till we were ankle-deep in rilling silver water.

The king thrust his chin upward, his face boyish in moonlight. "That's the way to imprison time, Alex," he said, awed. "After I've conquered the Holy Land, I, too, will build great structures, conquer the future with a throw of stone."

I said nothing, but shared his reverence. The magnificent curves above us seemed an ancient cathedral. He pulled me deeper into its shadow so we could get a different angle. After a long time, he sighed.

"Well, I think it's impressed forever on my mind now. How about yours?"

"I'll never forget it, Your Highness," I answered soothly.

"God's feet, boy, this Roman bridge has almost made me forget my purpose. I came to thank you."

"Thank me?"

"For saving my life today."

"Oh, that—'twas nothing, My Lord."

"Nothing to you, perhaps," he said dryly. "I value myself, and I believe there are others who feel the same."

I was glad darkness covered my flushing face. "I mean I did little—anyone would have done the same."

"I hope so, but in any case, I'm grateful."

He then helped me climb up the rocky drop till we came to his horse.

"Your Highness," I asked nervously, not knowing if I were presumptuous. "Who are the Albigensians? Why were they so angry?"

"Just another fanatic cult that grows like weeds in this clime," he answered without rancor. "The south cultivates such stubborn weeds—they are the religious counterpart to the rebellious barons in these regions."

"Then they're not the Antichrist?"

"Frankly, I've never paid much attention to their beliefs, though 'tis my impression that they're too Christian if anything. They're celibates, ascetics, zealots. However," and his voice grew hard, "the real issue was the assault on my person."

"Aye," I agreed, not satisfied but sensing I shouldn't pursue the topic further.

"Come, give me your hand."

He pulled me onto his horse in front of him.

"You should stay in my pavilion, now that I've replaced the Scot as your guardian. A young boy is not safe with some of the scum who follow our Crusade."

I fervently—and silently—concurred. And I hoped the ruffians in the bush had heard him, especially when he said that he was my guardian.

18

HE CITY OF MARSEILLES SENT OUT LEGIONS OF mosquitoes to greet us. No respecters of rank, the bloodsuckers made brothers of us all. Furthermore, the fiery heat turned sultry, drowning us in our own sweat. Our flesh stuck to saddles, to clothing, to itself, rancid as butter.

In late afternoon, a small group of us sat on horseback with the king on a hill overlooking the port. Richard's face glistened white as snow under his angry bites and a miasma of pests was feasting e'en as he sat. Mixed with his welts were hard whelks of an uglier sort, much as those he carried on his backside, and his eyes glittered supernally bright.

"God's feet, where's my navy?" he thundered hoarsely.

Unable to answer, we all stared at the small fishing boats dotting the Mediterranean's flat sheen.

Maurice de Craon, a trusted knight, tried to calm the monarch. "The path is treacherous by sea, my Lord. 'Tis said the violent headwinds in the Straits of Hercules can hold up travelers for weeks."

Richard's eyes were hard as granite. "From March to August? That's a mighty blow e'en for Hercules. 'Twill go better for my captains if they're blown to the pearly depths than if they return to Richard without excuse."

Grimly he urged his courser on.

News of the tardy fleet awaited us at the palace where the royal party was to be housed. Two ship justiciers, Robert de Sable and Richard Canville, had decided to divert their ships to Portugal in order to help the king there fight the Moors. However, the Crusaders had attacked the Jews as well as the Moors, raping their women and taking their property; finally the looting and mayhem had spread e'en to the Christians! The King of Portugal now sent a message to King Richard in protest; the Moors and Jews were under his direct protection. Lisbon prided itself on the peaceful coexistence of its divers nationalities, and he demanded *immediate* apology and redress from the English king.

I had the ill fortune to be with the king when this message arrived. His skin blotched hideously, his breath came in short labored rasps, his eyes set forward as if they would drop from their sockets. Horrified, I couldn't move. What was wrong? Was he dying? As he rocked his head, tried to unclench his jaw, fought for words, he was suddenly racked in a dreadful seizure. So large was his body, so violent his shaking that the whole world quaked! I screamed and threw myself upon him!

"Get out of here!" Mercadier hurled me out the door which was immediately slammed shut.

I lay on the floor where I fell and thought my heart would break. Not the *king*, the king couldn't die!

"What's wrong?" Sir Eduard pulled me up. "Alex, tell me what's wrong."

In broken syllables I choked out what I'd witnessed.

"Come, quick!"

Eduard jerked me down the narrow stairs into the anteroom

where Sir Gilbert lolled against the arch leading into the street.

I clung to Sir Eduard. "What ails the king?"

"He has some sort of dreadful affliction, no one knows what," the page explained. "All of us close to him witness it from time to time, but 'tis death to say you do. Do you understand?"

"No."

"Let him say whatever he wists," Sir Gilbert sneered. "The king's pet can do no wrong. Go back up, Alex, and hold the monarch's hand."

"Gilbert, must you always be such a toad?" Sir Eduard asked sharply. "The boy's a noble orphan, has just lost his brother and he's hardly old enough to be a rival! For God's sake, show some decency."

With that Sir Eduard walked away and disappeared in the crowd, leaving me alone with Sir Gilbert.

"I daresay Sir Eduard's correct, as usual," Gilbert intoned. "Certainly you mustn't be seen around the palace if you've had the misfortune to witness one of these seizures. 'Tis the one act the king would not tolerate, even from you. My advice is to get away as far as you can. Go to the waterfront—you'll be safe there."

For once I accepted his words.

I scuttled down the steps and into the streets of Marseilles. 'Twas already twilight; a few torches were lit at the corners, but there was no abatement of crowds. Men, hacked and marked like pirates, staggered drunkenly with locked arms while coarse toothless hussies tried to waylay them. Timidly I edged along the streets, ducking into doorways when rough varlets came near, but they were difficult to avoid. Unruly, jug-bitten mobs swarmed the dank steaming alleys like gray rats ready to attack.

I know not how long I wandered, hours mayhap, but somehow I found myself finally on the waterfront where I huddled terrified behind a barrel of fish. In the distance, red lamps on sardine boats cast flickering glows upon the black water, but on the quay sailors lurched and fell in puddles of vomit, grunted, shouted insults, bared knives and fists. I dared not move, dared not stay. Then I was spotted.

"Look ye, lads, 'tis the king's pretty boy come to sell wafers on the side!" I recognized the guttural voice from the aqueduct!

A reeling churl with a dirty cross on his chest reached for me, stumbled and missed. With drunken eyes and drooling mouth, a scarred face rose again over the barrel's edge as he gurgled foul curses.

A companion leaned by his side and crooked his finger, wheedling. "Come on, waferer, try a good honest Lincolnshire prick for flavor. Don't be forelore, 'tis pleasant swonk."

He grabbed my arm and pulled me into the street where a small crowd gathered to witness. I was shoved back and forth between them as they continued to jape. Feeling like a beaten dog, my mind went blank with dread.

"Can your horn make toot?"

"Or do ye horn the toute?"

"Oh, look ye, the pretty fop weeps. Do ye miss yer Richard?"

My knees cracked on the paving stones as I was wrestled into a kneeling position, my arms held tight from behind. All I could think of was the gray clabbered skies over Maisry's body, the kites circling, the crash of Sir Roland's armor as he undressed—vivid as yesterday.

A blurred dark figure in front of me dropped his pants, pulled his tunic up to display a fat hairy belly resting on purplish parts. It grew closer—I shut my eyes and mouth tight, stopped breathing.

"Force it open, Jamie."

Fingernails scratched my jaw as a thumb tried to pry my lips apart.

"Aaaaoooo!" Swish! And a splinter of bone!

I felt a spurt of warm blood.

"They've took his hand! Who the Devil are you?"

"Stop, in the king's name."

Mercadier!

I looked up at a circle of towering horsemen.

"Spare us, for God's sake. Mercy! We dint know he war with the king!"

"He's not hurt. Ast him!"

"We're Christians same as you . . ."

I was lifted onto one of the horses, heard the slash of swords.

Three men sank into puddles of blood, screaming and clutching. They had neither eyes nor balls.

"DO YOU KNOW where you are, Alex?" Louvart asked.

I nodded. "The palace."

Mercadier sponged my face. We were somewhere in candlelight. I knew not how we'd arrived, nor what the hour.

"You're not hurt, Alex," Mercadier told me in his foreign accent. "They didn't undress you, did they?"

I shook my head mutely.

"He's himself again," Algais said. "Best take him to the king now."

Mercadier stretched his mouth in a thin smile. "When the king learned you were on the streets, he sent us looking. He wants to see for himself that you're all right. Can you come?"

I nodded.

The king was being leeched by his physician when we entered the royal chamber. I was sufficiently recovered to note that, although pale, Richard was better.

"Alex, thank God! Where was he?"

"By the docks," Mercadier answered, then went on in the langue d'oc, a tongue I cannot follow. The king glanced at me from time to time during the recital, his face horrified. He asked Mercadier a few questions, then lay back and closed his eyes.

The physician removed the basin of blood and bandaged the king's arm. "You must rest now, Your Highness."

"Impossible," the king said sharply. "If I don't rent ships, we'll rot in this mosquito swamp. The Pisanos come soon to bargain. But leave me now—I want to talk to the boy."

They turned to go. "Oh, Mercadier, we thank you."

The captain flourished and went out with the others.

With deeply shadowed eyes, King Richard studied me, then held out his bandaged arm. I stumbled close, was gathered against his body which smelled like my own father, and felt tears rush down my cheeks. He crooned in his strange language and I didn't need to follow the words.

"Do you want to tell me what happened?" he said finally in

French. "First, how did you happen to go to such a dangerous part of town? Didn't anyone warn you about the waterfront?"

I felt a surge of anger but shook my head. Let someone else expose Sir Gilbert; I didn't want a writhing, eyeless figure on my conscience.

"'Twas a mistake. I was looking for Sir Eduard and got lost."

Gradually I tried to repeat what had been said. When I got to the "king's boy," I saw Richard's angry whelks return.

"*They said that of me?*" His body trembled. "Did you understand them, Alex?"

"No, Your Highness. I—I never sold wafers, have not even been an altar boy."

There was a shadow of a smile. "I see your Scot succeeded well. In future I, too, will be more vigilant, but I am a very busy man. Therefore I want your word that you'll not go abroad alone henceforth, not even to church without telling Sir Eduard or Sir Gilbert."

"Yes, Your Majesty."

Sir Roger then entered to announce that the Pisano ship captains had arrived and I was dismissed. As I left, I saw Richard's face again go through one of his remarkable transformations as he turned a beaming welcome to the guests.

I HUDDLED in my mosquito-infested room through a long sleepless night. What had that sailor wanted? And *why*? Over and over I relived those few moments and prayed for a rush of tomorrows to erase memory.

Never had I missed Enoch so much. I'd grieved for his sprightly companionship and the provision he'd given, but not till this very hour had I fully appreciated the protection. Because I'd never understood the danger. Well, now I knew. Horrors I couldn't fathom, as strange and dreadful as the rape I'd witnessed of Maisry.

Oh, Enoch, Enoch.

By morning I was sick with apprehension, afraid to venture out, yet unable to stay in my fetid privy-pit of a chamber another instant. The king had graciously dismissed me from duties that day, but where could I go? I stood in the arch and stared at the teeming street. At the next square I saw the towers of a church and decided to seek sanctuary there, where God might give me comfort. I told

Sir Eduard that I was going and sidled gingerly along the cobbles.

The familiar mildew smell and dank shadows of the church made me feel a little better almost at once. 'Twas a huge edifice with many niches and chapels and I didn't know which saint would be best for my purpose. Fortunately a chubby priest stood collecting alms and noticed my hesitation.

"May I be of help, child?"

"Yes, Father. I'm sore troubled by the evil in the world and . . ."

". . . and? Don't be afraid, my boy."

"The loss of my brother."

"A loss indeed. How did he die?"

"He drowned—in the Rhône River." I had a hard time saying it.

"Drowned?" The priest became excited. "Did you see him die? Bury his body?"

"Well, no, but he drowned e'en so. I did see him float away and we searched for four days."

The priest put down his money plate and clasped both my shoulders. "God has led you to the right place, child. I'm certain we can help you as we have hundreds of others. You know, of course, about St. Lazarus . . ."

By now he was guiding me along the dark nave and talking in a whisper so that he wouldn't disturb the faithful who were at prayer.

"The man Our Lord raised from the dead?"

"The very same. After he was raised, he sailed to Marseilles and became our mayor for forty-seven years, dying at the advanced age of ninety. He became famous as a miracle-worker in his own right, for he raised the dead again and again. Especially, because of our location on the sea, *sailors who'd died of drowning*!"

I shivered with awe under the mysterious vaults. "Do you think . . . ?"

"'Tis for the Lord to decide, but you should try."

We turned and walked through a cloister, then into a small chapel where the father stopped me.

"St. Lazarus is buried here in that crypt. His jawbone is on display and is without doubt the most powerful relic in Christendom. It will cost you two deniers to see it."

How I wished Enoch could have witnessed my readiness to part with silver for his sake! The priest opened a dull metal box and I gazed on a brown moldy bone with two broken snags.

"Those are the teeth that smiled at Our Lord Jesus," the priest told me. "I'll leave you here to pray."

I knelt on worn stones and tried to think what to say. Certes I should pray for Enoch's entry into Heaven, in case the absolution didn't apply in his case, for he hadn't been a zealous Crusader. On the other hand, what would he do alone in Heaven? For I was sure there would be no other Scots in that hallowed place. I supposed there was no harm in praying for a miracle, though I hated to waste my deniers on such a fruitless mission. Still, that was what the father had instructed.

While I was trying to formulate my words, two older women came and knelt behind me. I listened to their mutterings and realized they were saying a variation of the Rosary. I would do the same.

"Hail St. Lazarus, I pray for the return of Enoch Boggs; hail, St. Lazarus . . ."

The drone of my own voice and the comforting coolness of the place made me happy to pray for hours, except that the women kept nudging me. Finally I instinctively reached back my hand and pushed, just a little and very politely.

"Alex! Alex!"

Again I elbowed back—then the use of my name struck me!

And the voice!

"Enough, I say. Ye havena turned monkish on me, have ye? Cum, I've muckle to tell ye."

I whirled, faced a blinding light in which stood the living soul of Enoch Angus Boggs!

"I did it!" I screamed.

And fell in a dead faint toward him.

AFTERWARD Enoch told me the troubles he had with the hysterical priest who claimed that his return was miracle number four hundred three. The two ladies who'd been praying agreed, saying they'd heard my plea and that was that: Enoch's name went into the books.

As for me, I was near toty as the priest. People crowded around to see the "angel-boy" who'd brought back the dead, for an innocent "little child shall lead them" and "come ye as a little child to enter the Kingdom of Heaven" and I was perfectly willing to testify that 'twas true. Hadn't I seen him sucked under the waves with my own eyes? Hadn't I looked for him for four days?

Finally even Enoch agreed and dragged me out of the church, protesting that if he'd been dead almost three weeks, 'twas time for a good haggis. He led me to a small garden behind the square where Firth and Twixt were tied, brought back from the dead as well though I'd forgotten to pray for them. There he unwrapped a haggis, warmed it over a small fire and told me his tale.

"That war a swift current in the Rhône sure enow, but not to a Scot what learned to swim in the gorges and tarns of the highlands. 'Twas the beasts that detained me, fer they couldn't get footing and kept shooting ahead like greased arrows. 'Twas ten miles or more before a villager helped us walk out."

My excitement waned somewhat. "Only ten miles? Why didn't you come straight back?"

"Ten miles, aye, but two days and a night. 'Twas a long time, bairn."

"You were struggling in the water for two whole days? Without stopping or eating?"

His bright blue eyes oped wide. "I'm surprised myself that we made it, now that ye point it out. O' course, I war plannin' to rush back but Twixt war a bit lame."

I frowned. "E'en so."

"Well, thar was another reason. We'd lost all our supplies. Now ye saw yerself how mean the Crusaders be when they're hungry. I thought to myself, I'm in virgin land; I'll fill the coffer fer young Alex."

The word "virgin" roused a suspicion.

"What was the villager's name? The one who helped you."

He was caught off-guard. "Poll." Then hastily. "That be Paul."

"Poll, Polly. A pretty wench, I trust." I pushed away my haggis.

He let out his breath. "Aye, but also helpful. She gave up her best layers for our larder and e'en slew a lamb for haggis."

I got to my feet, trembling. "So you did all this for poor little

Alex, wallowed in some hussy's pigsty while I was near starving on the road, traded my safety for that miserable Gateway to Hell." And I brought forth the vocabulary I'd learned from him. "You tikel pisspot, you lickerous erse, sour-breathed sticked swine, drunk nose, crocked routing . . . Go back to your bawd! I don't need you any more!"

He grabbed me hard. "Alex, 'tis not seemly that ye be jealous! A man's a man, ye should knaw that!"

"*Jealous*!" I bawled. "Jealous! Of *you*? Nothing would make me happier than if you'd settle down and marry one of your foul dancing girls. Didn't I tell you to stay with Dangereuse? You're right, jealousy be a toty idea! But you're my sworn *brother*! Blood comes first! You're a disgrace to the MacPhersons!"

'Twas the ultimate insult and he blanched.

"Waesucks, lad, ye have reason. I swear I didna mean to desert ye. I knew Ambroise was wi' ye, and the king has taken ye into his household. Tell me, did ye suffer?"

"Aye, I suffered sorely but I didn't die." And I suddenly saw his purpose. "*That's what you wanted*, isn't it? You left me to die so you could take Wanthwaite! I'll bet you didn't lose the writ!"

His telltale hand flew guiltily to his vest.

"I see through you, Enoch Boggs. You came down to Marseilles hoping to be told that I'd fallen by the wayside. *I'm* the miracle! I'm the one who survived a living death! So go back to Scotland! I don't need you any more!"

"Ye've tinted yer reason! To tell ye true, I didna think of ye at all—at least at ferst. Ye're anely a wee lad wi' no understandin' of a man's lust, but . . ."

I blazed out: "Don't understand lust! *Me*?" And I brayed without mirth. "Don't talk to me of lust!"

I threw down my food and ran blindly into the empty midday streets. Back to the palace and the privacy of my hot stinking hole. I didn't look up when Enoch walked in a short time later, knelt in front of me. I buried my hands under my arms so he couldn't hold them.

"Look, bairn, I knew ye'd be safe wi' the king."

I still didn't look up.

"I belave ye've forgot our oath of brotherhood—that we would permit each other freedom in love."

I glowered at him under my thick fringe of lashes, then turned away and refused to talk more.

THE FOLLOWING MORNING Enoch was summoned to the king's chambers. He wasn't there long, but when he emerged his face was as red and wet as a boiled lobster.

"What did he say?" I asked eagerly.

The Scot was too angry to speak and struck the wall viciously, thereby jarring a thousand mosquitoes from their daytime sleep.

"Did you tell him about Polly?" I prompted.

"Kape yer stupid mouth closed," he growled.

We walked into the street. I waited, knowing he couldn't be quiet long.

"He claims that he assigned me to look after 'his royal charge,' that be ye in case ye wonder, and I hae neglected my duties. As yif I didn't knaw ye long before the king!"

"True." I was grimly pleased. King Richard had given him what he deserved.

"He laid out rules lak he doon fer his sailors: yif I don't obey, overboard wi' Boggs. Or Mercadier will be turned loose on me."

And I was no longer pleased; this was serious, for I knew well that my slightest complaint would be translated into sure death. Certes I was furious with the Scot, and I had reason. Still, given a choice of having him alive or dead, I'd learned the past few days that I needed him more than ever, treacherous unfaithful beast that he was. I would simply have to take care: threaten Enoch with the king's wrath if he got out of control, but say naught to Richard.

I'd been puzzling so hard that I hadn't noticed where Enoch had led us till my shin brushed a fish barrel and I saw with horror that we were on the waterfront. Immediately I tried to hide behind the Scot's kilts, but I was already too late. A drunken yeoman reeled directly at me with upraised fist!

"May you burn in Hell!" he cried.

Instantly Enoch's thwitel was out, his legs braced to fight.

"Git gang or ye're a dead man."

"Put down your popper, Scot. The pretty boy don't need the likes of you, not when he's got the king. Just watch to your own pouch, that's my advice."

Enoch kept his dagger poised. "What do ye mean?"

"I mean ye can have yer stinking Crusade. John Little will not serve no king what cracks nuts for a waferer."

"That be a woodly thing to say, dangerous as well."

"But true. They cut Pat's balls off, threw 'em to the sharks. Jamie's as well." His voice broke and tears streamed down.

"Air ye claimin' that the king did such? But why?"

He pointed at me. "Ask the licker there. The king guards him with one of his mercenary butchers. Watch your stones, that's my advice."

As he reeled away, Enoch slowly lowered his weapon and looked at me.

"Well, we ha summit to talk about."

"He acts as if he's the abused one!" I protested hotly. "They tried to kill me, right there by that barrel of fish, and would have too if Mercadier hadn't happed to come by."

"Happed?"

"Well, he was looking for me." And I told him every detail of that awful evening, making it clear that it was actually his fault for deserting me so. All the time he kept a queer look as if wondering about something else. When I finished he took my arm and led me back to the little garden behind the square where there was some privacy.

"Alex, tell me sooth, befar Mercadier come upon ye—did those scoundrels touch ye?"

"Aye," I whimpered, "they pushed me and pulled at my clothes, kicked at me as if I were a mad dog."

He sat entranced, whistled, looked upward, whistled again, then spoke in broad Scots which meant he was upset. "I dinna knaw exactly hu to put this, bairn. Ye say they kicked ye lak ye *war a dog*."

"Aye. A *mad* dog."

"But—think befar ye jangle—did they touch ye like ye war *a weasel*?"

"A *weasel*?" I gazed on him with wonder, remembering my father's pet weasel at home named Sly. "You mean wrapped me around their necks?"

"Nay." He looked pained. "There be an ancient saugh: *As nicht turns to day on God's easel/Swa boys chaunge to girls in the weasel.*"

A cold wind blew straight from the firth to my innards. How had the Scot guessed my secret?

"I'm a boy," I whispered.

"Aye, I knaw ye're a boy," he said impatiently, "but . . ."

"But what?" I sat on my hands to conceal their shaking.

"But whar there's a hole there's a worm."

His words were significant, enigmatic, and he looked at me as if I were sick.

"I haven't eaten any apples. Didn't you tell me they were too green?"

He sighed heavily. "Boy, thar be men and women as ye ken."

Why wouldn't he leave this dangerous subject? "Aye."

"And they mun gae twa by twa, na matter quhat happed to yer mother and friend; 'tis in the way of nature." He scowled darkly. "But when men don't have wenches to satisfy their call—wal, betimes they dig ore in black earth."

Something stirred in my memory. "The Albigensians?"

He was vastly relieved. "Aye, ye ken my meaning then."

"Aye, Buggers from Buggeria."

He began to stand. Anxious as I was to be finished with this threatening subject, I couldn't quite let it go.

"What does it mean?"

Again he sighed deeply.

"I dinna knaw exactly how to tell ye." He put his arm over my shoulder. "Ye see, in Scotland we hae no such evil wights."

"Soothly?" 'Twas the first good thing I'd e'er heard of Scotland. "Why not?"

"Wal, ye shuld knaw a wee bit of our history. The ferst man to conquer all of Britain—this be in the olden days—was naturlich a Scot. He should hae ruled the whole island, England as well except . . . that he war a sinner in the manner we're speakin' of. Sae God sent him to Scotland and sayed as hoo the Scots mun be ruled by England until they could get rid of this sin in their blood. And that's why we have no such sinners today. Do ye follow?"

Not at all. I'd never been so confused in my life.

"You mean like Adam was thrown out of Eden?"

"Quhat a thing to say!" he cried, outraged. "Ferst, Scotland *be* Eden and, second, Adam's sin war normal, whereas that king . . . God doesna like kings who . . ." His voice trailed off, and he looked at me, speculatively. "Alex, ye sayed the king took care of ye."

"Aye. He, Ambroise, Sir Eduard—all were kind. But the king most of all, of course."

"How so? Tell me facts."

"I slept in his pavilion, he held me . . ."

"While ye slept?"

I thought about it. "Only once, the first night."

"Now think carefully. How war ye both dressed?"

Again my skin bumped. That same question. "In my clothes, which were wet as I remember. The king was as most men, without clothing."

"And ye slept. Air ye sure?"

"Yes. What's wrong?"

"I hope *I'm* wrang, bairn," he whispered, "or I be slow as a snail in a snowstorm. I'm thinkin' aboot what that varlet said."

He kicked at puffballs in the grass, bit his lip in vexation, studied me in silence. Then he grabbed my hand and pulled me up purposefully.

"Where are we going?"

"Cum to the church. I need to thank old stick-tooth fer a miracle myself."

WHEN WE RETURNED to the palace, we ran into Sir Gilbert under the arch.

"Well, Alex," he purred, "I hear you had a bad experience down by the waterfront, and after I explicitly warned you about the place. Next time you'll heed me."

Before I could sputter reply, Enoch put himself between us. "There'll be no next time fer ye, ye envious viper. I'd take great pleasure in defanging yer smirking mouth. Do ye take my meaning?"

Sir Gilbert paled. "No need to threaten me, especially when you dump your brother into my lap. Look after the whelp yourself if you're so concerned."

The page turned as quickly as he could and shuffled away.

"Thank you, Enoch," I said.

He set his mouth grimly. "'Tis anely the beginning, bairn."

19

 ICHARD ARGUED WITH THE WILY PISANOS FOR A week about the price of his hired fleet, though everyone said the ship merchants of Italy were worse than the Jews when it came to money. Whatever the final settlement, the king was visibly relieved to announce that we would be sailing on August seventh. Half our company, led by Ranulf de Glanville and the Archbishop of Canterbury, would sail at their own expense directly to the Holy Land; the rest of us would proceed at a leisurely pace toward Messina in Sicily where Richard hoped to pick up gold and supplies inherited by his widowed sister Joanna, Queen of Sicily. There, too, we would combine forces with France again.

Enoch and I sat on our cramped deck-space aboard the king's ship, the *Pumbone*, on a bright windy day and heard the bells tinkle for Mass throughout the twenty galleys and *buzas* surrounding us. The King raised his mighty arms and shouted *"Annuit coeptis"* and we were off! Sails whipped like laundry, waves dashed, sailors sang in joy. We had barely gotten used to the roll and pitch of our deck when we dropped anchor to camp at Nice; the king planned to sail only a few hours each day in hopes that his own fleet might o'ertake us.

We put ashore for two days in Genoa where the king visited King Philip who was sick with the gripes. Richard returned in a black rage; Philip had again raised all his querulous complaints about Alais, the Vexin, and even about the weather. Furthermore, he'd ended his vitriol with a demand that Richard give him five of the Pisano galleys, then threatened to leave the Crusade when Richard offered only two.

Again we sailed southward, and this time 'twas a marvel that we moved at all, so glassy the sea, so lethargic the breeze. The shore rolled by us magically, as if on silent wheels. It took us two weeks to reach our next port, Salerno. Here King Richard planned to stay ten days, for he was determined to conquer his chronic physical ailments before he launched his campaign in the east. Therefore he rode off with his counselors to the Salerno Medical Academy, the finest institution in the world.

When the king returned, his eyes were as tragic and hollow as those of the cursed heroes of that southern land. Never had any of us seen him in such melancholy humor, almost a sickness of the spirit. Naturally we were exceedingly curious to know what had brought about such a plunge in the king's mood. Then Ambroise told me that the great doctors had diagnosed Richard's ailments as a curse from God: two ancient curses had tainted his family and thereby destined Richard himself to become the Devil incarnate. No wonder the king was desperate. However, there was hope. The doctors were sure that in time they could cure the monarch, rooted in the past though his disabilities might be, by the powerful tool of exorcism.

And gold.

The king spent two silent days brooding, then announced that he would go hunting. However, he cast cold eyes around the company and added a fateful word: alone.

Pandemonium followed. Even knowing the king's choleric humor, the lords protested vehemently. 'Twas unheard of for a great monarch to risk his life by venturing alone amidst hostile people, they said, meaning that the king's mood virtually guaranteed some dire incident.

"These rabble are insurrectionists, mark me well," warned the Bishop of Evreux. "They would delight in bringing down their overlord."

"I don't believe there's a true knight in the entire country," Baldwin of Bethune added. "Therefore they will attack in a pack, as wild dogs. Chivalry is unknown here."

Richard listened impatiently. "I want to be alone, and that's an end to the subject."

Even Mercadier could not prevail. "I can follow so discreetly that no one would know I am there."

"*I* would know, Mercadier, which is all that matters."

The whole company fell into a deep gloom.

Richard gazed around himself, rattled. "I see what I must expect in Jerusalem—an army of women. Well, I will appease your fears just this once. I will be protected by my page."

He pointed to me.

For one brief uncomfortable moment, I was the center of scathing attention. Then the counselors conceded to Richard's wishes.

"Alex, arm yourself well against my enemies," the king ordered, so everyone could hear. "Meantime we'll see if we can find you a little gerfalcon, in case you're not in combat the whole time."

"Yes, Your Highness," I said happily.

Soon Enoch had pulled me to our patch of deck and was whispering furiously in my ear. "Ye'll nocht go forth into this treacherous trap with the king alone."

"You heard. No one can stop him."

"Hark to what I say: someone can stop ye."

"Are you advising that I disobey the king?"

"Nay—and neither will I," he said mysteriously.

Let him squirm and let the others deride my assignment. I might not be able to fight off attackers, but I had a plan to save the king nonetheless. Fate had decided that I was to accompany the monarch; fate had therefore decreed that I cure him. I twisted my mind to the purpose, devised and discarded a dozen plans before I found the perfect one. Now all I needed was a period of peace and quiet with Richard, and he would be a new man.

King Richard looked healthy and happy as we pranced away at dawn. Dressed in hunting green with no royal insignia, his skin tanned, his hair streaked gold from the sun, mounted on a shining black courser, he could have been a magical monarch from elfland. I, too, had shed the Plantagenet red for my heather tunic Pax had made me, and I trowe that our "disguise" did give us a great sense of freedom as we splashed along the verge of the retreating tide. I pressed Thistle to keep apace with the king's doubled image in the water, for he urged his stallion to a gallop.

Then he turned inland, leaping over ditches and hedges before the eyes of startled peasants where they bent to tend cane and grapevines. We thundered across fields, down lanes, past villages, faster and faster. 'Twas midmorning by the time we climbed a narrow mountain valley cut in twain by a roaring fall. Although the sky was bright overhead, half the valley was already cast in gloom deep as night and we stayed on the sunny side. 'Twas as unlike England as the bottom of the sea. Black-trunked knarry trees twisted out of rocks, then sprouted leaves more gold than green and the air was filled with a luteous haze. Strange flowers abounded in tiny crevices, and in the meadow delicate pastel stars clustered on miniature bosks.

Below us we spotted a blue heron fishing in a stream at the bottom of a ravine. King Richard removed his falcon Penchant's hood but held his jesse. Then he let forth a mighty shout as I beat sticks against a hollow tree, and the heron took wing!

"Track, Penchant!" The king flung his bird.

The heron lowered its head, its stout wings pulling its weight slowly aloft as it tried to outfly the hawk, but Penchant's swifter pinions cut the air like butter as he rose easily above his prey, flying in tight circles till he was exactly positioned. Then the stoop! Struck like lightning in a volley of feathers and blood! Tangled bodies dropping into the pines as we edged our mounts down to bag the bird.

Richard grinned like a boy. "Your turn, Alex. Let's find another waterfowl if we can. If one is here, there must be others."

He hooded Penchant again and I made the little gerfalcon ready, biting my lip in excitement. We rode for some time without seeing anything but warblers, when of a sudden, a huge white bird rose from the trees.

"Track, Skyrow!" I shouted with a fling.

My valiant little hawk streaked like an arrow up the steep, easily topping the prey. But then the white bird gave forth a raucous cry, turned a red beak sharp as a sword.

"Alex, it's a crane!" the king called. "Careful, he'll—"

The crane thrust his head straight to his body and forced the hawk to give chase. Twisting and turning at sharp angles, the crane soared and dipped as the sturdy falcon followed close. Below, we urged our horses to follow the chase over the uneven ground. For a half hour or more we raced so. Finally the gerfalcon prepared to stoop, but by this time the crane was three hundred feet at least, a dark blue spread being attacked by a silver dot! The dive! The crane swerved—a miss! The gerfalcon fought to recover, climbed again— the crane was out of sight.

"What a heart!" the king cried. "A worthy little bird, but out-classed. Cranes are wily quarry, hard even for Penchant."

Keenly disappointed, I accepted Skyrow back on my leather glove and attached the jesse.

The king hugged me briefly. "Come, let's go to a lower meadow for warblers. There you'll see what a staunch hawk you have."

In a short time I'd known the thrill of the kill many times over and could hardly believe it when the sun shone directly overhead and I saw that our bags were full. We prepared to find a meadow where we could build a fire. The king rode forward while I trailed behind, a warm suffusion spreading in my chest-spoon that I sud-denly recognized as happiness.

Then the king stopped and waited. Without a word he took my hand and we continued slowly together through the unpathed for-est. Fragrant pines mixed with large-leafed planes and twisted black oaks to create a green mystery, pierced occasionally by a slanted ray of sun. Unseen in the boughs a bird traced our passage with a four-noted song like a thin fife playing. The king whistled a contrapuntal tune as our horses' heads bobbed in rhythm.

Suddenly we emerged on a high promontory overlooking the sea, a calm stretch of glitter under an intense sky. We sat there a long time, our spirits in perfect communion. Again we rode slowly into the shade, the air so pungent that it made me toty. We were rocking on our horses as tangled limbs moved overhead.

"Wait," said the king, "I think I hear a stream."

We dismounted, trod on a carpet of small blue flowers toward a cluster of rocks. I followed the king where he squeezed between boulders and we were in a perfect enclosure of stones and trees cut by a stream with a small weir. In the mist above the fall, a rainbow arched.

"Too perfect to be true," Richard said. "Almost makes me believe in my sister Marie's fancies. Come."

He sat on the flowers, hypnotized by the rainbow, and gradually his happy mellow humor turned melancholy. I respected his silence, but felt more and more anxious. Finally, he was overcome by despair and stretched out on a sunny patch beside the brook, covered his face with his arms as I gathered wood for a fire, cleaned the birds and plucked them, improvised a spit. Soon a thin line of smoke rose to the intense blue above, the birds crackled on the flame, and my stomach grucched happily. Let him sleep for now, I thought, and we'll talk later.

When the first birds were done, I shook him gently and handed him the juiciest woodcock on a stick. He pushed it away.

"Get me my wine, on the saddle."

He drank deeply from the leather flask, leaned back and closed his eyes again.

After a short hesitation, I ate the three birds that were cooked, and put on more. I took care to eat silently, not sucking or smacking, so the king could sleep. The second spit was ready—should I wake him?

Suddenly he sat up. "Did you hear something?"

"There are squirrels in the trees."

He lay back down, but I knew he didn't sleep because the muscle jumped in his cheek. Still, best not disturb his thoughts. Yet his thoughts disturbed me forsooth; I felt them like a cold draft chilling my spirits. Possibly this opportunity would be lost after all. I berated myself for arrogance, the sin of pride. How could I have thought I could reach the king—earn his eternal gratitude—when no one else could?

He spoke without opening his eyes. "Do you know the hour?"

"We're out of range of bells, Your Highness, but the sun runs midway past Nones methinks."

He sat again, sighing, brushed leaves from his hair. "I'm loath to leave."

"We could t-talk," and I cleared my throat to take the wobble out. "Enoch and I've seen many wonders since you've been gone. Would you like to hear about them?"

I took his lack of reply to mean that he didn't mind at least.

"A guide told us about a Greek hero named Oedipus, whose ghost lives in a theater here. Well, 'twas a most interesting tale for it treated on a . . . a . . . ."—*Deus juva me*—"a family curse."

His hard eyes raked me, but still he didn't speak, so I faltered on.

"It seems that the pagans believed in curses, as some do now, only I think that betimes such curses cannot be true. 'Tis like the relics, you see, where one contradicts another."

"No, I do not see," he said coldly. "What are you trying to say?"

My head was beginning to sweat under my hat. "Well, for instance, if the Devil appeared to someone on a particular Friday and someone else far away said he'd seen the Devil at the same time, one of them would be wrong, that's what I mean."

He lost interest because of my meandering, drank from his flask again and prepared to lie back. I rattled on with shallow breath.

"Some doctors claim that a person is the Archfiend because he comes from a cursed family with witches as ancestors, and therefore this person gets ill—to pay for all the sins."

The flush began at his throat and worked upward, a faint line of whelks appearing at his jaw, and I spoke rapidly before he could stop me.

"But I say that this person couldn't possibly be the Devil because I personally have seen the Devil. Therefore, you see, the doctors are wrong!"

His choler suddenly subsided, an encouraging sign that I was making headway.

"You've seen the Devil?" he repeated slowly, brows up.

"And he looked nothing like you," I affirmed boldly.

"And therefore—forgive me if I seem slow but I'm overwhelmed by this information—the doctors of Salerno are mistaken in their diagnosis and I need no exorcism after all?"

"Aye, that's correct. They may think you're the Fiend, for I'm sure they're honest men—but I am witness to their error. I saw Satan—very close to, touched him." I shuddered.

The king smiled briefly—instantly relieved, I trowe—but then became solemn again. "So you say, but you, too, might be mistaken. Tell me the details."

But I'd divulged all I could and still keep my own soul intact.

"Forgive me, My Liege, but I'm sworn to secrecy. On my honor as a baron I swear to you that I speak the truth: you are not the Devil for I have seen him in person."

"God's balls, Alex, you can't tease me so! I'm your king!"

'Twas the first time he'd sounded normal since his sojourn and I thrilled to think that my plan was working. How lively those blue eyes, how twitched the lips!

"I command you to tell."

Caught between duty and Hell, I ventured a little further, for this might not hurt. "Well, have you—do you know Fat Giselle? Or maybe have heard of her?"

"Fat Giselle?" He caressed the name. "No, I believe not. Should I have?"

"Well, Dagobert said that everyone in France knew her. And then of course she knows all about you, even your thoughts."

"*Whaaat*?" He bent forward, now fascinated by my revelations. "Good God, I hope not. How does she know?"

"She is a—she has—certain powers," I said lamely.

A chill returned to his manner. "Is she by chance a spy for King Philip?"

"Oh no, not at all." Though I did recall her speaking to the other witches about some sort of protection they received from the King of France.

"She's more a sorceress, you might say, with second sight."

"A witch?"

Averting my eyes, I nodded. *Deus juva me*, I hoped I was not going too far, for 'twas not part of my plan to lose my soul in the process of saving the king.

"And that's how you know about the Angevin curse?"

Again I nodded.

"How my great-grandmother flew out of the window on a broomstick? Yes, well I don't want to demean Fat Griselda, but 'tis common knowledge."

"Giselle," I corrected him. "Anyway, that's how I know you're not Satan."

"I'm glad that my own private soothsayer thinks so well of me," he said dryly, "but I confess I'm surprised that the topic was raised. I mean, imagine, dear Alex, if I should say that your Scot had assured me that you were not the Archfiend from Hell."

For a moment I thought he might be mocking me, but no, 'twas much too serious.

"Well?" he prompted.

"She didn't exactly raise the topic," I mumbled.

"Ah yes, you said that you'd touched the Devil." He reached forth and caressed my cheek, making me quiver like one of the poplar leaves overhead. "Now that would convince me and only that, if you'll tell."

"If I do—Fat Giselle threatened that—"

He removed his hand. "Well, for a moment I hoped, but I see I was wrong. You're like all the others, love me when you want something—in your case, Wanthwaite—but otherwise care little for your king and his suffering."

Again a brief bitter smile twisted his lips, but was instantly replaced by an expression of such wanhope that it broke my heart.

Farewell, immortal soul. "'Twas because I wanted to meet with you that I went to that awful place on rue de Gratte-con."

"Gratte-con?" Now his lips soothly twitched and I hurried on.

"Aye, where Fat Giselle and Zizka live, for she said she could get me an audience with you. However, the thunder o'erwhelmed my knocks on the door and I fell backward into her chamber where a coven was in progress."

'Twas hard to get to the point, for the king insisted that I repeat every word the witches had said, how they'd looked and behaved. I'd forgot the exact invocations but remembered the gist.

"But all the time I sensed we were not alone because of the smell. There was incense and the sweet spice of my wine but something else, evil and pungent, but also familiar."

"You tantalize me. Was it Satan?"

"Aye, behind a black curtain. When they brought him forth, I recognized the stench at once for 'tis the same as most goats."

"Satan was a *goat*?"

"Aye." I was surprised at his surprise, for everyone knows that Satan often appears as a goat.

He bit his lip, his eyes sparkling eagerly. "Go on, I must hear more."

I felt my face heat and I stared at my feet as I talked, o'erwhelmed by fear and humiliation at my heretical act.

"We lined up on all fours to—"

I told of each witch's prayer, then came to myself.

"I gazed straight into the pit of Hell and thought I must swoon. 'Tis not easy to be wicked."

"No?" the king drawled.

"But I knew I must see you—must get Wanthwaite. So I closed my eyes, held my breath and kissed his fud."

There, 'twas done, I stared glumly at the heavens waiting for them to crack, and sure enough heard a dreadful thumping and ripping as the Devil bent to take me.

But he took the king instead!

Shocked out of my wits, I saw Richard tumble flat to the ground and go into a fit! *Benedicite*, what had I done? He choked, gave forth strangled cries, beat the ground with his fists, kicked his feet. I threw myself on him in terror.

"Oh stop, My Lord! Please! Should I get some wine?"

He continued to rant breathlessly, then rolled to his back, his face bright red, his eyes full of tears, two poplar leaves sticking to his wet lips, and he couldn't breathe.

"I'll get some water!" I scrambled to my feet, but a gesture stopped me.

He continued to pant, beat the ground, screwing his face till his eyes closed. Then I realized that he was *laughing*.

I settled back on my haunches and waited, amazed. He went on and on until I thought that it must be the ague after all, only a peculiar form I'd never seen before.

I shook his head gently to help him recover. "I don't think you heard me aright, Your Highness. I made obeisance to *Satan*."

At which he went into wilder paroxysms, so I could do naught but sit grimly and watch him curl, uncurl, clutch his sides, howl and collapse. Finally he gasped out a request that I tell the whole tale again, omitting nothing.

Stiffly, I tried to oblige though he interrupted constantly.

After a very long time, he was exhausted and had to stop. He then sat and hugged me tight.

"Alex, you've helped me more than you know. I'm convinced

that you really did see Satan and I know as fact that you've never kissed my fud, so I couldn't be Satan."

I froze like ice at such a dreadful statement and was glad he couldn't see my face.

"And I'm well on my way to health again, enough at least to feel a ravenous hunger. Are there any birds left?"

I watched him greedily devour three wizened robins and hoped I'd been right to make such a sacrifice. Certainly he did seem better, though he'd missed the point of my confession. Well, God works in mysterious ways, the priests say, and if I could be an instrument in his salvation even at the price of my own soul, I guessed that on the Heavenly ledgers 'twas a small price.

Inwardly I couldn't help worry about my mother and father, however. They wanted to meet me in Heaven, that I knew, and now we'd never see each other again. I was moved by a dreadful woe where my soul used to be. But at least I'd get them out of Purgatory, thanks to the king, and therefore 'twas important for their welfare as well as mine that he stay alive. As for my own descent into Hell, I would think of that later.

The king finished his repast, washed his face and prepared to leave. He lifted me to put me in my saddle, but held me a moment.

"Thank you, Alex, for your confidence. Laughter is both cheaper and less painful than exorcism, I believe, and probably more effective. Put a high fee on your services; you deserve it."

And he kissed me, all the fee I wanted ever.

We had come inland farther than I'd realized and now trotted through Mileto, then on a dusty path toward a mud-colored village, and beyond that in the distance the band of blue sea. Richard called to a passing shepherd and learned that the village was Gioja.

'Twas a mean affair when we entered it, inhabited by the same creeping dark insects Enoch and I had gotten to know all too well. They stared sullenly at the great king who might as well have worn a suit encrusted with diamonds for all he seemed to melt into the populace. So accustomed was he to adulation that he didn't notice how people dropped their tasks and gawked, nor that their eyes shot black hatred at his back. However, I knew—and felt fear. As we left on the far side, my breath, which I'd been holding, was exhaled in a great sigh. Suddenly the king drew rein.

"Alex, do you hear something?"

"Aye, a bird squawking."

"Not a bird, a falcon!"

I listened again; he was right. A falcon crying in terror as men and women yelled at it. The screams came from a collapsing stick hut on our right.

Richard's face paled with anger. "How dare such peasants keep a royal bird. Hold my horse and Penchant—you'll have a proper falcon yet."

He dismounted and bent low to enter the sagging door of the house. Inside, his deep voice took command for a short time, then there was a howl of outrage from the bird's owner, and other voices joined the fray. I couldn't understand the local argot at such a pitch but 'twas easy to grasp that the king was being cursed and defiled. His imperious commands rose as well, but he was outnumbered.

He backed out the door, a fine falcon clutched in his leather glove as his free hand tried to fend off the impotent blows from a miserable family of Griffons.

Then metal gleamed and they weren't so impotent.

"Give me my hawk, get back on your horse and ride fast, or you're dead on the count of three," a toothless wight said clearly enough in a patois of Latin.

In a flash, the king thrust the new falcon at me and pulled out his long flat sword. 'Twas the weapon he was famous for and no knight would face him so, but these people knew nothing of his fame or knighthood. Four other daggers flashed. I held all the falcons on their jesses and drew my father's dagger. For a moment we all froze.

The toothless Griffon made his move, struck like a snake, but not as fast as Richard cleaved his mighty sword. The Griffon ducked, the sword hit the wall and broke to its handle!

We all stared, shocked. Instantly I recalled his broken staff and wondered what the omen meant. The disarmed king threw away the useless fragment and picked up two rocks as the Griffons pressed close, grinning malevolently. Once, twice, the king fended their thrusts with his stones—then they drew blood from his arm. Worse, from behind, a host of vermin crept close, armed with knives, sticks, rocks, anything at hand. I slipped my dagger to the king, but 'twas not a good defensive weapon against a mob. Desperately Richard threw, feinted, felled two assailants as four more took their place.

Then a chilling unearthly cry from afar. A thundering cloud of dust descended upon the road whence we'd come and I saw a familiar gaveloc wave in the air.

Enoch!

He rode his horse straight through the mob as he screamed the highland war-cry and shot blades every which way. Then back again, rearing Firth to trample a few of the enemy as he stabbed and pierced, making such a racket that he seemed truly inhuman. Terrifying and deadly in equal parts, he drew the Griffons from Richard and forced them on the defensive. Instantly the king was mounted again and we all were away.

We galloped straight for the sea without looking back. Only when we reached a gray shingle did the king whirl and stop. We both stared at Enoch who grinned back, his white teeth startling against a face painted blue with woad.

"Oh, thank you, Enoch," I blubbered. "You saved our lives."

Almost at the same time, the king blazed, "How dare you follow me! After I'd given orders! Traitor!"

Before Enoch could answer, the king spurred his mount and ordered grimly, "Come."

The Scot and I glanced at each other, then rode after the tall green figure as he cantered in the shallow waters of the lapping sea. He went inland only once, to make a wide swath around the town of Bagnara, and continued along the shore away from our ships. Loping side by side, Enoch and I looked at one another occasionally but said nothing; the Scot's face under his bizarre paint was tense. Finally we reached a group of fishing boats dragged onto the sand and Richard dismounted to speak to two fishermen who were unloading their catch. They handed him some fish for a coin, then continued to talk as Enoch and I sat waiting. Richard walked back to us.

"Dismount at once," he ordered. "They've agreed to row us across the Far. We'll spend the night by the lighthouse there."

More and more alarmed by the king's strange acts, Enoch and I looked across a sea channel to a high rocky strand where a lighthouse perched. The king instructed the fishermen to get word to our ship when they returned but to hold our horses and hawks until morning. One stout fellow took the birds and bridles while the other one manned the oars of the heavy wooden dory. Enoch and I waded after the king, then sat ankle-deep in slimy water floating with dead bait as the first man pushed us off the sand. Listening to oars creak in rhythm to a sea chanty, we moved slowly through the blue-black waves. Except for his blowing hair, the king's figure was chiseled and still as death.

Beached at last on the stony spit, the king instructed the fishermen to return at dawn. The dory scraped away and Richard led us up the slope, doubling in a forked path against the steepness. Sharp rocks cut our feet cruelly and the wind howled through our tunics but the king kept his brisk pace. More than an hour passed before we stood in the deep purple shade of the Far's lighthouse, our skins now streaming with sweat from the exertion. At least we were protected from the wind here.

The king had maneuvered us when we stopped so that Enoch stood against the wall with me between them. Frightened already by the king's mood and now by his stance, I noted that his fingers rested lightly on my father's dagger. Enoch, too, was aware of danger and subtly shifted his weight so that the thwitel in his sock was close to his right hand.

Richard's control was more ominous than his usual rage. "Scot, you disobeyed me."

Enoch, too, was controlled, placating but not unctuous. "That I did not, Your Highness. You ordered that you were to hunt alone, and you did. And I obeyed your command given in Marseilles that I was never to let Alex out of my sight. I believe that you have not rescinded that order."

"Don't quote me against myself!" the king shouted in a sudden burst of fury. "We are not in a fancy disputation which can be won by twisting the argument! You spied on me, pure and simple!"

"I followed the boy; I didn't spy."

"Spied! *Spied*! Lurked in the woods, peeped, eavesdropped. Don't contradict! As for Marseilles, I ordered you to protect Alex against rogues in the streets."

"Aye," Enoch said evenly, "and there be rogues in these woods as well."

"God's feet! What am *I* for? When he's with me, *I* protect him!"

Enoch pressed his lips and remained silent, but all of us must have thought of the recent scene with the falcon. When it was apparent that the Scot wouldn't answer, Richard continued.

"The truth is that you have set yourself up as watchdog over Alex against me! I am your rogue in the woods!"

Wild though his accusation was, the bitter snap of his words made me queasy with fear.

"I was protecting him against danger," Enoch said finally, his French very accented, his forefinger twitching. "The natives here are unlawful."

"Against *me*! As if I were the danger! Answer me like a man, by God, or you'll answer otherwise."

Enoch's eyes shone blue in his sweating blue face.

"Only you can answer that," the Scot retorted, then added sarcastically, "Your Highness."

And the king's hand rose.

"No!" I screamed. I flung myself in front of the Scot. "Don't! Please don't! He's my brother—the only family I have!"

Two voices shouted together, "Alex, move!" and "Bairn, git gang!" and rough hands pulled me but I clung to the Scot's furry vest.

"You'll have to kill me too! I can't lose him again!"

I was dragged this way and that between them but burrowed into the Scot like a tick.

Finally I heard the king pant behind me, "Alex, I order you!"

I turned blurred eyes. "Please, Your Highness, if you believe that I saved you today, grant me the Scot's life in return! I gave up my hope of eternal life and any possibility of meeting my parents in Heaven, and I don't mind, but I can't give up my earthly family as well. Please!"

The king stared at me as if I were woodly. "You gave up *what*?"

I glanced at the Scot's stoic face, at the king again in warning. "You know, Fat Giselle and what I told you—my soul is forfeit."

Richard frowned, then to my great relief lowered his dagger. "I don't want to appear ungrateful for your sacrifice, Alex, though I hate for this villain to be the beneficiary."

"I'll defend myself!" Enoch assured him.

I pinched the back of his arm as hard as I could, digging my nails deep. "Thank you, Your Highness! You are the most gracious monarch alive!"

And I flung myself upon him, hugging his knees as I knelt. I could fairly feel the locked stares over my head, but the dagger didn't rise again.

"I'm letting you go now, but I do not consider the matter closed. Do you understand?" the king said icily.

"Perfectly," the Scot answered.

"Good." But his voice trembled with fury. "I will not forgive your suspicion concerning Alex. Take warning: I'll not be clement a second time."

But he was being clement now, which was all that mattered. I prayed that Enoch keep quiet, which he did. In the silence that followed, I wondered exactly what the argument was. Could the Scot soothly believe Richard would harm me? And why? I'd given the king no reason for anger.

Richard continued. "As for my order in Marseilles, it applies only when I am not with the boy. Do you understand?"

"Yes, Your Majesty."

The men still eyed each other, their faces full of words unspoken. Then Richard added, almost as an afterthought, "We thank you most graciously for coming to our aid this afternoon."

Enoch imitated his sarcastic cadence. "'Twas nothing, Your Grace, since you had the situation well in hand."

"I was betrayed by my sword," the king replied defensively.

"Yes, Your Highness, but your royal skill in battle would have prevailed. I merely followed the rules of chivalry by aiding my king." The Scot bowed.

Richard nodded shortly. "So be it. Now, if you will excuse me I will go examine the straits below. A runner informed me that my fleet has finally arrived, and this height gives me good vantage to see. Scot, cook these fish for us, for I am suddenly famished. Alex, you come with me."

He kicked the string of fish toward Enoch and strode away along

the lighthouse wall. Quickly I turned and saw that the woad
streamed like a waterfall down Enoch's face, but he managed to grin
weakly.

"Good work, wee brother. Ye showed yerself a true Mac-
Pherson."

And I ran after Richard's long shadow.

We stood on a small ledge at the top of a cliff which dropped to
the seawash a thousand feet or more. Gulls circled below us, their
faint screams piercing the silence. The lowering sun blazed through
a grate of horizontal clouds so the sea seemed liquid fire. The king
shaded his eyes, frowning.

"Do you see anything, Alex?"

"Smoke, I think, in two places, there and there."

"Volcanoes, Stromboli and Mount Etna, for that's Sicily to our
right. But I meant on the water. Wait—I think—God's feet, there
they are! Look you, boy, two hundred strong, Saladin's defeat sailing below us!"

I grabbed him in alarm as he leaned forward, then squinted to
see miniature ships dotting the straits, a fairy fleet, I trowe. Now
the king began to jangle excitedly as if his former melancholy, his
near brush with death and recent choler had not happened. I marveled once again at his swift shifts of humor and tried to shift my
own responses, with less success for I was still trembling inwardly
at that raised dagger. Would he actually have murdered Enoch? He
would have *tried*, that I believed, but 'twould not have been easy.
Again I shuddered as I thought what might have resulted, one or the
other dead or both wounded—and the aftermath. Too awful to
conjure.

Finally the king's monologue was stopped when we heard Enoch
bellow behind us, "Dinner!" By now radiant smiles played on
Richard's face and he could hardly tear himself away from the
happy scene before him. As we rounded the corner of the lighthouse, however, he paused and his expression became grave again.

"Wait."

I looked up, apprehensive at his tone.

"I apologize that I was slow to understand why you were so
fearful to confess today. 'Twas not a matter for levity, was it?"

Mortified, I dropped my head. "Fat Giselle made me swear to

Satan that I'd lose my immortal soul if I told."

"I see."

Now what I'd dreaded was surely coming; no good Christian would knowingly associate with the Antichrist.

I felt his hand cup my chin, was forced to look into his face.

"But you were willing to sacrifice yourself in order to cure me of my family curse?"

"To prove it couldn't be true," I corrected him.

For once he seemed not to wear a mask and those blue-gray eyes would have penetrated to my very soul if I'd still possessed it.

"So you traded eternal life for my peace of mind."

"Yes, Your Highness."

"To relieve me of my curse." His opaque eyes shifted restlessly over the horizon. "Are you sure I'm worth your sacrifice?"

I responded eagerly, "Of course. You're worth anything."

His brooding eyes fastened on me again. "You know, there's a second curse on our family, namely that none of us can take pleasure in children."

"Well, I'm not . . . that is, that must apply to your own children."

"Indeed." He gave forth a harsh mirthless laugh. "Ask my father, wherever he is. What would you think, Alex, if I confessed to you as you did to me today that I, too, have traded my immortal soul for damnation?"

I stared at him, expecting that he must have kisssed Satan in spite of his protestations earlier.

"For I murdered my own father."

The words swung around us like bodies on a hanging tree. In vain I sought some sign of a jape, but he was deadly serious.

"Yes, that takes your wind, I can see. Frankly it takes mine as well, though I have no regrets. It was his life or mine, and he ran to the point. Nevertheless . . ." He leaned against the wall, his face sickly. "Nevertheless, you can understand my lack of enthusiasm for begetting heirs."

All words that came to my lips were quickly swallowed as fatuous in the face of this monstrous confession. I thought of my own father, how I had loved him. Had the king once felt so for King Henry? When and why had he changed?

The sunset cast a pink glow over the king's figure, which seemed carved into the wall; his hair blew straight back. Despite his words, his thoughts were far away in time, whether past or future I couldn't tell. After a long period, he noticed me again and pulled me against him, so that we both gazed out to sea, and he ran his hand through my hair.

"What do you say, Alex? If I permit myself to love you, will you turn on me one day?"

"Never, My Lord, never!"

"So you say now," he commented bitterly.

I turned around, staying close to his body so I wouldn't fall into the sea below. "I mean it."

He slid down and crouched at my level, fastened his strong arms around my back.

"Suppose I refuse to give you Wanthwaite." He smiled at my reaction. "You see?"

But how could he withhold Wanthwaite? Why would he want to? Then I realized he was simply testing me.

"I don't love you because you can restore my home, Your Highness."

He continued to stroke my hair, tried to keep it from blowing in my eyes. "No? Perhaps not, but a king can never be sure."

Suddenly I felt a flood of sympathy, for wasn't this just what I hated about being an heiress? Would no one ever love me for myself and only myself? Enoch—who befriended me with ulterior motive.

"I'm sure, Your Highness," I said with real conviction this time. "You—you are . . . I mean I would never love King Philip if he could give me a thousand Wanthwaites."

He laughed and put his forehead against mine. "Irresistible argument. You are now the only person whom I love—you and my mother."

But I was filled with apprehension again. He might worry about my fealty, but I worried about whether he would love me if he knew I were a girl. It seemed he might be giving his affection to a child who'd already betrayed him.

"What troubles you?" he asked, his hand sliding to my chin.

"I'll never turn on you," I repeated, "but . . ."

"Go on. Don't be afraid. But what?"

"Well, you don't know me . . . I mean, you learned only today that I have no soul. I may have other lacks—just as serious."

He stood again and pulled me up with him, so he held me tightly in his arms.

"I'm glad you mentioned character . . . deficiencies. I, too, have major sins."

"Not like mine!"

"Hush, you don't know." He was depressed. And sad. "You learned that I killed my father. There are other things . . ."

I looked deeply into his gray-blue eyes, layered in depth after depth like the sea, the deepest I'd looked into anyone's eyes since my mother's.

"I don't care," I said.

"Neither do I." He smiled. "In any case, love is always an act of faith. Give me your oath of fealty, Alex."

We swore to each other to be faithful, to love each other forever. We were not brothers—I know not what we were—and we didn't exchange blood. But we sealed our vows with a kiss, sweet and lingering. When we parted, both of us had glistening eyes.

"I thought you'd fallen into the sea," Enoch grucched as he came around the corner.

Richard put me down, but kept his arm around me as we walked back to the fire.

20

 S WE ARE SEEN, SO ARE WE ESTEEMED."
Richard's words rippled through the fleet down to the meanest ranks. Therefore were we the most splendid armada assembled since the world began as we sailed the boiling waves across the Straits of the Far into Messina. Painted sails, poops bursting with music, glittering shields, festooned pikes and glory everywhere! Leading this splendor was Richard in royal red, riding his crimson castle with spangled cape flying, Apollo dropped from the sky. I stood on the deck of his galley the *Trenchemer*, gazing up proudly, for this was *my*

doing, my reward for selling my soul, and I hardly knew whether to thank Satan or God.

"Do you see King Tancred? Or Philip?" the king called from his perch down to the Earl of Leicester.

The earl peered at the approaching shore and shouted back, "No, My Liege, not on the beach. Could they be inside the city gate?"

We all lined the rail to search along the strand for royal insignia. In spite of my pleasure in the king's health, I chilled at this close view of Messina. A snowy-white city spilling down a steep scarp, backed by tiers of purple-blue mountains in the shadow of the forbidding Mount Etna. A high wall enclosed the city, and the space between the wall and the sea was crowded with men shouting and waving.

"Are those our own Crusaders?" Richard called to Lord Robert again. I noticed that the king's cheek now twitched with his telltale muscle.

"I believe so, My Liege. They wear our crosses."

The king was openly exasperated. "But why are there no Messhinites? No royal welcome?"

There was no answer.

"I see a welcoming party," I whispered to Enoch. "Look you, bishops with gold crosses, a red carpet, horses."

"Landed by Richard this marnin' so he'd mak a good show when he rode in the streets. There be our own Bishop of Evreux—see?"

The oarsmen turned us alongside the pier, the plank was lowered, fanfare blared forth. King Richard strode down, waving and smiling to hysterical cheers and the *Te Deum* as tapers were lit, the whole thing staged by Ambroise; we were performing for ourselves. Only the Crusaders on the beach were spontaneous and they were woodly with joy, for they were also part of Richard's army, common men who'd marched from Marseilles to await us here.

"King Richard, save us!"

"Food, for God's sake, give us food!"

Enoch frowned at their cries as we took our places at the back of the king's household, and he pointed out that the king's captains were protecting us from the rabble much as they had in Tours. We began to move forward.

"In Jesus' name, mercy! Give me bread!"

A scarecrow grabbed Thistle's bridle and Enoch whipped him off.

"Get to the other side of me, bairn." And he raised his gaveloc.

Perplexed and frightened, I peered around the Scot to watch this frenzied mob. English and Norman they might be, but they were desperate enough to kill. Then I saw two other wights, truly scarecrows in long black tunics and strange square hats, curly black beards falling almost to their knees. They, too, shouted, made obscene gestures with their fingers, pulled down their lower eyelids.

"Dirty dogs! Put *that* in your mother's swinehole!"

"We want no filthy rats here! Go back to your sewer!"

"Be those Messhinites?" I asked Enoch. I knew this was the name applied to inhabitants of Messina.

"Aye, that they be," he said grimly, "but they're also Greek Christians, that is, Griffons from the Byzantine Church. Think what the other Messhinites mun be like, the Arabs and Jews."

As we progressed, more and more of these hideous Griffons joined with the mob till 'twas difficult to go forward. Then we came to a dead stop.

Mercadier and Algais thundered back, shouting orders. "Make a phalanx! Wall your horses! Two lines, and keep the center clear! *Move!*"

Enoch pulled Thistle's muzzle against Firth's haunch; everyone else did the same with their horses till we formed two living walls protecting an aisle in the center. To my astonishment, King Richard soon high-paced down the opening, his face a crimson profile of fury, then the clergy and great lords.

"Follow the king!" Louvart shouted.

And our lines doubled to the center as we trotted rapidly back to our ships.

King Richard was already in his mail, long shield with its three lions in hand, sword, mace and flail beside him. The Bishop of Evreux rang a bell for silence; the king spoke from his forecastle.

"We've been refused entry into Messina by order of the Sicilian king, a usurper called Tancred, and King Philip of France. Our Crusaders who arrived before us have lived outside the walls without food or drink while the French grow fat inside. My sister"—for the first time, his voice shook with rage—"Dowager Queen Joanna of Sicily, is held like a common prisoner in Palermo, her dowry stolen by these traitorous kings. I've spoken with six lords who will accompany me with their knights. The rest of you will stay here on board ship until I return. *In the name of St. George!*"

He raised his fist to a great cheer! Everyone scrambled to make ready.

"Are they going to fight?" I asked, my voice trembling with fear.

"Nay," Enoch replied, "they're gang to kick the Morris dance."

I'd never seen a battle, but I'd seen the results and felt sick. The king was almost ready, his great white horse saddled and draped in mail. I watched him ride away from Messina, prayed he'd turn and wave, but he didn't. Then I sat on the silent deck: my father, turning thrice, speaking to his steward, riding through Wanthwaite's gates.

Two interminable days later the triumphant Richard returned, and this time he waved as he rode past the *Trenchemer* on his way into Messina, for he'd gotten entry for all of us. Beside him, riding cross-saddle, her gown trailing the ground, was the most beautiful woman I'd ever seen, Queen Joanna. She, too, waved imperiously, smiled Richard's own radiant smile, then followed her brother. Quickly we all prepared once again to ride into Messina, but this time there was no effort at pomp. If we were esteemed, 'twas because of Richard's sharp sword.

KING RICHARD'S WRATH was directed at King Philip. He sent the French monarch a command to attend him the following afternoon. Sir Gilbert was forced to use me as page for the occasion, as Sir Eduard was ill from the water.

When I arrived in the chamber where Richard lived, Gilbert greeted me with eyes cold as river ice.

"I hope you have no lice in your hair," he sneered with his customary courtesy. "Bedding with beasts has made you filthy."

I had just laundered my clothing. "I have no lice," I replied, "having washed my hair with lemon not one hour ago. However, I can understand your concern. After all, my hair is very thick. 'Tis a pity that yours grows thin on top."

"A sign of my powers in other ways, I assure you." But I'd hit my mark—his face grew red. "You will pull these oak trestles to the center of the room while I go downstairs for cakes."

And he won the gambit, for the oak trestles were too heavy for two strong men. I had to go seek porters to help, but by the time Sir Gilbert returned, I was draping the linens and arranging goblets.

"Get me a tray—no, idiot, the silver one." He put his hands on his hips. "Now I'm going to give you just one instruction, only one. And I hope you can muster sufficient wit to follow it."

From his portentous tone, I thought I would be ordered to serve while hanging from the ceiling.

"You will serve the French, and only the French, which means King Philip, for I believe he comes alone. Do you understand?"

"King Philip, yes. I suppose if there are twenty English in attendance, I'm to let them expire of thirst."

"The English are my concern. I assure you, none will expire, but if they do 'twill be from some malady caught before they came here. Quiet, now—the king." He turned a flushed deferential face to the door.

". . . a Judas to our cause," came Richard's voice from below, and my heart speeded. This was the closest I'd been to the king since our hunt.

His footsteps shook the walls as he climbed upward; then he swept in with his sister Joanna.

"*Benedicite*, Richard, no one told me you were so like our father," she said in a deep throaty voice.

Her sandalwood mixed with his sweet woodruff in a powerful royal scent, and her train made a swath as she turned to help herself to one of our cakes. She was an uncanny double of her brother— tall, golden-haired, confident and faintly mocking.

"What mean you?" he shouted. "I'm nothing like Henry!"

"No?" Her brows shot up. "Not in appearance, perhaps, where you bear Eleanor's stamp, but the Angevin temper?"

"Blast the Angevin temper! Are you telling me I should permit insults from a reptilian hunchback and a French ferret? Damned if I will, and if that's like Henry I put my foot in the boot."

The queen smiled and stroked his angry face. "No offense, dear brother. The Angevin temper is a useful flare when all is darkness, but I miss the beguiling pretty boy I left in Poitiers. Soft luminous eyes, sweetly arched lips, an angelic disposition, the same but not the same. None of Henry's crude choler then, but perhaps the seed lay dormant."

"We must flower or wither," the king agreed dryly.

"Unfortunately." She nodded. "Who would have dreamed then that the next time we met I would be the disinherited widow of a whoremonger king. I was only a bride of twelve, and you were nineteen."

Nineteen! And I was now twelve. . . .

"You have changed more than I have, Joanna," the king said, smiling back at her. "You are a beautiful woman and a queen. Yet methinks you still behave like a child."

Instantly her face twisted in Angevin wrath, again exactly like his, and her voice rasped. "You dare to speak to me so? When I've suffered disinheritance, imprisonment and worse?"

The king continued to smile. "Suffered? Or permitted? How could you allow that freakish Tancred to steal your gold? Are you so naive that you do not make proper arrangements for a treasure?"

She whirled and struck our trestle with her palm. "Give me wine."

I was closest and dared not disobey. I poured wine into a silver goblet and offered it to her trembling hand.

"I believe," she said with controlled sarcasm to her brother, "that you must look to yourself if you would fix blame for the loss of my gold. If you had not tarried on your journey, had not permitted the King of France to arrive before you, I might have been a free woman and kept my gold as well."

Richard's face was now grim. "You confirm what I suspected. That French traitor! Conspiring with Tancred to thwart the Crusade. And stealing! By God, I'll pound his balls to powder! My word, Joan. This is Richard speaking."

He put his arms around her and she returned his embrace.

"I believe I like you, brother."

He gazed into her eyes like a lover. "If the times didn't dictate otherwise . . ."

Bitter bile shriveled my tongue as I watched this tender scene between brother and sister, and I hated Joanna despite her charms. She had no right to stroke and kiss the king in that manner when he was her brother. No wonder the Church is so strict toward consanguinity when such women be abroad. And why hadn't Richard looked at me? Was he so dazzled by this enticing sister that he'd forgot what he'd said on the Far? He was going to defy his family's curse about pleasure in children, a mysterious curse, but I understood that he loved me, aye, more than he cared for this *sister*.

Voices below signaled the arrival of the French company and Richard stepped back, then came to our trestle for a quick swallow of wine. Sir Gilbert handed him his goblet, and when the king smiled briefly at me, I forgave all. He took his place beside Queen Joanna.

King Philip entered the salle alone and without ceremony, tossing a comment to an unseen functionary in the hall. As I had noted in Vézelay, he was wiry in build, about ten years younger than Richard. I now recognized in his light splenetic voice and royal bearing the same arrogance that Richard carried: both men were kings to the tips of their long pointed boots. I also realized that whatever Philip lacked in grace or size, he made up with an incisive intelligence. There was an assurance in the set of his lips, a penetrating grasp in his steady eyes—albeit one was milky—a positive cadence in his speech.

King Richard knelt to make obeisance.

"Rise, brother, and tell me your . . ."

His voice faltered and Richard looked up, puzzled. King Philip was gazing at Joanna. There was a long silence and the English king slowly rose again. What had happened? Did the French king suffer from some strange malady such as Richard had?

No, the cause of his paralysis was the beauteous queen. I too studied her, much alarmed. She must be a witch, though she looked nothing like Fat Giselle, and I had good reason to be terrified of witches. I peered at her hands to see if she held an amulet, at her lips to see if she breathed out a spell, but there was nothing.

"I would like . . . who are you . . . I want . . ." Philip gasped unintelligibly, his face waxy pale.

Richard's brows shot up and he lifted his sister's delicate hand for presentation. "I would like to present our Liege Lord, Philip, King of France. Philip, this is my sister, the dowager Queen of Sicily."

Philip leaned to the hand rapturously as brother and sister exchanged meaningful looks over his head, and I realized I had just witnessed a man falling in love. 'Twas exactly as the verses and songs described: Cupid had shot a bolt through his eye and enchanted him forthwith. Yet Joanna must be credited with the miracle as well. Again I wondered what she had done and studied her. Was it something I might learn?

The French king stood, stammered out a few ecstatic syllables.

"We are delighted," Richard answered when he paused. "This is the sort of greeting we had expected when we arrived."

King Philip reluctantly turned from Joanna to her brother, and both his expression and words changed to their original coldness.

"We could hardly welcome an invasion, Richard. You have entered Messina like an occupying force. Your men raid, rob and worse. Just before I came, I was told of a poor woman called Emma who was raped by your knights this morning in full view of a dozen witnesses."

Richard pursed grim lips. "Not knights, but hungry foot soldiers. Nor did they rape. They demanded the bread which they had just bought. Emma and her brothers refused to give it to them. My men are hungry, Philip."

"Yes, so King Tancred understands," Philip replied acidly. "Hungry for gold."

Richard's skin blotched as it had in Marseilles. "If you refer to Joanna's gold, Philip, we are hungry for justice. That gold was her wedding dower."

Joanna bit her lower lip and entered the fray. "I beg you, My Liege, to return my dower. Otherwise, I may not wed again."

Philip lapsed into his former state.

"You will wed again, I assure you. Your beauty, grace, utter enchantment . . . You are . . . I myself would . . ."

Richard's face became speculative.

"My sister is indeed a wondrous queen. Nevertheless, the point remains: give her her gold."

Joanna shot him a warning look which he seemed not to heed.

"By depriving her, you deprive all of us. The queen has pledged her dower to me for our journey."

"What, pledged?" Joanna cried in open amazement.

"For *you*?" Philip dropped the queen's hand.

Even I was dumbfounded. Richard might be a great warrior-king, but he was no diplomat. Why hadn't he kept his plans for the gold a secret? I would never tell Enoch what I really intended.

Philip's bedazzled smile had turned to a grimace. "In which case, I too shall receive half her dowry, as we agreed in Vézelay. Share and share alike."

"Of plunder," Richard retorted wrathfully. "I'll see you in Hell before I let you touch one denier of our gold."

Our gold! *Benedicite*, Richard was no better than Enoch. A pox on all brothers and their greed. To take *all* of Joanna's dowry and fight over it with the French king, as if she didn't deserve a coin. I adored the king, aye, and he was like my own father, and I was jealous of Joanna; yet she was a woman and so was I!

"Richard, I did not . . ." Joanna blazed, but he stopped her with a peremptory hand. His Angevin temper had now taken over.

"I wrote to Pope Clement," he continued to Philip, "and reported that you had broken fealty here in Messina. I demanded your excommunication."

"I wrote a similar letter from Vézelay," Philip fired back, "demanding *your* excommunication. You have clearly broken your holy pledge to wed my sister Alais."

Richard bared his teeth in a travesty of a smile. "Did you also tell him *why* I broke my promise?"

Enthralled by this hint of a dark secret, I eagerly awaited King Philip's reply. I waited in vain. He pressed his lips like white worms under water, and Richard had won.

But Queen Joanna wasn't finished. She placed her hand on Philip's arm. "Enough of threats and pleadings. My Lord, I trust your honor and know you will not fail me."

He managed to keep his voice steady in reply. "My Lady Queen, by my royal office which I hold with God's will, I promise that your dower shall be delivered forthwith. *Teste me ipso*."

She rewarded him with a long significant smile, and the atmosphere became less charged.

Richard waved a hand in our direction. "Sir Gilbert, Alex, wine and refreshments if you please."

As we served, they spoke of other things, mostly the prevailing winds, for King Philip was most eager to sail to Acre in the Holy Land. I hovered close to the queen, sniffing her sweet sandalwood. I could easily see why King Philip had been so smitten, and Richard too, *Deus juva me*. In a short time, the French king begged to be excused and took his leave, warmly from the queen, hardly at all from her brother.

"Holy St. Martin," Joanna gasped when he'd left. "Eleanor would have been proud of me tonight. In order to *produce*, try to *induce*; if that fails, *seduce*. Such did I learn at the queen's knee. Here, boy, refresh me."

I took the proffered cup, glancing at Sir Gilbert, and handed wine to the queen.

"Why, what a pretty imp," she remarked, gazing on me. "But so young. Hardly weaned, I'd say. How old are you, lad?"

I always had to think. "Nine, Your Highness."

"A babe. Richard, best get this bait out of Messina before the sharks feed. He's the kind of tender morsel that starts a riot in this city."

The king ruffled my hair. "I've made it my special task to guard young Alex myself."

"Oh?" Her brows shot up in a perfect parody of the king's. "Fortunate Alex."

But he was already thinking of other things.

"The sweet opiate of your person appears more effective than my threats with Philip. What say you to ruling France?"

Joanna rolled her wine in her cup and smiled wickedly.

"I'll say aye if you will. A double wedding, I with Philip, you with Alais."

"Joanna, I mean it. What say you to Philip? He'll make you the most powerful woman in Europe."

I held my breath; 'twas the first time I'd actually witnessed the dispensation of a royal lady.

"Thank you for such unexpected largesse, but I think not. 'Tis not my pleasure to spread my legs for a pasty Cyclops to secure your Vexin. Especially when you can pump sweet Alais at the same well."

"Who speaks of pleasure, Joan? Our aim is security along the Norman border, for which the Vexin is essential."

Her mouth tightened and her words came with asperity, recalling Sister Petronilla to my ear. "Your aim, not mine, for I care nothing for that swampy plain. When I was twelve, my father sent me to rule William's harem in Palermo; I went, because a king held my dower. Now I'm older and have my own dowry and I'll decide."

"Your confidence outrides your horse," drawled Richard. "'Twill be my gold."

Joanna smiled broadly and clasped her hands behind her brother's neck, then leaned backward to gaze on him. "But Richard is not Henry and will give me what is my due. Let's strike a bargain: you may have my gold and more, *as a loan*; in return, you'll get me dispensation to accompany you on your Crusade; reimburse me in full when we return to Europe; then find me a lusty stud to fill my womb. What say you?"

"God's balls!" Richard stamped a foot and laughed. "You are my own sweet sister. You offer me a headache in exchange for the world, yet deflate argument by implying that to do else would be like Henry. Well, 'tis done. Let's to Jerusalem, Joan!"

And she leaped to his waiting arms.

With that embrace I was back to my first emotion: jealousy which twisted my heart to a lemon peel. I hated the odious forward queen, didn't want her on our Crusade. Hadn't Richard said that no women were permitted? He might be a great king but tonight he'd proved himself a mere man as well. *Produce, induce, seduce!* How clever she was to disarm her victim by showing her claws, for she'd conquered Richard as surely as she'd conquered Philip. And unwittingly taught me a lesson as well, though I knew not how I might apply it.

They parted finally, smiled with nauseating tenderness and left without a backward glance. No sooner was the door closed than I felt a sting across my cheek and almost fell with the blow!

"How dare you strike me!" I screamed at Sir Gilbert and would have hit him back except that he held my arms.

"You served the English queen!" he panted. "After I told you to serve only the French!"

"She asked me, you fool! I'm going to tell the king that you hit me! He'll have you punished, see if he doesn't."

He let go of my arms. "You do that, and I'll tell the king what I know about *you*."

Stricken, I searched his yellow eyes for a clue and suddenly remembered how he'd clutched my crotch in Vézelay. *He must know that I was a girl.* What else could it be? I ran from the room.

"His poison be venal, bairn. Did ye knaw that Sir Eduard just departed fer England?" Enoch said later when I'd related the scene.

"No! Why?"

"I canna tell ye the particulars, but this Sir Gilbert kapes pages coming and going lak sinners to the priest. The king's household be Gilbert's ane private court."

"Do you think I should tell the king?"

Enoch knotted his brow. "Certes ye shouldna be whipping boy to the king's slubberdegullian, but ye must time yer complaint. Fram what ye said, the king has mighty problems here in Messina." He thought further. "Wait till ye have better opportunity, that's my advice."

21

 HREE DAYS LATER QUEEN JOANNA AND HER train left our palace to live in the Abbey of Bagnara which Richard had taken for her. At first I was relieved to have her away from the king but soon suffered from the same ennui as every Crusader in Messina, for we were all prisoners in this hostile territory. Enoch reported near mutiny in Richard's ranks.

"Sum say the king be under a sorcerer's spell cast by the Antichrist and canna move. Most of the lot sold all they had to crusade and they dinna keer to spend it wintering in this pissmar."

"It's not winter yet."

"Aye, on the sea 'tis winter. The next fair breezes come in March. That's as soon as we can sail."

I, too, was impatient and nervous. Other Crusaders might be spending money, but I was spending something much more precious: time. For me, getting older each day promised disaster. I examined my body anxiously several times from morning to night, terrified if I found an insect bite. How could I be sure? It could be unwanted hair coming on, or—worse—a bulge.

Fortunately the king was mindful of his promise to govern my education and I attended classes in chivalry and courtesy given alternately by Sir William de Courcy and Sir Jordan de Homez, and Sir Roger taught me such arts as carving meat with my left thumb against the haunch, but time hung heavy.

Therefore I near swooned with delight one day in late autumn when Sir Roger summoned me to accompany the king on a rare sojourn into the countryside to exercise his horses. Enoch went too to watch the prize destriers, but he rode separately from us. There were several lords, however: our instructors in courtesy plus Wigain de Cherbourg, Geoffrey Rancon, Aymeri Torel and others I couldn't name. I was astonished that King Philip's most valued lord, William des Barres, also joined us. He was a dashing nobleman, almost as tall as the king and garbed in dazzling raiment of peacock blue. He smiled affably but everyone was uneasy to have King Philip's best friend in our midst, almost as if he were a spy.

Copper-green hillsides rose above the sedgy marshes and the citrus was tinged with gold from the low autumn sun. Our Roman path lay under the purple shadow of Mount Etna so that we felt winter's nip, though Enoch said there would be no snow. The jingle of the bridle bells, the friendly rumble of men's voices and the very fact we were no longer within Messina's hostile walls put everyone in festive mood.

After the king had gifted me with his radiant smile, he rode with his peers and I was left to listen and enjoy by myself. We didn't pause until Haute Tierce when we reached a small level plain by a

Greek amphitheater, apparently our destination. I served the king while the others ate whatever they had carried with them. There was easy jangling and japing as the knights lounged on the seared grass. Then, after a pleasant rest, one noticed a growth of canes behind a column.

"Look you," he called. "Canes such as we used to joust with when boys. What say you to a game?"

Some demurred, still too sluggish from their food, but others mounted and began a leisurely imitation of tilting spears. Then the French William des Barres spoke to the king.

"We hear, Your Highness, that you have a boy you're grooming for your court. Has he yet been trained with the quintain?"

The king glanced in my direction and smiled. "He's too young."

"I began when I was only eight," des Barres insisted. "What say you that I fashion the quintain and you instruct your young charge what he should do? 'Twill be a useful and pleasant diversion."

Richard sensed a note of challenge and bowed to the French lord.

"Come, Alex, let me speak with you."

So I walked slowly to the king who smiled reassuringly and described the technique of placing the lance in an adversary's chest-spoon.

"'Tis a formidable weapon, much too heavy and long for you to handle, but we'll fashion a light facsimile of cane, and the quintain is simply a pole dressed as a man, not a moving target and in no way dangerous. The worst that can happen is that you'll miss. Are you ready?"

"Aye, Your Highness," I said, my eyes swimming with pleasure at his attention.

As Richard carved the cane, he also talked: the lance was used principally in tournaments, for in actual battle it was good only for a single thrust, then must be replaced by the sword or mace. Of course the Saracens fought in a different manner but that need not concern me. The lance could be eighteen feet long, was made of oak and steel and had to be manipulated by one arm only. In the spurt toward the enemy, 'twas necessary to hold it against the body for balance, then at the last minute to raise it and thrust it toward the chest, by no means using one's own body as ballast as that would be suicide. The impact of the strike was taken in the stirrups, so I should throw my feet forward and upward with my knees straight. Therefore the skill was in speed, aim, free thrust—all to be coordinated as one act.

The lords remembered their own training and lined up to urge me on in my first ride. Though the lance was only cane, 'twas awkward to an extreme and shook in my grasp. I pulled Thistle behind my line, placed the cane against my side, took aim against the quintain now dressed as a "man" with a stick "arm" to which a broadsword had been tied for verisimilitude.

"Go!" called the king.

I knew at once that I wouldn't succeed: my start was tentative, my gait wrong. I didn't even bother thrusting but turned back to try again. Now I was excited and wanted desperately to please King Richard.

"Go!" he called.

This time 'twas right. The wind whistled steady in my ears, the lance rose like a falcon and hit. I was thrilled at the contact, right in the chest!

"I did it!" I shouted.

Then was struck myself from the rear as the world went black! I lay on the ground face-down and wondered dazedly what had gone wrong. I was still conscious but too stunned and breathless to speak.

"God's feet, what happened?"

"Air ye hurt, bairn?"

Hands tried to lift me and I screamed in agony.

"*Don't touch me!*"

This time I did swoon, though only for a moment. Then feebly I beat away the hands that were trying to tug down my baggy pants.

"No, no, don't," I wept.

And they stopped.

"He's been struck by a broadsword on his lower back!" the king cried. "Let me see that quintain. Who put it on a swivel?"

In a great distance, I heard a mix of laughter and denial.

"It was the accepted method where I was trained," William des Barres's voice claimed. "If you'd warned him, it could not have happened."

"Because I thought you *chivalrous*, such a warning never occurred to me," the king answered hotly.

Des Barres became offended. "Be careful, Your Highness. I cannot accept a slur to my chivalry."

"You are a disgrace to chivalry and henceforth are barred from our Crusade! I should have known when you broke the pledge of parole in Aquitaine last year, and now a second offense. To arms!"

Still lying on my stomach, I saw that Richard and des Barres now both held canes which they were using as spears, but in deadly earnest. The lords' faces were pale and worried as they saw Richard thrust, then thrust again with such accuracy that des Barres had to drop his cane and cling to his horse's neck. The king loosened his own saddle with his blows and quickly jumped upon another steed to continue the fight. 'Twas the Angevin temper in action and for the first time I was convinced that he was from the Devil after all. His face was fixed in madness which must end in death, his own or the Frenchman's. Finally the other lords tried to intervene, the Earl of Leicester to the point of grabbing the royal reins. Richard whipped him savagely and screamed, "Leave me to deal with him alone!"

At last William des Barres understood the depth of his wrath and rowled his spurs in a fast retreat!

"Get thee hence!" the king shouted after him. "And take care that I see you no more! From this time I am enemy to you and yours forever!"

A profound silence fell upon our company, only that I thought I heard an ancient wailing howl through the arena from the old gods.

'Twas the last sound I heard clearly until we were in Messina where I was waked by my own voice screaming. I was in dreadful pain but that wasn't the reason I cried: I didn't want anyone to remove my clothes.

It started with Enoch who tried—gently—to pull down my braies and look at my buttocks. He retreated when I threatened to kill him if he touched me. However, I agreed to piss into a cup he left by my bedside.

Then came King Richard. He knelt on the floor so that his face was level with mine where I lay on my stomach on a bench.

"Alex, you must believe me, this injury will be avenged if it's the last thing I do."

I believed him.

"The Scot says you have no blood in your urine, so I know you'll recover soon. Nevertheless, I'll send my own physician, Orlando, to examine you.

"Alex?" I felt his hand on my cheek. "I'm sorry that you have to suffer on my behalf."

"Your behalf—?"

"By being my Achilles heel."

"I don't understand—Achilles."

"Achilles was a great warrior who was dipped in water so he couldn't be harmed, but the god held him by his heel. Therefore his enemies attacked him on his vulnerable heel and eventually killed him."

I gazed uncomprehending, vaguely insulted to be called a part of a foot even if 'twas Richard's foot.

He saw my puzzlement. "You are my heel because I care for you, and whoever harms you harms me as well."

Warmth flooded through my tortured body. Then his face came close, his lips brushed mine, and he left. The Scot replaced him.

"*Quhat hermis ye hermis me as weil*! Quhat schitten bullar, say I! Ye tal me quick and ye tal me plain what the king meant."

"He feels grateful because I saved his life!" I shouted, then groaned at the pain and grunted out the rest. "'Tis more than you feel though I saved your life as well!"

"*Ye* saved the king? *Ye* saved me? 'Twas my burly brand that saved the twa of ye yif I recall!"

"Aye, but you spied on us and you know it! I saved you by weeping and pleading or you'd be dead!"

His eyes narrowed to blue slits. "Why would I spy on ye?"

"You tell *me* quick and plain. I think you're afraid the king will give me another writ. Besides, you're jealous."

"Jalous? Jalous? Have *I* e'er told ye to pour my nappy? Or serve my farls?"

"Enoch, please, not now," I implored. "If that pisspot Orlando touches me I'll die and it will all be your fault! Tell him he's not to come near."

The Scot's broad furry face bent close. "Ye carry yer woodly modesty too far. 'Tis nocht seemly to be so ashamed of yer terse; ye mun learn to live with yer deformity and not advertise it to the world. After all, there be many a wight canna crack boast about the inchwarms ridin' their stones, but what of that? Such shame be a form of vanity."

"You don't understand!" I bawled hysterically. "My terse be longer than yours for all I'm a wee boy. But I cannot disturb the relics I carry between my legs on fear of death!"

"Relics, be they! Waesucks, Alex, ye're worse touched than I thought. All men be summit bewitched by their own balls but donna call them haly relics!"

My face broke into earnest sweat for at that moment I honestly believed what I was saying. "My father—I have relics of my father and mother in a special belt I made to carry them with me always. Vials of blood, scrolls, hair and much more. The last thing my father said before he died was that if I disturbed them for any reason, he and my mother would go straight to Hell and I would soon join them there. Here, feel for yourself."

I led his hand to my inner thigh and placed his palm across my quilted pad.

His eyes misted with sympathy. "Aye, bairn, I ken yer problem. A dying man's words be the same as a curse. Try to sleep now and I'll head off Orlando."

He left; I collapsed.

He woke me and 'twas already dark. "'Tis settled, bairn. I hae talked wi' King Richard hisself and convinced him that I were physician enow. And here's the best of all: he's sending us to Bagnara whar we'll be safe with Queen Joanna. We can go abroad thar when we wist and I'll find some Arab Infidel to learn us his tongue in case we're captured. What say ye now?"

I smiled weakly and said naught. Part of me was much relieved to be leaving this prison-palace crawling with jealous churls; the other, my faithful liver, quivered and chilled at the thought of being away from Richard.

THE MEAN JAPE of the quintain was not the only way des Barres had insulted the king: Richard brooded over his taunted omissions in my education. Therefore less than a week after we were established in Bagnara the king arrived with a young knight called Sir Roderick of Penrith to teach me the military arts.

"Sir Roderick has great skill," the king said. "He won his spurs last year when he was only fifteen. Besides that, he's blessed with patience and a sweet temper."

The knight hung his curly brown head and blushed deeply at the praise. Instantly my fickle liver began to warm. I liked tanned skin that was lightly freckled and the English turned-up nose.

"You're from Penrith?" I asked. "I believe that's not far from my home near Dunsmere village."

He raised his head and smiled, his teeth as small and pointed as daisy petals. "Aye, close on Dunsmere."

He spoke Saxon!

"I want the boy to become adept first with the sword, then the mace. We'll wait on the lance. Test his horsemanship and see to it that he rides several hours daily. Practice with the bow as well, though he'll rarely use it."

"Yes, Your Majesty," Sir Roderick promised.

"Good. I'll check his progress each Saturday, time permitting. Now, Alex, come give me a tour of your living quarters, for they must be suitable."

I led him to a suite of sunny chambers where we found Enoch carving a wooden ball. The king greeted him with strained civility.

"I see that you are living in luxury," he said. "Certainly better than my cramped, infested quarters."

"Aye, 'tis adequate, Your Highness," Enoch answered with equal strain.

"Where's your Lady Barbara?" I asked. 'Twas a sore point between us, his dalliance with this new doxy. I turned to the king. "We share quarters with Enoch's inamorata which makes us also cramped and infested." Forsooth I left when the Lady Barbara arrived, and I bitterly resented it.

Enoch looked murder at me, but the king smiled tolerantly. "'Tis to be expected during such a long sojourn. Would my other men were so harmlessly distracted."

Which made me doubly angry, so I drew attention to the

wooden ball. "Your Highness, can you guess what this is supposed to be?"

"There are many objects with such a shape. What is it?"

"The world!" I jeered. "Enoch has enrolled us with a heathen Arab called Ibn-al-Latif who insists that the world is round!" And I awaited his derisive guffaw. Instead, Richard studied Enoch, this time with more interest than tolerance.

"Is this true? What is his evidence?"

"The movement of the heavenly bodies, the curve of the sea," Enoch replied laconically.

The king weighed the ball in his palm, glanced speculatively at the Scot, then put the ball down and courteously withdrew. As we walked back to the field where Roderick awaited us, the king took my hand.

"When I come on Saturdays, Alex, I shall expect a full accounting of what you learn from the Infidel."

"Yes, Your Highness."

I watched him stride away, thought I couldn't bear . . . couldn't bear . . . that he believed I was a boy! *Benedicite*, what ailed me! He *must* believe that I was a male if I was to escape with my writ some time, and yet . . . Our vows on the Far, the searing touch of his lips, my liver, I know not what, had cast me beyond the affections of a small boy. What could I do?

What could I do? Some ungovernable force within me answered the question despite my mind's severe injunctions to *be careful*. The following week when Richard appeared at the field to see what progress I'd made, I deliberately mis-shot my arrow.

"God's feet, Roderick, how have you taught the boy? Look you, Alex, you must step with your weight on your right foot, so, and lean back as you raise the bow. Let me show you."

He stood behind me, his arms over my shoulders to put the arrow in place; I turned my face against his shoulder, lost my balance and he had to catch me. He was all business, but I had my moment of embrace albeit with false motive. I managed to make him hold my hand over the poignard as well, to lift me off the horse and I clung for a moment. He gave the civil kiss of farewell first to Roderick, then to me, only my kiss held longer. A flick in his eyes showed his awareness as he pulled away.

During the week, I studied with Roderick, with Ibn-al-Latif, but mostly from my list of the rules of love, from which I derived a wicked plan to make the king jealous. Again he came to the field and I repeated my tricks, only this time with Roderick.

"Come, Roderick, support me as you did yesterday, for this sword is too heavy by far."

Roderick complied.

"I think you should have a lighter weapon, Alex," the king commented. "You have a nice thrust and good footwork, but should point with the saber instead of the broadsword. Do you have such a weapon, Sir Roderick?"

He did not.

"Then I'll bring one next week. Now let me see your horse maneuvers, for that's the other area in which you excel."

Again I requested that Roderick ride behind me as he'd been doing all week. I deliberately smiled at him, whispered in his ear and laughed, leaned my cheek on his, and had the satisfaction of seeing the king frown.

"Be serious, please. We have no time to waste," he said.

Roderick complied, but I'd enjoyed a small victory.

That afternoon, the king asked me to join him and his sister in a pleasant ride in the hills. Although Queen Joanna always ignored me, her usual indifferent manner to the lower ranks, I enjoyed being with her. Soothly she was the most charming female creature alive and I secretly mimicked her when alone as I had copied Enoch in the English woodland. Behind a hedge, I strolled in undulating swings using my stomach as ballast, leaned my head over my shoulder and tried to imitate her throaty laugh. Some day, I swore, I would amaze the king. She and Richard shared a store of private japes from the past and parried verbally throughout our saunter in a way I couldn't follow, though I laughed too. Toward the end of the afternoon, they spoke of me.

"What do you think will become of the pretty popelot?" Joanna asked in her lazy, affected drawl. "Could such a lad become your successor?"

The king smiled at me. "Anything is possible. You recall our great ancestor William the Conqueror was a bastard."

"Methinks this boy seems more delicate than doughty; he would need your help. I suppose such help might be forthcoming, given the proper circumstances." She gazed quizzically at the king.

The king no longer smiled. "I don't jest about such important matters, Joan, even with you. You know my plans for the succession very well."

She shrugged and took his hand. "All I meant was that the boy is at that peculiar crucial age when anything may happen, all things are possible. Don't you agree?"

Richard looked at me with warm eyes. "Yes, a golden age, the ripening time. Believe me, I will guide him well."

Joanna laughed in that elusive throaty manner I'd not yet mastered. "Oh, I believe you, brother. Why shouldn't I?"

All this time, neither had said a word to me directly but I didn't mind. I floated back to the abbey, my fantastick cells reeling with impossible dreams. If I could be king, why not queen?

SO, SURREPTITIOUSLY, I tried to signal my king that I was really a female, but it was Enoch who received my messages. He caught me one day waving an imaginary fan and laughing archly over my shoulder.

"Quhat air ye doing?" he cried. "Who's in the bushes?"

He parted the shrub behind me to expose emptiness, then turned perplexed. "Have ye gone toty? Quhat's wrong with yer voice that it sounds so hoarse?"

"Nothing. I had a tickle which made me cough, that's all." And I deliberately hacked to reassure him.

But he wasn't fooled. He sighed heavily, and took my arm to pull me to a nearby bench. "Bairn, methinks the time hae come to introduce ye to the pleasures of the flesh."

Sweat formed at my hairline and on my lip.

"Did ye e'er notice that thatched cot on the left as we gae to Ibn-al-Latif's?"

"I believe so, yes."

"And that bonny wench with the mole above her lip?"

"With dark red hair?"

"That's the one, Anna by name. What say ye to sportin' a bit with the finch, just friendly?"

"No . . . no." I shuddered, chilled to the bone despite my sweat. "I couldn't."

"Couldn't?" His eyes turned suspicious, angry. "Why nocht, Master Sweetlips? Ye make calves's eyes at Roderick which I doona like. Better be a man than a slummock. Cum, I'll show ye the tricks."

And I told him the truth. "Enoch, such an act . . . breeding . . . swiving, dighting, fucking . . . is still rape to me. I'll never, can't . . ."

He studied me at length. "I doona believe ye, but mayhap ye're nocht ready. Nine be young, I grant ye."

He left me alone to brood. Soothly the Rules of Love suited me perfectly, I thought, for the lady teased her swain out of mind, made him want to die for love, but as nearly as I could fathom, that was as far as it went; she granted him nothing. Love was perpetual yearning, a game with no ending, for consummation brought satiation and death to love. Aye, for me, the rules were tailor-made, for I could never forget the bloody deaths of Maisry and my mother, could never connect such acts with love. Therefore was my passion for Richard perfect for my needs: 'twas constant yearning, constant titillation, and with no possible consummation, for he thought me a boy. I laughed to myself—in my own manner without throatiness—to think how surprised he would be to know the truth.

'TWAS AFTER CHRISTMAS before Richard visited again. And I was distraught. Had he tired of me—after he'd sworn fealty? My disposition grew antic, up and down, round and round. I wept in secret, shouted when crossed, slumped into such deep melancholy that Enoch began to dose me with his hideous remedies again. Life was dreary, life consumed me, life was a bitter jape.

One day while I swallowed ox-bile, Enoch said casually, "'Tis said in Messina that the king shocks the town wi' his debauchery."

And I spit the black poison into his face.

"That war a mean trick, you evil sludge-pit!" He struck me on the cheek so that I reeled away. "Since when did ye think the king an angel? Havena ye heard it said since the beginning that he war filled wi' foul appetites?" With these spiteful words, he wiped his face clean.

"It's not true! And who are you to judge?"

"I be better than ye! You doona see me bletherin' and drooping day and nicht till I drive everyone lunatic! Straighten up, or I'll gae back to Wanthwaite wi'out ye. Ye're too tinty to run an estate."

I didn't straighten up, of course, but I managed to conceal my grief better thereafter, for I took the threat seriously. Then one day I saw Mercadier ride past our rooms and, fast behind him, the king. I was about to throw down my stylus and run after him, but he didn't turn my way. All day I awaited his summons, but none came. The next morning, I was up early and when I saw him ride out with Joanna alone, my heart broke.

Enoch hadn't seen Richard's arrival, *Deo gratias*, for I couldn't bear his snide jeers; I tried to settle down with the Arabic language, but 'twas impossible. Soon we were bickering and snarling at each other till I was near tears. Enoch put down his stylus and regarded me speculatively from his round blue disks.

"Be ye ailing, bairn? Is summit bletherin' ye?"

"Aye, you, you bother me," I snapped. "Can't I ever be alone? I need to think."

"Gae think, then, 'tis the age. Soul searchin' be best near to water. Why don't ye walk along the beach?"

Surprised at his apparent understanding, I mumbled an apology for being so cross and went to get food from the kitchen. Shortly thereafter I'd left the abbey behind me and walked, head down, southward on the sea's shingle. When alone at last, I permitted the scalding tears to o'erflow down my cheeks in sobs as I thought of how solitary I was. No one in the whole world loved me, even knew who I was, least of all the king. Oh, I realized 'twas madness to expect him to care for me as I did for him, with all the pressures of his Crusade and vexations from King Philip, but after all, he'd volunteered in Marseilles to take close heed to my welfare; he'd claimed he cared for me on the Far and I needed him. Wanted him. It wasn't fair, to raise my hopes so, then forget me.

'Twas sultry hot under this southern winter sun, hid though it was behind a thin layer of high clouds, and soon I stopped to take off my shoes and braies. Like Wanthwaite, I thought, that last day, only there I'd trod on soft new grass while here coarse sand scraped the tender area between my toes. I walked slowly, picking my way around rocky promontories, and was surprised when I stopped to see how far I'd come. Now I was truly alone, physically as well as spiritually. I sat in the partial shade of a wild broom growing on a hummock and stared moodily out to sea, a motionless pewter sheen except for the listless heave of the horizon. Ubiquitous gulls circled above or floated in the shallows, attracted by the sweet stench of fish; occasional schools of sardines riffled the surface; sand fleas danced at my feet while oval beetles iridescent as opals skittered in fast starts and bewildered stops. In vain I sought profound thoughts about my sad condition: my mind remained blank as the sea. The sun finally drove me from my lethargy. I stood, pulled my baggy pants as high as they would go with the weight of my treasure, tied my tunic firmly around the whole as an apron and waded into the frothy tongue-licks.

Cold as the Wanthwaite River that last May, a fearsome under-tow even at ankle depth, a change of color not too far out—the drop-off. I stepped back to the shore, felt the breeze on my wet feet, waded again and found the water warm. Something shadowed the bottom; I bent and picked up a long horn-shaped shell. Instantly a blue-black slime wiggled from its depths across my hand and plopped into the water. I screamed and dropped the shell, then picked it up again. How beautiful! A lustrous pink lining swirling out of sight. I put it in my tunic and continued looking. When my apron was soggy and loaded, I carried my prizes back to the broom and sat to eat my bread and cheese.

Sweat trickled down my neck and somehow sand had gotten into my hair. I sucked a lemon to quench my thirst, then rubbed it across my nose where my skin felt thin and pulled. I went back to the sea. Time truncated and suddenly I saw my faint shadow fall long across the transparent wavelets; my skin had white spots when I pressed with my fingertips. Now almost hip-deep, I waded awk-wardly against the receding sea, bent to pull sea-pods off my legs, and when I looked up again King Richard stood by my hummock, watching me.

At first he seemed a Greek statue, one foot forward, his hair cut shorter than the last time I'd seen him, and I froze on my own shifting pediment.

"I've missed you, Alex," he said.

"Me—me too." I tried to wade forward and fell into the water.

The next thing I knew, he'd picked me up, dripping wet though I was, and carried me to the dry sand. His heart thumped like the sea, his laughter filled the empty air.

"I'm glad to see you haven't grown up in my absence, Cupid."

"No." Feverishly I tried to unknot my tunic to conceal my legs but it was too wet, and I noted to my horror that my plunge had made my false penis stand forth like a stiletto against my wet linen. I crossed my legs in vain to conceal it, then hunched forward.

"Joanna and I saw you from the hills and wondered what you were collecting." He picked up the shell.

"You may keep that as a gift if you like," I mumbled. "'Tis called a king shell."

"Thank you, I'll cherish it." He blew through it, making a hollow tone, then sat on my hummock pulling me down with him. I bent my knees so that my willow receded somewhat. I was toty with embarrassment, happiness and I know not what. Flowings and poundings shook my body, the bees buzzed on the yellow blooms around us as I tried desperately to think of something interesting to say.

"And what's this one called?" He picked up the first shell I'd found.

"It belongs to the sea snail and changes color if you hold it in the light. See?"

"Ah, you're right. May I have it as well?"

I nodded, beginning to breathe normally again.

"'Tis a perfect house for the king of sluggards, which is what I am called, you know." He looked at me brightly. "Tell me, Alex, do you mind our long delay in Sicily?"

"Oh no," I lied fervently, "I love it here—and I'm learning so much."

"Refreshing," he said. "Tell me about your studies. Have you tried the crossbow?"

I blushed furiously. "I meant my studies with the Arab philosopher."

"Sit still, you have a tick on your leg." He leaned forward and picked an opal beetle off my leg, then rested his palm on my thigh. "What subjects?"

I gazed at his tanned hand, his carbuncle ring on his forefinger, the squared nails. Though I was hot, my skin had goosebumps, A bee landed on the carbuncle ring but the hand stayed put.

"What interests you the most?" he prompted.

I looked at him blankly, trying to remember the question. His eyes . . . I must say something.

"Well, the body, aye the body, I mean they know . . ." But I didn't want to tell what they knew, wondered why I'd brought up the subject.

"Know what?"

"The stars, astronomy not astrology, from Egypt or Greece and the world is round," I hurried.

"I'm interested in the body." He looked at my legs. "Does he explain why you have such pearly skin?"

I gazed at his hand, a branding iron.

"No, but he showed us a drawing, a map of the body inside and out and . . ." I blushed again.

"The curve of your legs is quite feminine."

My hair prickled. "Then how the blood is made like the water of the sea."

"Your bones, delicate, like your namesake."

"My namesake?"

Again his eyes.

"Alexander the Great. You looked so like him that first night in my chamber. He's my own personal hero, you know. My God, how I idolized him when I was your age. Do you have a hero?"

"Aye," I breathed.

We looked at each other and somehow couldn't look away. He had never been so vivid, eyes blue and dazzling white, golden skin, lips.

"Your eyes," he murmured. "I can't fathom them, traceries shifting, like snowflakes. What are you thinking?"

I forced myself to look away before he guessed.

He continued to study me, I knew, but I said nothing.

"Such a balmy day, peaceful after Messina. I could lie here forever."

He lay back against the hummock and gently pulled me with him, thus stroking his hand *straight across my willow*!

"Oh!" I shot back up, heart bursting.

"What's wrong? Another tick?" He leaned solicitously forward and put his hand on my leg again.

"No-no, a thorn in the sand."

"There." He brushed the hummock with his free hand, pulled me back and *again his hand stroked my prick*! Aye, *stroked*!

"Tell me more about your studies."

His teeth translucent blue at the edges, seven grains of sands like jewels on one brow, eyes pale and dark triangles with me in their black mirror centers.

"Aristotle—biology—the ocean—chemistry, but no demons."

"We know there are no demons, don't we?" He moistened his lips and waited, but I couldn't reply. After an unbearable silence of just looking and breathing, he said, "I should go back."

"Aye." I sighed deeply, nearly swooning with pleasure. "No, don't."

"Are you ordering me to stay?" he teased.

I shook my head, couldn't speak, gripped by an illusion so strong that I must hold it forever. My father—going away . . .

"Alex, what ails thee?" A hand gripped my shoulder. "Are you ill?"

"My father—father," I whispered.

The king grew very still. "Do I remind you of your father?"

"Aye. No. You're very like. Only not really."

"Go on, don't be shy," he encouraged softly.

I wasn't shy—'twas the mix of pain, poignant grief and joy together. Memory. Lying in wait, all that still lived of my father.

"When I was little—" I faltered. "When I was little, my father rode me in front of him for the hunt. Inside his arms everything was still, outside everything moving, the sky, the earth. I was so frightened and . . . stirred. Then afterward he brought me to a cave on our river. Our place, he said. And he lay on the grass, lifted me high . . ." And I stopped, thinking.

"Go on."

"'Tis silly, I know, but not to us. He tickled me, called me his Tickle-Bones, and we worked out a secret kiss, just for us."

Time moved forward. "And the last day . . . he held me so . . . and if I'd only known . . ."

The colors of the sky pooled crimson.

Then gold, and I was looking downward, held high in the king's long grasp as he lay back on the sand, my father, not my father. My breath grew shallow.

"Oh, please, Your Highness, don't . . . I didn't mean . . . and I'm too heavy."

He lowered me slowly to his chest.

"You're as light as a This-tell."

I lay without moving, heart palpitating, and I hunched my back slightly so my willow wouldn't dig into his stomach. His eyes were half-closed but alive.

"Tickle-Bones."

Hands under my arms, fingers exploring.

"Ah—I can't help—" And I convulsed breathlessly.

"There? There?"

One hand moved, the other held me firmly into his body as I thrashed wildly, stabs of delight shooting through me.

"Oh! Oh!"

I squirmed helplessly but he wouldn't let go. I cried *mercy* to deaf ears as he rubbed and dug at all my spots. I rolled this way and that, shrieking with laughter.

Then he ceased but still held me tight. I was gasping, sprawled, legs spread and my willow punctured me, so must touch him as well but I could do nothing about it.

"Wait, that's not all. Now give me the kiss."

I raised my head, startled.

"Tickle-Bones." He moistened his lips.

Again my heart raced as I bent to obey. Forehead, cheek, cheek, chin.

Lips.

Lips open, a touch of flame. I raised my head, eyes.

"You're a very strange *boy*, Alex," he whispered. "Do you know that?"

"No!" I denied quickly, heart thudding. *Benedicite*, I *had* finally revealed myself in that kiss. "In what way?"

'Twas as if we were both bewitched, our lines rehearsed, for I sensed the next words that came had been said before. "For one thing, you're old for your age . . ." Aye, twelve instead of nine. "Sensitive, delicate in your feelings . . ."

A girl, if he but knew. My breath stopped.

"And there's this." He shifted his body subtly so that my willow dug us both. I stared with uncomprehending eyes.

"I don't understand—Your Majesty."

He raised his brows. "I think you do, Alex."

And I did. Anyone feeling my prick dig so must recognize that it was false.

"You . . ."—I could hardly speak—". . . *know?*"

"Of course."

"But how? When?"

He smiled. "You sound like one of my sister Marie's courtly lovers. Well, let's see. Since you bent your sweet smooth backside and farted in my face?"

I lowered my crimson face onto his chest. Of course! That flimsy Cupid attire, and I hadn't worn my fortune belt, hadn't yet constructed my false prick. He'd known I was a girl since the beginning! I felt a fool for my long pretense and had a thousand questions about why he'd waited so long to reveal what he knew, but I was too mortified to ask.

"Don't be shy, Alex. You've nothing to be ashamed of."

I raised my head. "You're not angry?"

"God's feet, why should I be?" His smile was faintly cynical. "I'm hardly in a position to cast stones—I, too, dissimulate."

But he wasn't a girl forsooth.

"And you're not going to—do anything? Not going to tell?"

"I assure you that telling will be the last thing I do. We have a secret, just we two."

"Aye." I felt so strange I knew not what to say or do. The king knew I was female, had been privy to my disguise all these months. I could only conclude that he'd accepted the fact because of his generous heart. However troublesome it might be to take me with him, 'twas safer than leaving me with some unknown husband.

He cupped my face with his hands. "So you think of me as a father."

"You . . . you . . . no."

"But I could be, am old enough certainly."

"Aye."

His eyes were serious. "And you're young enough to make conversation difficult. Different. I don't usually . . . I mean, I care about you, Alex. Cherish your—delicious sweetness—don't want to hurt you. Do you understand?"

I didn't really but knew he was complimenting me. "Aye, Your Highness."

"I wonder." He shook his head again. "When we're alone, call me Richard."

"Yes, Ri-chard."

His eyes made me toty. "Will you kiss me again?"

He held my face, closed his eyes.

Parted lips, soft as vair, moist within, then his tongue. Startled, I tried to draw back but he held me firm. His tongue pushed gently, his teeth on my lips, then his tongue on my teeth, deeper, deeper, I felt I was choking, but it went on and on and grew easier, sweet as honeysuckle, deeper and moving. His hands slid to my hips as our mouths held and we began to move, sway to the sibilance of the sea, pounding together.

"Do it to me," he whispered.

And my tongue was in his mouth, strange sensation and I let him guide me as we tossed ever higher, engulfed, frantic to get closer and I felt his hands fumble with the knots in my wet tunic, then there was a great shudder and the king groaned, seizing me so that I couldn't breathe, kissing me passionately, hurting, then he pulled my head into his damp shoulder and held me very tight, speaking in langue d'oc.

We lay a long time as the sea roar receded; our breathing became normal again. I watched the broom through his hair, the bees. Then he raised my head and we looked at each other.

'Twas more shattering than ever, as if we were naked. His eyes . . .

"Alex?" he said again. "I am a powerful and aging king, you are a nine-year-old page and I love you. Can you understand that?"

I nodded.

He smiled ruefully. "So can I, but no one else would. I love you." And his smile turned to pure joy.

I smiled as well.

"And you?"

I put my forehead on his cheek so he couldn't see me. "I love you," I whispered.

He clutched me hard, then released me.

"Now we must go before your Scottish sheepdog comes herding, or Mercadier rides out to see if I've been devoured by Griffons." He bit my ear gently and whispered again, "I love you."

We both beat the sand off our clothes. Then the king bent to give me a lingering kiss of farewell.

"I promise that we'll be together soon, my *jeune premier*. I miss you already."

And he strode toward the abbey, paused at the promontory to wave, and was gone. I unknotted my tunic which now came undone easily, gave my willow a vicious whack in the process and gathered my shells. This is the turning point of my life, I thought dizzily: the king knows I'm a girl and he loves me. 'Twas what I wanted above anything and didn't want at all. I loved him, aye, I knew I did, and he'd said he loved me. But did we mean the same thing by love? Would he abide by the rules? I thought of his arching man's body, those shudders, and had to sit again from weakness. A bird beat in my throat as I remembered. *Benedicite*, he couldn't . . . wouldn't . . .

I thought I must die.

22

NOCH MIGHT NOT KNOW OF THE KING'S VISIT, but I feared he would guess what had happened by my face. I must have changed; my guilty excitement must show in every pore. With wanhope of concealing what had transpired, I skulked like a dog who's devoured the chickens, my head and belly both low. Then the Scot carped and I changed my tactics.

"Time fer treacle and halwei," he said, "before thee faloweth to a burdie."

"What?" I asked, for I'd been thinking of Richard.

He spoke more clearly. "I say, time fer medicine and herbs because ye're droopin' like a young girl."

Instantly I went back to my old ways, swaggering and speaking boldly in Enoch's own manner, and he was satisfied. Inwardly, however, I was wet and warm as Richard's tongue, now tingling with pleasure, now shriveling with fright. I lived that scene on the beach a thousand times: thrilling, heating, pulsing. For now 'twas enough: it sufficed. Then—I know not when—I began to yearn for more. I played in my head new kisses, new words, new movements between our bodies. Yet I balked at the memory of that hand fumbling with my wet tunic. If the king had gotten it loose . . . and next Saturday . . . here my liver burst and spread hot lead through my body, whether of fear or desire I couldn't say.

Then Saturday came and went and no king. He'd said that he would return soon; something urgent must have kept him. Another Saturday, another, another. My spirits drooped. Yet he *was* king, I must remember that. Many things—indeed almost everything— must be more important than I was, though he had declared he loved me. What could be more important than love?

Then I thought he must be making arrangements for me to travel with him as a girl. That must be it—'twas too dangerous for me to continue my disguise! He needed dispensation from the pope, of course. But would he get it? Yes. For wasn't Joanna traveling with papal dispensation?

Betimes I worried about Wanthwaite. *Benedicite*, what must my father's spirit be thinking? 'Twas one thing for the king to find me a husband, another for him to take me as his own lover. Yet I was sure that Richard would honor his word about my castle, now more than ever.

And more Saturdays. All my arguments failed. With slow horror I faced the obvious fact that the king had toyed with me. Kissed me, sugar-talked, almost seduced me, all as a game. *He'd* dallied by the rules, all right, and I'd succumbed like a fool, though I was forewarned. I was hurt, humiliated and ashamed. Of all the fancies

I had imagined, this was the only one I'd omitted: that he would forget me! Finally I could no longer dissemble to Enoch and was forced to swallow his tonic, though I discovered by the taste that it was gillyflower juice and feared that this time the foul liquid would make my breasts grow.

When I finally received the king's order to come back to Messina, I was so deep in my slough of despair that I didn't want to go.

'TWAS A BITTER CHILL DAY toward the end of February. Enoch and I stared upward at the forbidding wooden tower Richard had constructed called Mategriffon, or Kill-the-Greek. Both of us were reluctant to enter.

"'Tis not an inwiting donjon," the Scot observed soothly. "A good war engine, for ye see it con be wheeled to a wall for archers to shoot into the enemy's camp, but a strange place for the king to live."

"Aye, but no worse than that palace he had before, and possibly there are no rats."

Whereupon we entered. Inside, pine torches hissed from the walls, filling the dank space with more acrid smoke than light or heat. Listless knights lounged everywhere, dressed in fustian and furs for warmth, their armor rusting in careless heaps beside them. Sir Roger told us to report to Sir Gilbert on the fourth floor above: the king's chambers were on the fifth. We climbed a ladder-stair with rope banisters and found the pages in a small chamber at the back of the tower. Sir Gilbert told me with his usual malevolence that I'd been summoned solely because the two new Pisano pages, Antonio and Giorgio by name, didn't yet know the protocol. I gazed with surprise at the Pisanos for they seemed Sir Gilbert's choices and I'd thought that the king took a personal interest in his attendants. However, I could make no claim of knowing the king's ways at this point and the two Pisanos were extraordinarily comely, if a trifle coarse in my opinion.

"Is there some special affair?" I asked Sir Gilbert.

"The French king and his court will arrive soon for an important parley." He glanced at my tunic. "I hope you've bathed recently."

I refrained from reply. He could see that I was clean and fragrant as a spring flower, and I'd made myself a new woolen tunic of very pale gold edged discreetly in the king's red. In truth, I wanted to impress my lord, *Deus juva me*, in spite of his ill treatment of me.

I saw him the instant we entered his chambers. He was dressed in white wool trimmed with vair, a gold clasp at his waist, a plain gold crown on his hair which was once again to his shoulders. He was talking to the Archbishop of Rouen and didn't turn around though my heart pounded so loud in sorrow and yearning that he must hear it. Sir Gilbert shoved me rudely toward a series of trestles so magnificently appointed that I knew that the forthcoming conference was of first importance. The wooden walls were likewise dressed in tapestries and thick furs for both beauty and warmth, but naught could withhold the sea wind which billowed the hangings and swayed the entire structure. At least what heat there was in the tower rose to this room.

Quickly the chamber filled with nobles in King Richard's train, the Viscount of Château Erald, the Castellan of Bruges, Count John of Seis, Robert of Leicester and many more. All bowed to the king, exchanged a few words and made room for still others pouring through the door. Sir Gilbert pushed us pages til and fro with wine and cakes while porters brought trays from below, yet with all this activity never once did my eyes leave the king. Several times he turned and each sight of his face tugged my breath as if I were on a gibbet. He had changed, looked more serious, glowed but in a different manner from when he lay on the hummock, more ascetically, aye, that was the word, a white flame in his simple dress and burning expression. Fanfare sounded below and somehow the Norman-English crowded themselves into one side of the chamber to make way for the French. Richard stood on his throne platform alone.

King Philip and his court entered with appropriate flourishes and I trowe that his nobles were as great as Richard's, though I recognized only the Duke of Burgundy. King Philip ascended his throne opposite our king and waited for his court to find places, then held out his hand for Richard to kiss as he surveyed his person with insolent eyes.

"I hope, dear brother, that you are fully recovered from your recent scourging."

I looked at King Richard, startled. Who would dare scourge our king?

"Completely, I believe," he replied in the deep voice I'd so longed to hear.

"Make a second confession for us, please do," King Philip teased. "All of Messina wants to know what you meant by '*peccatum illud*,' and so do I. Come now, you're among your peers, and we have a brotherly curiosity. To stand naked and confess in public, then to leave us hanging, 'tis not kind."

Naked? Confession? "*That sin.*" My heart began a foreboding bounce. What had transpired since I'd seen the king? And did it pertain to what we'd done?

"My original statement was perfectly clear," Richard responded with remarkable calm. "I said that the thorns of my evil lusts had grown higher than my head and there was no hand to pluck them out."

And I dropped my tray of cakes!

'Twas a dreadful clatter and everyone jumped. For the first time King Richard's eyes swept past me though without recognition while Sir Gilbert glowered over me furiously. Immediately I plunged to the floor to pick up the cakes and continued to listen. If he mentioned me by name I swore I'd hold my breath and live no more.

King Philip picked up the thread. "Next time, call on me. Nothing would delight me more than to pluck the thorns of your evil lusts. Of course, I would still demand more details."

"*An refert, ubi et in qua arrigas,*" Richard quipped lightly.

As I crawled under the table for an almond pastry, I translated: *It matters not where and in whom you put it*. It mattered to me! I wondered if Sir Gilbert would notice if I just stayed here, but an exploratory kick from his pointed boot assured me he would. Miserably, I stood again.

"Perhaps," King Philip conceded with the same edged cynicism, "though we might differ on that point. You should have shrived yourself years ago, Richard, and saved all of us grief. Tell me, what moved you to become a penitent now?"

I gauged the distance between me, the door and Sir Gilbert: if the king pointed to me, I was prepared to dash.

Richard's smile illuminated the room. "I confessed in order to prepare for marriage."

To me! said my imbecile heart as I reeled giddily, though I knew it must be to Alais, for he'd cut me out of his life in public confession. Hadn't told me, hadn't come to see me all this time, while everyone else knew! Sir Gilbert thrust a jeweled goblet into my hands and indicated that I should serve King Philip.

"Don't bandy words, Richard, I warn you." I sidled timorously toward Philip's throne. "Nothing would please me more than your wedding, but I'll not be mocked."

King Richard shrugged innocently, but his smile was close to a leer. "I've never been more in earnest. I need your release from my vow to marry the Princess Alais so that I may marry the choice of my heart, the Damsel Berengaria of Navarre."

King Philip sprang to his feet and shrieked, "Never! Never! I'll see you dead before you desert Alais!"

On each *never* his arm swung wildly, the second swing catching the goblet of wine I carried and flinging it across the space to Richard where it spilled down his white tunic like blood. Neither king noticed the accident but Sir Gilbert yanked me back by my hair and hissed, "This is your last night as page, you fumbling idiot!" *Laudatur, Maria*, thought I, then swallowed the bitter bile welling from my spleen and huddled in the enshrouding billows of the blowing tapestries more forlorn than I'd e'er been in my life! *I am an aging king and you are a nine-year-old page and I love you.* Liar! Liar! The choice of his heart, *Berengaria*!

King Philip recovered his poise more quickly than I, but then he was more experienced with the English king. He whirled, talked briefly to Burgundy, then presented a face set in wrath but controlled. "Yes, my spies informed me that Sancho the Wise's daughter traveled in our direction with your Queen Mother Eleanor. I believe they've reached Brindisi now. Am I right?"

Richard nodded. "Awaiting my word to come on."

"So," France mocked, "'the choice of your heart,' is she? About as convincing as your confession, a paltry princess with neither beauty nor land. And for this union you risk certain excommunication. The interdict. Foolish, false Richard, smitten by passion at last, ready to expire for love in true troubadour fashion. Except that Pope Clement will never release you from Alais."

Deo gratias for the French king, his intelligence, his welcome information of Berengaria's ugliness.

"If your spies had traveled farther north," Richard responded smoothly, "you would have learned that Pope Clement has just died."

Philip gasped anew and 'twas instantly plain that this was a coup for England. Our lords watched the muttering French expectantly, slyly witnessing King Philip's struggle for composure.

"The oath to God holds," he replied after only a beat. "And in any case, I will not release you! You will marry Alais, or you'll marry no one!"

Two bishops now whispered to Richard, but he shook them off impatiently. "I will marry Berengaria and you will release me. You know the reasons." His pleasant tone had become ominous.

Now I prayed that King Philip would not force the issue, for I saw clearly that I wasn't yet out of danger, though soothly I didn't see what Richard had to gain by mentioning me now. However, I understood nothing except that I was betrayed, and that alone made me frantic.

Philip's voice matched his hard ice-touched eyes. "Take heed that you go not too far, Richard. Some words cannot be forgotten or forgiven."

Obviously several people knew Richard's intentions, for he was immediately surrounded by murmuring counselors while the French king sat alone.

"Your last chance, Philip. I will return Alais's dowry."

Even that brought no rise from waiting France.

"I cannot marry the French princess because she is not a virgin," Richard said in cold, measured syllables.

An aspirated moan ran through the room. Not a virgin? Alais? But she was betrothed . . . Then I remembered the Rules of Love. Doubtless in her long wait for Richard, she'd met some comely knight.

Philip was motionless. "You speak without proof," he hissed.

Richard countered sharply. "Alais came to our court when she was a child. By the time she was nine, my father King Henry and she were lovers!"

King Henry and Alais! At nine! My present age—supposedly! *Deus juva me*, and my father'd sent me to seek this Old King's help. Poor Alais! Raped as a child, forever a child in an old lady's body.

"A lie! An infamous, venal lie!" King Philip shouted as the whole French court went wild in a babble of protest and the ominous clink of swords.

King Richard's voice rose. "When she was twelve she bore him a stillborn child and still he stayed with her. He imprisoned Queen Eleanor in order to carry on his unholy dalliance."

His unholy dalliance! What about Richard's with me! For that's what he'd intended, wasn't it? If I'd borne a child . . . I staggered and would have dropped another tray if I'd had one. What a dreadful fate!

"If you speak the truth, why did you fight for her?" Philip blazed. "Why did we join arms to force the marriage? Or did you conveniently discover this affair after the king died?"

"I used Alais to make Henry fight. Think you I would make such a tarnished whore my queen? Think you that I would hurt my own mother more than she has already suffered? And drop that sanctimonious sneer, for you, too, had an ulterior motive in our joint rebellion, to divide and conquer England!"

Now they were both enraged and all I could think of was poor Alais, seduced as a child, ruined at twelve, isolated, hopeless, now a prisoner—and why? Did she ask to go to England? 'Twas easy to shift from this litany to poor *Alix*—and who knew King Richard's present purpose with me?

"And now you use her again to avenge that slut you call your mother!" Philip cried. His indigo robes with their subtle *fleurs-de-lis* had made his face seem pale when he'd arrived, but now 'twas a flaming red above a dark blue sea. He wasn't armed but the Duke of Burgundy stood close, his hand on his hilt.

Richard rose, filled with wrath at the slur on his mother. He towered over France, his heavy voice thick with fury. "The Duchess of Aquitaine, the Queen of England, suffered marriage with your eunuch-father, betrayal by your whore of a sister, imprison-ment by my father, but that's all, with God as my witness. You'll apologize."

"How can a child be a whore?" Philip ranted. "An old man in his thirties rapes a nine-year-old and she's a whore? Only a family of devils could see it so!"

I expected King Richard to at least glance at me now after these awful words which fit us so neatly, to gesture some way that it wasn't true of us, could never be. But no, he hammered back at King Philip. "That whore hasn't been a child for the last fifteen years. She seduced a powerful old man, tried to ruin his wife, and by God she made me the laughingstock of Europe! Not even a Frenchman would wed such a trollop!"

Abruptly King Philip sat on his throne again, his eyes slits. "I refuse to hear more calumny against my own sister, especially from the lips of such a notorious lecher. Your accusation does not con-stitute proof."

Yet I believed King Richard, and I think everyone else did too, even the French. I believed the acts between Alais and Henry, that is, but I didn't believe the venal motives he gave the French prin-cess. Why did no one mention love? Wasn't it possible that Henry had loved her and she him? Maybe their passions had outstripped their reason. *Deus juva me*, I could understand!

"Twelve witnesses—including Queen Eleanor—will give testi-mony before the new pope unless you release me now," Richard asserted.

King Philip's steady stare was chilling.

"There speaks Angevin gold," he replied. "You have bled your country to bribe and coerce your way to power, even at the cost of humiliating your liege lord. I thank God that my own father is dead, that he's not here to witness the continued wiles of his adulterous wife and her serpent son. Nor to hear poor Alais's cruel maligning from a family of child-molesters!"

My own wail was swallowed in the general outcry, *Deo gratias*, for 'twas now clear that King Philip knew—and therefore everyone must know—about the king and me. The act was bad enough, but to speak of it in public so!

King Richard heard the insult to his person and the line of red whelks began to gleam on his jaw, but calming whispers from his counselors restrained him.

"Alais seduced Henry, by God!"

Aye, I admitted miserably, I seduced Richard as well, by leaning on him and kissing him, but I'd thought he loved me.

"But you twist facts to your own ends. Witness your expulsion of the Jews from Paris in 'seventy-two on the basis that they were child-molesters."

"Jews and Angevins," Philip said, "an apt comparison."

"After you had appropriated all the Hebrews' wealth and property," Richard went on relentlessly, "they were suddenly invited back to Paris. Now you call me and my family child-molesters for a purpose as well. Speak plainly, Philip, what do you want?"

"The Vexin *first*," Philip answered.

And I released my breath. How cleverly Richard had led him away from that odious topic of abusing children, though at the same time he hadn't denied its truth.

"Never the Vexin." And they were back on familiar ground. "That territory has been English since my brother wed."

"The Vexin *first*," Philip repeated, "and I assure you that it will be mine. Gold for our humiliation and certain guarantees which we will present in our own time."

Now other counselors joined the argument as I sank into a vision of Richard with horns and cloven feet, for he *was* cursed, he and his father both. Yet he had lied when he'd said that his father had never had pleasure in children; he'd been betrayed by his sons but Alais has given him carnal pleasure. *Benedicite*!

King Philip suddenly seemed pressed beyond endurance and abruptly rose to take his leave. Richard stood as well. Once again the French king's face was marmoreal white, his manner icy.

"Wait, Your Highness," Richard said. "I'm yet to hear from your lips: '*I release you from your betrothal vows to my sister*.'"

If possible, France paled still more. "With my own lords and bishops as witness, I release you, Richard." He smiled bitterly. "And I release my sister as well, from her ignominious imprison-

ment in Rouen tower, from the martyrdom of suffering your de-
bauched person in her bed."

Our king couldn't resist. "And me from suffering hers. However, at least she would have received all of England in return."

Philip swayed as if on a boat. "How little you understand the
Capets. Alais cared nothing for the English Empire, never, not
when she was a child and not now. She cared for peace—as I do.
And with Alais gone from your bed, peace goes as well: first the
Vexin, then peace for all time, for mark me well, England, today
you have suffered a victory which will haunt you always. If Alais is
not your wife, we are no longer brothers and our countries are enemies forever."

He bowed and walked from his throne but was stopped at the
door by Richard.

"One last word, My Lord. Call you *this* peace? How could it be
worse?"

Philip smiled enigmatically. "You will see, Richard, you will
see."

His submerged threat gave me gooseflesh though I had nothing
to do with such matters, *Deo gratias*. I had sufficient problems of my
own.

Richard stood silently until he was certain the French king was
out of earshot, then turned, clasped Leicester and laughed aloud.

"St. George be praised, we have our way!"

Leicester's smile was tight. "Indeed, Your Majesty, but 'tis more
prudent methinks to await Philip's terms about the dowry, especially the Vexin; for I fear he'll change his mind."

Richard could not be repressed. "Did you see his face when he
heard that Pope Clement was dead? Let Philip discover what it's like
to parley without Rome on his side. I'm going to light a candle to
Clement, God bless his rotten soul." And he laughed again.

A bishop glanced at Leicester. "As the saying goes, My Liege,
you have won the battle but taken on full-scale war in the process."

"Nonsense," Richard scoffed. "France has always hated England, always been at war. This is merely the latest skirmish and the
day is ours. Admit it! Banish those long faces!"

The lords and bishops attempted to comply, but 'twas an effort. William de Fortz was the next to express his reservations.

"I fear, My Liege, that he has declared war, is your sworn enemy."

"*England's* sworn enemy," Rouen corrected him, "which is more serious. Philip's anger goes beyond a personal vendetta and will last as long as he lives."

"Then I promise to outlive him," Richard said lightly. "I'll wager my span against his, for I am Eleanor's son."

And Henry's too, I thought grimly. Child-molester! I scrubbed at a spot on the table linen, eager to be quit of this loathsome tower and its traitorous king. If only I could steal my writ from Enoch this very night.

"When do you expect the ladies?" asked Gilbert de Vascueil.

"As soon as I can get a ship to Brindisi to transport them; I hope before Lent so that I may wed at once. But if the pope's release takes some time, I'll get a dispensation and transport the new queen with me on the Crusade. Think! England's future heir may be conceived in the Holy City!"

I felt nauseated. Let him procreate in the middle of Jerusalem's golden streets if that's what pleased him, so long as I didn't have to watch. I hated him! Hated him!

After a long, wearisome time the English, too, prepared to depart and me with them.

"Wait, pages," the king ordered.

I stood behind Antonio who was very tall.

"Thank you for your tactful attendance on this difficult occasion. And I must remind you—especially the new pages—of our rule of discretion."

Sir Gilbert vowed we'd all be quiet.

"Very well, you are dismissed. All but Alex."

"I'll attend you," Sir Gilbert said eagerly.

"I want a word with Alex."

Sir Gilbert smirked. "Ah yes, of course, Your Majesty. I have already dismissed him from your service for his gaucheries tonight. I humbly apologize."

He flourished his way out and I set my jaw, awaiting the worst.

"Don't make that mouth," the king said in his old bantering fashion. "I merely wanted to have a cup with you. No, stand still, I'll serve *you*—it may be safer."

He walked to a cabinet, then the trestle, and pressed a thin knobby old goblet of wine into my hand.

"Will you drink a toast to my marriage?"

He drank; I didn't.

"Alex," he said sternly.

I looked at his shoes, the same pointed red velvet pair he'd worn at Chinon.

"I hope you'll be very happy," I raised the goblet and stopped, fighting a gagging in my throat, "with the choice of your heart."

"I'm still waiting for you to drink, Alex." His brows were high, his smile bemused.

I poured the noxious liquid down my gullet where it landed like lead. The goblet tasted of rust.

"Good, now I'll tell you a secret. You've just imbibed from a magic cup, for that was King Arthur's own goblet, excavated from his tomb in 'fifty-five."

I felt his vibrant expectancy and stayed silent. A pox on all kings and their goblets.

"And I want to give it to you for your very own." His sentimental voice.

Before I could stop myself I asked suspiciously, "Why?"

The question caught him off-guard. "As a gift, of course. I enjoy giving presents to . . ."

Our eyes suddenly locked as they had on the sand and he stopped. Cast back into that mood of intimacy with this new ugly knowledge between us, I became reckless. I would not be a "whore," bought off by old cups!

"I don't want a gift—*Richard*." I saw his dangerous flush but didn't care. I banged the cup on the trestle.

"There'll be no discussion," he said angrily. "Take it!" He put it back into my hands.

"Thank you. Is that all, Your Majesty?" I was equally choleric.

"No."

Again I watched his feet, saw him go for another glass of wine, return.

"Look at me, Alex."

I did, found his face no longer jocular or sentimental, but troubled.

"You know that I don't want to hurt you. What you heard today has nothing to do with what I feel . . ." He smiled ruefully. "I am a king."

"I know that, Your Highness."

"I doubt it, but at least try."

His voice and words were both extraordinarily soft for his person and had a devastating effect upon me, for my anger melted to a grief I felt I couldn't bear. If I didn't escape at once, I would burst into tears.

"May I please be excused?" I barely managed to choke out.

"Not yet, not until . . ." His hand fell lightly on my shoulder. "What can I do to make you happy?"

"I want to go home!" I sobbed. "Please, Your Highness, give me another writ—just for me and not the Scot—and send a note to your justicier. I want to go back to Wanthwaite!"

I saw the consternation on his face. "And leave me?"

"I have no role in the Crusade," I implored, "and I'm only a nuisance to you. You have to worry about me when you have so much to concern you. And besides, since . . . I mean, now that you're . . ." But I couldn't bring myself to mention his marriage.

He didn't answer at once, seemed to consider. I held my breath.

"You would be perfectly safe if I put you with the queens."

Aye, put all his women together, I thought bitterly.

"No, please, Your Majesty, I don't want to travel with the queens. They have a reason—a purpose—and I haven't."

"You have exactly the same reason that they have," he replied coldly. "Namely that I want it so."

And I knew I'd lost, but I had to go on.

"But you also want me to have my estate, have often told me so, and I could begin my life again. You've already given me so much, taught me so many arts—I'm sure I could do it. Please!"

"God's balls, have you no respect? Not another word! You'll do as I say! I mean that, Alex, and if you want your precious Wanthwaite, you'll obey."

I gave up, lowered my head, woebegone.

He put his hand under my chin, made me look at him again. "You seem to have forgotten that murderous Osgood of Northumberland . . ."

"Osbert."

"Osbert, a ruthless scoundrel as I remember him. That hasn't changed, Alex, nor has my promise. I swore that you'd be reinstated and you will; I swore that you'd be educated in my household up through your winning your spurs and you will; and you will crusade."

I didn't answer, lowered my eyes.

"And yes, I also remember that I swore to protect your innocence. And I have. Since my scourging, I, too, am innocent in God's eyes. We start anew, little Alexander, and I swear you'll be safe—even from me." His words were firm, but not his tone. I caught a lack of resolution masked by his strong oath, the way I sometimes go too far in a lie. He'd also sworn that he loved me and would see me again. His image blurred in my gush of tears.

"Christ! My Eros," he groaned as he lifted me to his shoulder, "don't remind me of what I've renounced. Do you think I don't know?"

I breathed deeply of sweet woodruff and didn't answer. His hand stroked my head.

"Nor is the irony lost on me. *Alex, Alais*—even the names are similar."

"How can I survive in a war? With all those men?" I asked brokenly.

"I'll put the Scot with the women as well; he knows what to do. Besides, no one dare touch you when I . . ." His voice trailed off. Then he pulled me back so we looked at each other. "Shall we kiss goodbye?"

He cupped my head in his hand and drew me into a passionate embrace which stirred and confused me utterly. If Berengaria was the choice of his heart, what was I?

"Now go, before I forget my scourging entirely."

He dropped me and I ran out the door.

And was nearly stabbed in the stomach by Enoch's raised thwitel!

"Put that silly thing down!"

I half-slid down the ladder to our dark corner below as the Scot scrambled after me.

"WHAT HAPPED IN THERE? Why was King Philip wrathful? Why did ye stay afterward?"

He was stunned at the tale of Alais and King Henry.

"Such a hizzie as that," he marveled. "I'd rather make hough-magandie with a broom. Still, there's no accountin' fer a king's cardiacle passion."

But 'twas the announcement of Richard's forthcoming marriage that intrigued him most. Again and again he had me repeat every word till I was sick of the subject.

"The choice of his heart. Hmmm. It mun be true yif she's nocht rich nor bonny nor powerful. What elsit? I mun have him wrong." And he waxed cheerful, whistling and humming.

The strain of the last few hours and the telling of it now took their toll on my vital spirits. I curled on my goatskin and felt Enoch place a squirrel cover atop me.

"Be as be may," he said softly, "'tis good news that the king be gang to take a decent wife to breed an heir fer England."

"Aye."

"And that he's put us on the dromond with the queens, a buss round and flat as a lily leaf. We'll float to Jerusalem safe as yif we were in our mothers' arms."

My eyes were already closed. When I opened them again it was to hear my own voice sobbing and screaming. A fearsome nightmare had sat on my face and I thought I would die. Enoch cradled me in his arms, *safe*, I thought, *safe in my mother's arms*, and I clutched him by the shoulders, then had to laugh when I got a mouthful of beard. If he were my mother, I was a bear cub.

Nevertheless, in the morning I still felt uneasy and vulnerable.

"Here," I said abruptly, "I want you to have this."

He held King Arthur's cup with awe. "Nay, bairn, I canna take such a valuable gift. 'Tis yers."

But he'd take half of Wanthwaite.

"I want you to have it and there'll be no further discussion," I echoed the king.

"Wal, yif ye're sure." He rubbed the dull metal. "'Tis the mast highlich gift I e'er received and I'll treasure it always." His corn-flower eyes were moist and before I could stop him, he leaned forward and smacked me on the lips. An honest kiss forsooth with no insinuating tongue wagging inward.

"Howsomever, Alex, now that ye've made yer decision I mun tell ye that King Arthur would be happy yif he knew. Aye, fer he were one of the greatest lairds that e'er came out of Scotland."

"He was *Scottish*?"

"That he were." He leaned over confidentially. "And I'll tell ye summit more, betwixt us twa, he were bore close to our clan. Aye, Alex, I canna swear but 'tis said that he were a MacPherson! But we mustna crack boast . . ."

"Perhaps it will bring us good fortune," I said moodily. "He looked for the Grail; we look for Jerusalem."

He contradicted me sharply. "Nay, bairn, *we* look for Wanth-waite and this Crusade be a necessary diversion, that's all."

Then, in my tinty state, I made the mistake of confessing to Enoch that I'd asked to be excused from the Crusade and how the king had replied.

"Withouten me?" he asked.

"Of course not," I lied. "I asked for both of us."

"Hmm." He narrowed his eyes. "He doesna want to lose control of Wanthwaite, for there's money to be made. Especially to pay for his Crusade."

"Do you think we'll ever return, Enoch? Tell me soothly."

He placed a heavy hand on my knee. "I plan that we shuld, but I canna guide our stars, sae listen. Yif anything haps to me, I hae sent our writ to Malcolm in Paris."

"When did you do that?" I flared.

"When we ferst come to Messina. One of my clansmen carried it fer us. I gave Malcolm instructions to guard it well, but he would give it to ye yif I were gone."

"Would it do me any good without you?" I asked. "You know I've not read it."

"Well, ye mun have a guardian but Malcolm will see to that. We'll keep it in our clan, ne'er fear."

"And if something happened to me, could you use it?"

His eyes were cold as the grave in spite of his grin. "Not yif King Richard knew, but I'd see that he didna learn aboot it."

I understood him well, him and the king too, both my "protectors." The king would protect me so long as I went on his Crusade, would give me Wanthwaite on his own terms and otherwise keep it to himself. Enoch would protect me so long as my presence helped him gain Wanthwaite, but if I perished he would move on his own. To give the Scot his due, I no longer thought he would kill me himself or permit someone else to do it, but I knew that he would marry me off to whomever he pleased when he learned I was female.

I was caught between the suck and pull of two powerful forces, Enoch and the king.

23

HE KING'S WEDDING DAY, 12 MAY 1191, IN THE city of Limassol in Cyprus, whence we had been diverted by storms. Day bright as diamonds, blue sea baubled with gay galleys, air filled with music. Feast day of St. Pancras, St. Nereus and St. Acilleus.

And my thirteenth birthday.

I stared balefully at my three companions, Enoch where he lay snoring and the two red-bellied lizards that crawled across our faces in the dark. All the king's household had been summoned to serve on this great occasion or nothing could have stirred me, for my head beat like a clapper. I dragged myself from our mean dank hole onto the balcony that o'erlooked the jungle garden, a paradise for reptiles

and insects with its festering piles of rotting fruit. To think we'd
spent weeks at sea, only to be blown to this miserable backwash.
Soon I minced through the slapping leaves and fetid water leets to a
giant water wheel where I could bathe in my leisure. By the time
Enoch stood yawning above, I was the king's own fastidious page
preened in special finery to serve the new queen.

Together the Scot and I walked through meandering reeking
paths to a Roman villa where the first part of the ceremony would
take place. There we separated, he to check with the horsemen, I to
strew flowers on the trestles. Varlets were still clearing vegetation
from the garden here and throwing rushes on the dank ground. Ambroise barked orders to musicians while bishops supervised the arrangement of their altars and tapers. A goodly number of lords
arrived before we were ready, their polished armor mirroring the
rising sun and adding to my head's throb. Then long horns sounded
in the distance to announce the approach of Berengaria's train.

Enoch rejoined me to stand in respectful line with the others.
My head drooped a little, but I could still see through my lashes:
two fat gentlemen in black and yellow, ambassadors of Sancho VII,
King of Navarre; Queen Joanna in Plantagenet red and Sicilian
green; and Berengaria, bride to my king. How woodly to have
dreamed that I might have stood in her place now, when even she
was considered too low of rank, too poor for a king. But at least I
was beautiful and he loved me.

"How would you describe the future queen?" I asked Enoch
softly.

He stroked his beard. "Her hair hangs on her head richt
smertly."

"Do you include the hair on her upper lip?"

"Alex, dinna be snell. 'Tis namore than a shadow from her
nose."

"Which is too long forsooth. If I were writing with Ambroise
now, I'd tell of her moonish pallor and cowpat eyes."

"For shame, to backbite with swich privy invy."

Aye, for she was the choice of Richard's heart. And she was
magnificently garbed, better than I'd ever seen her, I'd grant her
that. Her tunic was blue silk semé richly embossed with *fleurs-de-lis*,

girdled with jewel-studded gold, draped with a gold mantle banded in heavy orphreys of embroidery and sparkling gems. On her head she wore a flower circlet of verbena intertwined with gold, from which fell a white veil as long as her flowing dark hair.

Shrewd, I thought, to cover her face.

Then a gasp went through the crowd. The king had arrived, surrounded by splendid lords and clerics, but who could see them? Richard blazed alone in this company, the rest of us mere ornaments in his frame. His rose-colored silk-satin tunic sparkled with silver and gold spangles cut as suns, stars and crescents, over which was draped a scarlet robe heavily embroidered with gold with the Plantagenet lions in snarling stance; both garments were clasped by an elaborate plaque belt encrusted with jewels. On his head he wore a snug scarlet cap embroidered in gold and a *fleurs-de-lis* crown. Add to all of this his dazzling smile, his sapphire eyes—what need to say more?

We all moved forward at the chaplain Nicholas's signal to witness the first part of the ceremony, during which Richard and Berengaria knelt silently before the altar as the wedding contract was passed for representatives from England and Navarre to sign. Next the guests were asked for donations. During this period I had a perfect view of the king and gazed on him with wonder. Was it true that he'd once held me in his arms and said he loved me? This greatest and most beautiful of men? A woodly fantasy. Father Nicholas stepped between us for a moment and whispered to the pair, whereupon they exchanged rings. Then Richard raised Berengaria's veil and gave her the ritual kiss. I leaned forward, agonized, trying to see if he'd used his tongue. I couldn't bear it. A signal was given at the door and the crowd outside shouted acclamation: Berengaria was queen! And my world was shattered.

But she still must be crowned. Father Nicholas stepped aside as the Bishops of Evreux and Auch took their places before the royal pair who now stood and faced each other. Speaking in Latin, King Richard gave his wife the whole of Gascony south of the Garonne as well as vast holdings in his empire. His voice was low, his gaze serious (but not adoring as it had been with me) as he made Berengaria the most powerful woman in all of Europe.

Thus ended the civil service. Now to the church.

We formed a procession to march to the Latin Church of St.
John where the great apostle's bones were interred. 'Twas claimed
that Lazarus also lay there, which must be an error since I'd seen his
jawbone in Marseilles. To the rhythm of sacred bells and chants, we
wended a slow way past wattle-and-daub huts, now hung with curtains of flowers, crumbling earth walls covered with silk, and trod
on Oriental carpets to protect us from camel droppings. Another
crowd awaited us at the church and there a full half of our guests
would have to wait outside, for the edifice was small. Fortunately I
went with the king's personal household, but Enoch had to stay
behind.

Black and musty as a tomb, the church's interior gradually shimmered with ancient elongated saints caught in the tapers and an
anguished open-mouthed Christ emerged above the altar. Male
voices rose from the shadows to chant the antiphon *Missa pro Regibus*
as I knelt on the floor, clutched by an awesome chill at the holiness
of this ancient tabernacle, the closest I'd yet come to the Holy Land.
The Bishop of Evreux sat on his episcopal throne before the rood-
screen, flanked by cantors with staves held high, while King Richard and Queen Berengaria prostrated themselves full length on the
floor at his feet. Then the royal pair rose, sat on faldstools before the
bishop, Berengaria the closer. The chorus changed to a swelling *Salvum fac Reginam* as Berengaria carefully removed her veil,
dropped her cape and opened her tunic to reveal her dusky breasts
to the bishop, small pendulous pouches with large nipples the color
of figs. *Benedicite*, if I couldn't grow better than that.

When the queen was bared, the bishop dipped his fingers in an
ancient Grecian urn by his side and marked a cross on her forehead
in oil, then a cross on each breast. Another priest carefully removed
the oil with a linen, then burned the cloth on a silver platter. After
the fire had subsided, the Bishop of Evreux placed a gold scepter in
the queen's right hand and intoned:

"Accept this symbol of royal authority."

During the fifteen prayers that followed I was sure that Richard's eye flicked downward to those breasts at least once and I
thought I detected a slight shudder at what he'd purchased.

The bishop placed a rod topped with a cross in her left hand.

"Accept this symbol of royal justice."

He pulled her clothing back into place, placed a *fleurs-de-lis* crown similar to Richard's on her bare head, repeated the *Benedic Domine fortitudinem* and made Berengaria Queen of England in the eyes of God. But not in my eyes, never in my eyes, this usurper of love who'd never set foot in England. The king took her hand, smiled, turned to the door and they passed solemnly through it to a great shout, "*Vivat reginam! Vivat reginam!*" Hail to the queen indeed.

Sir Gilbert gave me a sharp nudge to get me on my feet. "How did you like the ceremony, Alex?"

"'Tis a glorious occasion," I said. Then shuddered. Alais Capet's words long ago in Chinon. Well, the king himself had said that our names were similar, likewise our fates.

Back at the Roman villa, solemnity ended as everyone strove to become merry and drunk as fast as possible. Every oven in Limassol had been called into duty for the festivity and I spent hours carving sheep, goats and lambs. Wild turnips and beets were piled high as a man's shoulder, loaves marked with crosses were heaped on the tables, but most important were the goatskins of fine Cypriot white wine for the repeated toasts. When our meat was ready, the *cor l'eau* sounded, ewerers passed towels and the merry guests took their places, Berengaria for the first time climbing to the highest dais to share the king's bowl. Lutes, pipes and drums vied with church bells in a noisy clamor; glittering conversation and laughter drowned both as we took platter after platter of viands to the tables. Then the earnest drinking began and soon drained goatskins made a wall for our open kitchen but there were plenty of full ones to bring on and we continued to serve throughout the entertainment. Aye, and to serve ourselves as well, one sip for the page for every goblet filled, and the sips mounted up rapidly.

Ambroise had brought us our first Turkish dancers, though we'd heard of them since Paris and Dangereuse had claimed that one of her choreographies was Oriental. Not so. I stopped on my rounds to gaze open-mouthed at the sight of ladies dancing on their hands, their skirts overhead, their smiles upside-down moons. Soothly 'twas not merely the acrobatic skill, however, that made them such marvels, for they were as graceful as bending flowers no matter how contorted, their toes miracles, their gyrating bellies, even their nasal whines as they jerked their heads to punctuate their rhythms. 'Twas strange, exotic, exciting.

By the time they were finished, our own company was sufficiently drunkalewe to take the floor. The smiling king leaped lightly to the center and held out his arms to Berengaria. Shyly she followed, her black eyes dew-bright, and I swallowed the better part of a goatskin of wine. Berengaria was back on her throne and the king reached for Joanna. Both were skilled dancers and so matched in beauty that the court applauded loudly when they finished. One after one in proper order the king gave each delighted lady a turn as the other men waited. Then everyone danced in joyous abandon as I steadily tippled.

"Jine the fun!" Enoch shouted as he whirled by. "The best nakryn noise with pipe I've heard since Scotland."

Magically his doxy Barbara was in my arms and we floated a foot off the earth, I trowe, both of us giddy as larks. Then we tippled, pressed our dripping lips together and she was gone with Sir Roderick. Swaying slightly, I asked one of Joanna's ladies called Blanche for a turn and was surprised when she accepted. I'm a bonny dancer, I thought, lithe as a cat, light as a bird, and soon we were having a merry spin. She kissed me in gratitude and we drained another goatskin together. Then she was off with a knight and I sought another partner and another, getting so dizzy and gay that I could hardly speak, but I could still dance. Tapers were lit and I hadn't noticed when it got dark.

With the darkness came greater abandon. We danced closer, rubbed our bodies and the Devil take us, and I noted that the ladies appreciated my hard prick which had grown stiff and unyielding in the dry climate. 'Twas toty to be a mock-boy and merry and what did it matter? I could seduce as well as the next, *up to a point*, and I laughed giddily at my own secret wit. Now I was struck in the eye by a piece of bread. Everyone had loaves, everyone threw chunks in a silly game, laughing and laughing. We were drunk as mice, happy as canaries. And all this time I watched the king.

Now began a kissing game. We English were often teased for our custom of kissing and this night we deserved the jibes. We kissed when we danced, when we met, when we passed one another, when we separated and for no reason at all. Now there was no discrimination between men and women, all kissed all. No one is as great a lover as I, I thought, and I kissed with lips slightly parted as I circled the floor. Barbara, Beatrice, Sir Gilbert (before I saw who it was), Helen, Queen Joanna, Barbara again, King Guy, Robert of Leicester, Sir Roderick (where I lingered).

And King Richard.

"Well!" He kissed me back. "Is that a congratulatory kiss?"

"Aye."

"Thank you, give me another." But he was gone.

After that I was forced back to the wine to restore my spirits. Betimes I was still kissed but didn't participate much. Once I was grabbed so hard that teeth clinked with teeth like goblets.

"Ye'll ne'er win fair lady wi' fangs!" Enoch cried. "Now this be a breme kiss!"

And he lifted me as Richard had done formerly to give me a sample of his successful technique.

"Soothly, you're *good*," I admitted, my eyes wide with surprise.

He laughed. "That's sae ye won't accuse me of forcin' myself on the wenches. Ye'll soon be enjoying yer own conquests, I can see, and I'll tell ye my secrets, share and share alike."

He was off as the stars turned in wheels, flames shimmered and I laughed and laughed and laughed or wept and wept and wept.

Lewd figures crept from the corners, beat tambourines and stroked their huge mock-pricks. I admired their creations, thinking that soon I would make mine in like manner, then was pulled with the company as we all stumbled up the stair to the bedchamber. Here the lascivious songs and movements were more bawdy and I felt myself heat along with everyone else at those shooting tongues, those fondlings. They advised the king to enjoy his "merry fit with a hot iron" but to stay on top, warned of the monarch of old who'd pricked so deep that he'd disappeared in the ditch and was ne'er heard of more, told Berengaria to fill her cup, that many a pole be staked on an ale. The king was there with his queen, laughing and laughing. And they went into the lighted chamber where we could see the bed strewn with flowers. He took off her cape and flung it to the floor, turned and laughed as the bells jingled. With horror, I saw that he was lost forever. Forever.

He kicked the door closed.

And I pissed in my braies.

Benedicite, no warning at all! No twinge! Never since I was a babe! Mortified, I clutched my knees tight and fought not to look downward for fear others would look too. I could feel the warm liquid on the inside of my legs, atop my feet. Was there a puddle? Finally, nonchalantly, I dropped my goblet and bent down to pick it up.

Across my right foot was a streak of bright blood!

NOW COMPLETELY SOBER, I crossed my legs and inched my way into the shadows to outwait the frolickers. Not till all were yexxing so hard that they could no longer sing did the crowd gradually disperse. When the last taper had rounded the corner, I bent forward like a hunchback to better squeeze my parts and hobbled to my room knock-kneed and pigeon-toed.

Deus juva me, what a mess! Everything besmottered. I tore up my outgrown Plantagenet tunic and began to repair the damage, but 'twas a long, tedious, nauseating task complicated by sharp pains in my cod as if the flux were coming on which it finally did. *Deo gratias* that Enoch was distracted by his doxy, for I needed privacy this night. And for many to come. That long-ago preview on Dere Street had finally flowed to a genuine deluge. I tried to remember Magnus's song about Eve's curse: a few days once a month? Well, no difficulty remembering this date, and if I could get through the next few days I would have four weeks' grace. But then some decision would have to be made, for I could not foresee disguising my condition long—especially from Enoch.

I'd just emptied the slops and tidied the evidence when the Scot stumbled in at dawn, still drunk as a mouse.

"Come, bairn, fer the second day of revelry be aboot to begin. 'Twill be murrier than the first fer we start foredrunk."

The wedding celebration was to go on for three days all told, but for me 'twas finished.

"Please make my excuses, Enoch, and tell Sir Gilbert that I've got stomach cramps and cannot serve."

"Waesucks, I hope ye didna drink the water."

That I most soothly had not.

"I'll send ye sum hot broth later."

"Thank you, Enoch."

Listening to the pipes and kettle, the gay laughter of the dancers, I laundered my money belt and when it was dry sewed an additional hammock in the middle on which to place my rags. Finally I curled up and slept. Though I felt weak and sweaty, I wasn't ill. When the hot broth arrived, I felt better than ever. Nevertheless, I was glad that Enoch stayed away a second night as well.

On the third day I rejoined the party and found a stunning deterioration in the mood. Slack mouths, blood-veined eyes and foul breaths revealed bilious cods and aching heads, though once sufficiently jug-bitten the guests grew merrier again. Most of all, I was astounded at King Richard and Berengaria. She sat on her dais alone, a stricken effigy, pale, her eyes staring marbles. By contrast the king was edgy, pacing back and forth, not drinking, talking to his knights about Isaac Comnenus, the ruler of Cyprus, who still hid in the mountains and whom they must conquer. Neither looked at the other; neither made merry.

Benedicite, if this be the result of conjugal love, I'll take my chastity vows forthwith.

The pattern of eating, drinking and entertainment repeated throughout the day, except that everyone turned cups a little earlier and a little more heavily so that by midday there wasn't a sober Englishman in the court. Except for the king.

He approached me where I sat on a low wall. "What, not tippling today, Cupid?"

"No, Sire. I'm not accustomed to such luxury."

He glanced around moodily. "Many a sour gullet and rancid breath here today." He turned his haunted eyes my way again. "How are you feeling? Did you get the pomegranate juice I sent?"

Startled, I said I had. "I'm sorry—if I'd known, but I thought Enoch . . ." But of course the Scot had sent broth.

"He told me you were ill."

Again he stared, his eyes dull moonstones. He seemed to want to say more, then didn't. The look became long, uncomfortable. My unruly liver heated exactly as if the king weren't married, and I saw how weak I was.

Shortly thereafter a messenger broke into the party and went directly to the king where they conferred briefly. Then the king signaled the music to stop, raised his arms to make an announcement.

"My lords, arm yourselves at once!" His face lighted with new exuberance. "The tyrant Comnenus has been trapped in the mountains close to Nicosia. Meet me on the strand within the hour." He smiled and spread his arms in mock apology. "Ladies, forgive me for ending our celebration so unexpectedly. I would never forsake you, if I had a choice, but we must conquer this island for future security in Jerusalem."

He didn't glance at his queen.

Abruptly 'twas done. Lords and knights found wits to tramp back to their quarters while the ladies collapsed forlornly. I went back to my own dank cell. There I had an awful shock. The red-bellied lizards had smelled my blood and were squirming atop my discarded rags! I kicked and flailed till they'd scurried into corners, then threw away the attraction. 'Twas a timely lesson, for shortly Enoch came to arm and I realized that my condition required utmost discretion.

I WAS LEFT in Limassol with the women and a skeleton staff while the men, including Enoch, fought in the mountains close to Nicosia. At first I was glad for the privacy which gave me the opportunity to construct a new prick, necessary because the old one was worn out and also fouled with blood. It occurred to me I would have to do this every month henceforth. It also occurred to me that I couldn't. Somehow, I must leave the Crusade before my secret was discovered, and the most probable person to find me out was Enoch.

He was gone four weeks, the longest we'd ever been separated, and for a while I felt so normal again that I began to hope that this instance would prove a false warning, as the time on Dere Street had been. Then I began to have two strange itchings on my chest, as if I'd been bitten by some giant invisible insect. Scratchy and painful, the bites drove me mad. One day as I was rubbing myself, I felt hard round bumps. Breasts! I jerked my tunic up and stared. Aye, nipples growing like beansprouts! I clapped my hands hard on the offending bulges. What could I do?

One day when Berengaria was out of her chamber, I sneaked in to gaze at her French looking glass. *Benedicite*, soft pointed triangles, mountain peaks where there'd been a flat plain only yesterday! Was it possible? Then I noticed the queen's soiled laundry in a basket and picked up the top garment, a bandeau. Tentatively I placed the strip of cloth around my chest and saw what its purpose be. So this was how women controlled their bobbing bosoms. By nightfall I wore one as well, pulled so tight that it constricted breath. At least it reduced my expanding mounds to proportions that could be covered by blousing my tunic.

The mirror also gave me a second shock. My face seemed to be changing, growing more oval, delicate, and my eyes appeared huge. Was that also a symptom?

At the end of a month Enoch returned and so did the bleeding.

I greeted him nervously. "Did you capture the tyrant?"

"Aye, anely Roderick war wounded."

"No! Seriously?"

"I think nocht, because I keered for him. He took an arrow in his right leg, but it didn't sliver the bone."

I didn't construe Enoch's statement as vanity, for we'd both learned about hygiene from Ibn-al-Latif. Then I became aware that the Scot was staring at me.

"Waesucks, ye've changed."

"Changed?" I laughed, a high-pitched whinny. "I don't know what you mean."

"Neither do I." He touched my cheek. "Mar pearly . . ." His eyes narrowed speculatively. "Boot ye should . . ." He touched his own cheek which bristled with beard. "Mayhap ye're beginnin' to— though ye look mar pasty than ever. And yer voice be higher . . ."

"The men in my family mature late," I asserted hastily.

"Aye, I see that. Anely . . ."—he groped for thoughts or words, I wasn't sure which—"anely, ye're maturin' in the wrang direction."

I made up an excuse to get away before he could notice more, for

I'd become keenly aware of my own female odor; whether it actually existed or whether my fear made it so, I wasn't sure. In any case, I'd practically bathed in oil of cinnamon to cover it.

Aye, I must find some way to escape.

Almost at once, an opportunity arose which solved my immediate problem of exposure to the Scot. Father Orlando sought my help in caring for King Richard who had contracted a severe case of the fever which had swept through the entire army. Could I relieve the physician at night?

I entered the chambers at sundown, just as a sneering Sir Gilbert was leaving. He, too, had a touch of fever, however, and could remain on duty no longer.

"The king is prepared for the night," Father Orlando told me. "I've given him juice of the poppy for sleep and I don't think he'll wake. If he does, however, offer him wine or fruit; bathe his head if he's hot. I'll be in the next chamber."

After he'd left, I checked the sleeping monarch whom I'd seen only from afar since his return. He looks thin, I thought, and the lines in his face are sad. I pulled my pallet to below the window, then opened the shutters to the night air which was against Father Orlando's orders, but I was following what I'd learned from Ibn-al-Latif who scorned Christian healing methods. Then I dampened a cloth and gently bathed the king's forehead. He muttered, opened his eyes briefly and slept again. After a time, I stretched onto my pallet and was soon asleep as well.

I woke groggily to the sound of argument. At first I thought it came through the wall from outside but as I became more alert I realized 'twas the king's voice. But with whom could he be arguing?

I took a taper and went to his bed. His waxy eyes glared upward; veins in his temple swelled like roots of an oak.

"I'll not tolerate double dealing!"

Still not thoroughly aroused, I sought his contender in the shadows.

"You cheated me! Sacrificed my oath for humiliation! Made me a man and have unmanned me! Call Yourself God?"

Awake at last, I almost swooned at his blasphemy. "Hush, Your Highness, you're dreaming. I'll go for the doctor."

But his great hand caught me in a vise.

"*Deus absconditus*! So be it! *Richard abscondito*!"

"No, no, take back your words. He doesn't mean it!" I looked upward to God. "God has *not* abandoned you, My Lord!" Nor had the king abandoned God, as he swore. Wasn't he on the Crusade?

I made a sign of the Cross before his face to ward off the Devil.

"He has betrayed me!" insisted the anguished king, beating his head on his pillow.

"You are on your Crusade and have fallen ill, but you'll soon be well again. 'Tis only a passing—"

"*All fathers betray their sons*!" The king drowned my plea. "Did not even God forsake Christ when He needed Him most? Yet I was foolish enough to trust Him! But never again! *Never*!"

By now he was sitting upright and shouting. I dared not leave him but hoped Orlando would hear and come to my aid.

"You've met Your match in Richard! Never again will I go whimpering to a cross! I have loved You and served You, only to be stabbed by Your own spear! But no more! If You doubt that I can deal with fathers, look to Henry!"

I clapped my free hand over his mouth and implored him. "Please *stop*, you have a fever and know not what you say! Oh please, Your Majesty."

At last he leaned back on his pillow, but his eyes rolled upward alarmingly and he would not be silent. He pushed me roughly aside.

"Did I not cry out my sin? Did I not crawl at the feet of those milksop priests? And still my lust burns unquenched. Alive on wood but dead on silk, all *ludus* lost."

His words were ever wilder, though I thought he must refer here to his wooden bed and silken quilt.

"How can the ax strike without its blade? How can the piper make music without his pipe? God has a sense of humor, you see."

At last he acknowledged my presence by turning his glazed eyes upon me.

"Riddle: How can a king scorch God with a thunderbolt?"

"I know not."

"By wasting creation."

He laughed hoarsely at his own wicked wit.

"Second riddle: Where lights the Angevin eagle when he's stripped of his beak?"

"I know not, Your Highness."

"On Jove's hunter." Again he laughed.

"Riddle: Where lives the Angevin lion when he loses his fang? Answer: In the cave of the hyena."

'Twas dreadful to see a great mind break so and I tried once again to pull from his grip so I could fetch the physician, but he held ever harder.

"Tell me, are you Ganymede, Jove's cup-bearer?"

"Whatever you say, Your Highness."

"Then fill the Holy Grail; it's drunk to the dregs."

Suddenly he released me and I quickly poured him a cup of wine which he accepted without drinking.

"Tell me what you think of this ditty. 'Tis to the tune of a jig I made up long ago:

> *"I confessed and was wed;*
> *I was wed and was dead,*
> *Lost my polyhedral head:*
> *Sole son of my mother,*
> *Sworn foe to my brother,*
> *Despised by my father,*
> L'homme sensual non pareil
> *To all but Berengaria;*
> *Thus my acroterium crumbles,*
> *Thus England's king tumbles!"*

He smiled with bright expectancy.

"'Tis a passing brilliant verse, Your Highness, but methinks your judgment wanders and you need help. May I get Orlando, please?"

"*Oc e ne. Oc*, I need help, *ne*, you may not get Orlando. I believe you lied to me."

"Me, My Liege? Never!"

"*Oc*, you said you were Ganymede when I myself baptized thee Alexander the Great. I dub thee, Alexander!"

And he poured his wine o'er my head, then laughed fiendishly to see it drip.

"Now we begin again. Are you Alexander?"

"Yes, Your Highness," I gasped.

"Good, and I am your lord who henceforth will not deny you. I now give you permission to cure me."

Almost too terrified to speak, I yet must try. "Yes, Your Highness. What can I do for you?"

"Erect me again. Give me a Greek column, a swollen entasis which will not fall. Will you do that, Alexander?"

"You know I'll support you, Your Highness."

"Good, then there can be no issue. But the Devil's will be done. We ride our incurable disease to Jerusalem, there to capture the Cross and perish on wood, for I've eaten too many rabbits. So be it, *teste me ipso*."

Whereupon he turned fretfully away and was soon asleep, leaving me to cope with my besmottered tunic and brain as best I could. I finally concluded that the king in the grip of his fantastick cells was keener that most men with all their wits. There seemed an underlying pattern of profundity in his wild utterings, if I could but decipher the language.

THE NEXT MORNING Father Orlando sensed that something had gone amiss and questioned me carefully about the king's state of mind. Richard was sleeping heavily by then. Faltering, I told the physician that he'd raved a little but that his mutterings had been too outlandish to understand.

"'Tis the leeching methinks," Orlando said. "Betimes it has that effect upon fevered brains. The demons become angry and howl forth in their demented tongue. Think you that his utterings be sacrilegious?"

"No," I lied. "I could not understand much but I know he twice addressed God the Father."

I was then dismissed to rest, though my own fantastick cells were much agitated. When I came back on duty Orlando reported that the king had been rational enough all day to receive reports of his fleet's preparation. Again His Majesty slept.

Or so I thought. As I pulled the shutters from the window, I heard, "Thank you, Alex. I daresay the air is putrid in here."

I walked to his bed.

"How do you feel, Your Majesty?"

"Better."

Indeed he looked much improved, partly because he was groomed. His hair was clean, his eyes wide open, his scent better under a heavy layer of sweet woodruff.

"Do I repel you?"

"No, Your Majesty."

"Your first lie, for of course I do. I repel myself."

Soothly my heart raced and my breath grew short as I tried to reassure him. Yet I dared not reveal my true feelings.

He was gazing out the window. "The watery star weeps tonight. Do you know why?"

I followed his glance. "You mean Venus?"

"She weeps for the loss of her son Cupid who is interred in Famagusta." He looked back at me. "I can sympathize with her grief."

There was naught I could say, but I pulled hard on my stomach muscles to control my liver.

He reached for my hand. "You promised last night that you would cure me."

I was amazed that he remembered. "Aye, if I can."

"Oh, I think you're my chosen physician, all right. As the poet says, '*A cock has great influence on his own dunghill.*'"

He smiled but I saw no humor in the comparison.

"Every good physician begins with a diagnosis. What is wrong with me, Alex?"

"You have the fever."

"A symptom, but not the disease. Come, don't hide behind your tender age. You have a head, two eyes, a tongue."

A tongue—aye, well he should know. I saw that I'd overestimated his improvement: he was still in manic disposition.

"You have the disease that everyone has, a plague, but I know not its name."

He released my hand, folded his arms behind his head.

"Let me help. Listen, 'tis a song my great-grandfather wrote:

"Do I sleep or do I wake?
Only you can tell—
My heart will soon break
For I am not well,
And I care not at all.

"I am sick and will soon die—
My heart will cease—
Only one doctor can stop my cry,
My illness appease
When I am not ill at all."

His low voice faded into silence. I cleared my throat.

"A very provocative lyric. Is it another riddle?"

"A paradox. I am not ill but seek a cure, for the cure is worth the pain when that cure be pleasure. I can no longer defy necessity." He pressed my hand so hard that I winced.

"If you tell me what to do, then I will do it," I promised again, much confounded.

"What more can I ask?" His brows shot up in their old cynical pattern. "If I choose the supple body, can I also expect the subtle mind? Well, so be it. I'm no philosopher, but I can read. Alex, I am my own holy trinity: flesh, air, and the part which governs. You will treat the governor: in short, we are to be lovers."

I gasped and pulled back. He couldn't mean it!

"But doesn't it go against—? And your queen!" I cried involuntarily.

"Enough, Alex. Such matters are my concern, not yours."

I nodded, swaying with shock.

He lay back and closed his eyes. "I should think you would be flattered to find yourself so irresistible," he said bitterly. "As for me, well, I suppose every general must face one defeat. Richard, felled by a delicate child—nine years old?"

"I've just turned ten."

"Ten! God help us."

As I writhed at my own lie about my age, wondering if I dare admit the truth, he took my hand and opened his eyes. To my amazement, they seemed to glisten, almost as if filled with tears, but no doubt 'twas some trick of light. He raised my hand to his lips, kissed it and smiled wryly.

"At least if I were ten as well, I would say I had good taste, for I believe you are a rare combination of intelligence, integrity and warmth. And that you love me for myself. Am I right, Alex?"

"Soothly I love you for yourself."

"Good." And he forgot me again in his own dark thoughts. "In any case, we do not choose our destiny but follow our stars." He sighed, pressed his lips. "Once I am fully well and in the field, you will move into my pavilion and live with me. Do you understand?"

"Aye."

"Oddly enough, the confusion of battle makes a perfect cover for us, but in any case we have Ambroise, Mercadier and the other captains as our honor guard. Naturally we'll be discreet and you'll be quite safe from discovery."

"So they know that I'm—?"

"Of course."

Strangely, that was a relief.

"Should I tell Enoch?"

The king rose to his elbows. "*Enoch*! By no means!"

"But 'twould make it easier," I protested unwisely.

He became agitated and tried to rise. "I order you not to tell that suspicious cur!" He added coldly, "Whatever our relationship, Alex, I am king. Your king and lord as well as your protector." He closed his eyes, breathed deeply, frowned. "I will get rid of Enoch."

Get rid of Enoch? A chill frisson shook my vitals and I was sore afraid.

"Don't be upset, dearest." He carried my captured hand to his lips. "We have turned our corner at last and will not look back. I need not your diagnosis to know my disease: 'tis simple, I do love thee."

Deeply offended, I pulled my hand away. To be called a disease! The king reached his fingers to my face and smiled.

"Sorry, Alexander, I amend my words. 'Tis not my love *per se* which has caused my sickness, but my perception of it as a sin."

He continued to stroke my cheek in silence as I pondered his ominous words. I couldn't stop my heated liver from leaping, but my vital spirits trembled with fear of this sinful passion. Sin. Was it also a crime?

"Go to now, Alex, and let us sleep." He kissed my hand.

I curled on my pallet and listened to the king's even breathing, but I believe I slept not at all that night.

THE KING'S INTENTION to make us lovers complicated my own plans. I didn't take care of him after that night, so had no opportunity to ask him exactly how he planned to conceal my emerging sex traits. Nor did his peremptory tone invite questions. And how was I to explain the whole matter to Enoch? Wouldn't his beginning suspicions about my sex be compounded by the king's carnal interest in me?

Benedicite!

The test came immediately when Enoch learned that we were now to sail on the *Trenchemer* with King Richard instead of the buss with the queens.

"That's a fightin' galley. Why do he nocht take sum older page to serve him?"

"I don't know."

"Air ye servin' him in the field as well?"

"I believe I am, aye." I squirmed, uncomfortable, twisting myself to hide my breasts, and trying at the same time to ascertain the wind's direction so he wouldn't smell me.

"Do ye hae worms, Alex?"

"Oh no!"

"Then sit still and listen."

I did, but he was quiet a long time, then sighed heavily.

"Ye war e'er a winsome bairn, but now ye be *pretty*. I doona like it."

Neither did I, I agreed fervently.

Deeper than the problem of discovery was the very fact of consummation. I thought of my airy fancies in Bagnara as if they belonged to a different person, a child. What I faced now was reality, and I had a good example of what that meant in Princess Alais. The possibility of a bastard babe, a life of secrecy, a ruined character if I ever wanted to marry, the king's tiring of me, the loss of Wanth-waite.

If I truly loved him, would any of this matter? For the first time, I wondered. I was no longer a child, so couldn't deceive myself with fantasies of unconsummated love—especially with the king's state-ment still ringing in my ears—but I seemed not to be entirely adult either, for consummation frightened me. I was drifting in my own Limbo, neither one thing nor the other. Or perhaps I could have loved more easily if I'd felt secure in Richard's affection. But how could I when we didn't live in the same sphere? He was powerful and mercurial; I was a young, lowly damsel, completely at his mercy.

24

 BOARDED THE SHIP TO LEAVE FOR THE HOLY Land with great trepidation, for the time for depar-ture couldn't have been worse: I was bleeding again. Was the rest of my life to be measured out in seg-ments between bleedings? Were all great events to correlate with this loathsome monthly horror?

King Richard straddled the metal ramming beak of the *Trench-emer* as it rose and fell on the waves.

"See what I mean?" An oarsman nudged his mate. "Looks to be his own prick."

"Stiff as a poker, hot as a forge."

"Clinks all night it do, striking ore."

"Aye, poor queen. All night and all day too, swives her bolt upright."

"No wonder the poor wench looks so pale and with them black circles."

"But marriage agrees with him, our merry king, God bless him.

Could almost pity the Antichrist Saladin. He's met his match in Richard."

At that moment the king stepped down and waved.

"Heigh-ho, Your Highness! Good health to thee!" The delighted sailors waved back.

But Richard's smile was fixed on me where I sat cross-legged on a cask of herring. I tried to resist, but lifted my hand as well. Enoch watched the exchange with murder in his eye.

Sometime later, our eagle-eyed lookout called from the mast, "Land ahoy! Holy Land to the luft!"

We all scrambled quickly to the rail for the first sight of God's home, but we saw only a smudge. An hour later we discerned details. Shading my eyes against a searing glare, I looked beyond bare dunes to wave after wave of windswept sand. On the distant horizon, forbidding rocky hills cut the sky.

"There be the land of milk and honey," Roderick commented dryly. "Fields like emeralds," I said.

"To think that God could have chosen Scotland," Enoch added. "Mayhap He didn't want Jesus to like His home on earth too much."

Most of the Crusaders seemed as disappointed as we were at this first view of the Holy Land, though a few muttered that every country had its barren spots, that surely the area around Jerusalem would be beautiful beyond words. Only the king was undismayed.

We danced along the dead shore all afternoon on our way to Tyre. King Richard could not stand still for three heartbeats together but rushed from one end of the galley to the other, talking incessantly, touching his men. I had my share of touches and comments but as the day waned I felt alienated from the euphoria of crusading. Perhaps it was because I was a girl, or because I wanted to go home, or mayhap 'twas because of Roderick.

Enoch and I worked hard on Roderick's leg which had developed a seepage. We combined a mix of Enoch's former experiences in battle and our lessons from Ibn-al-Latif in our treatment. Enoch washed the leg with sea-water, then wine, then sewed it as neatly as Dame Margery could have with wine-soaked thread. Finally he placed it where the sun would dry it and prepared a poultice of herbs and lemon-juice for the night.

"I'll carry ye ashore," he promised the poor knight, "for ye mun give the stitches time to heal. Yif there be a stick of wood in the city of Tyre, I'll make ye a cane to use in Acre."

"Thank you," Roderick groaned. Then when Enoch went to empty the slops, "Your brother's a saint, Alex."

"A *saint*!" I brayed. "Then Saladin be the Angel Gabriel!"

Roderick shook his head and reproved me. "For shame, Alex. Everyone notes what a devoted brother he be to you. I've heard it said that never did a man love his own child more than the Scot loves thee."

"The Scot may love me, but he loves my land more. He's stolen my writ from the king so he can claim my castle alone. I tell thee true, Roderick, that he stays with me only to usurp my title and land—if that be love."

Roderick shook his head, still toty from the wine I'd poured into his gullet for pain.

"Well, be as be may, you've both been friends to me and I'll ne'er forget. Later you must tell me more about your estate. My uncle is a powerful man in the north and mayhap he can help you."

By this time Enoch was back and our conversation ended. Then the exuberant king drifted close and sat with us a few minutes. We should put on our best dress, he explained, for we must make an impression upon Tyre. The governor there was Count Conrad of Montferrat who wanted to be King of Jerusalem once Richard had won it back.

"He's bound to give us a royal welcome," the king prophesied, "and we must display our power to establish future authority in this area."

He'd already alerted others as well, to judge by the knights' sudden efforts to shave, comb windblown locks and make themselves neat. *As we are seen, so are we esteemed.*

God dropped our wind directly before the port of Tyre. For the first time we saw signs of human habitation in one of these great forbidding fort-towns, for the water bobbed with boats of commerce, and camels waiting to be loaded lined the quays. King Richard sent his priest Nicholas, the Earl of Leicester and Baldwin of Bethune to convey the king's greetings and ask permission to enter the city. As we waited impatiently for their return, Richard ordered the musicians to strike up a sweet air to celebrate our entry into God's land. It seemed an eternity before we saw our small craft row toward us alone.

"God's feet, did he send his emissary with our men?" the king asked his counselors. "I expected a small fleet."

Then our own messengers were back on deck, all red-faced with anger.

"Count Conrad regrets that he cannot permit the English king to enter this city," Leicester reported in a voice of steel.

"The *count* cannot permit the *king*?" Richard repeated, all euphoria gone. "Explain yourself."

Baldwin continued. "He says he takes his orders from King Philip of France, My Lord. It seems that King Philip sent a runner from Acre with strict orders that on no account was Conrad to permit you the hospitality of his city; and Conrad says he does homage to France, not to England."

There was a long silence as Richard's lips pressed thin and white with anger, and his voice chilled the furnace air. "Mark me well: This Conrad will never become King of Jerusalem. As for King Philip, God help him."

He told us to camp outside the city walls on God's own ground, unpolluted by the presence of the Infidel. Again the musicians struck, this time "The Wood of the Cross." As the voices resounded, the grim king prepared to disembark first.

Loaded like a mule, I staggered in the soft hot sand after Enoch who carried Roderick in his arms. *Deo gratias*, Sir Gilbert had advised me that he and the Pisanos would serve the king that night. We pitched our tents in a line under the shadow of the high buff wall of the city, not that we needed shelter for warmth but against the heat and blowing grains of sand that cut us like needles.

I patted the sand into a hummock so that Roderick could rest his back comfortably, then helped Enoch prepare our supper. I shared with Roderick a wooden bossie of porridge mixed with sodden mutton, which was not too bad washed down with methiers of strong ale. Then as a special treat, Enoch gave us salted lamprey which encouraged more drinking, with a dessert of marrow bones, "guid fer healin' the wound." Satisfied at last, we lolled on the sand gazing seaward where the sun flopped like an egg over the horizon, leaving us in instant darkness.

"The moon looks big with child," Enoch observed. "The way she bulges, could be twins."

Instinctively I touched my twins' caul where it rested on my right thigh.

"Aye," Roderick agreed. "From the size of those fat stars, they could be baby moons. At home they're different, more blue and scattered, like slaeberries."

"Aye," we all agreed. "And yet," I added, "these must be the selfsame stars."

"Nay, ye're forgettin' yer astronomy, bairn. Ye've ne'er seen the Southern Cross in Wanthwaite but there it be, Cygnus with Alpha Lyra on the left. We're on the far side of the glabe."

"What's a glabe?" Roderick asked.

"Globe. Enoch means that the world is a round ball and we've sailed around a curve so that the sky is different."

Roderick began to laugh helplessly and begged the Scot to tell further outlandish tales. "It takes my mind off my leg."

The more Enoch protested that this was a scientific fact learned from a great Arab philosopher, the more gleeful Roderick became. "So are we walking upside down then? Good! I can use my hands instead of my injured leg." And he beat the sand in his mirth.

Actually I, too, wondered why we were right side up when the globe showed us to be sideways, but Enoch explained that an Arab called Yaqat was working in Palermo to find the reason.

"Be as be may," I said, suddenly solemn, "I wish I were in England. That was the land of milk and honey if we'd only known."

"Aye," they agreed, and were silent.

Then Enoch began a familiar song of the north and Roderick and I joined in, despite our mix of dialects:

"When winter's breath has ceased to blow
And March's clouds away do flee,
And wandering worms stir roots below,
Whilst icy weirs go flowing free,
Then cracks the woodruff's notes,
Then bleats the newborn lamb,
Then swells the threstle's throat,
Then swonks the maukin' ram:
Tulay! Tulay! Tulay!

"When every spinney blooms with spring
Hearts'-ease, days'-eyes, red pimpernel;
And April's dews the combes do bring
Primerole, speeds'-eyes, green moschatel;
Then warms our hearts so gay,
(Our hearts were sore a-cold)
Blood runs in madding May,
(Our blood so winter-palled):
Tulay! Tulay! Tulay!

"When summer heats our feet to dance
Mid fruiting blooms of bough and bower;
And long white nights our hearts do trance
In panting love, Nature's dower;
Then twines each girl and boy
In garlands with a kiss,
And bursts their bounds with joy
To crown their year with bliss:
Tulay! Tulay! Tulay!

Spellbound by our own song, it seemed to me that the spangled curtain of night parted just a crack so that I saw the green upon green of bending trees in the park, the greensward glistening in a rising mist. Then another voice broke my trance. King Richard was approaching. Was he coming to take me to his pavilion? But I couldn't . . .

"Excuse me," I mumbled. "I'll be right back."

"Waesucks, bairn, yer eyes be full of stars," Enoch called after me, meaning that he'd seen my tears. I threw myself into a hollow and let them soak into the greedy sand.

"Don't let me stop your singing," I heard the king say. "That was a lilting carol in the English style, I believe, very sweet."

"Scottish, Your Highness," Enoch corrected him.

"The same thing." Richard laughed derisively. "But I thought I heard a boy's treble as well. Was it Alex?"

"Aye," Enoch replied.

And there was an awkward pause.

"Sir Roderick, how is your leg? Draining well?"

"Yes, Your Highness, thank you. Alex and Enoch are fine at physic."

"I've noted as much myself." Another pause.

"When I write London, I'll see that your uncle hears of your courage." Then the king continued casually. "Where is young Alex?"

"Well, to say sooth, Your Grace, the young scamp war sickened by the sea, sae his cod be slack as a sock. Quhat with the noxious fumes fram his stomach and the bilgewater from his bowels, I sent him into the sand. 'Any tom-cat would shame you,' says I, 'have the decency to bury yer flux in a hole whar it won't offend honest Crusaders.'"

The king seemed as astounded at this description as I was.

"'Tis hard to believe, when he appeared perfectly well not two hours hence. Have you given him some potion to help?"

"Aye, verjuice mixed with grinded earthworms. 'Twill do the trick in time."

"I see." The king hesitated and I feared he was going to wait to check my condition himself. "Well, tell him I asked."

And with more courtesies on both sides, he strolled away.

"I didn't know Alex had the gripes," Roderick said.

"Ye were too drunkalewe to notice. I didna want to shame the lad before the king but, 'tween us, Alex sneaks eels when ye're not lookin' and makes himself sick. I've told him and I'll tell ye that ye mun be keerful about eat and drink in this Holy Land. 'Tis said that the flux killed more Crusaders than the Turks did last time round."

I squirmed in my hollow listening to these outright lies. What possessed the Scot? Why had he painted such a revolting image of me? What would the king think?

Then I had a revelation! Enoch attributed the flux and gripes to me because he smelled my bleeding. *Benedicite*, I dare not crawl back to my goatskin if that were the case. I dug a hollow in the sand for sleep, wallowed in self-pity, rubbed my eyes with fists and got sand under my lids.

But I forgave the Scot, for whatever his motives, he'd saved me from even greater mortification by protecting me from the king. 'Twas true that Enoch's nose was as sensitive as a wolf's, but Richard, too, was exceedingly aware of odors, as Sir Gilbert had warned me often enough.

How would I ever survive this Crusade? What antic god had put me with the king?

WE DRIFTED SLOWLY down the Ladder of Tyre, our oarsmen abetting the dying Arsur wind while most of our fleet still lay becalmed in Tyre's harbor. Gradually the rocky line of mountains along the shore receded inland and we reached Acre's plain, close upon the actual city. By late afternoon our year of travel came to an end, for ahead a great stone promontory thrust into the sea like a hand beckoning us to enter its deadly port. High on its ramparts tiny white figures gazed down, the enemy at last.

We turned out to sea to avoid a welcome of Saracen arrows, then inland again just south of the fortress-city where the Christians held the field at the mouth of a river. The *Trenchemer* listed to port as we all crowded the rail to behold the welcoming army, lords and knights who'd been fighting since the pope first issued his call. Swarming like bees atop one another, waving, cheering Crusaders rent the skies in a roar of welcome to the king who was to bring victory at last. Richard stood on the forecastle, a scarlet extension of his scarlet ship, and shouted assurances of what he would do. "We will take Acre in a month! Jerusalem before the rains come! Be home by Christmas!"

No one ashore could hear him, but we did and my own heart

bounded in hope at those words *home by Christmas*. Was it possible? Would I be gathering fir and holly for Wanthwaite's hall this year? Enoch deflated me.

"'Tis the ferst time I've heard the king speak with swich nicetee," he remarked caustically. "He mun have quaint crekes up his spangled sleeve yif he thinks he can do in four weeks what others couldna in four years."

"Four years!" I exclaimed. "You must be wrong. I've heard two."

"Acre fell in 'eighty-seven, this be, 'ninety-one. Do ye need my abacus?"

"Why? Are the Crusaders outnumbered?"

"There be six thousand Saracens in Acre, a hundred thousand Crusaders with more coming all the time. No, the king may think the battle's safe in a poke, but 'tis the world that will pipe. Besides, 'tis a bad omen to crack boast."

Just then there was a rustling on the shore to make way for a mounted party and King Philip arrived. All our faces turned to King Richard: his eyes narrowed, his lips twisted, but he waved and simulated a broad smile. King Philip flourished his banner in reply, his white face a blur. Then the two kings were lost as Richard descended to his bark and the crowd took over. The waves were alive with swimming Crusaders who threatened to pull the king to the bottom of the sea in their enthusiasm. Music struck from various parts of the shore in a competition of sounds, clerics waved holy banners and held silver chalices high, many knelt and wept, others waved jugs and staggered in joy as the whole world went mad! Now Richard was held aloft, laughing, touching, making the sign of the Cross, then was lowered onto his courser, the great stallion Fauvel, captured from Isaac Comnenus.

He leaned forward to kiss King Philip. The horses turned and they walked slowly toward Toron Hill where the kings were camped.

Meanwhile, I was arrested by the unexpected presence of women on the shore. Dressed in noble tatters of silks and satins, ermines, sporting gold brooches and jewels, they also carried bows on their shoulders and walked on bare feet. Their unkempt hair floated free in every shade of yellow, brown and red indicating that they were Europeans, and their shameful cleavage showed skin that had once been pale but was now brown as leather. Several carried falcons, and hounds swarmed at their feet.

"Who are all those women?" I asked Enoch.

"By my skull, Alex, ye have a keen eye. They mun be refugees from the fall of Acre, but take care. Aye, I've noted the glintin' in yer gray eye and know ye mun have nightspills, but watch yerself here, boy, and stay chaste. Venery in these parts and ye may wish yerself a lipper."

By the time Enoch and I joined the royal train, the kings were far ahead and most of the crowd with them. Roderick attached himself to a knight with Lord Mortimer's army and we lost sight of him. Well, finally we were in the Holy Land—treading its "streets" paved with cracked earth, breathing its sullen haze with the malodor of rotten eggs.

From the empty slope of the beach we climbed to a haphazard improvised city built in the style of an ant colony. Hundreds of artisans plied their trades in clay holes: iron-mongers, hammering carpenters, doctors and women in hospitals, shepherds guarding sheep in pens. It took so long to wend our way through this labyrinth that the sulfurous sky had darkened to brown by the time we emerged on the other side.

There we found Roderick leaning wanly against a pile of earth, his face twisted in pain.

"Here, lad, ye've attempted too much," Enoch said. "Alex, take my wrist, there, and the other one as well. Cum, Roderick, we'll carry ye."

With faint protest, the poor knight had to accept our hammock seat as we struggled up the rise to Toron Hill. E'en though Enoch took almost all the weight, I staggered and we were slowed to a crawl. I became aware of rats scurrying in dry palm fronds, occasional sharp cracks around us. We could now look downward on a hollow area dotted with bonfires, torches and tapers, each surrounded by a cinnamon glow cut by long shadows of skeletal Crusaders dancing deliriously to syncopated drums and fife. From somewhere ahead rose the solemn swell of "The Crusader's Hymn":

> *"Hear us, O Christ our King,*
> *Hear us, O Thou Who art Lord of Kings,*
> *And show us the way.*
> *Have pity upon us,*
> *And show us the way."*

Enoch tugged on my arm and we pulled Roderick with us into the dark, for the Scot had seen someone he knew from Paris. Soon we stood behind King Richard's pavilion where another Scot told Enoch in broad dialect how we should protect ourselves in this wilderness. Enoch translated: we were to keep a fire going night and day in the center of a ring of sharp stones, for the swamp below was infested with poisonous vipers which might crawl into our mouths by night; however, our stone islands would attract scorpions and we were never to thrust our hands into shadow or walk with bare feet. For water, dig about a foot down almost anywhere, but never drink anyone else's water for all was contaminated. Don't bathe in the river which is full of crocodiles (two-and-a-half Crusaders were devoured last week). Sleep with a dagger at hand lest the enemy try to kidnap you in the night. Watch food and drink, for both are oft poisoned. (His own face gave truth to his list of horrors, for the famine fever had taken all his teeth, his breath would make a camel blanch, and his sunburned eyes peered from dark shriveled sockets.) He also gave us the shocking news that both Ranulf de Glanville and the Archbishop of Canterbury had died of fevers because they'd not followed the rules. As for the battle, the chivalrous Saladin had held back this day because of King Richard's arrival, but wait till the morrow.

When I finally lay down to sleep later in our own sharp circle, I was stiff as a plank and gazed with wild fear at the fuzzy burr-stars floating above Acre's pall, listened to slitherings in the dark. Since I was bleeding, I trembled with dread. Would serpents be attracted to my menstrual flux as those red-bellied lizards had been? Then there was panic in the horse quarters—doubtless a Saracen had sneaked by. Blood puddled between my legs but nothing would make me venture into that darkness. I wondered how long I could live without sleep.

Or just how long I could live.

25

 MUST HAVE SLEPT, FOR I WOKE WITH A START. The stench of nightearth had sent me into a fit of coughing and I sat upright to get my breath, thereby releasing the flood again. Objects were barely visible in this predawn hour and nobody stirred. Cautiously I moved a few feet from our tent to take care of myself.

I'd barely finished when the sun hurtled like God's thunderbolt across the sky and exploded at the foot of our hill.

"*Judgment Day!*" I howled.

Wild with terror, I leaped on top of the sleeping Scot.

"Wake and ask to be forgiven!" I screamed. "We're going to Hell!"

A second sun with a tail of foul gas shrieked through the air. Shadowy forms rushed by, a steady pounding began, shouts, drums rolling, somewhere the skirl of a bagpipe, everywhere a chaos of din and disaster.

"Greek fire," said Enoch, pushing me aside. "Best eat a farl and drink a little sour wine. Micht be yer last chancit."

"You mean we're going to die?" I cried, grabbing him again.

"I mean we're about to crusade and, aye, 'tis a risky business."

He forced Roderick and me to swallow his cakes, whereupon the knight saw one of Mortimer's men in the distance and bid us a hasty farewell. By now Enoch was strapping his wooden shields fore and aft.

"You're not going to fight!"

"I'm going to study the situation. Ye stay put till I cum back."

"When?" I yelled into the mists as he ran away.

Suddenly he turned, grabbed my cheeks in his greasy hands and kissed me on the forehead. "By my faye, Alex, betimes I'd rather have a schitten kite fer a brother than ye, boot we're stuck twaye and twaye. And I do love thee."

Again he was gone. Nothing he'd done since I'd known him had ever so alarmed me. Never would he have shown affection if he e'er expected to see me alive again. I sat paralyzed by the ramifications, then was knocked out of my sorrow when a leather bucket dropped into my lap. I looked up at Sir Gilbert.

"Collect piss and bring it back to soak hides," he said. "King's orders."

"Collect piss? How? Where will I find it?"

He smiled malevolently. "You milk a man as you would a cow. As to where, in the battlefield below. The trenches are filled with bladders just waiting for you. Hurry now, for the king has already assembled his war tower, Mategriffon, and wants it covered with piss-soaked leather by day's end. 'Tis the only way to guard it against fire."

As he left, I saw that he, too, carried a pail. What a woodly assignment, necessary of course but hardly heroic. Still, if the king had said I must . . .

I gripped my leather bucket uncertainly, disoriented by the noise and bursts of light above, unable to make out forms in the dust clouds below. Finally I retraced our route of the previous night and when I reached the point where Roderick had been lying against the mound, I saw a path twisting into the battlefield. Foot after foot trotted past me, quivers filled with arrows, crude wooden shields in place. I edged to the top and stared downward. *Benedicite*, a field potted and trenched as if a thousand moles dug there, filled with dusty heaps and mounds that at first I couldn't identify, then saw they were corpses. Aye, fat bloated horses, men in all stages of decay, smelling of glue and rancid butter and burnt sugar combined. I held my breath and slipped into line.

Immediately I was hit from the rear and fell in a frightened heap atop a knight whose eyes and tongue were gone, his body streaked with kite-shit that made him look like a marble idol.

"Be ye daft? Get into a trench!"

I looked around, dazed.

A bowman was shaking his fist. "Don't get in the line of bow-shot, boy! Stay down!"

I wormed my way across a carpet of corpses to the nearest trench, then bumped down on an uneven stair of crumpled bodies. For a time I sat in my macabre hole not remembering why I was there, then pulled myself upward by a bone-shank and approached a busy bowman. I tapped his shoulder timidly.

"Do you have to piss, sir?"

He brushed my hand away and took another shot.

"Because if you do, I'd appreciate it if you'd give me your piss."

He turned in disbelief. "What did you say?"

"I'm collecting piss, sir."

"And I'm the King of England! Heigh, Joe, come here!"

Another varlet struggled along the trench.

"This lad here wants your piss, Joe. I told him that you piss pure honey and he wants a suck!"

A knot now grew around us.

"I need piss," I said desperately, "to use against the Greek fire."

"Nothin' like it," one nodded sagely, "and if that fails, try spit."

And they all guffawed.

"Tell you what, we'll form a pissing brigade. Ready now, one, two, let her go!"

He pissed on another varlet's feet.

"That's not funny, Bob!"

"Why, you're an ungrateful fellow that says so, when I've saved your stinking feet from the fire!"

"It's for King Richard!" I cried. "The king needs it to protect his war machines!"

There was an uneasy silence.

"He do wear the king's colors."

"And I have heard of pissing on hides."

One by one they each contributed a few drops, but I saw that 'twould be weeks at this rate before the king's huge tower was covered. I went the length of that trench with little luck, then hesitantly peered over the edge to the next. To my astonishment, I saw Enoch. I sat by a decayed chest to consider. I had about three cups of piss now, hardly enow to count, so I might as well use them to best advantage. I waited till there was a momentary lull, then ran to Enoch.

"Git ye doon!" he cried. "Didna I tell ye to wait by our tent? Ye'll be killt!"

He squatted beside me.

"Aye, but King Richard said . . . he ordered . . ." And without saying more, I dipped a cup of piss and poured it over the Scot's head. He gasped, sputtered, turned red with blue veins.

"Quhat the— Damnatioun! I'm all droukit in pisswater!"

"So you won't catch fire," I said. "I don't want either of us to burn!" And I poured a cup over my own head.

He tore a rag from the corpse, shook off the white worms and wiped himself vigorously. "Ye're a woodly blastie, bairn, and I belave the battle hae tinted yer reason. Cum, I'll take ye back to the tent."

"No, 'tis what the king ordered, only I can't get enough for Mategriffon so we might as well use it." And I explained my order.

He listened dumbfounded to my words, then shook his head. "I wouldna believe it except that ye couldna wende such a thing. Stay low."

He peered cautiously o'er the edge of the trench, then took my hand and pulled me onto the field. There he crouched between me and the fearsome wall with his shield protecting both of us as we started to run. We'd gone only a few feet when I was swept up from the rear and Enoch pushed flat to the ground.

I gazed down from King Richard's horse.

"How dare you bring the boy here!" the king shouted and raised his sword.

Enoch struggled to his knees. "Ye sent him here, Your Highness. Aye, and on swich a woodly task!"

"Sir Gilbert!" I piped as loud as I could o'er the noise all around us. "He sent me, Your Highness!"

"What?" The horse reared and the king fought for a moment to bring him under control.

"Sir Gilbert—to collect piss for Mategriffon!" I pointed to my empty bucket where I'd dropped it.

"From *soldiers*?" Richard forgot Enoch in his shock. Without further talk, he spurred his horse to a leap and soon we were riding up the hill back to the city, leaving the Scot in his trench. Once we were out of bowshot, the king reined his destrier.

"Let me understand, Sir Gilbert told you to go into the field and collect piss from the fighting men? Think carefully, for I don't want to make a mistake."

Nor did I, for I heard the threat, but what could I say? Enoch shouldn't be blamed. "Aye, to collect it as you would milk from a cow." I hung my head, embarrassed.

By now a small crowd had gathered to touch the king, but Richard paid them no heed. "And said that this was *my* order?"

"Aye."

I glanced up, saw the red whelks, saw death in those eyes. By then he was sufficiently calm to notice my stink, however, and hastily slipped me to the ground. "My other pages were instructed to prepare the hides, but they got their piss from horses, not men."

Of course! Why hadn't I thought of that? Because of Sir Gilbert, that malicious demon! King Richard was looking at me with the bemused affection I knew so well. "Alex, you'll serve me tonight." He flourished his sword through my miasma of flies. "Only see that you clean yourself. We need no more pests around our person."

"Yes, Your Highness."

And he was gone.

MY HAIR WAS still damp from a cleansing plunge in the sea when I entered King Richard's pavilion. A Pisano was already serving wine to the king and his guest of honor, the Count of Champagne. Quickly I picked up a tray to help.

The parley went on half the night, it seemed, and was soothly most serious to judge by the courtiers' faces, though I followed little. I gleaned only that Henry of Champagne was nephew to both King Philip and King Richard, that King Philip had cheated the young count in some manner and that King Richard was going to restore money and favor.

"You will have four thousand pounds unencumbered," the king said, "plus food for both men and beasts for the duration of the Crusade."

Champagne fell to his knees.

"No, no obeisance, Henry," our king rebuked him graciously. "You've earned it by your solitary siege this past year."

Gradually the business was finished and, one by one, the great lords begged to be excused. Finally there was only Champagne and he, too, was poised to leave. The king accompanied him to the door.

"No, 'tis fitting that you tell the Pisanos of our offer," he said. "After all, they know and trust you."

"Henceforth you are their leader," Champagne responded in his respectful manner, and he, too, left.

The king and I were alone. Belatedly I wondered if this would be our first assignation and my legs became weak.

"Well, Alex, you look recovered from your strange baptism," the king drawled, his eyes sparkling. "Your nemesis, Sir Gilbert, will soon discover the terrors of the field himself. I've made him a common foot soldier."

I gazed upward at his stern face, not knowing what to say. We both understood that Sir Gilbert wouldn't survive more than a day in that gutted valley of death.

"Come, child, help me to my bed."

His heavy hand rested on my shoulder and we walked awkwardly to his pallet covered with leopard skins. This, then, was the beginning? I couldn't think, had no time to think. He sank onto the edge of the bed, turned me so we looked upon each other. His figure blurred in my eyes, his handsome features approached and receded as if he were under water, and I thought I would swoon.

But 'twas the king who collapsed at my feet.

26

E KNEW RICHARD WOULD LIVE, *DEO GRATIAS*, BUT he was a very sick man. His physicians pronounced that he had *leonardie* as well as *arnoldia*, both complicated by his old ague and its concomitant high fever. Not only was he losing his hair and nails (*alopecia*), but his face was a mass of watery sores concentrated around and inside his mouth; his gums bled, were receded, and 'twas predicted that he would soon lose all his teeth.

Withal he was like a wounded beast howling with rage and 'twas not safe to come close or try to appease him. When Orlando bled him for his fever, Richard hurled the basin against his tent making a huge ugly stain, and he cried aloud, "Blast your stupid leeching! Get me out of here! I must do my Lord's work!"

Then in the very next breath he would blaspheme his Lord: "My God, do your worst! You'll not defeat Richard! I have a lion's heart to defy You, a fox's head to outwit You! And I and I alone will win Jerusalem! Let the Devil aid me if You will not!"

His priests crossed themselves quickly and Father Nicholas wanted to exorcise his demons but the king wouldn't hear of it. *Exorcise God if you would have my enemy*, he cried, *for He has made me a second Job*!

Throughout the night I huddled in a corner of his pavilion, willing to do *anything* if I could reverse his symptoms. At dawn King Philip entered the tent.

He bent over the sick king and studied his face. "Well, Richard, I believe you are ill after all."

"Your faith is touching."

"Would you like me to send my priest?"

"It depends. I'm not ready for a final absolution, if that's what you have in mind."

330

"Calm yourself, coz, I meant to exorcise whatever demons escaped your confession in Messina."

Richard rose on one elbow. "Are you willing to hold back our attack for another day? For I assure you that this setback is temporary."

"Well, so it may be." King Philip turned and from where I sat I could see his mocking signal to the Duke of Burgundy. "Yet you know that such a postponement could be disastrous." He smiled down on Richard. "I refer, of course, to Saladin. If he learns that you are ill, he will attack with all haste."

At that moment there was a rustle outside the pavilion, an exchange of angry voices in a strange tongue, a low mediation and the flap opened to admit a Saracen carrying a large basket. Richard's interpreter Henfrid de Torn followed.

"The Sultan Saladin sends you his deepest sympathy on your illness," the interpreter said, "and hopes you will accept this gift to aid in your recovery."

A cloth was drawn back and everyone gasped. Lying on a bed of crushed ice and snow was a pile of luscious fruit: melons, grapes, figs, dates and others that I'd ne'er seen before. Most remarkable was the ice, which the Saracen said had been run from the mountains to lower Richard's fever.

"He'll send this daily until you are well," Henfrid informed Richard.

"So much for secrecy," Richard said dryly, "and for enmity as well. I'm impressed by the quality of my adversary who sends me a sincere token to speed my recovery while my brother would have me expiring from my own sins."

"Perhaps you misapply the word *brother*," Philip said coldly, "for I remember well that you abjured that relationship at our last meeting. Moreover, you may have more in common with Saladin than you think, for I believe he, too, is filled with sweet blandishments and perfidious acts. But now, if you'll excuse me, I must go to the field."

"To attack?"

"Yes."

"Forget your bitterness for a moment, Philip, and listen to me:

this is a tactical error. Obviously Saladin knows our depleted strength. He will slaughter you, or waste your best effort with minimal reply."

"Enjoy your fruit, Richard." The French king left.

"Curse him." Richard lay back, exhausted from the parley.

His doctors then hastened to pack Saladin's ice on the king's brow against the rising heat, though Richard's linen pavilion was designed to permit the breeze. I was jarred from my miserable stupor when the king mentioned my name.

"Alex, you'll stay with me for the next two nights."

Flattered and relieved, I agreed to serve.

"Yes, Your Highness."

Orlando gazed askance on my frail bones. "He's very small, My Liege, and methinks knows little of physic."

"Who does?" was the king's bitter reply. "At least he'll not pray over me. At sundown, boy."

THE NIGHT PASSED without incident. After a good sleep on both our parts, I left the king's tent at dawn.

It took me over an hour to get back to Enoch's tent, for I'd finished bleeding and must construct a new prick to replace the one I'd just discarded. When I arrived, I found the Scot burning my bloody rags in the fire!

I sat hurriedly on the ground before I should fall. After a long silence, I forced myself to look in his face. He was frowning but seemed not suspicious. I couldn't refrain from asking him, "What are you burning?"

"Someone left an old bandage in our camp."

I made no comment.

Finally my poor rags were gone and he added wood to the flame, then heated oatcakes.

"What did you do last night?" he asked blandly.

I choked on a crumb. "Nothing. That is, I slept. The king was drugged."

"I hope ye didna kiss him." He turned burning eyes. "'Tis a good way to get the fever."

"Why should I kiss him?" I cried, aggrieved. "He's sick!"

He made a face, didn't answer.

"He wants you to take me to some high place in the tent city where I can watch the field. King Philip may attack today, and the king wants Ambroise to have a report for his history. Ambroise is still becalmed in Tyre, you know."

"I knaw." His eyes still burned. "Ye can't tell a catapult fram a butter churn."

"But you can instruct me." I smiled, forcing my dimples, and saw it was the wrong tactic.

"Dinna play henhussy wi' me, Alex." He rose, and it seemed to me his eyes raked my torso with unusual interest.

Benedicite. I couldn't wait to get my new prick in place.

At the town's center, Enoch learned that the highest point was the church belfry. After considerable meandering, we found a mean structure with a second story and climbed up an outside stair to the shaky bell tower.

"Nocht bad," Enoch mused as he gazed out on the vista before us. "A mighty good view."

I tried to pay heed as he described the nature of the terrain. We were looking into a round valley shaped somewhat like a Greek amphitheater with the hills of Toron on our right forming one side, the hills of the tent city another (though it sloped down to the sea), the sea itself the third, and the long high wall of Acre the fourth. Acre was a square city surrounded by a double wall, open only to its enclosed port which was like a curved hand with a tiny strait between thumb and forefinger. On each finger, however, rose a high tower, one called the Tower of Flies because of human sacrifices, and the strait was guarded by a heavy chain. Nevertheless, Christian ships dominated the sea all along the coast and no Turkish vessel could break through the blockade to bring the besieged city supplies. Christians held all the hills as well and 'twas hard to see how the Turks survived. Saracen swimmers sometimes sneaked in at night, or Saladin sent camel trains in the dark, but very few got by the Christian watchmen. 'Twas suspected, Enoch explained, that the outlying fruit orchards and pastures somehow supplied the trapped Turks.

His voice trailed off, and he fell into a trance.

"Alex," he said hollowly. "Do ye recall our oath of brother-hood?"

"Aye, very well."

"We're to gi'e each other freedom in love."

I nodded, waiting breathlessly.

"Boot . . ." He bit his lip and his eyes were a startling blue in the clear light. "Boot it doesna apply yif one or tother be bewitched."

"You mean has a spell put on him by a witch?"

"Alex, doona lat anyone touch ye. Do ye hear? No one! Yif sum painted Willie tries, come right to me!"

Again I nodded.

He stared at my face, my figure, and seemed bewildered. "Ye're . . . tempting."

I cleared my throat, waved to the field. "I would have thought the Christians would have won by now."

"No," he said with relief, "'twas not that simple . . ."

Despite numerical superiority and greater mobility, the Christians were also entrapped. They, too, depended upon the outside world for food, and the only Christian stronghold capable of supplying them was Tyre; yet last year Conrad of Montferrat had refused to send grain, with the result that over thirty thousand Crusaders had starved. That's why Richard had taken the time to secure Cyprus, a grain-rich island close by. Furthermore the fortress of Acre was formidable. The inner city—where we could see spires and waving poplars—was not only protected by two walls, the outer one measuring fifteen feet in depth, but also by a moat which was too deep and wide to span. The Crusader assault against the wall was concentrated in the valley below us and while we could see many pockmarks where our stones had hit the outer wall, no real progress had been made in four years of trying.

Nor were the Christians the only aggressors. Far in the distance, we could see the smoke of another tent city called Tell-Ayadiyeh where Saladin had his headquarters on the road to Damascus. The Christians' greatest dread was that he would attack their rear and push them into the sea. Our men had built a huge trench around our entire area, but it was nothing that a nimble horse couldn't jump. And while Christians outnumbered Arabs in this small valley, Saladin could call on eight hundred thousand allies or more.

"How do you know so much?" I asked Enoch in awe.

"Waesucks, lad, 'tis fundamental to survey the country around ye. A good part of victory be in the choice of battleground."

"Think you this was a good choice for the Crusaders?"

He didn't answer at once. "Depends. In any case, 'twas the anely spot Saladin didna take so I reckon 'twere good. Now let's talk of strategy."

I gazed down on thousands of crouched figures in their trenches shooting haphazard arrows at Turks well beyond bowshot. "They look like so many dung beetles," I said.

"Aye, yif human dead be dung. The burial squads cannot keep up with the supply, as ye can tell by yer nose."

"Where are the knights?"

"What could knights do? They be trained for hand-to-hand combat, ye know that. They'll be good when the wall tumbles, nocht before."

"I don't see any signs that it will ever tumble. When was it built?"

"I canna say, but I'll find out. But we air assaulting the wall e'en so. See there, that stone caster beyond the rock."

"I can hear it anyway."

"And another on yer left. See?"

Indeed the field was dotted with machines of various designs, called *petrariae* by some, *beliers* by others, in any case different-size catapults (or mangonels) which fell into two groups no matter how they were named: the smaller ones designed like giant crossbows with low trajectories, best for hurling huge spears; the larger more like slingshots with high trajectories, best for throwing stones and casks of boiling oil over the wall.

"What exactly is Greek fire?" I asked.

"We doona have the exact formula, but we knaw it has naphtha and sulfur in an oil mix. It explodes upon contact and canna be put out by water. It clings to whatever it touches, like burning glue."

As he spoke, a small machine burst into flames right before our eyes and covered the field with a thick black smoke.

"They'll beat us in the air!" I cried.

"Nay, lad, the battle will be won underground. We mun mine the wall and make a breach."

"How is that possible?"

"Some luckless wight will dig a tunnel to the foundations, fill the hole with oil and brush, light it and blow himself and the wall to Hell. A martyr for king and country."

I shuddered for this poor unknown mole.

"I mun gae work on the king's machines," Enoch said abruptly. "Will ye be all right here alone?"

"Of course." In fact, I couldn't wait to be alone.

"I'm nocht sure. Bairn, ye would tell me yif . . ." He stopped, uncertain and a little embarrassed.

"You could come back for me at the end of day," I said.

"I mane to. All right, then . . ." He climbed down the ladder.

I took my parchment and stylus in case he looked back on me before he left and wrote a description of the terrain. Then I walked to the window to gaze across to where King Philip was preparing to attack, despite King Richard's warning. At that point—I know not whence, or how I could not have seen the varlet—something whizzed by my ear and rattled on the floor behind me. Puzzled, I turned and saw an arrow lying at my feet!

It was a Norman arrow.

I picked it up in wonder, still not grasping its significance. I thought it was a mistake; someone had bad aim. Only slowly did I realize that no one has such poor aim that he shoots an arrow backward over his shoulder! Acre's wall stood in the opposite direction. Furthermore, no arrow yet made could whiz from the field below to where I stood.

Someone had shot at me intentionally. And at close range.

Instantly I fell to the floor. Nothing more happened. I listened for sounds. With Enoch gone, I was vulnerable both from the window and from below. I crept on my stomach to the edge of the platform and with enormous effort pulled the ladder up to my floor. There, anyone wanting to approach would have to shout.

A pox on writing about King Philip's attack. By the end of the day he would have won or failed, and I would make up what happened between. Nothing would make me expose myself at that window again.

I then took the secret cache of materials I had gathered this morning and began laboriously to construct a new prick.

DID ENOCH NOTICE my new shape? I thought he did, but knew not whether that was good or no. For the first time, I wondered if I'd erred in judgment. True, the new member I'd devised was more clever by far than my former models, its subtle swelling much closer to the real shape, but 'twas also true that it hadn't been there this morning.

If he noticed at all, Enoch immediately forgot my transformation when he saw the arrow.

"Yif ye're right, someone wants ye dead," he said. He sighed deeply. "Alex, air ye sure we must crusade to get Wanthwaite? We could leave for Paris—there be many ships sailing til and fra—pick up our writ, and git rid of Roncechaux through Assize court."

"Not with Osbert as judge," I reminded him. "Northumberland won't give up his own land."

"I'm willing to do the ordeal," he reminded me in return. "I'll fight Roland in single combat."

And leave me with half an estate. Besides, I'd made a promise to Richard. . . . I turned away.

When I turned back, he was still studying me. "Be it the king quhat keeps ye?" he asked softly.

"I don't know what you mean."

KING PHILIP had lost his battle. His favorite machine called "Bad Neighbor" had been destroyed by Greek fire. Whether from disappointment or God's vengeance, the French king now became sick with King Richard's malady. The loss of both leaders cast a terrible pall on the fighting. Then through sheer force of will, King Richard rallied and took over the leadership, though he couldn't walk or ride. He governed from an improvised hammock with a webbed canopy, which he called a *testudo*. His first order was to raise the foot soldier's pay from three aurei to four aurei per month, thus wooing the volunteer army from Philip.

His second command was to swale the orchards and groves around the city in order to starve the men of Acre. Soon smoke and soot garbed us so we looked like Bedouins.

His third, and most ominous, was to summon Enoch.

"Lord Enoch, you have the best engineer's mind in my entire company."

"Thank you, Your Highness," the Scot answered warily.

"You are also acute and brave."

Enoch merely nodded.

"Therefore I would like your opinion. How can we best break the stalemate of Acre's battle?"

"You have to lower the wall," Enoch answered promptly.

I began to get the drift of Richard's questioning and suddenly recalled: *I'll get rid of the Scot.* And Enoch: *Some luckless wight will blow himself to Hell.* How diabolical of the king!

"Exactly." The king nodded approval. "At what point?"

The Scot studied the situation briefly in the field below us. "'Tis obvious. The largest tower at the corner there, on the southeast."

"Right again, what we call the Accursed Tower. And how should I proceed?"

Don't answer, I signaled mentally. *Pretend you don't know.*

This time Enoch frowned for some time. "You'll tunnel in a northeasterly direction at least twenty feet under, for the girth of the wall indicates a base of fifteen feet or more. Then you fire the tunnel and collapse the wall's foundation."

Richard gave the Scot a fixed look. "Do it."

"*Me*, Your Highness?"

"My best engineer."

"Except that I've had no experience in sapping, Your Grace. With your whole strategy riding on its success, and with the considerable risk of life to your men both above and below, I humbly suggest that there may be someone better for the task, someone more knowledgeable."

The king became as angry as his depleted energies allowed. "Someone with courage, you mean. You have your order: see to it!

And don't lag your foot unless you would lose a foot. I mean to be in Acre within the month."

Enoch's lips pressed tight, he bowed and walked quickly away.

I ran after the Scot as he strode and caught him at our tent where he swilled a methier of ale, his eyes blank.

"*I'll* speak to him!" I cried. "You're right, 'tis woodly to attempt such a task for the very first time. And you told me yourself that 'twas sure death!"

Enoch shook his head. "Spare yerself the blither, bairn. The king knows what he wants. There's an expression among these kings of chivalry in breme battle; I believe 'tis '*enfants perdus*,' meaning that some men be 'lost children,' expendable. I be yer lost child."

NEVERTHELESS, I did speak to Richard the very next day.

"You show your ignorance, boy. I've given your brother an opportunity for great glory. By George, I envy him! I can't imagine a better way to die."

"I don't want him to die!" I protested without thinking.

Instantly the king's visage froze. "The Scot is expendable; Acre is not. His sacrifice can serve double purpose."

I looked at him, appalled. Could he possibly believe that I would want the Scot *murdered*? For I clearly saw now that that was what the king was about, the deliberate slaughter of my Scottish friend. Didn't he know that I needed Enoch?

I started again to speak, saw the king's eyes as he looked around, and fell silent. But I prayed, Please God, don't let Enoch die. God had so favored me in my recent prayers that surely He must grant this.

I DECIDED not to tell Enoch of my failure with the king but to try to cheer him however I could. When I returned to camp with this intention, I found him standing by the tent, a puzzled expression on his face; in his hands he held two dead pigeons.

"Are you going to make pigeon pie?" A great favorite of mine.

He spoke portentously. "Alex, these birds be murdered."

"Of course, but that's a strange way to say it. We don't eat live birds."

"Murdered," he repeated. "Poor little martyrs fer our sakes."

I thought the strain of being Richard's sapper had made him woodly.

"Sit down, Enoch," I said as kindly as I could. "Let me cook the pigeons for a change, and you talk to me about the history of Scotland."

"The dinner be prepared," he said stiffly. "There, liver and oats, but doona touch it yif ye value yer life."

"What?"

"I'm tellin' ye, these birds ate of our meal and promptly died. Someone hae poisoned our food." He tossed the pigeons into a ravine. "By the smell, I'd say with monkshood."

I sat down weakly. "The Saracens. Aye, 'tis said they sneak into camps and pick off one Crusader at a time by all sorts of devious means—poison, scorpions, snakes."

"Aye, mayhap." Enoch remained standing. "Anely I be not so sure that the Saracens be the best suspects."

King Richard?

No, the king would never stoop to such lowly perfidious tactics. Nor would he chance that I might eat the poison instead of Enoch.

It must be the Saracens who'd chosen our camp by chance. I sighed with relief. Terrible as it was, it was not likely to happen again.

DEO GRATIAS, KING RICHARD wanted his tunnel to succeed more than he wanted Enoch to perish. Therefore he selected another group of *enfants perdus* to sacrifice so that his own sappers could work in peace, namely King Philip's sappers who dug in another direction. He explained exactly how he was doing it.

"Now, see there, Alex, to your left, the entry into Philip's tunnel. He's chosen the wrong goal so it's expendable, and a concentration of fighting close to his tunnel will distract the Saracens from our more important digging."

He thereby ordered four lords to assemble their knights and make a foray in a manner which pointed like an arrow to King Philip's men.

"But won't they die, Your Highness?"

He shrugged impatiently. "Probably, but that's the difference between strategy and random death. Hundreds die here daily, but if we carefully select which men will die and for what purpose, we make their deaths a stepping stone to victory. Diversionary tactics lose men, but don't waste them. You see?"

I wondered if men so used would agree, but I kept my counsel. The king glanced at me obliquely.

"I spoke to Enoch, by the way. Since you were so vehement, I gave him a choice."

"Oh, thank you, Your Highness!" I cried. "When will he be replaced?"

"Why, never. He wants the job, just as I thought. Or," he amended, "he wants the reward."

"What reward did you offer?" I asked, much amazed.

"Ask him."

I waited a decent interval, then dashed to find the Scot and do just that.

He was evasive. "Aye, yif I live and yif I get back home, I'm to have reward."

"Yes, but what? Gold?"

He turned his look on me, his eyes still blank and almost hostile. "Put it this way, bairn: yif I want to stay in the Holy Land at all, I have to dig this hole. Then I also get reward. Yif not, I have to leave."

There was a long silence as I absorbed his hidden message: the king would be rid of him one way or another and, though the Scot knew it, he had elected to stay with me. I turned away to hide my grief.

DAY AFTER DAY Enoch grew grimmer. He never laughed or japed, rarely talked. He descended like a mole each morn before sunup and climbed out marrow-weary, black with ooze and powdered with dust, his eyes heavy, his spirit depressed in a way I'd ne'er seen before. Other Crusaders spoke of him as a marvel of ingenuity and labor, soothly a wizard of mining, but he took their comments with stoic disregard. It frightened me to see him so and I mourned for his former abrasive self. King Richard might replace knights and bish-

ops in his game, but Enoch was unique. Hadn't I learned it when he
fell into the Rhône? I didn't need the same lesson twice. But what
could I do?

King Philip's tunnel was fired and made a breach in the wall at
the cost of two hundred seven Frenchmen dead, including his engineer Jean de Brun. The Saracens stood in the crack and jeered at
the Christians who still couldn't approach the wall because of the
deep moat at its base. But, as Richard pointed out, the breach had
its encouraging effect, and every day he urged his men to scale the
wall. The point here, he explained, was that the *enfants perdus* were
the advance for the men who *would* get over the wall and were thus
preparing them spiritually for the Herculean task.

Twice the king had relapses of his disease while Philip continued
to improve. During these periods the French king took command,
but on the day Richard's tunnel was to be fired the English king was
there.

I helped Enoch prepare, rubbed his woad onto his back and legs.

"This micht be farewell, Alex."

I saw that he was serious and felt my heart thud to my feet.

"The king is certain you'll succeed—I've heard him say so.
Soothly Enoch, many times."

He nodded, lips twisted. "Aye, that we schal. The tunnel will
blow, the wall will fall. But it still micht be farewell. As a Scot I tell
thee true: my chances be about the same as a snow blizzard this
day."

Fanfare blared in the distance and he took my arms.

"List to me lad, and hear me good. Yif I die today, *doona continue
on this Crusade.*"

His blazing eyes frightened me near to a swoon.

"What do you mean? Where would I go?"

"Home, home to Wanthwaite. Gae to Malcolm first in Paris and
ask him to help. I mun gae, so pay heed: there's a bundle tied under
Twixt's pillion for ye to use for expenses yif it cums to that."

He was offering me money. I felt such a mix of gratitude, terror
and astonishment that I couldn't speak.

"Buy passage on the next ship. And Alex, forget the king. Nay,
dinna deny that ye dote on him—anyone can see it. Ye're a silly

bairn and he's a great hero sae it's to be expected, but such a fate be nocht in yer stars."

"What fate?" I couldn't help asking.

"I doona think I need to explain. Promise!"

To keep him from worrying more, I promised, for I, too, couldn't explain. Yet, I remembered well from Messina, the king had warned me that if I tried to leave the Crusade I would lose Wanthwaite.

The Scot took my cheeks and kissed me, then ran down the hill. I washed off the woad and somberly followed him.

I joined the king at his pavilion where he mounted his litter to be carried onto the field while foot ran beside him supporting his *testudo* overhead, a hurdle roofed with wicker-work and hides. I took a quiver of heavy steel quarrels for his arbalest, for there was an opening in his bombproof for him to aim his deadly arrows. Enoch had been furious that I was to go into the field but I wore my helmet, could crouch behind Richard's shield; there was an inpenetrable aura around the king which made all of us close to him secure.

A declivity had been dug for his leopard skins with a good view of where the tunnel would explode and we all kept our eyes anxiously on the spot. The Muslims were still at prayers, the Christians should have been at Matins. We watched, silent, hardly breathing.

Enoch's still alive, I thought, but three heartbeats from now he may be dead. What would the world be like without Enoch? Once before I'd faced the possibility and almost died myself.

Then it began, an uneasy rumble and sway in the earth's gut, an explosion of smoke and fire to rival Mount Etna as flames shot upward carrying huge rocks as if they were feathers. Right before us the Accursed Tower cracked, shuddered, leaned and stayed at an impossible angle as soldiers below scurried away from its imminent fall and Turks in the gap behind stared with disbelief at their sudden exposure.

"Good work!" the delighted king shouted. "Into the breach, men! Climb the wall!"

Meantime I turned to the tunnel's entrance awaiting the emergence of the first sappers. Soothly they must have survived—no bodies had shot upward. Yet how could they live through such hellfire? One by one they crept out, blackened, exhausted, exhilarated men.

And Enoch was there!

"He's alive!" I said triumphantly.

"Of course," Richard replied, then registered my tone and continued coldly. "I surmise that he didn't tell you what his reward is to be, Alex. You should follow the Plantagenet method of dealing with the Scots and learn to use them, but never trust them."

I wanted to answer, but this was not the time. Also, a thought stirred that I'd repressed in my fear: Was Enoch's reward connected to Wanthwaite? Was his willingness to risk his life more connected to my property than to me?

BY LATE AFTERNOON the king was waxing angry, for no one could reach the wall across the wide deep moat.

"After them, you cowards! Pull it down! Two gold bezants for a stone off the wall!"

Spurred by gold, several Pisanos gave their lives for naught. Knights tried to leap their horses o'er the ditch and were rewarded with Greek fire dropped directly on their heads, turning them into burning effigies!

"Three bezants! For England and St. George!" the king shouted.

"I'll enter Acre today or die trying!" a brave knight cried as he spurred his mount forward.

"Albert de Clement," Richard said. "He'll triumph if anyone can."

We watched Albert scramble on foot down the moat, somehow emerge on the other side, start a hand-over-hand ascent up the sloping stone. Reach the top! Go over! Moments later a Saracen appeared wearing Albert's helmet. The king took careful aim and shot him through the heart.

"Four bezants!" Richard cried.

Our arrows brought down so many Saracens that the moat began to fill with dead bodies.

"Use the bodies as a bridge!" the king called.

Darkness fast descended. Trumpets sounded the end of the battle and knights retreated for well-earned rest. But not Richard. He sent me to his pavilion to fetch refreshment while he conferred with his captains.

The moon floated full o'er the scene of carnage and despair. One by one, silent Saracens appeared on their parapet, let down ropes to descend so they could collect their dead. One by one King Richard and his knights picked them off and slowly, slowly, the moat was filled. Guards were placed to make certain our bridge of corpses remained in place, and the king finally retired.

AT DAWN the sick king was again in place.

Mategriffon was pulled to the edge of the mushy ditch. Finally the mules were whipped, the monstrous structure crunched o'er human bones and gore right to the wall's edge. Tun after tun of Greek fire struck the piss-soaked hides to no avail, and now the Crusaders could shoot directly into the city.

Then there was fanfare behind us! From the hills thundered white clouds of Arabs on their magic steeds. "Aid for Islam! Aid for Islam!"

For a moment the Crusaders quailed, were thrown off balance. What we all dreaded more than anything: Saladin attacking our rear!

"Take heart and fight, you cowards!" the king bellowed hoarsely.

E'en so, 'twas a scene of panic. Drums throbbed without end, horsemen leaped howling through smoke o'er the heads of foot in the trenches, green banners flowed. All kinds of strange men: dervishes whirling like madmen in their red skirts, Egyptian mamluks in mail, black Kurds with long shining scimitars and painted shields, saffron-cloaked *Halka*. Everywhere a melee of noise, confusion, cries, the clang of sword against sword, animals neighing in terror, the pound of stone on stone.

"Christ and the Sepulcher! Christ and the Sepulcher!" chanted the foot as they took deadly aim at the horses' bellies when they leaped the trenches.

"Islam!"

"Christ!"

But our king had anticipated the fearful tactic and now waved his banner thrice to waiting knights on Toron Hill. Men of steel, lances held horizontally before them, rode in tight formation as one body down into the fray. The Saracens were trapped. Now mayhem intensified. Through rolling clouds of dust we watched the panicked white eyes and bared teeth of stalwart destriers as they took mortal wounds, great knights slowly tumble to the ground in clattering heaps, and everywhere the flow of blood. At last, hours later, the Saracens regrouped the remnants of their gaudy forces and limped back o'er the hills whence they had come. And we turned once more to the wall.

Richard sent the signal to intensify the battering of the tower where it leaned as if jug-bitten. One great *belier* tower after another was put into action, drawn closer to increase the damage; another shudder and 'twas down! A roar filled the skies!

Hour after hour the fighting continued without letup, ever fiercer, ever deadlier. Then King Richard rose from his pelt.

"My horse!" he demanded.

Nothing could stop him. Followed by Leicester, Hugh le Brun, Andrew de Chauvigny and the Bishop of Salisbury, his great figure rode into the swirl and scream of the battle. I didn't breathe for an hour as I watched. His long arms turned like windmills, his shield in one hand, his broadsword in the other, as heads rolled at his feet. Never had anyone seen such a sight! E'en the Turks paused, awed by his invincible prowess. On and on he rode, right up the wall I trowe, a powerful god-king and no one could stop him.

Into darkness he fought as bodies piled high in the moat, towers pulled to the wall one after the other, stones peeled away like fish scales. Then there was a giant shout in the darkness!

Acre had surrendered!

It was July twelfth, almost exactly one month since our arrival. King Richard had kept his word.

27

ICHARD PAID FOR HIS MAGNIFICENT LEADERSHIP with a brief relapse in his health, but he was still able to dictate the terms of peace. He ordered all Turks to leave Acre forthwith except for three thousand emirs who volunteered themselves as hostages until Saladin should fulfill Richard's demands for a huge ransom of gold, a return of Christian prisoners and the True Cross. However, our wise king set a deadline for the sultan so we would not be bogged down in Acre forever.

I was witness to these exciting negotiations as the king now kept me near him in his pavilion. Once his hot eyes beamed from his pale face and he whispered, "We'll have a palace instead of a tent, Cupid."

Then that same day a runner arrived from Tyre with the news that the queens had left Cyprus, their buss was expected at any moment. Caught utterly off-guard, the king's face became suddenly unmasked and for a fleeting moment I witnessed such childish terror as I'd never seen before in the most timorous soldier. 'Twas gone in an instant but left an imprint like that from looking directly into the sun.

Quickly he recovered and expressed his pleasure, saying that a suitable palace must be found for the royal couple, glancing at me as he gave the order. For days afterward, I pondered that panicked expression, much perplexed. That the king might be repelled by his queen I could understand, or irritated, or bored, or resentful. But fear? From a king notorious for not knowing the meaning of the word? How had poor little Berengaria managed to strike such terror in a lion's breast?

FOR ONCE the king's favorite adage "As we are seen, so are we esteemed" couldn't apply to our entrance into Acre, for we marched through empty streets. Enoch and I rode directly behind a group of bishops who broke into loud sobs as we passed the many churches in this Christian city. Pointing to whitewashed walls, they bemoaned the mosaic saints lost under the paint, or they keened loudly for the empty altars, or the rounded minarets set atop Christian towers.

"You'd think they'd found quhat they expected," Enoch commented dryly. "Circumcision blood in the baptismal fonts and worse on the altars."

"Maybe you're just not as Christian as they are."

"That I'm not," he agreed cheerily. "'Tis said King Richard canna be Christian because he's from the pagan south, you and I canna be Christian because we're from the pagan north, which leaves the field to those in the middle."

"*I'm* Christian," I asserted, not liking the association, "even if the Scots are not."

For the first time in days he laughed aloud. "Ye? Ye're naught but a pagan Celt once removed, ready to worship a tree or a stone as quick as a saint, and believe in kaelpies and kongons."

I didn't want to argue the matter. Soothly I would agree that most of the Crusaders were more interested in lechery than praying, for our ranks were e'en now being depleted as the men broke to run to the port where 'twas rumored that boatloads of women from Tyre had just landed.

Also, I must admit that I was more intrigued by Richard's reaction to his queen than I was by the reaction of any bishop. Berengaria rode a fine roan mare next to Richard on his Fauvel, and she had the bearing of royalty if not the beauty. Her sharp chin thrust upward, her close-set eyes dropped demurely downward. She gave no glance to her husband but I saw his uneasy eyes fall obliquely on her as the telltale muscle in his cheek quivered. A spiritual malaise cloaked his victory and subdued everyone's joy.

IT WAS the rest period after Haute Tierce and the king was alone. Silk curtains gave his chamber a pearly luminescence and I had the giddy thought that the king looked like the scarlet streak of blood inside an egg.

"Come close, Alex, I'm not asleep."

But he should have been, for his eyes were deeply shadowed. I placed the mail pouch beside him.

"Ambroise sent these, Your Highness. I believe 'tis mail from England."

"Let me see."

I noted that his new nails had grown back very pink after his illness, that his hands trembled.

"Ah, a letter from my queen mother. Suppose you read it to me while I rest."

Breaking the seal on the rolled parchment, I watched him covertly. He had lost his symptoms but appeared under mental strain. Berengaria. Had she spurned him? 'Twas rumored around court that she preferred her ape Alphonso to the king. I didn't believe it. If anything, 'twas the king who did the spurning.

"Alex, are you gathering wool?"

"I'm sorry, My Lord; I'll read."

"No, wait. Come here, love." He held out a hand. "I daresay you think I've forgotten our conversation in Limassol, don't you?"

"No, Your Grace, I know you're much occupied, and now . . ."

"The queen is here," he finished dryly. "Yes, just so. However, let me assure you that nothing's changed, just postponed. And not for long. Do you understand?"

"Yes, Your Highness."

"I pledge to give you fealty, disinterested affection, and now love." His deep voice throbbed. "Tell me it's the same with you."

My lips parted, breath became shallow, heart raced. "Aye, just the same except . . ."

He frowned and waited. "Go on. Another confession?"

"Aye, in a way. Nothing important but it's worried me since I want to be truthful, as you wist. My father thought I was too small for my age, too small for a boy that is, so he suggested that I say I was three years younger than I soothly was."

"Three years?" The king grinned, more sunny than I'd seen him of late. "So you're really . . . ?"

"Thirteen."

"Thirteen! I'm delighted and feel somewhat less guilty. Is that all?"

I nodded, my heart light.

"Then let's kiss on it and you'll read."

I leaned over him and he clasped me so I fell upon his chest. We kissed over and over, a dozen, two dozen times, abandoned and happy.

Then he placed me upright again. "Now, read."

"To Richard Plantagenet, King of England, etc.

"'I plead with you to quit your Crusade and return to England.'"

"What?" The king leaned forward. "Let me see the script. God's feet, 'tis Eleanor's all right."

"Shall I continue?"

"Yes."

A bare foot touched the tiled floor as he propped himself higher.

"'Come quickly before this once rustic isle disintegrates to a refuge for every scoundrel in Europe and turns to a nest for insurrection, banditry and usurpation.'"

"'Usurpation'?" the king exclaimed. "She must mean John. Damnation!"

"'But to specifics. The injustices of William Longchamps have pressed the common people to the point of mutiny against the Crown. Indeed, ruffians rule the forests and roadways in the name of "civil order" and many commoners are grown to prefer their rough justice to that of the appointed justicier.'"

"Where's John in all this?" the king exploded. "He's the canker in the body politic."

I waited, then continued.

"'Obviously the only noble with sufficient stature to offset Longchamps's acts is Count John. Need I recount his methods? He has seized Tickhill Castle, refused York entry into England and in various ways antagonized all the great barons who now see themselves caught between unacceptable factions.

"'Therefore have the barons finally been forced to unite themselves as a third power in this triangular struggle.'"

The king interrupted grimly. "Those traitors!"

"'My own fear resides with this last group, for I can see how you might defeat Longchamps or John when the time comes, but if your lords challenge the very concept of kingship, then that is a battle of new dimensions and one that will not easily be won.'"

"Which guarantees civil war for a hundred years!" Richard exploded.

"'Such chaos must attract outsiders who will prey on our weakness. Therefore you cannot be surprised to learn that your brother Count John is in constant touch with King Philip. We have intercepted six of John's letters confirming that they conspire against you, though unfortunately we know not the direction of their plans. Poor John is such a fool. To think that Philip would do aught for him, after his plots against Henry, his betrayal of you.

"'Richard, the case is urgent. No one knows better than I your commitment to Jerusalem, but you have no choice. Send me word by the next ship that you come. Send me as well news that your queen is with child. Such an announcement is gravely needed in your beleaguered nation which sees itself threatened, with the king fighting a perilous war and no heir to carry on.

"'I await your missive with God's blessing. Yours . . .'"

And she signed off with the usual formalities.

I rerolled the parchment as Richard tapped his bare foot. I dared not look at him after the last directive. After a time, he sighed and spoke to himself.

"If I can get Berengaria with child, that should purchase me four months of grace. With God's help, I could take Jerusalem in that time. Or at the worst, I could secure the coast cities for a later try."

There was a sharp rap at the door.

"Court is convened, Your Highness," a voice called.

"Help me with my shoes, Alex. Philip has chosen this ungodly hour to insist he has something of great import to relay. Would I could show him this letter." He made a sour grimace.

As I followed the king, my own mind was tumbling with thoughts. *Only four more months if he could get Berengaria with child.*

"Hssst, bairn, hssst!"

Startled, I looked o'er my shoulder and saw the Scot gesturing wildly from a niche. I was at the end of Richard's train as it marched toward the chamber to meet King Philip; I slipped away.

"What's wrong?"

Enoch held a tin plate of cocky-leeky wrapped in fig leaves. "Did ye eat part of this?"

"Not yet. I had to read a letter to the king."

He sighed deeply with relief.

"'Tis laced with monkshood."

"But which—?" I gazed, comprehending now that 'twas not a single incident, but a plot.

"Quhich of us be the intended victim? Aye, that's the question. Then we'll know *who*. Put yer mind to it, Alex."

"Aye," I gasped. "I have to go now."

I ran after the king and spent the first part of the next hour turning the problem in my mind.

'TWAS THE LARGEST, most ventilated chamber in the palace but 'twas oppressively hot at this hour, especially with so many people crowded together. All the great lords had been summoned for this auspicious occasion. They stood languorously, their eyes heavy, their hands waving palm fans to move the air. King Philip was already on his throne.

Kisses were exchanged between the monarchs, a prayer recited, and we all settled to see what King Philip would say.

"Richard, I am an ill man. Very ill. So say my physician and my astrologer."

Richard's disgust was palpable.

"I don't want to contradict your stars, coz, but I tell you plain that your counselors do you wrong. However, if you think you suffer, please accept my sympathies."

He then sat back and endured a long harangue of symptoms as courtiers buzzed around us. I heard one say that if Philip died in the Holy Land, 'twould be of fright. Richard looked inward as he waited, his face suspicious.

Suddenly Philip brought everyone back to sharp attention: "Therefore I have written to the pope."

"To Celestine?" Richard leaned forward. "To send you an elixir for your gripes?"

"Don't scoff, Richard. I'm serious!"

Richard waited, alert.

"I asked a release from my vow to crusade."

Richard leaped up, his face apoplectic! "I'll kill you with my own hand before I permit such perfidy!"

Two bright red spots appeared on Philip's cheeks but he sat firm.

"I am leaving Acre forthwith to return to Europe."

"You may deceive popes," Richard cried, "but never me! That you suffer from cowardice I believe! And of treason!" His voice had risen to a howl of rage.

"'Twas not *I* who threatened to kill *you*." Philip shot back. "Nor was it I who bled my country of gold in order to purchase loyalty."

"Are you speaking of Champagne?" Richard demanded. "Tell him, Henry, how he cheated you!"

Before Champagne could utter a word, Philip continued. "And the Pisanos, the Genoese. You bribed them to follow you."

"*Paid* them, sir, when they'd gone two years without wages."

"And you wasted weeks of valuable time and countless lives in order to plunder the Kingdom of Cyprus."

"*Kingdom* you call it? A tyranny! As for plunder, it's all going for the Crusade!"

"Truly? Then who purchases your splendid raiment that you wear like a peacock? What gold underwrites a fleet of hundreds? I, too, could sail in golden poops if I wished to be a pirate."

Both men were now standing nose to nose, their counselors helpless to stop them.

"To what purpose would you sail so?" Richard cried. "You prefer to manipulate like slime. You order your puppet Conrad of Montferrat to thwart us at every turn! Did he not starve Acre last winter by refusing to send wheat? Why did the two of you refuse me entry into Tyre?"

"To force you to fight! You would tarry, would ride through streets with flourishes, anything to preen yourself with adulation."

"Conrad is a usurper!"

"Be careful, coz," Philip slithered his words with obvious enjoyment, "how you speak of your future partner. For I plan to put the French command in Conrad's hands during my absence."

King Richard stopped, astounded.

The Duke of Burgundy entered the fray with trembling dignity, tears in his eyes. "You surprise us, My Liege. None of us in your court knew of your plans to depart. We have no fealty toward Conrad, have never sworn him homage."

"Of course you did, when you swore to me." Philip's milky eye wandered somewhat. "You will command in the field, of course."

"Under my leadership," Richard blazed, "but taking commands from Conrad. Is that your scheme?"

Philip smiled. "A necessary precaution, coz, for Conrad withstood Saladin's attack for four years. We fear that you are too soft with your Turkish enemy while Conrad knows his true colors."

"How soft? By taking Acre? By making stiffer terms than you wanted?"

"However, I assure you that I will take half our ransom gold and half of the True Cross."

Again order dissolved.

"Half the Cross? A desecration!"

Richard waited, his eyes glinting.

"Answer, Philip, how am I soft on Saladin?"

"You took fruit and ice . . ."

"But gave nothing in return."

"Have received a fine Arabian stallion."

"Again without recompense."

Philip sat on his throne again, his voice hardly above a whisper. "And you promised your sister Joanna in marriage to the sultan's brother called Safadin, then offered this un-Christian couple governance of Jerusalem. Deny it if you can."

'Twas Philip's biggest bolt and the effect was stunning. Richard's own court reeled at the disclosure, none more than I. He *loved* his sister. How could he?

But Richard didn't deny it. "So, still smarting in your poor rejected heart? How ironic, you long for Joanna, I flee from Alais— the gods are sportive. Nevertheless, let it be on record that I tried to persuade my sister to wed you, France, but her mind is strong. However, she clearly understood how she might aid our Crusade. After all, Alexander wed ten thousand of his men to Arabs. Joanna agreed if Safadin would convert to Christianity and he refused."

"The betrayal of our Crusade!" Philip cried.

"Do you take me for a fool, Philip? Do you think I don't know your real reason for quitting our adventure?"

"My spleen, my bowels . . ."

"Put Greek fire in your bowels! How soon do you plan to attack England?"

Now Philip blanched; the court hummed ominously.

"Why would I want your miserable gloomy isle?"

"Why indeed? Except that you declared war on me and mine forever. Oh yes, we heard you in Messina but thought that we were safe for the duration of the Crusade."

Philip's mouth twisted in a derisive smile.

Richard now rose and signaled his court to do likewise. "We shall be in constant touch, coz, in hopes of dissuading you. In the meantime, let me assure you if you plot with my brother John to unseat us from our throne, you will not live out this year."

In a derisive breach of decorum, he moved to leave the chamber. When he reached the door, the French king called sharply.

"Wait, Richard! I neglected to tell you my date. I plan to sail July thirty-first, Saladin's deadline. And Richard, I'll need two of your galleys."

I trotted after the English court toward another chamber at the far end of the palace where they planned to parley. My own head was swimming at this deadly news. If Philip left and Richard stayed, the Crusade would surely go on till I was an old lady.

But if Richard left now, I would soon be in Wanthwaite.

ENOCH WAS WAITING for me when the session was over. I'd been so intrigued at this new turn in events that I'd momentarily forgot the poisoning.

"The Crusade will fail," Enoch announced flatly, after hearing my news.

"But why? Everyone knows that King Philip's no fighter."

"No, but he has an army, and Richard canna do without it."

Then he turned the subject back to the poisoning of our food, and I told him what I had concluded on my own while listening to the kings parley.

"'Tis *I* someone wants dead, Enoch, not you. Soothly he—or they—don't care if you live or die, but I'm the intended victim."

"Why do ye say so?"

"Because of that arrow. Remember?"

Comprehension crossed his face and I knew he agreed. "But why?"

I dared not tell him. If I thought Sir Gilbert still lived, I'd say he was our villain, but he had disappeared and must be slain. Furthermore, even alive he'd never once used a bow.

I suspected that Queen Berengaria had hired a killer to murder me as her rival. After all, 'twas said that Queen Eleanor had poisoned her rival, the fair Rosamond.

WE WERE CLOSE to the deadline for Saladin to deliver gold and the True Cross. Every conference grew more malignant as Philip prepared to leave; every day waxed more tense as Saladin remained silent as a tomb. The hostage emirs huddled in the *Locus Veneratum*, waiting; I huddled in our leather tent waiting, terrified by our unknown enemy.

"'Tis melancholic fer yer spirits to brood," Enoch advised. "Come doon to where I be repairing the wall."

"It's too hot there."

He squatted in front of me. "Air ye certain that ye want to march to Ascalon, bairn? 'Twill make Acre same like a fair."

I couldn't answer.

He looked at me a long time, seeming to know that I was bound to the king.

He stood, started away, then turned back. "No sense drenchin' in yer own woes. Go see Roderick. He's in the Hospitallers' hall where they're treatin' his wound."

Within the hour, I was inside the hospital. The space was dim and putrid, like climbing into a dead camel's cavity. When my eyes adjusted to the dark, I saw I was standing on a floor among writhing, whining men in various stages of decay. The only upright figures were physicians exorcising demons or priests giving absolution. Appalled to think that Roderick had fallen into such a rank pit, I began gingerly to step between grasping claws and piles of filth to try to find him.

"Here, Alex, here!"

"Roderick?"

Crunching on brown beetles feeding on pus and excrement, I made my way to whence the voice had come.

"Oh, Alex, I'm so glad to see you! Will you take me away?"

Only the voice was the same, for certes this shrunken cadaverous pile of bones with its huge panicked orbs could not be Roderick! Holding my breath against the gluey stench of his seeping wound, I knelt beside him.

"Of course I'll take you with me. Enoch will have you well in no time." I fanned vigorously at the flies. "What's wrong with your head?"

"My demon resides there," he explained, pulling at a dirt-crusted rag on his forehead. "It entered through my leg, then fell in love with me. My skull is a mass of mind-sores."

"May I look at your leg?"

"It needs cleaning," he apologized.

"I can see that."

I plucked at the stiffened bandage, looked at him, smiled and gave the mess a hard tug. Off came the rag and the skin as well, but Roderick didn't e'en flinch. I tried to ignore what this might mean and told him to wait, I'd be right back.

Outside I breathed deep of the fresh air, then ran to the square of St. Gidius where I purchased wine, water and embers. Soon I was on the floor beside Roderick again heating my father's dagger o'er the coals.

"I've got fresh rags," I said brightly. "You'll feel better in no time."

"You won't disturb my demon, will you? He's mean . . . as the Devil." He laughed feebly.

I scraped at the infected area almost down to the shank, then to the edges till I struck firm flesh and made Roderick scream. Slowly I poured wine into the blue-yellow gash, then wrapped wine-soaked rags around the whole to keep the insects off.

"You've learned a lot, Alex," Roderick whimpered.

"Aye, I helped care for the king. Now drink this water, as much as you can—it's safe here in Acre. I'm going to look at your head."

There was naught amiss with his head except that his curly mat moved with vermin. I washed it with the water that was left, then added wine for good measure.

"Rest your weight on your good leg, Roderick, and let me pull you to a standing position."

We tried, but he screamed in agony when he tried to sit up and collapsed backward.

"I'll bring Enoch later," I soothed him. "Remember how we carried you on our wrists?"

"Don't leave me! Please! I'll die if you go. Just give me a brief time to regain my strength from cleaning the wound."

So I sat silently beside him as he closed his eyes. His wound appeared gangrenous to me, but naturally I didn't say so.

"Alex, am I going to die?"

I squeezed his hand. "Not at all. Do you want to try to stand again?"

"Aye, but first promise me something. If I die, my people should know that I perished a hero, for I killed two men in Cyprus, you know. They'll make an effigy for my tomb."

"You are a hero and will be again, many times o'er."

"Here, take this ring to my uncle and tell him, Alex. Will you promise?"

"Didn't the king say he would send word?"

"But the king may die."

The words chilled me, e'en as I added mentally *and so may I*.

"How would I find your uncle, Roderick? Does he dwell in Penrith?"

"No, he's Bishop of Durham, easy to find. Everyone knows."

I took the garnet ring and slipped it onto my finger.

"And Earl of Northumberland."

"What?" I looked into that wasted face, thinking I'd not heard aright. "Did you say somewhat about the Earl of Northumberland?"

He banged his head to one side. "My uncle Hugh de Le Puiset is Earl of Northumberland."

Now I recognized that he was raving and knew not whether to humor him or to correct him so that I could get my facts straight.

"Try to be clear for a moment, friend. Your uncle cannot be the

Earl of Northumberland. But is he soothly Bishop of Durham?"

"Bishop of Durham and Earl of Northumberland, made so by King Richard's own appointment."

"King Richard?" I forgot Roderick's state of mind. "Oh no, you're wrong. I know the Earl of Northumberland and his name is Osbert. The king and I have discussed him many times."

My stridency gained the poor wight's attention. "*Benedicite*, I *know* my own uncle! And the king knows him as well. They're cousins, marched side by side in the king's coronation in 1189. Richard made Uncle Hugh Justicier of all England until Longchamps could arrive from Normandy. Ask anyone if you doubt me. Ask Leicester, ask King Richard."

"I believe you, Roderick," I said, my head reeling. "Certes the king knows your uncle. But we were speaking of Northumberland and *your uncle is not Earl of Northumberland!*"

"Alex, I hate to say so but you're a fool. Why are you so stubborn about a well-known fact? When Richard came from Poitiers to take the crown, he raised money for his Crusade by putting up all titles and appointments for sale, no matter whether the people who possessed them wanted his act or no. He said he'd put up London if he could find a buyer."

Aye, I'd heard such rumors in Paris.

"I know not what happed to the former Earl of Northumberland—Osbert you say—but I believe he must have been dead. In any case my uncle Hugh bid ten thousand pounds for the title, more than anyone else for anything, which be woodly since he is so old. The king said, 'Ten thousand pounds! What a clever workman am I to make a new earl out of an old bishop!'"

He lay back exhausted as I recalled other words of the king's.

"Wait, Roderick, don't doze now. I must know. Mayhap someone else appointed your uncle and Richard learned of it later. Think!"

"Don't be tinty, Alex. Richard did it and knew exactly what he was doing. Hugh helped Richard and his brothers in 'seventy-three when they invaded England through Scotland to o'erturn King Henry."

"Scotland!"

"Aye, with William the Lion, the Scottish king. My uncle believes in the Scottish cause, and therefore Richard knows Hugh can deal with the chieftains."

"And Richard?" I implored. "What does he think of Scotland?"

Before he could answer, two men approached us, a doctor and his assistant.

"Well, Roderick," said the taller of the two, "you look much improved. You must have repeated the charms against the Devil as I instructed you."

Roderick smiled. "Aye, that I did, Father Thabit, but my spirits have been raised as well by my friend here, Alex of Wanthwaite. Alex is going to take care of me."

"Fine, there's no medicine like a good friend."

Dr. Thabit gently pushed me aside and knelt close to Roderick's head. His purple robe had trailed in both new and old filth and gave forth a medley of noxious odors, his red gloves were bloodstained, his hood and biretta were snowed with scalings from his blistering head. His long, cadaverous face was kindly but tired, his voice near a whisper, possibly because of a throat ball which rode up and down his neck as he spoke. When he took off his gloves and pressed his hands against Roderick's temples, his fingers were yellow, his nails broken and black.

Roderick watched him anxiously. "Am I going to live?"

"You are promised eternal life for the service you have given Christ, my lad, so put all fears behind you." The doctor gestured to his assistant, a hefty Hospitaller with half his battle gear in place, lacking only his shield and helmet. He carried an ax and a leather sack.

"The salt and the block, Geoffrey," Dr. Thabit said calmly. "Now, Roderick, you may feel a bit of pain for what I have to do next but 'twill last just a second and 'twill cleanse you forever of your Devil, thereby assuring you of entry into Heaven." He put his gloves on again.

"Methinks he need not worry about entering Heaven for many years to come," I interjected uneasily.

"None of us worries about entering God's Kingdom," the priest chided me gently, "for 'tis what we desire above all things. I simply want to prepare Roderick, to cleanse his soul as we must all be cleansed." He gestured to his helper. "Geoffrey, put the block under his head. There, Roderick, now close your eyes whilst I make a mark on your face, so, and think of the eternal life. I'm going to exorcise your demon first and when you wake you will behold God."

Why not behold *me*? I became more and more nervous at the preparations. Geoffrey drew a piece of charcoal from forehead to chin down Roderick's face, then lifted his ax.

"What are you going to do?" I asked him directly, and reached for Roderick's cheek.

Father Thabit kicked my hand back, raised his cross, and chanted: "*Audi ergo: Satana, vitae raptor, seductor, exitator dolorum, recede ergo in nomine Patris et Filii et Spiritus sancti, Amen.*"

He lowered the cross in a swift movement as Geoffrey swung his ax and split Roderick's head like a melon.

"No! No!" I screamed too late.

Father Thabit knelt and muttered more Latin "... *quid stas, cum scias, Christum Dominum* ..." as his busy gloves tugged at Roderick's brains which spilled like congealed yellow pudding onto the floor. When the cavity was empty, the father rubbed salt into the cranium, then used my shoulder to pull himself upright again.

"A good clean job," he said, "and none too soon. The brain is tinged with Saturn's color, you'll note."

"What about the leg?" Geoffrey asked.

"Yes, take it. Best be safe."

Father Thabit shook bits of brain off his red gloves and tottered to his next patient while Geoffrey hacked at the leg, showering me with bone chips.

He held the bloody shank aloft. "Have to bury this under a cross at once or the demon will enter someone else."

I ran into the blinding street clutching the garnet ring.

I CROUCHED STUPEFIED in the shade of a carob and twisted Roderick's ring around my finger. The shock of his death gripped me for the rest of the day, but as the shadow moved to the other side of the tree I began to respond anew to his terrible testimony. The Bishop of Durham was Earl of Northumberland, made such in 1189 soon after I'd fled my burning home. Appointed by King Richard no later than November.

I'd met the king in June 1190, and I remembered the scene perfectly. The summer lightning, the wind becoming an urgent whisper, then my assertions of Northumberland's crimes. Richard had turned: *Are you sure? He was ever a faithful earl*; then, *When was this? Ah, that explains it*. At that very instant the king had decided to deceive me! Knowing full well that I was in no danger whatsoever for my life and that Hugh of Northumberland would honor the king's writ, Richard had deliberately and knowingly forced me to forgo my estate and accompany him on this woodly Crusade with the vague promise that he and he alone would decide the matter when we returned.

Why? What on earth could his motive be? I thought and thought about it, but could not answer. He'd been attracted to me even then, but I had no such silly vanity as to think that a great king can be pierced through the eye by Cupid as the legend says.

Whatever his mysterious reason, the fact spoke for itself: he had lied and continued to lie, though he knew my desperation. I thought of Messina when I'd begged him for release and he'd invoked Osbert's name to keep me as captive, or even here when he'd again said that only he could restore me. I was certain of his perfidy, but would check with Ambroise just to make sure.

And who else might have known? Enoch? Aye, there's another rat's nest. Enoch and Richard hated each other as persons, yet on the political level they might have some sort of understanding. Did Enoch know about Northumberland? Casting my mind back, I didn't think so but couldn't be sure. Then there was the reward Richard had given Enoch for sapping the wall, something so valuable that the Scot had been willing to risk his life for it. I knew Enoch too well to think he'd tell me what it was for the asking, but I also knew the Scottish temperament sufficiently to know he'd talk till next year about Scottish history. I'd start with that.

"RODERICK'S GREATEST FEAR was that his family would ne'er hear of his valor on the field." I held up the garnet ring. "He gave me this to carry to his uncle Hugh de Le Puiset. Have you e'er heard of him?"

Enoch fingered the ring and sighed. "A pretty stone. Poor Roderick. Aye, ye mean Bishop Hugh of Durham."

"The same. A famous man according to Roderick and friendly to the Scots. Roderick claimed he helped your king when he invaded the north."

"Aye, when my father was killt."

"Your father? You never told me that."

"Ye niver asked." He looked bemused. "At the Battle of Wark, when we crossed the Tweed."

"And the English won?"

"Well, aye, technically."

"Were you there? Was Richard?"

He raised surprised brows. "The king were sixteen and went to the conference in Paris but not to the field. I were six."

"Six! Oh, Enoch, I'm so sorry. Why, you're an orphan too!"

"Nay, lad, my mother still lives, and I had twa older brothers."

Gradually it was coming back, how he had been steward to his older brother, now dead.

"What think you? Is Bishop Hugh friends with King Richard today?"

"Friend and cousin, and both men be friends to Scotland. King Richard hae promised sae that Northumberland will be part of Scotland as soon as he returns."

"*Northumberland will be part of Scotland*?" I cried. "Never!"

Enoch stared at me queerly. "Ye should be glad, since ye have Scottish blood."

"And is Bishop Hugh willing to help with this robbery?"

"How dare ye call it robbery!" he shouted, his choler rising. "Northumberland be Scotland and I'll hear namore of your traitorous blather."

I studied his scarlet face. Honest outrage or cunning evasion of the facts? I couldn't be sure.

"THE COLOR OF BLOOD." Ambroise turned the garnet against the light. "Poor Roderick."

"What worries me," I prattled, "is how I'll e'er find his uncle, Hugh de Le Puiset. Methinks my friend bestowed too much confidence in me for I know naught of any Hugh."

"I think Roderick can rest in peace," Ambroise said, "for you appear to be most resourceful."

"Roderick said he was famous. Famous for what?"

Ambroise shrugged. "Wealth, a patron of the arts, an amiable disposition rare when combined with learning and power, but I suppose your friend was referring to his titles. He's Bishop of Durham, of course, and Earl of Northumberland."

Casual damning words. I caught my breath in pain. At last I knew the truth. Oh, Richard, how could you lie to me!

The troubadour was sharp. "What's wrong? Why that stricken grimace?"

"I—I just recalled that he is also very old. Mayhap he'll be dead by the time I get back to England. I wish Roderick had given me a second name. How long do you think this Crusade will last?"

Ambroise's cheerful countenance grew serious. "I don't know." He copied a few more words. "But whatever you do, don't ask the king his opinion."

"I wouldn't. But why?"

"Well, boy, you and the king are very close, I believe. Therefore you should be aware of his melancholy humor and problems, for you are in a position to help him. He's changed here in Acre."

"Changed?"

"Come here, Alex." He went to the window seat and gazed out on a clump of rat-infested palms. "You're very young and may not understand the import of my words—but follow them anyway, for I trust that you have the king's well-being at heart." He studied me, then went on. "Many of us who've been with him since the beginning are concerned at changes we observe."

"He appears well."

"In body, yes, but . . ." I could see the transparent layer o'er his pale eyes as he looked outward; then he turned back to me. "He's suffered a series of incalculable blows. King Philip—not just a temporary aberration but a shift in his life scheme, from peaceful administration to total continuous warfare. Leopold of Austria, another mortal enemy and ally of King Philip's. The Crusade, now to be waged with half an army."

"Half? How so?"

"Richard knows well that Philip will pull his forces at some crucial juncture. Our king travels with a viper at his breast. And already Saladin is exploiting the situation by not exchanging hostages, thus tying Richard to Acre."

"I see." Though my mind was on Northumberland.

"Then there's Queen Berengaria."

And he had all my attention.

"It's an open secret that the marriage is a failure, although our king tries valiantly to cover his disappointment."

"I suppose you mean because there's no issue."

Ambroise sighed heavily. "God knows, the king has tried. Queen Eleanor must be blamed, for she selected the princess from a list Richard prepared. He'd met Berengaria once at a tournament where he fought with her brother Sancho. Eleanor thought to secure his southern border by the match. But who could have known that such a healthy young woman would prove barren?"

"Barren?"

His eyes commanded me. "Yes, *barren*. After all, the king has a son in France, Philip by name."

"Philip! For Philip of France?"

I could see from the troubadour's stiffness that I wasn't responding with proper decorum.

"Of course, Philip and Richard were once close friends, you know."

No, I didn't know anything, I decided, in this contradictory, circular world. Roderick had been right: we were walking upside down.

"And for all these reasons, the king has changed? In what way?"

"Well, he was ever a merry monarch, a poet of the south, and I fear he's become bitter. That's where you must help, Alex: I think you are the only light-mote in his eye today."

I bowed my head to conceal my own bitterness. No doubt Richard did love me in his fashion, but his fashion was to twist facts to his own ends.

Osbert of Northumberland.

28

 WAS SWEPT OFF MY FEET IN A CLOUD OF SWEET
woodruff.

The king pressed his cheek against mine and
whispered, "Have you missed me, Alex?"

"Aye, yes," I muttered, gazing fearfully down
the empty corridor of the palace.

He turned, kicked open the door of a small closet and placed me
on the cutting table there. The musty air swirled saffron through a
yellow bit of silk pinned to the window to hold out the blowing
sand.

"Elusive Eros, we'll be on our march in two days. As soon as
Saladin sends the ransom that will free the hostages, you will share
my tent."

I studied him. Ambroise was right: Richard's face had changed,
delicate downward lines around the mouth, eyes heavy and red-
rimmed. Before, I'd always seen the younger Richard lurking
behind his actual years, now I saw the older man approaching, a
cynical, calculating warrior.

He caught my perusal. "Why that look? Are you ill?"

"I've been fine, Your Highness."

He held my cheeks and gazed. "Don't lie to me."

Both thrilled and chilled at his perception, I tried to deflect him
from the truth. "Well, I didn't want to worry you, but Enoch—"

A voice outside the door called. "King Richard, Your Highness,
are you there? We're in the conference room." 'Twas Champagne.

"Begin without me, Henry. I'll be there shortly."

Footsteps retreated.

The king stood and bent over me. Some trick of the light
through the silk turned one of his eyes to pure gold. That's my
mote, I thought dizzily, the light beam that gives him hope.

And he kissed me. 'Twas the first time in weeks that we'd touched so and 'twas the same but not the same, my body more responsive but my mind more detached. Richard had again become mysterious, a figure in a dream.

Subtly he'd shifted me so that I now lay on the table. The light was obscured by his head as he leaned over me so that his face was again transformed to its youthful beauty.

"Alex, I want . . ." he whispered.

My heart leaped in fear but I seemed unable to protest. I felt his hand slip under my hips, then lost its pressure against my fortune-belt. Again he kissed me.

"Where's the king? Have you seen him?"

Footsteps hurried past. The king raised his head, sighed.

He kissed me once more, then clutched me fiercely to his trembling body, his voice now gruff.

"Alex, I do love thee. Perhaps no more, no less than others before, but with a difference: you're all I have to give me comfort now. Swear that you love me."

"I love you."

"And you'll be loyal."

"I'll be loyal."

"Forever."

"Forever."

"And I love thee."

He was gone.

I lay looking at the yellow square of daylight, Saturn's color, the color of perfidy, treachery, jealousy.

Not that I'd been lying exactly: it was just that I no longer knew any truth except that my heart was squeezed dry.

WE RODE to the enclosure between the double walls of Acre where the emirs awaited some sign from Saladin. Tonight we would camp in the foothills; in two days' time we would march for Ascalon. Already the knights were in full mail for marching but they also wore linens tied across their faces in the Saracen fashion, for we were in the midst of a sandstorm. Hills changed contours before us, brown palm fronds whipped erratically at our horses' feet and the wind's howl was abetted by the abrasive rattle of sand against metal armor. Yet the sun shone withal, a shrunken baleful eye staring at a world twisted out of shape and deprived of all color.

Three thousand emirs huddled in the square as we surrounded them. The leaders Mestoc and Caracois immediately approached the king who bent forward to parley. I couldn't hear, nor did I have to: Saladin was a week past his deadline, but everyone expected he would come today for he'd been sent an ultimatum. Enoch leaned over and tied cloths around Thistle's and Firth's eyes to protect them. We put our hands to our faces for the same purpose.

The king then dismounted so that he could hear better. I saw his teeth in a broad grin as he ripped away his mask. He liked these Saracen men for their skill and daring in warfare. Moreover, somewhere they'd learned the rules of chivalry better than some Christians, the king had remarked caustically. Aye, the king could appreciate chivalry.

The sun's pale iris had disappeared entirely behind the swirling ochre dust, but enough light penetrated for us to see our own short shadows: 'twas Nones, which the bells soon confirmed. And still we waited. The emirs were now all crouched in one direction, their heads turned to the eastern hills. King Richard was back on his horse. Twice, knights approached him and exchanged words. I thought of King Philip, at this very moment riding through Acre's empty streets to board his waiting galleys.

Horses were pawing restlessly; a few knights had dismounted; the emirs spoke to each other in their strange tongue. The king raised his hand and fanfare sounded. We all looked upward expectantly to see Saladin approach.

A scream made us turn.

Two knights had plunged their pikes into the soft undefended bodies of the crouching men!

"Stop them! They've gone woodly!" I shouted to the Scot, but he shook his head in a daze.

"The king's command."

I didn't believe it! I whirled Thistle to gallop up to Richard but found my bridle held firm in Enoch's grasp.

"Stay out of it, bairn. 'Tis planned sae," he said harshly.

No! No! No! No! The old protest drummed in my head. And with the same result.

I heard Richard's voice shout something and turned hopefully. Surely he would stop the carnage!

No, he'd ordered a search for gold. Torso after torso was ripped by daggers as gloved hands plunged inside to pull at stubborn intestines. Most knights didn't know a stomach when they saw one so livers and spleens were sliced open before coins were found in the gullets.

The whole slaughter seemed to go on forever but actually took less than a half hour. Finally the bloody knights relinquished the field to the soaring kites and remounted their horses, jabbering excitedly about what they'd found. Again the trumpets sounded, the company turned back to the city.

The king rode close enough to touch. His face was bare again and I saw that his smile was a grimace of death, teeth bared, eyes hard. He must have planned this immediately after caressing me in the closet. I turned away.

Finally there were only Enoch and me—and three thousand corpses.

"At least they didna have souls to lose," Enoch said. "Being Infidels."

I had a sharp answer on my tongue until I saw his heavy ironic expression. "A Christian act," I concurred in the same tone.

Then I noticed a spurt of blood from an emir's neck was soaking Thistle's hoof, and pulled my horse back.

Enoch noticed it too. "What say you that we cleanse our beasts and ourselves in the sea? Mayhap we can wash off the day."

"Like Pontius Pilate." I had to get away from the mutilated heap, so reminiscent of Wanthwaite, albeit on a larger scale. Yet my horror was the same.

Quickly we headed down the slope toward the Mediterranean, pushed by the gale at our backs.

WE WADED OUR HORSES into the shallows and gazed out on the sullen leaden swells beyond. The water was turbid from roiled sand, sibilant under the steady howl of the wind.

Enoch dismounted, dropped his clothes and held Thistle for me.

"You go ahead. I'll join you in a minute," I said.

Sick at heart, I watched him struggle through the surf and plunge into the sea. For a brief moment, I envied his strength and freedom. He might be a Scot, but he was a handsome specimen without his distorting Scottish kilts and he could strip naked without worry. In former dips, I'd always kept my clothes on, waded discreetly so that the weight of my treasure would not suck me under. Now I felt besmirched in every pore by both sand and horror, felt I must immerse myself in a total baptism in order to be fresh again. I guided Thistle to the protection of a huge boulder where I removed my treasure belt and false prick; I quickly weighted them with a heavy stone and then, wearing only my light tunic, ran to the sea.

After the first delicious dive, I stayed far under, scraping along the bottom like a ray. Above me in the sand-filtered light, I could see Enoch's arms and legs moving in slow graceful arcs. Then I, too, surfaced, half-floating, half-swimming in desultory movements as I tried to order my thoughts. At the center was King Richard, master of lightning transformations from angry tyrant to seductive lover, but never before had I seen such a complete change. Passion turned in an instant to murder. I knew he would explain the deaths as a political act, but I'd heard him often praise these emirs as men of exceptional courage and honor who'd voluntarily offered themselves as surety for Saladin's word. Political or not, Richard knew many of them personally, and liked them. *Enfants perdus*, lost children, expendable lives. I wanted no part of such thinking. When human life can be sacrificed so casually, who is safe?

The Acre massacre must be a stain on the Crusade, whatever the ultimate outcome. And a stain on King Richard forever.

"Cum, Alex, time to leave!" Enoch's glistening figure waved to me from the beach. Too bad he was about to transform himself back into a Scot, I thought again, for in his naked state he could rival any man alive.

I heard a distant clang of bells, took one more long dive, and waded ashore, shading my eyes against the bladed blowing sand.

When I rounded the boulder, I found Enoch holding something in his hands.

"Be this your treasure belt, bairn?" he asked.

Benedicite—how could I deny it and still get it back?

"Uh—aye. It makes me too heavy to swim."

He raised and lowered it judiciously, weighing it, counting the coins if I knew him. "Aye, ye mun carry a fortune between yer legs." He laughed heartily at his bad joke. "How much do ye figure?"

"I never counted," I lied, "but it's mostly deniers."

"Sum gold though?" His gimlet eyes glinted greedily.

"The important thing is that it also contains my parents' relics," I snapped. "Give it to me, please. Soothly I feel naked without it."

"Aye, I recall in Messina hoo ye cried out that ye couldna take it off or yer parents would go straight to brimstone." He held it out, but when I reached, retracted it again. "What be this woodly string of sticks?"

"String of sticks?" I gazed on the jointed willows as if I'd never seen them before. Indeed, I tried to pretend to myself that I hadn't, hoping that I could imagine some new function for them.

"Aye, they mun poke ye something fierce yif ye wear them close to yer balls." He drew the contraption closer. "Waesucks, it stinks."

I laughed giddily. "Aye, 'tis a bit besmottered, but . . ." *But what?* I stretched my dull brain. "But it protects me," I ended feebly.

He was turning the false penis this way and that. What did it look like to him? "I doona see how old willows can protect ye."

"From—horses!" I said, as if inspired.

"*Horses?*" His face was a study of disbelief.

"Well, of course, such a—er—stick wouldn't help everyone, but you see I'm different."

"Different how?" His eyes involuntarily fell to my crotch where my wet tunic clung close and I quickly put one leg forward to obscure the outline.

I could have bit off my stupid tongue for using the word *differ-*

ent, but there was no help for it now. "That is, I suffered an injury on a particular part of my—er—prick, and it needs protection."

"When did this hap?"

"Oh, a long time ago!" I sang out. "My horse Justice, back at Wanthwaite—er—bit me."

"*A horse bit yer terse!*" His eyes widened.

"Not exactly bit—I mean kicked." I felt I would swoon. "Kicked so hard that it felt like a bite, if you take my meaning."

The Scot now stared at me, more intrigued by my words than my false member. I looked back with a vacuous brightness, trying to read the comprehension or lack of it in his eyes. Again he put one hand on the willows, put his other below the belt, and tried to balance them in what I saw must be the position they rode between my legs. The willows rose in a close proximation of a prick, or so it seemed to me. Enoch narrowed his eyes, turned the whole in profile, looked back at me with the first stir of real suspicion.

"As I understand it, this willow mun slip o'er yer terse. Lat me see how ye wear it." He finally handed me my poor disguise.

"That's absurd," I said firmly. "No prick could squeeze inside that narrow pipe as you well know. It once served to hold off horses, as I said, but it's grown too brittle by far." Quickly I broke the willow off and threw it toward the sea where, *Deo gratias*, the wind carried it into the surf. Then, using the same manner I'd done on Dere Street to fool Magnus Barefoot, I reached up from under the hem of my tunic and fastened the belt in place, protected in the act by my garment.

Enoch was now roused. "Alex, in almost three years, I've ne'er seen ye wi'out yer clothes. Why is that? Be there somewhat wrong wi' yer parts?"

"If you haven't seen me, you haven't looked," I argued back. "I've been without my garments many times."

"No, ye have nocht!" Amazement shone in his face. "I doona knaw quhat ye look like!"

And he lunged toward my tunic.

I spun away terrified!

He stumbled after me, not sure but close to sure that something was amiss. Bewildered blue eyes raked me from head to foot, hands reached to catch any part of me. We feinted in grotesque circles as I tried to think of a way out.

"Ye're nocht *Alex!*" he cried.

"Alex! Is that you?" Sir Roger's voice sounded from the dusty swirls, almost upon us. Then his welcome figure loomed above.

"Sir Roger!" I screeched in relief. "Are you going to the king's pavilion?"

"Yes, we're late."

"I'll go with you!"

I was already on Thistle and spurred my horse to a rear to avoid Enoch's reaching hands.

I thundered into the sand-screen as fast as I could.

"Wait!" Sir Roger called.

"Alex, wait!" Enoch echoed. "Be ye a . . . ?"

But I was too far away to hear the last word.

SIR ROGER AND I worked feverishly to make up for the fact we were late, and we finished setting up the goblets just as the king's fanfare announced his arrival in camp. I was grateful for the hard tasks which took my mind off the emirs, off Enoch, off the coming night of love. *Benedicite*, I hoped I would never live through such a day again.

The king was accompanied by great lords, already in heated discussion about the massacre.

"Saladin will go down in infamy for his dastardly act today."

Saladin? I looked in amazement at the speaker, none other than the temperate Champagne.

"Yes, 'tis difficult to comprehend the Infidel mind. No Christian king would murder the cream of his own army. And we thought he was a chivalrous leader!"

The king, I saw, was halfway in his transformation from Death to Great Monarch. His mouth was still fretted by bitterness, his eyes still heavy, his speech lugubrious. "'Tis not Saladin, 'tis Philip who is at fault," he announced.

"How so, Your Majesty?"

"Once France defected, the peace terms no longer had to be honored. Obviously we could not march the emirs in our ranks to Ascalon; just as obviously, we no longer have sufficient army to guard them in Acre. The strategy was to hold us in Acre until Saladin could raise the eight hundred thousand troops he's called." He threw his heavy cape on the bed and sat on his throne.

Strategy, always strategy. The question was, did he enjoy the act of murder? This afternoon I'd thought he did. If so, I would soon be copulating with Death. I handed him a goblet of wine.

"I daresay the pope will approve," a bishop opined uneasily, "since the purpose was holy."

Richard turned cynical eyes. "If we take Jerusalem, he will approve."

"You're absolutely right, Your Majesty," the bishop agreed hastily. "The pope has great faith in you."

Richard's lips twitched; then he turned to his advisers. "Look you, we agreed in conference on this awesome act. I suggest that we put it behind us now and turn our attention to the more pressing matter of our march to Ascalon. If I am right about Saladin's recruitment, we face formidable odds on the narrow stretch along the sea. We'll go in triple file, mounted knights closest to the sea and our following ships. Here is the map . . ."

Well, these were momentous decisions, I knew, but soothly of little interest to me. The Scot's unfinished question hurled at my back occupied all my mind. If Enoch knew I was female—and I was sure he did, if not now, then within the next few hours as he thought things through—then my whole situation was changed. He would see and grab his advantage. Which meant that he would leave for Wanthwaite *at once*, knowing that I could not dispute his male sovereignty. He would bring an army, challenge Sir Roland to the ordeal of single combat, the absolutely legal way of attaching my estate.

What could I do?

Enlist the king's help. 'Twas unfortunate that I had to ask on the heels of his own disasters, but there was no other way. So as he plotted how to defeat Saladin, I pondered how I might outwit the Scot.

I had arrived at my own strategy long before the king finished planning his, and I thought the parley would go on until dawn. Finally, however, close upon midnight, the first lord rose to take his leave. Soon others followed and in a short time Sir Roger and I were busily cleaning the pavilion, laying out the king's sheets and robe.

Then Sir Roger and the king carefully rolled the maps and placed them in a chest. Two of the wax lanterns had been extinguished and the one that was left cast an eerie light across the swelling canvas which rose and fell in the wind like a great heart.

The king accompanied Sir Roger to the exit of the pavilion where they stood talking earnestly for a few moments. Then the secretary untied the flaps and bent low into the wind; before the king could close the opening, the wax lantern flickered out and we were in darkness.

"God's feet, help me tie the flap, Alex!"

I groped my way across the inky space, hit the side of the tent and edged to where the king stood. He tied the upper part, while I sat on the ground and tied the lower. Then I rose and he grasped my shoulder.

"Where's the ember?" he asked. "'Tis said that darkness is a friend to love, but I believe we need a *little* light."

"One of the bishops told Sir Roger to remove it, Your Highness. He was afraid of fire in this gale."

"A presumptuous prelate, I might have guessed. Well, we shall be night partners then." He laughed and led me to his bed.

The simultaneous loss of human voices and light isolated us. I heard anew the fierce winds wailing about us, an anguished sobbing chorus of tortured souls, calling in the darkness.

I thought of the emirs.

"What's wrong, love? Why that frisson?"

"Nothing, Your Highness."

"Call me Richard. Night is a great leveler." Again the rich laugh.

Death is the great leveler, I thought, and I wished we had light. True, the king had diminished to a disembodied voice, a single hand, but he was emblazoned in my mind's eye as a skull-like grinning face riding past the pile of dead hostages.

"Ah, there we are." He sank onto the edge of the bed. "I don't suppose you're clever enough to get us a cup of wine in this pitch."

"I'll try."

I made my way along the bed, from the bed to the partition

where the wine chest stood. I took a goblet and a flask, thinking it would be safer to pour after I reached the king. When I groped my way back, I touched a muscular leg.

The king was naked.

"None for you? We'll share a loving cup."

He took the flask and poured, sipped and pushed the goblet toward me, spilling a little.

"If you were in my state, wine stains wouldn't matter. Let's make you comfortable."

His hands groped at my neck laces.

"I'll do it, Your— Richard." I stepped away, took off everything except my tunic which was still slightly damp at the edges. 'Twas as far as I could force myself to go.

"Where are you? Ah, there. I've poured more wine and you must drink it, as a good omen."

I sipped it as slowly as I dared. Gradually I could see the faint pale outlines of the silk fenestrations. Richard was a ghostly mass next to me.

But if 'twas hard to see, the sound was terrifying. Canvas cracked like sails, metal objects outside crashed, rolled, thumped. And that mournful keening howl. We were sailing through a pitching universe, enclosed only in a flapping charnel tent.

"You're still dressed!"

"Just my tunic," I stammered.

"Are you afraid?" His whisper made me start, for 'twas directly in my ear.

"A . . . little."

"Come, let me hold you. Don't be shy. It's natural to be apprehensive the first time, but I promise . . ."

He lifted me onto his lap, lay back so that I fell awkwardly to one side, pulled me across his chest.

"You *are* frightened," he said, laughing. "Your heart strikes like a stone caster. Here . . ."

He held my cheeks, pulled my face close and kissed me softly, languorously.

"Alex, I love you. Pagan Eros, adorable . . ." His kisses grew more probing. His tongue . . .

I was dreadfully hot. The blackness was furry, suffocating, and his skin was sweating. I couldn't think of him as the king, or even a man I knew—his mouth enclosed me—and I wished desperately to escape. If only Enoch . . .

His hands took my bare calves, kneaded them gently, slipped upward to my thighs, my buttocks . . . and stopped. He turned his face away and my nose was buried in his neck, breathing in sweet woodruff, but he was not my father.

His hands no longer caressed—but explored, almost like a doctor's—where my treasure should be. And stayed, feeling. I leaped slightly. I was extremely sensitive, but also terrified by the peculiar quality of touch, as if I were an alien object. His hands slid upward under my tunic, felt my rising nipples and instantly withdrew.

He plucked me off his chest as if I were a snake. Leaped off the bed.

"What trumpery is this!" he exploded. "You're . . ."

Trembling all over, I clutched the sheets around me, not knowing what to say.

He grabbed me by the neck and shook me.

"Who put you up to this! By God, I'll kill the traitor!"

I lost breath—grew weak—couldn't speak for choking! Death, he was Death! The wind's sobs turned to laughter—waiting! My parents!

"As you value your life, *answer me!*"

"You're hurting me!" I gasped.

He loosened his grip and I fell to my side. Disoriented, I wondered desperately if I could escape under the cover of darkness.

Again those awful hands, on my shoulders now. "I'm waiting."

"I—don't—understand. You said you knew, said . . ."

"Said I knew what? When?"

"That I was female, said you knew . . ."

"God's balls, would I make a *girl* my page? Bring a *girl* on the Crusade? Devil's slut that you are! Spy! Now *talk*, God damn you!"

He sat with a heavy crash, pulled my hair so that tears came.

"I'm Lady Alix of Wanthwaite, ran for my life dressed as a boy as my father told me, had to escape Northumberland who'd killed his wife to marry me . . . Northumberland . . ."

I paused, *God damn him for the liar that he was about Northumberland!*

"This father you've touted as a hero—deliberately instructed you to lie to your king?"

"No! No!" I sobbed. "Not my father—you were the only one I was to tell!"

"But you didn't, did you?"

Contemptuously he pushed me away and I rubbed my poor sore head.

"No," I whispered.

"Because you could get more out of me by feigning to be a winsome, flattering boy, clinging and simpering to make a fool of me! I'll ask one more time and you'll answer or live not another day. *Who put you up to this?*"

"No one!"

"Zizka?"

"He never knew!"

"Ambroise?"

"No!"

"The French?"

"I don't know a soul in the French army. I . . ."

"That leaves the Scot, the pair of you, traitors!"

"No!" I screamed. "No, he doesn't know! Except . . ."

"I'm waiting."

"He may have guessed today—and he's angry, just as angry as you . . . only, the difference is . . ."

"Only?"

I could hardly go on, but I had to. "*I thought you knew,*" I whispered. Otherwise . . . how could he have thought he could make love to me? All these months . . . the many scenes, now returned with vivid clarity, of happy eyes, kisses, whispered love . . . and he'd thought I was a boy! I shivered in horror, the darkness a deep pit and I was falling, falling. Other words—"*Better show him, Pat; get on your knees, boys,*" "*Try a good Lincolnshire prick for flavor,*" and Enoch's elusive explanation of a sin when men don't go "twa by twa" with women. I knew now I would never leave this tent alive, for I had indeed stumbled into a scorpions' nest of secrets.

The king turned away—his foot inadvertently kicked his goblet. "What made you think I knew?"

I turned hot, sightless eyes in the direction of his voice. What could I say? Innocence—my only defense—and true.

"I know now I was wrong, Your Highness, but, you see, I loved you with a dreadful passion and my excuse is that I saw what I wanted to see. So when you said in Italy on the hunt that you loved me—that you were willing to take a chance in loving a child, then talked of Alais later and your father, I thought you meant you loved me as he did her."

"God help us," he groaned. "Go on."

"In Bagnara—on the beach—you"—I gritted my teeth and forced myself—"touched me and *said* you knew. When I asked when you'd first known, you said when I'd played Cupid—and soothly it would have been possible, since I was without disguise at that time."

"Disguise?"

I covered my face with my hands and spoke in muffled tones through my palms. "I—constructed—a false prick." I waited and when he made no answer, went on. "After you told me I was going to crusade—I had to take some measures, in that crowd of men. It fooled everyone, even Enoch."

"Go on," the sepulchral voice ordered. "How did you shape this article?"

I told him in fine detail.

Then there was silence.

The king groped along the floor seeking his goblet, picked it up and walked to the chest for a fresh flask of wine. In the meantime, I collected what clothes I could find and put them on. When he returned, he, too, had on his white silk robe.

"Wine—Alix?"

"No thank you, Your Highness."

There was another long silence between us, but I was keenly aware of many other things, like a blind animal whose senses are alerted. I heard the thin rustle of silk as his arms raised his goblet, heard wine sliding down his throat in long swallows, heard his heart and his breath. Smelled him as well, the strong musky horse-smell beneath the sweet woodruff. And sensed his thoughts—that there was a greater problem here than my discovery.

Finally his words came, almost expected. "Well, little Alix, our show is finished. Did I frighten you?"

"Aye," I said cautiously, "just a little."

"I've been planning this test for some time. Do you understand why?"

Suspecting a trick, I remained silent.

"Of course you know that I am surrounded by spies and traitors at all times. Every one of my familiars is subjected to an—er—examination to be sure he—or she—is exactly what he seems. 'Tis a sad but necessary part of my security."

Another long silence. "Don't tell me you believed me! Of course I knew you were a lass—often joked with Joanna about it. Otherwise . . ." His voice had strained jocularity and I knew this time I must answer.

"You did frighten me some, Your Highness," I admitted quickly. "You're a remarkably skilled actor." Which was indeed true, except for this performance. Brise-Tête could have done better.

He sat on his bed and continued, thus making an error that I could easily have corrected: he went too far. As an accomplished liar, I knew the secret was to tell no more than was absolutely necessary. But the king was anxious.

"I confess I had a second motive. I knew your knocking heart might crack a rib if I didn't desist. You were frightened by my advances, weren't you?"

At last I could be honest. "I believe I've feared—men—since I saw my mother killed."

"How did she die?"

To underscore my fear, I told him graphically what had transpired. Again my heightened awareness revealed to me he was not listening, but that my description gave us both time to gather our thoughts.

"Poor child. The example of our parents does affect us, does it not? The sins of the fathers . . ."

I frowned, for my father had not sinned, then realized he was speaking of Henry II. A black melancholy thickened the natural gloom.

"Well, we must sleep. I promise not to . . . I mean, I won't . . ."

"Like a courtly lover?" I prompted.

"What?"

"My book on the rules of love says the chivalrous knight does not touch his beloved until the lady gives her consent."

He made a sound of relief. "Exactly so. Yes, from my sister Marie. I believe the expression is that we lovers worship from afar, as sycophants before a shrine."

"Aye." He had no fear of receiving a signal from me to make love.

"Then, my dear, shall we sleep?" He dropped his goblet on the floor and lay across the bed. Gingerly, I hung on the outer edge, my mind as awake as it had ever been.

"Alix—did you say that the Scot learned your secret today?"

"I believe so, Your Highness." And I told him of Enoch's discovery, his reaction.

For the first time in more than an hour, the king chuckled dryly. "One thing never fails—you are a most droll creature, whatever your sex."

I waited.

"However, the Scot's knowledge creates a dilemma. Will he continue to care for you?"

"I believe he'll go back to Wanthwaite," I said bleakly. "He may even try the single ordeal—get a legal hold on my land."

The king raised himself on his elbow. "How would you feel about that?"

"I couldn't bear it! Do you think . . . ?"

I hadn't the courage to ask him for a favor.

Then to my astonishment, he leaned in the dark and kissed my lips—a chaste kiss by his standards, but startling nonetheless. And repellent. For me, a shadow thick as Acre's wall lay between us, real for all I couldn't define it.

"Ask, Alix. I believe you want to go back to Wanthwaite and are afraid that I will be hurt by your desertion."

"If I could have my own writ guaranteeing me sovereignty without the Scot."

He lay back. "Done. See Ambroise tomorrow and have him write it. I'll sign and give it my seal as soon as you bring it."

"Oh, thank you!" I cried, overwhelmed by relief.

"I think we owe each other that much," he replied. "Good night."

"Good night, Your Highness."

We lay quietly a long time more, my mind full of thoughts.

"I wish I could see you," he said plaintively. "It's all so . . ."

Sudden, I finished for him.

"Tell me, Alix, is there some part of you that's disappointed?" he asked.

I was glad there was darkness, for the gloom veiled my despair which must show otherwise. "Yes."

"In what way?"

I felt I was skirting a quicksand waiting to suck me under. Yet something within demanded honesty.

"I was thinking of our oaths by the lighthouse, on the Far. Do you remember?"

"We swore to love each other—to never betray."

"Yes. You said your family was cursed by children who turn on you. I promised I'd never turn—but I warned that I had a lack." Of a small pendulum between my legs, such an insignificant organ but essential for the king's love, it seemed.

"You should have been more explicit."

"I grant you. But you see, what I miss—since you did ask—is the sense that you love me. I never knew till now how I depended on . . ."

Tears streamed down my hot cheeks and I couldn't go on. But that was the truth. The king was formidable, dazzling and frightening, inscrutable, cruel, brave beyond words—all secondary to the fact that he loved me. I could accept almost°anything except this terrible loss.

Rough arms pulled me across the bed and held me close. To my amazement, I thought the king wept as well, though 'twas impossible to say whose tears were whose. He pulled me tight against his body which shook with deep sighs, like repressed sobs. He held my head against his neck, stroked my hair and didn't speak.

"Alex." He kissed my hair.

I reached a hand and touched his cheeks.

We were comforting each other.

"I'm going to—miss you," he said.

"Yes."

"I meant it—I did love you."

"I know. I too—"

And we could hardly bear to put it in the past. An elegy. The darkness reduced us to two lost people, *enfants perdus*, timeless, ageless, sexless even, but filled with such yearning.

We didn't want to part and gradually we fell asleep so, clasped as close as we could get. If we moved in the night, it was always together.

We woke in predawn gray.

Richard rose on his elbow and looked down on me. 'Twas August twelfth and yesterday had been August eleventh; this was Richard and this was Alix; but a millennium had passed during the night and we were strangers. I stared with wonder at eyes I could not fathom, at a mask which concealed another mask, layered back and back to I knew not what. Except that it was an awesome secret.

Richard seemed equally confounded. He twisted a curl on my forehead against his finger, licked his lower lip, studied my face as if it were written on vellum, frowned in concentration.

"Alix?" He smiled with his mouth, his lower lip more thrusting than usual. His eyes remained aloof, smoke-screened.

"Good morning, Your Highness."

"Richard," he corrected. "How could anyone think you were a boy?"

'Twas a rhetorical question.

He sat up, heavily, held his head in his hands.

"Stay there," he ordered. Soon he returned with wine and bread. Deeply inhibited by the unspoken, we broke bread and ate. He finished first and stared openly as I drank my dregs.

"Alix, good morning." He bent and kissed me. We both measured the kiss: neither hit nor miss, a trial shot. "I, too, was recalling in the night our vows on the Far. Remember?"

"Yes, Your Highness, to be faithful . . ."

"And to love—whatever surprises might be in store."

That I was a girl, that he was . . . ?

He laughed uncomfortably. "I suppose all lovers must accommodate to age and sickness, but few have our trial . . ."

I hung my head, wishing he would leave.

"Love is faith," he said quietly.

I raised my head.

His eyes glowed somberly. "No matter what revelations or changes, faith is steady."

"Yes," I agreed. Except that nothing had been revealed or changed except perception. I'd never *been* a boy, no matter what he'd thought. And, the silent sentence unwound in my head, he'd never been a man.

He kissed me again, more passionately, lips slightly apart. And I thought I caught the sparkling mote in his eye. "Alix, we don't march for another day. After you get your writ from Ambroise, you'll come back and bed with me again tonight."

I nodded, frightened almost out of my wits.

If he saw, he pretended not to. He lifted me against his chest in the old way—only this time he deliberately crushed my tender breasts against him—and kissed me once more. Then he laughed. "I always knew you were a sweet damsel!" he said, almost as if he believed it.

He put me down, took his sword, and stepped out into the dim morning light. Instantly he was surrounded by clamoring voices.

I LONGED TO FLEE that odious tent, but nevertheless stayed long enough to be sure Enoch was not about. First I watched the king walk away with his bishops for a hurried Mass; then I went from one fenestration to another and gazed through the netting into the camp. I finally spotted Enoch's leather tent to our rear and a concentrated study showed me the Scot was away from the tent, probably tending to his horses. I slipped out the front.

Fortunately my horse was tied under the king's canopy with his many steeds, and I soon led Thistle behind the cover of scattered tents to a path parallel to the main road back into Acre. It was a little more dangerous because it was on higher ground and therefore open to the Saracens, but better screened from our own camp. When I thought I was safe, I mounted and rode as fast as I dared toward the city. I wanted to get that writ from Ambroise, signed and sealed by the king, and into my own treasure belt before Enoch could stop me.

The sun still had not risen by the time I passed the pile of dead emirs, now food for circling vultures. I spurred my nervous steed around the corpses as quickly as I could and soon we were clopping through the quiet streets of Acre toward the Castellum where Ambroise lodged. We reached it without incident, but I didn't ride directly into the courtyard. Instead I sought a hiding place for Thistle and finally tied him to a carob tree behind a mosque, across the way from the king's former headquarters.

I waved to the few guards still on duty, entered the main court and walked silently along the arched corridor bordering the garden. No one was about, and I began to organize in my head exactly how I wanted my writ to be worded.

Suddenly I was grabbed from behind!

Instinctively I responded with the holds Roderick had taught me. Wound a foot around the ankle of my assailant. Raised my elbows sharply against his arms. Bent forward. And felt him slip. I twirled and saw a gross shadowy churl, was overwhelmed by his vomitous stench, but most of all saw his dagger. No time for observations. This was my life! Using every strategy I'd ever learned of wrestling and swordplay, I fought with the determination of Richard, the wildness of Enoch, and almost at once had felled my opponent who dropped to the ground like a ripe fig. I jumped on top of him before he could recover.

And looked down on the ravaged face of Sir Gilbert.

"*Benedicite*!" I gasped. "Are you still alive?"

"No thanks to you," he snarled, and tried unsuccessfully to spit on me.

I stared in amazement as the saliva coursed down his boiled cheeks, so covered with sores that I could hardly find skin. And his smell! Worse than the stench in the hospital where Roderick had died. No wonder I'd been able to topple him with such ease. With a guilty pang, I started to rise. Instantly he reached for his dagger and we were at it again, only this time I sliced his earlobe before I controlled him.

He sobbed like a woman. "You've killed me—I'll bleed to death. Oh, help me, help me!"

Soothly I thought he would die soon, but not from this measly wound. "If I let you go, will you promise not to harm me?"

"No one can hurt you, you iron-gulleted scorpion, or you would have died a dozen times over!"

"So you were the one who poisoned our food!" I cried.

He stopped sniveling long enough to peer up triumphantly from his mattered eyes. "Yes, either I or the Pisanos."

"Pisanos?" I thought of Richard's mercenary army.

"You know, Giorgio and Antonio, the pages we hired in Messina. They are masters at poison." Then he whined plaintively. "But why didn't you die?"

Again I let my attention drift at the revelation, almost disastrously, for the varlet was quicker than I recalled. After I'd knocked him back this third time, I took the precaution of tying him with my saddle rope and fastening him securely to a fountain nearby.

"Antonio and Giorgio." I came back to the point grimly. "I hardly know them. Why do they want me dead?"

Again he tried to spit, and this time he hit my shoes. "Simpering idiot, fox-eyes, filled with sniveling pretense. Master Melon-brain, we don't want you bedding with the king."

I stared like an idiot. These pages were *jealous*, which meant . . .

"Not that we're not willing to share," he went on. "We'd accept even his former love, King Philip, if that was his desire."

"*King Philip!* You're lying! He would never . . ."

"Wouldn't he?" he slavered at my shock. "His own father, King Henry, was dismayed when young Richard seduced the boy Philip. And with such indiscretion! Their affair was the talk of Paris." He laughed at my sickened expression. "Now if you would share. . . . You want him all to yourself and you've done it too. Very clever. Or was it your *pimpreneau*?"

"*Pimpreneau?*" I repeated dully.

"Yes, your Scot. He must call your moves. You're a fortunate fellow—the rest of us work without guidance."

"What moves? What has Enoch to do with this?"

His yellow-red eyes bulged from their sockets. "Is it possible he doesn't tell you? Being a Scot, he may want to hold all profits to himself."

"What profits? What are you talking about?"

He leered in delight to see me so discomfited. "Why, my dear, the Scot arranged your contract and made a nice sum. Did he share it with you?"

I was dumb.

"Then he dangled you before the king, forbidden fruit till the price was forthcoming. Richard had never had to deal with such a bargainer before, hard as any Jew. Finally he made his deal: you for the bed, but only if the rest of us were discarded. As for the amount of gold, only your *pimpreneau* can tell."

I turned and ran.

"Don't try to return to the king!" he called. "Giorgio and Antonio are guarding him well. And they have enlisted a dozen henchmen to help. You haven't a chance!"

I took his warning seriously, once away from the court, and sidled in deep shadows toward Ambroise's apartment.

HE WAS HUNCHED over his writing table when I burst in.

Without preamble, I announced myself. "Ambroise, I'm a girl."

He raised a sweet beatific smile from his work. "I know, dear. How lovely for you both."

"You—you traitor!" I cried savagely, and swept his vellum pages to the floor. "Aye, now you'll listen to me!"

I ripped at my laces, lifted my tunic and pushed my breasts into the troubadour's recoiling face. "Girl! Girl! Female! Woman!" I shouted.

He tried to rise from his stool, weaved this way and that, fell back, missed his stool and crashed atop his scattered pages.

"Oh, oh, oh I don't believe it. *Does the king know?*" His protruding watery eyes begged me to say no.

"Yes. He asked if *you* knew." Grimly I watched him struggle with his bubble-body which was now heavy as lead, slippery as butter, then reached out my hand to help him rise.

He crossed himself. "I swear I didn't—you must have said that I didn't, Alex."

"Lady Alix, if you please."

"Lady Alix?" He still couldn't comprehend. "God be merciful. What shall we do?"

I replied acidly, "I'm leaving this jackal-country this very day, and you will arrange it."

"What did the king say?" he asked, appalled as the truth filtered inward.

"Ask him. *Today*, Ambroise. I am not going to Ascalon, I will not stay here with Berengaria—is that clear?"

"What does the king prefer?" he begged piteously.

A most interesting query, but no longer relevant.

I crouched close so our noses touched. "Ambroise, forget the king for just one moment. *You* got me here under false pretenses; you cheated both your king and me. I know not what vengeance the king may take on you—though I promise that I tried to exonerate you—but I don't plan to pay with the loss of my estate or my life. Is that clear?"

He shook his head, his eyes livening somewhat at my statement about exonerating him, but still confused withal. "I cannot believe the king would kill you, Lady Alix, or take your land. He's most forgiving . . ." And then he must have recalled the emirs.

Without further palaver, I enlightened him about Sir Gilbert and the Pisanos, and about Enoch's nefarious goals.

"I must get back to England *at once*," I finished.

"You say the king promised you a writ?" He took up vellum and quill.

"Too late," I concluded, after much painful twisting in my mind about the Pisanos. "I dare not go back for his signature or seal— mustn't see him again—mustn't show myself to *anyone*. My life is at stake."

He leaned back, amazed. "You're much more forceful as a female, Lady Alix."

"I have more reason," I said bitterly. And more knowledge, I added to myself. The innocent girl had been replaced by an innocent boy; now both gave way to the woman.

"What do you want me to do?" he asked.

"Get me away this very day, secretly and safely, so that I may return to Wanthwaite."

"How?"

"That I leave to you. But, Ambroise"—and I leaned close again—"if you don't help me escape today, I will send word to the king tonight with a different tale about you than I told earlier. I'll say I was confused and frightened the first time, that you knew I was female and hoped I could change him."

He wiped his face with his sleeve, muttered a prayer and rose wheezing from his desk. "Here's the key to the door," he said. "Lock it after me, and I'll see what I can do."

HE BOUGHT ME PASSAGE on King Philip's galley, sailing back to France the following morning.

"You were fortunate," he said, "that one of Lord Coucy's men sickened and died this very day so there was space."

"I will be under Lord Coucy's protection, then?"

No, Ambroise knew Rigord de St. Denis, King Philip's historian of the Crusade, and had prevailed upon the writer to take me on ostensibly as a scribe, disguised in French colors of course. I would sleep topside, but my days would be spent below with the horses so I could be less visible.

"And my horse?"

"Naturally."

I nodded, satisfied. "What was the cost?"

He waved a fat hand. "A gift—from the king." He smiled, patted my head, almost as relieved as I was. "Oh, Lady Alix, you'll be interested to know that Enoch tried to buy this same space."

I pushed aside his hand and jumped up. "He isn't on the ship!"

"No, dear, but you cannot be too sanguine. I hear that Richard is sending a second galley in the wake of Philip's with his own spy aboard. After all, there seems little doubt that France will attack England, despite the pope's injunction."

What did I care about England and France? I leaped forward and grabbed Ambroise's silk blouse. "Enoch is going on that ship?"

"It appears that he is."

"*Deus juva me*," I moaned.

"Where's your horse, Alix? The sun has already set and it will soon be dark enough to leave." He twisted his few hairs nervously. "Then I must report to the king."

We stared at each other.

"This is our last chance to talk?" I whispered.

He nodded.

As Richard had said last night—it was all so sudden. After two years—three for me—to end like a flash of Greek fire. No, that wasn't it. To end in a manner which negated the whole time. Sex revelations, contractual revelations, and finally no writ. Empires were coming asunder over my head and my own little world was splitting underneath, a lesser star.

"Ambroise, I must know about Enoch. Did he take money for my contract with Zizka and you?"

"I believe not at first in Paris, beyond perhaps stealing some from you. Zizka surmised that the Scot was too gullible to see our—purpose. Naturally Zizka encouraged ignorance."

"The Scot is shrewd," I objected.

"So he proved in Chinon, but he didn't approach Zizka again. I believe he went directly to the king, getting his payment in the form of concessions along the Scottish border."

"What did Richard concede?"

Ambroise's pale eyes shifted away. "Some estate in the north." Wanthwaite!

He turned to the door.

"Wait! That's not all he offered the Scot." I stopped him. "When Enoch dug his mine to blow up the wall, something else was offered. Do you know what?"

Ambroise sighed with relief. "Yes, the earldom of Northumberland. Bishop Hugh of Durham is a very old man and the king plans to put Enoch in Hugh's place as Northumberland when the time comes."

My heart shriveled. Enoch had traded my body for a title! This was the "brother" devoted to protecting my "innocence"? No wonder he'd been dismayed at discovering my true sex—he'd been undermined in the most venal contract ever made. I wanted him dead.

Ambroise brought me back by a touch on my shoulder. "I, too, must say one thing, hurried though we are. Alix, think kindly upon the king."

I was almost too angry to heed.

"List to me well, for I've been with Richard more years than I care to tell. He loves you. No, wait, don't interrupt. I know what you think, but it's not like that. Richard is a giant in every way:

physically, spiritually, emotionally. But he's never been able to find a vessel worthy of his emotions. Until you appeared, Alix. You have the mind, the character, the person—everything to delight him. I believe you've been a revelation to him."

"Hardly that, since he thought I was a boy."

"Are you sure?"

I recalled his shock. "Aye, indubitably."

"Yet . . . he loves you. 'Tis true he was once seduced when he was a lad like you—'tis common in the military, has been since the Greeks. 'Tis also true that an inclination grew to an alternative, and finally to his only possible expression. Witness his difficulties with Berengaria."

"Why doesn't he change?" I cried.

"You know how he's struggled. After all, sodomy is a sin in the eyes of God, and Richard is a Christian king. Even the Saracens put a man to death for the act. Perhaps God is testing Richard in some way. For all his determination, the king so far has failed. Unless . . . perhaps . . . you."

I hung my head, remembering.

"'Tis impossible, of course, here, now . . . but if you could leave a message?"

Ambroise's honeyed words couldn't erase my shock of last night, Gilbert's revelations—the dead emirs.

Or Northumberland.

"Please, Alix?"

"I once did love him," I said grimly. "Once . . ."

"That's enough," he interrupted hastily. "I can embellish a little. And you left because . . . ?"

"I had no choice. Embellish that as well."

He turned ashen. "I'll say—that a nobleman gave me the message, but he doesn't want to be identified."

Or something even more convincing; I wasn't worried about Ambroise protecting himself.

At dusk we rode through Acre's back way to the port. There the black outline of Philip's borrowed galley loomed against the clear evening sky, a wax lamp on deck reflecting in jagged lines to the shore. There was great activity as Frenchmen loaded their gear. I waited in the shadow of the Tower of Flies as Ambroise waddled up the plank and identified himself. Soon he was back with the equally portly Rigord de St. Denis who carried a blue cloak of France to drape across my shoulders.

Ambroise and I stared at each other in the dim light.

"I'm sorry, Alix." He leaned forward and kissed me.

Angry as I was, I felt moved by his kiss. We'd been through much together. Then I led Thistle onto the lower deck and when I looked to the dock again Ambroise was gone.

I waited below decks until the movement above had ceased, then climbed up and took a post at the rail. The wind had died, the bright stars hung low and tracked the black sea. In the distant hills, fires burned in Richard's camp. Ambroise would wait till I was far at sea before he told his story, but the king already knew that I was not returning to his pavilion, had not brought the writ. I imagined his wrath, wondered how long it would last. Richard of the Angevin temper, a valiant warrior, a chivalrous king who lied and deceived when it suited his purpose.

Enoch.

My heart boiled to think of him. Monstrous traitor, hypocrite, thief, *pimpreneau*! My legs grew weak; my palms sweated where they clutched the rail. I swore to beat the Scottish snake yet. I had no writ, no army at my back, nothing but my bare wits, but that was enough. I hadn't come to Hell and back for nothing—I'd learned much from the treacherous rogues along the way.

Dawn came bright and breezy. I slipped down to hide with Thistle once again, but heard the sailors' shouts, the sail crack in the wind, felt the roll of the waves.

I was on my way home.

BOOK THREE

WANThWAITE

Perhaps a god will yet restore,
By happy chance, our bliss of yore.

HORACE

29

OD FAVORED THE FRENCH WITH A STEADY WARM
breeze and we skimmed o'er the lapis plain as easily
as a sea gull. I knew not what Richard's troubadour
had told Rigord, but the French historian hovered
over me protectively, announced me as his new
scribe and gave me parchment to copy his words as proof. Despite
my gratitude, my spleen boiled in rage as I read his nefarious lies
about King Richard, for he'd made my monarch the Devil incarnate, a bragging, vainglorious, ruthless traitor to God and King
Philip, who had poisoned Philip's wine and forced him to quit the
Crusade. I briefly considered editing the tale toward the truth, but
what could I do? My very life was now in Rigord's hands and I must
conform.

Deo gratias that King Philip suffered from seasickness. His keen
baleful eye would have discovered me at once although I believe
we'd not spoken a single word to each other. As it was, I was spared
all but his groans and retching which rent the air day and night.

When I wasn't scratching Latin on vellum, I went below decks
to be with Thistle, as planned. Both his familiar presence and his
safe stall comforted me in my terror of the French nobles around
me, many of whom I recognized. If I were discovered, first I would
be questioned, tortured if they thought I was a spy, then made a
prisoner until they could ransom me to Richard. A fate so painful
that I dared not dwell on it. Every time a knight came to check

his own horse, I buried my face in Thistle's mane till I was alone again.

One afternoon as I half-dozed with my arms around Thistle I o'erheard a most disturbing conversation between two nobles standing by the rail directly above my head.

"Vexin will fall easily," said the first.

"And give us a clear march through Normandy," said the second.

Just what Mercadier and Richard had always predicted. I missed something, then heard:

"Not before spring at the earliest and we'll be waiting."

"Or if not in France, he'll be captured in Austria where Leopold will be waiting."

"Think you that Count John will protest?"

"When we are putting him on England's throne? Hardly. But I hope the Whore-Queen Eleanor dies beforehand. She could make trouble."

"Women."

On another hot day while everyone slept, I sat below Thistle's belly and cautiously took off my money belt to remove some coins for my trip back to Wanthwaite. How clever I'd been to outwit the Scot about money, and I'd see him in Hell before I'd give him a farthing now. Let him eat his title of Northumberland if he hungered; he'd been more than compensated for the bit of cocky-leeky and haggis I'd forced down my gullet. As for our lodging in Paris, that was matched by the palatial rooms King Richard had given us. Aye, on that score we were even. But when I toted all his evil gains at my expense, nothing short of my conquering Scotland could make us even. So far, of course, his victories were only fancies and not yet in effect; therein lay my hope. If I could find Bishop Hugh first—assuming he was still alive, *Deo volente*—I would make a strong plea for my right to Wanthwaite. Certes Roderick's uncle was a just man and would support me, but only if the deed was done in Assize—and before he saw Enoch's royal writ.

Our galley blew apace toward Marseilles but not fast enough. Betimes I crept to the stern and squinted from one side of the horizon to the other. Every small movement made my heart quake till I saw that 'twas a fish's dorsal fin or a bird flying low, not a ship.

EXACTLY TWENTY DAYS after leaving Acre, we landed in Marseilles without incident. I thought surely that King Philip would disembark for Paris but Rigord informed me that the king planned to continue his journey by sea despite his infirmity, for he'd inherited the land of Artois from the Duke of Flanders and wanted to claim it against possible contenders. The historian kindly invited me to join them on their way through the Straits of Hercules and up the Atlantic coast to Boulogne where I could catch a ship to Dover; 'twas faster than land and, besides, Ambroise had paid my way. Much as I was tempted by the speed, I was more eager to get away from the French where I suspected that one nobleman had recognized me. Reluctantly I declined.

I was on the waterfront two days later buying salted eel for my lone journey northward when a large galley swung into port.

"'Tis one of Richard's!" someone shouted. "Look to the three lions!"

Wildly I lunged into the shadow of a portico of a stewe, and I could see knights crowd around the lowering plank.

One by one, they descended. Holy Fathers, most of them. Then a few wounded, then . . .

Enoch!

My heart belched, my mouth turned to dry cotton. I pressed deeper into the shadow, tried to make myself invisible as a fish by a riverbank. I know not how long I stood so but suddenly 'twas night and I'd been there since early morning. The Scot had stayed near the ship awaiting Firth and Twixt; I watched him eat a fish stew from a barrel, relieve himself into the sea, rub his hands and bend his knees to limber his body, and the more I watched, the more I hated. How unfeeling he was to look so red-cheeked and bright-eyed when he'd lost me. Well, there's no elixir like greed, that was obvious; already Enoch was counting my acres.

Finally he mounted Firth, took Twixt's bridle, and whistling his loathsome "Murriest May" song, rode past me close enough to touch with a lance. I waited a long time, then ran to the palace where King Philip's household was staying and asked the guard for Rigord. The historian was already in bed but came at my summons, a torch high o'er his hoary locks.

"What's wrong, Alex?"

"Forgive me, Sire, but is it too late to change my mind about going with you?"

He leaned forward to peer at me and I could smell that he'd dined on a strong garlic soup. "I believe not. Many nobles have chosen to ride directly to Paris, so we have deck space." He reached for my arm. "Come, you'll sleep in my chamber tonight. There's nothing to fear, boy."

I was sure that Enoch hadn't tarried in Marseilles, for he was on his way to Paris to pick up my writ; nevertheless I hid in Rigord's hot chamber until our ship was loaded and ready to sail. 'Twas with a great sigh of relief two days later that I saw Marseilles shrink to a shimmering cluster. That city was my nemesis and I prayed fervently that 'twas the last time I'd see it or be stung by its mosquitoes.

King Philip's contradictory fortune held, good in Zephyrus' hot steady breath, bad in his wretched *mal de mer*. The Straits of Hercules were known for their treacherous storms but we puffed past their awesome rocks and eddies with ease. Then we hugged the brown shores of Spain and Portugal, resisting the pull of the Atlantic and the unknown. But when we put in at Boulogne, the French king left to ride overland and took his good fortune with him—for the wind fell, the mists rose.

"I still have gold from Ambroise," Rigord said in farewell, pressing coins into my palm.

I watched him ride away, oddly moved to lose this last connection to the Crusade. Now I was alone, without Dame Margery, Enoch, Richard or Rigord. Well, I would just have to look after myself henceforth.

I joined the channel boat. We sailed for England with a heavy mist over the water which the captain assured us would soon burn off. However, the fog closed in quickly after midday and we had to use our oars as the captain studied his needle floating on a dish and the bell rang constantly to give warning. Our first sight of England came just before dawn the next day, the lamp burning atop Caligula's lighthouse, and a giant cheer of relief rose from the passengers. We could hear the screaming of the gulls, the steady pounding of surf; then the sun rose behind us and there were the chalk cliffs crowned with the jade forests of England.

I clutched the damp rail to watch. So many countries, so many miles, and all the time England was here waiting, the true land of milk and honey as poor Roderick had said that night outside Tyre. Somewhere in those rosy clouds floated the spirits of my parents, earthbound until I could release them. Somewhere far to the north Wanthwaite still stood.

BY THE SECOND afternoon on the London road I was so weary I could hardly stay awake. I'd lost a night's sleep on the Channel boat, had rested only a few hours in Canterbury. When I reached the crossing point at the Thames, opposite London's glowing sprawl, I realized that we would be landing on the strand close to Jasper Peterfee's inn where I'd left my wolf Lance. I decided to indulge myself with a good night's sleep in his company, though I knew 'twould be foolhardy to try to take the wolf on the road north. 'Twas like coming home to clop along the strand with its many fine kitchens and enthusiastic hawkers. I yearned for a fresh pigeon pie, a good sleep on my old goatskin, a cup of English ale. I saw the sign of the Red Fox readily enough, led Thistle into the court and reined tight.

There, still loaded with gear, stood Firth and Twixt.

In a flash I turned Thistle back to the strand and galloped toward Ludgate.

30

 AMNATION. I WOULD HAVE TO SLEEP IN THE fields outside London this night and risk outlaws, rogues and bandits. How had the Devil-Scot gotten here so fast? On his broomstick, I thought sourly.

I rose at Matins, while it was still dark, and began the upward climb on Icknield Street. By the time it was light, I'd left the rich mansions behind and was in open country. Briefly I wondered where Gladys Stump was now, recalled her raucous "Caaa! Caaa! Caaa!" and Enoch's ridiculous enthrallment. Would he had married the hussy.

I stopped that night in a village inn, and inquired to see if there was a northbound group I could join. Fortune's Wheel helped me, for I linked myself with a company of Benedictine monks heading for Durham, led by Father Thaddeus. He warned me that we must travel with all speed and take our beds as we found them: the whole country was embroiled in civil warfare—to linger might prove fatal. I assured him that I too sought speed.

Every step thereafter carried us into more hostile country. The fathers were alert to danger e'en though they pretended to ignore it and I felt especially conspicuous with my scarlet robes, a cardinal among crows, the one person who might be carrying gold. Therefore, I borrowed a black cape from the fathers.

Villages were now infrequent, as were houses. Occasionally we passed a mean thatched hut with a fetid pool before the door where wretched families watched our passage sullenly. Others were hostile, shook fists at us and called us "Bishop's lackeys." One morning we rode for many miles without seeing any sign of human habitation when all at once we came to a stop.

Father Thaddeus raised a hand to signal silence, though no one had spoken a word for hours.

Nonetheless we stopped obediently and virtually held our

breaths. In the distance we could hear shouts and the clang of swords; I judged that an army of about thirty was coming our way.

"Into the woods!" the father whispered harshly.

We needed no second order, but rode into the thick brush, dismounted some distance to our right, well out of sight but still able to see one portion of the street. Now the sounds grew in volume: taunts, screams, the clash of weapons. Then my educated ears told me 'twas over, one side gave chase to the other. In no time a gaggle of harried men rushed by low to their horses, their outfits a mixed motley, many of them bleeding and ashen of face. Still we waited. Almost on their heels came their victors, a group just as wounded and poor as the first except for their exultant shouts. Finally, cautiously, and after a long silence, we made our way back to the road to continue our journey.

Around the next bend we came upon the grisly sight of seventeen men hanging from the oaks which lined the street. Though their eyes and tongues bulged in death, the fathers rushed to cut them down, for their flesh was still warm. One lived a short time but the others were dead. We stopped to say a death Mass, tried to dig shallow graves in the frozen turf, had to settle finally for covering them with leaves and branches against ravening beasts.

"They're more sinned against than sinning," our holy father said. "Treason is abroad in the land."

As if the day's events were not enough to bloody our fantastick cells, we could find no inn by nightfall and were forced to sleep in the open under an icy drizzle which penetrated our very marrows. We couldn't rest comfortably without a fire, yet were terrified of what its light might bring us. We huddled around a tiny circle of smoke and prayed through chattering teeth for God's mercy, which for the holy fathers meant we should go to Heaven if slaughtered in our sleep, and for me meant that we should not be slaughtered at all.

Although we knew God was with us in this valley of death and repeated the psalm to prove it, we forced ourselves to a new pace and hardly stopped to eat or sleep. I gave Thistle handfuls of precious grain from my saddlebags when we paused for water, but it barely sufficed. However, I didn't complain. Danger was palpable and I was as eager as Father Thaddeus was to avoid it.

Then late one bitter afternoon, we rounded a curve and plunged into disaster. Green-clad archers swarmed like locusts over a dell, their stolen treasures spread on the hoary grass, while several bound merchants watched in terror. A fat friar was among the bandits and saw us before we could pull back.

"A company of scurvy priests, Robin!" he shouted.

"Ho-la, get the scum!"

They charged upon us on foot and instantly o'ercame the priests who carried no arms. However, I turned Thistle and prepared to dash back up the road alone.

A slender boy grabbed my bridle and I beat him about the face savagely. "Let go, in the name of the king!" I cried.

Instantly a large muscular man came to the lad's aid and pulled me rudely by the leg so that I started to fall. I loosed my foot from the stirrup and turned the fall into a leap, then hit Thistle's flank smartly to make him sprint away. By the time the man and boy turned, I had saber and sword. "Touch me and you're dead!"

"I'll take him!" the boy called, drawing his weapon.

The man grinned and shouted to his comrades. "Swordplay, men!"

I took my stance, sword and saber in position. I was determined to win at the same time that I saw I was hopelessly outnumbered. 'Twould take wits to escape this predicament, but winning came first.

My opponent held his sword at a flat angle before him, his arms stiff. Astonished, I wondered if this was the first time he'd fought. If so, my real challenger was the muscular man behind him.

I took one step back, then *marched* swiftly from the side. I tapped his hand and drew blood!

He cried out in pain and danced back, then forward, waving his sword like a banner.

More and more astonished at his lack of training, I easily avoided his wild gestures by feinting, then struck him again on the shoulder.

Again he cried out, but thrust his chin forward stubbornly and rushed at me and past me as the men began to laugh.

"Methinks you're outclassed!"

"Good work, stranger!"

Before he could recover, I thrust, but he whirled and avoided sure death.

"Want to quit?" his mentor asked him.

The stripling's eyes flashed. "Never!"

I smiled derisively, beat my blade on the flat of my hand to confuse him, thrust again and tore his tunic. I no longer planned to injure the wight; 'twould not be chivalrous to take advantage of him, or good strategy either. I admired his valor, and I feared his backers. I *marched*, *flèched*, and tossed his weapon into the air as easily as if it were a feather.

A mighty cheer went up.

I flourished this way and that, never taking my eye off the boy who was now embraced by the man. Something in their manner reminded me of Richard with me, and I shuddered.

"Are you hurt?" I heard the older man ask.

"Only my pride." The boy grinned bravely, showing dimples much like mine, and thrust out a hand to me. "You're the better man."

There was a roar of laughter at these simple words and I winced. Surely they didn't know I was female.

The friar now leered down on me, the most disreputable prelate I'd ever seen, what with his stained smock barely girding his bloated cod, an old piece of helmet topping his crown, bleary eyes and breath strong enough to make me drunkalewe on the spot.

"Where did ye steal that garb?" he belched.

I was about to say that the fathers had lent me a cape, when I saw that I'd dropped the cape and stood forth in full Plantagenet splendor. Remembering that some of these highwaymen worshiped the king, I decided to brazen it out.

"I've come directly from King Richard in the Holy Land where I served him as page," I said haughtily.

A murmur of excitement swept their ranks and the friar was pushed aside by my opponent's friend. He doffed a feathered cap and bowed low. He had dark curly hair to his shoulders, a crooked smile and cleft chin.

"Robin Hood, at your service. My men and I are keeping the king's peace in this dangerous wood during his absence. Have you heard of us perchance?" His black eyes gleamed eagerly.

"Yes, I believe I have." I affirmed to please him. He *could* be the "ruffian" in Queen Eleanor's letter. "And so has King Richard."

"What has he said of us?"

Before I could reply, an extremely tall man whispered in his ear and I tried to apprise my situation. I no longer feared for my life, but delay would be equally hazardous. Robin Hood was a vigorous, intelligent-appearing man with a courteous manner, but at least a dozen rich-clad merchants watched me from their bindings and my fellow travelers cowered in a group under the eyes of three archers, so I dared not trust the varlet. This was an outlaw cutthroat band and must be handled warily.

Robin Hood turned back, his crooked smile in place, his dark eyes still eager. "What is your name, sir?"

"Lord Alex of Wanthwaite, in the household of King Richard."

"You will be our guest tonight in Greenwood Hall, Lord Alex. You are the most excellent swordsman we've ever seen forsooth, and we want you to join us."

Permanently? My heart fell like a stone.

"I'm most flattered, sir, but I must decline. If you will release the priests, we shall be on our way, for we have orders from Richard to reach the north with all due haste. The Scots are expected to cross the border."

A small frown fretted my host's brow. "We have no use for priests, nor should you, a scurrilous lot of leechers. However, since you obviously come from the king, I'll release them to show respect for His Majesty. As for you"—his voice dropped—"I'll let you go in good time."

"And the merchants?" I persisted, wanting to help the poor prisoners. *Deo volente*, I, too, would regain freedom, though soothly I was frightened, especially that Enoch would o'ertake me.

"As soon as we've left with their purloined goods, the priests can do with them as they please."

He nodded to his men who were already collecting valuable pieces of carved silver off the ground and packing them onto their horses. Now my opponent whispered in Robin Hood's ear and the robber turned an astonished face to me, listened again, and smiled licentiously. A knot of fear formed in my gullet. Did the varlet mean to abduct me for reasons beyond my swordplay? Had I once again fallen into the hands of a man who loved boys? He swaggered toward me, hat in hand, his manner both deferential and mocking. "I've called for your horse, Lord Alex. Usually we blindfold our guests, but you will be an exception."

I bowed properly and slid my eyes to the boy for clues, but he continued to smile with strange vacuous delight. In almost no time, everyone had mounted and we turned to enter the dense forest. I cast one piteous farewell glance at Father Thaddeus who made the sign of the cross. *Deus juva me*, I would be back in his company, safe and sound, tomorrow. Then I had to pay heed to the way, for huge ivy-covered trees spread roots like traps, angled their low limbs cunningly to strike our heads off our shoulders. Robin's men rode silently as ghosts through this tangle, neither speaking nor cracking a twig. The leader turned back to accompany me. His teeth flashed in the gloom and he reached boldly to my saddle, whereafter each time I came back to the seat I sat directly on his palm. Now certain that my suspicions were correct, I almost broke my legs in an effort to ride in my stirrups and avoid my own saddle.

I was sweating from exertion by the time we finally came to a halt in a greensward. Instantly Robin Hood was on his feet and reaching upward to help me. I had no choice but to accept his arms, whereupon he slid me down the entire length of his torso and bruised my breasts. Too bad I no longer wore my false prick, I thought sourly, for he was deprived of that particular thrill.

The boy now approached. "Come, Lord Alex, I'll take you to a chamber where you may refresh yourself before dinner."

For the first time, I realized that we stood before massy structures of logs and woven branches which blended completely with the background. I followed my narrow-shouldered guide into an octagonal hall already lit with pine torches and set with trestle tables loaded with silver. At the far end of the area we climbed a narrow stair to a vast upper chamber dominated by a huge bed.

"This is Robin's chamber," the boy explained. "He's taken the liberty of ordering water to be heated for a bath after your long ride."

More and more uneasy, I stared at the fur-laden bed. "I would prefer to sleep close to my horse." Aye, and to ride through that pathless wilderness if need be.

"Soothly?" The lad was startled. "Well, of course, whatever you say. But I thought that before dinner you might like to clean yourself and change your clothes. Would you perhaps like a woman's tunic?"

'Twas my turn to be startled. "What? What are you talking about?"

The lad laughed gaily. "Forgive me, but I guessed immediately by the way you fought. You took particular care to protect your breasts."

Which made me angry. "I fought to protect my heart and chest-spoon as I was instructed. 'Twould not hurt you to learn the same lesson!"

"No offense, Lord Alex." He touched my arm lightly. "Perhaps 'twould be more honest to say I recognized a fellow female, for I, too, dress as a boy to ride with the men." And he stripped off a tunic to reveal himself a woman.

I must have looked as ridiculous as I felt, for the wench couldn't stop laughing, especially at my gauche study of her torso. Soothly her breasts were small knotty muscles, nothing like the swellings on my own chest, and I marveled anew at the variety of shapes the body could assume, recalling the naked witches in Paris.

"Would you like to borrow a tunic?" she asked again.

"Aye, I believe I would, thank you."

"Ah, here's your bath. Soak as long as you like, and I'll bring appropriate garb."

"Does Robin Hood know?"

"Of course. That's why you rode without blindfold. He's ever chivalrous to the fair sex."

She admitted two varlets with a wooden tub of steaming water, then ran down the steps after them, leaving me alone. I sank into the luxuriant suds, dazed at this turn of events. So my suspicions had been wrong. But wait! That hand under my seat had been no error. Robin Hood knew I was a woman, that was all. *Benedicite*, I wished I *were* a boy! No, for then I'd be a captive swordsman. Unless . . . more and more frightening. What were the brigand's intentions? And what was the role of this boyish girl?

She was back, already dressed herself in a soft green gown laced with gold, and with a similar one in her hands for me. Late-afternoon twilight entered the upstairs window and shone on her face. In boy's garb and from a distance, she appeared very young, for her body was straight and hard, her face clean-jawed and alert. When I perceived her close and as a woman, however, I noticed crinkles at the outer edges of her eyes, a slight discoloration of her teeth, and realized she was in her late twenties, not young at all. Also, she made a handsome boy, a plain woman. Her brown hair and eyes, sunburnt skin, extra-wide mouth and square chin were engaging, but not feminine. I took all this in at a glance, while she studied me with the same curiosity.

"Your skin glows as if there were a fire behind it," she observed. "How do you keep it so bright when exposed to wind and sun?"

Soothly I didn't know.

"And your hair." She fingered my wet locks. "Spun gold and silver combined. Your eyes are luminous as jewels. Do you have some magic elixir you could share?"

I heard the note of envy, though 'twas more sad than bitter, and shook my head. "No need, My Lady, for you are an elf from fairy-land yourself."

She brightened. "Do you think so? Robin assures me, but I feel alone without women and it's been so long . . ."

She then recounted her most odd story. She was Lady Marian Fitzwalter of Arlington Castle, only child and heiress to her estate. She had fallen desperately in love with Lord Robert Fitzooth of Locksley, a champion of justice for all. King Richard had called him the most noble lord in all England for his chivalry, and rewarded him with the earldom of Huntingdon. Richard, alas, then went to Jerusalem and his brother Count John promptly stripped Richard's men of their honors. In defiance, Robert became Robin Hood, and formed his own nation in the forest, dispensing the king's justice, robbing from the bloated rich and giving to the deserving poor. Marian, too, had defied her father, forsworn her inheritance, and followed Robin to his woodsy lair.

I listened to this fantastic tale, astonished and dismayed. Naturally I knew naught of Arlington Castle or Count John, but I did know about the Earl of Huntingdon. I had been in Chinon when King Richard signed the order making David, brother to the King of

Scotland, the Earl of Huntingdon. I'd heard it from both Enoch and Richard. Had Robin managed to deceive poor Marian? Or was she trying to impress me?

But that wasn't all.

"Robin and I want to marry, but above anything we worship Richard and Mary."

"Mary who?" I asked, not following her reasoning.

"Why, the Virgin Mary! We've built an elaborate chapel in Her honor and say Mass twice daily."

"Of course, I see. Only what does this have to do with Richard or marriage?"

I could barely see her flush in the fading light. "Robin and I have taken the vow of chastity until the king's return. Then and then only will we wed. Thus I am known as Maid Marian."

And should be titled "Made" Fool, I thought, remembering Robin's insidious hand. The Earl of Huntingdon who'd taken the vow of chastity and gave to the poor—though his own tables groaned with gleaming silver—and was "chivalrous" to all ladies. Poor credulous Marian. How could she be so old, yet so naive?

By now I was dressed in my tunic, crowned with a gold braid, and I stood before a cloudy mirror to study the effect. *Benedicite*, I didn't recognize myself in the glowing curving creature before me, as if I'd been touched by a wand.

"How did you serve King Richard?" Maid Marian asked from behind me.

I looked at my seductive image and considered rapidly. Either I would have to tell the truth, or render some fantastic tale such as she had told, or create a falsehood which would nevertheless seem closer to reality. I decided to protect the king by the latter course.

I sighed deeply. "We loved each other passionately, Maid Marian, even though it was against his purpose in Jerusalem, against God. We couldn't help ourselves."

Her dimples showed. "Please tell me all, and I promise to be discreet. I, too, love the king and need to know for my own future bliss . . ."

Perhaps she was convinced of my invention because she was so sheltered, but I believe I told a good tale besides. The yearning and passion were easy, just a slight exaggeration of the truth. When it came to our bedding together, I started with our assignation in the tent and ended with what I'd seen Enoch do over the years. 'Twas I who groaned under Richard's weight, that was all.

Tears trembled on her lashes. "How could you ever say goodbye?"

"He couldn't bring himself to expose me to the dangers of the desert," I lied glibly, then permitted a significant pause. "In any case, 'twas not goodbye, but farewell. You are not the only person awaiting his return to England."

Which I thought was a nice touch, just in case her nefarious Robin Hood had any intentions of detaining me.

"I will tell him we met you," she declared, "when he attends our wedding. Oh, Lady Alix, perhaps you will attend as well."

I refrained from smiling, poor wench.

We then descended to the great hall to meet with Robin and his men. Robin stood courteously as Maid Marian presented me by my true name, adding only "beloved lady of King Richard." I winced at her openness, at the same time that I noted Robin's appreciation of my exposed neck. Indeed, all the thieves leered and made me wish for my boy's braies again.

The dinner was suspiciously succulent, and I wondered again at the "poor" who benefited from Robin's good works. Maid Marian and I sat on each side of her love, while the other men ate at our table with no distinction in rank that I could see. Marian had identified the prelate as Friar Tuck, and he led the questions about the Crusade with a Little John and Will Scarlet close behind. Robin, oddly enough, showed little interest in his king, but a great eagerness to impress me by his own exploits. He recounted incident after incident—all the same, all to his own glory—which I must relay to the king. I quickly grew weary of the man's braggadocio and paid more attention to his manner toward Marian.

'Twas sadly lacking in courtesy and affection. If he cherished her at all, 'twas as a loyal audience, for she kept goading him to remember this event or that. Weary, I announced that I must retire.

"Not before you tell us where you travel and why," the unperturbed Robin said.

"To Durham to see Bishop Hugh, Earl of Northumberland," I answered coldly. "I have a writ from the king which the earl will enforce through the Assize."

Robin's black eyes twinkled wickedly. "Except that your king neglected to inform you that Hugh is no longer Northumberland."

"What?" I was so astounded that I sat again. "Is he dead?" *Benedicite*, my worst fear come true, that the old bishop would expire before I could reach him, that Enoch would become Northumberland.

"He's alive and fighting," Friar Tuck continued. "Hugh won't recognize the king's brother as archbishop, so the king stripped Hugh of his powers. However, the wily bishop refuses to renounce the title, though I believe he no longer calls the Assize court."

And I took wanhope. Better that no one rule Northumberland than that Enoch assume power. Aye, a limbo of jurisdiction might yet benefit my cause.

"If you need help, I could ride with my men," the oily Robin offered.

And siege a castle with a ragged group of archers? Conquer Enoch when he arrived? O'ercome a Scottish army led by a brute waving his odious writ? I carried Roderick's garnet ring as my writ which I'd been sure would be persuasion enough for Northumberland. Now I must discard this plan and go to my second scheme, more chancy by far.

"I take it that the Assize doesn't meet then."

No, they concurred.

"Are there any lesser courts in the region?" I asked the bloated priest who seemed a cut above his peers in intelligence.

"Local moot courts do such business as there is," he said, "though their strength varies from place to place, depending on how angry the people be. Those under bad lords, or under Count John, have little stomach these days for laws."

I remained standing, lost in thought, until Maid Marian asked me gently if she could show me to my quarters. I thanked her and bade Robin and the others good night.

"I hate to leave you here with the animals," Marian said later as we stood in the stable.

"I'm used to it, and it's warm. Thank you for the tunic." I handed her her robe, having dressed in my male attire once more.

"Please keep it for remembrance. And, Alix, may I ask you a great favor?"

"Anything at all." Poor wretch.

"Will you come stand with me on my wedding day?"

"I promise, God make it soon." God make it at all.

"Amen to that."

I gave her instructions of how she might find me and we kissed goodbye. I then stretched out on clean straw piled by the wall and began to scheme. All my hopes for Hugh of Northumberland were now dashed—what could I do? A twofold problem: to unseat Roncechaux; to find a legal claim superior to Enoch's royal writ. My brain grew weary.

I was wakened by Thistle's whinny and saw a shadow against the open arch. I took my father's dagger in readiness.

"Lady Alix, don't be afraid."

Robin Hood!

What to do? I didn't want to kill the rogue, which would invite certain death for me, yet I suspected his intentions. He sat beside me where I now crouched on my knees.

"Maid Marian has confided your great love," he said thickly. "Tell me, do I remind you of the king?"

"The king . . ."

"Aye." He reached forth and took my free hand. "I thought that if you pined for him, I might give you solace."

I could feel his hot breath on my cheek and leaned back. "No, thank you anyway. I've resigned myself to being alone."

"Nonsense, your kind is never alone." Before I knew what he was about, he'd wrested my dagger from me. "We'd be a good pair, sweet-cuds, both in bed and in the field. Swordplay in both places."

"What about Marian?"

"She'd be delighted. The poor wench is lonely and needs a friend." Without further ado, he locked me with one arm while that active hand reached under my tunic and found my nipple.

"No! . . ." And I was smothered by his lips as he pressed me into the straw, his hand working feverishly, his mouth sucking like a man dying of thirst, his legs pushing my knees apart. 'Twas so swift and expert that I thought I was lost.

Then his lips descended to my nipple as if to satisfy their thirst there, and at least my mouth was free.

"Stop! Oh please, stop! King Richard will never forgive you if you kill it!"

His head rose. "It?"

"I carry his babe in my womb, only no one must know. Our son will be heir to the crown—already pronounced so by Richard—and Count John would murder me if he knew. Don't harm England's hope, I beg you." And I broke into racking sobs.

He rolled off me carefully and straightened my garments in the dark. "Tell the king his secret is safe with Robin Hood," he said fervently. "I misread you, My Lady. I thought you were a camp follower of the king."

Quickly I rose, my fingers once more entwined about my dagger.

"I'll return you to the priests in the morning." And he left me alone, but not to sleep more that night, for my heart beat in my ears like a drum.

NEVER WAS ANYONE more relieved than I was to rejoin Father Thaddeus at dawn the next day; his manner might be brusque, but it was honest. With unspoken consensus, we moved as rapidly as we could to get away from Nottingham and Sherwood Forest with its dangerous inhabitants. Again we were forced to sleep outside, but at least I needn't fear a hot-tongued varlet stealing into my bed. Except that I had a dream.

In my dream I again stood by the lighthouse on the Straits of the Far with Enoch and Richard, only Richard held the falcon he'd taken from the peasant and the Scot held a huge white swan. The iron-eyed king cut a circle in the stones with his spur and set his falcon in the center. "I challenge your swan!" he cried. "Let the birds fight and winner take all!" And so the two feathered beasts were placed on the ground, the falcon with his tufted feet and small glinting eyes, the swan crouched low with breast outthrust, head curved back, and soon they were twisted in knarls of bloody feathers, screaming and hissing when a beak went home, and in a short time the swan was victorious. The king picked up the carcass of his bludgeoned bird and without a word faded into the elements. Smiling grotesquely from his blue face, Enoch pushed me with the huge white fowl. Instantly the beak and feet disappeared in a cloud of downy softness as I was embraced by the beast. Yet one part remained hard, for I was simultaneously penetrated in a sharp hot stab that made me cry aloud. Astounded by my own keen joy, I rocked with the bird, warm, secure, thrilled, praying my dream would go on forever.

I woke still spellbound, grinning like an idiot, my liver throbbing. And then guilt hit. *Deus juva me*, what sort of evil gripped my mind that I could have such a wicked vision? 'Twas the planet Jupiter's influence, no doubt, my body's distress, a *visium*-nightmare and not, *Deo volente*, a *visio*-prophecy. I slunk furtively to my horse hoping that no one could read my stricken face, but gold does not always glare and thoughts are secret if one is wise enough to stay quiet.

Aye, I might fool the holy fathers, but I couldn't deceive myself. As we pounded through the cold weary day, I tried to find an acceptable explanation for my vivid vision, and tried as well to push down the recurrent excitement it still caused in my nether parts. Macrobius teaches that contact with the dank earth can cause black bile to flow, thereby creating a melancholy humor as the natural virtue takes over. Be as be may, however, I couldn't ignore the disgusting stimulation of Robin Hood's lips on my nipple and over and over I wiped the offending breast viciously with my arm. But worse: that the stimulation should cause a sensuous arousal by *Enoch*! Never mind that he pretended to be a swan; 'twas the Scot and his terse I'd dreamt of to my everlasting shame. The liver is a most immoral organ and I wondered if 'twas possible to numb it with some sort of drug. Or, failing that, have it cut out.

The next day our progress was slowed by the steeps of the Pennine mountains where Enoch and I had cut into the forest. Spinneys gave way to knarry twisted tree sculptures rising from boulders, their shapes suggestive of clutching monsters and bent seers; the road, too, turned back on itself and narrowed at times to treacherous cuts along cliffs that dropped dizzily to sure death. Streams now became thunderous weirs which we crossed by clinging to ropes. We met no one, saw little wildlife except for circling hawks.

That night we stayed at the Inn of the Gray Falcon and I was appalled to see how Betty and Bibs had declined from their former hospitable selves to haunted fearful shadows, ready to leap when the wind blew. Bibs now carried a knife in his rope belt and the door was braced with a heavy log. They'd been bound and robbed three times but felt lucky to have escaped with their lives.

I jogged our hosts' memories about my previous stay.

"That was the beginning of our ill fortune," Betty whispered so that I could hardly hear. "That was when Jimmy . . ." And she gave way to tears. I'd noticed her son's absence, of course.

Bibs said heavily, "Your Scottish friend—or brother—was here two nights ago looking for you."

"Asked for you—or your sister, for he said it might be a lass." Betty frowned, confounded.

And I thereby gave up a night's sleep as I lay before the fire, turning feverishly on my pelt, watching the coals pale to ash. How had the Scot possibly gotten ahead of me? While I was with Robin Hood, no doubt, and I thanked the Virgin devoutly that at least he hadn't seen me. I hoped he was on his way toward Durham to see Bishop Hugh. If so, I could regain lost time.

Now we paced rapidly across dunes of thistle and gorse, site of my first bleeding. The unimpeded northern gales blew a cold rain into our faces, then icy needles and finally snow in tiny whirling flakes that rose in an updraft. Well did I remember that Enoch and I had been unable to find a croft for the first night and, sure enough, when darkness fell the holy fathers took uneasy refuge within a circle of rocks. There we built a huge fire, huddled close in our furs, and woke blanketed in snow.

Now the descent. I rode at the rear, trying to discover the point where Dame Margery had put me on Dere Street, but it all looked so different under its white mantle.

"Alex, come to!" Father Thaddeus called sharply.

I had dawdled to a standstill, gazing anxiously. We were on a curve with thornbushes on my left, a bank, but I wasn't sure. With a lurching stomach, I spurred Thistle onward. A half hour later, the irritated father again admonished me.

"I've come to my turn-off," I said uncertainly. "Thank you for your company."

He rode back to where I sat. "I don't like to leave you alone in this heavy wood, boy. You'll die of exposure within hours if you become lost. Is there no path? No sure sign?"

I dismounted. "Wait while I look, if you have time."

I climbed up the slippery snowbank, clinging to spiny bushes with my leather gloves till I could stand upright. The awesome forest was a maze of sinister shadows and black trunks, a haphazard limbo. I stumbled along the ridge of the bank, trying to remember. Then I paused, studied.

"Wait just one moment; I'll be back," I said to Father Thaddeus.

I sat and slid down the far side to the level, then lurched to a small winding form and brushed the soft snow off the top. My heart leaped: a drywall. Aye, now I recalled, we'd followed a drywall all the way. This was my thread to Wanthwaite.

"I found it!" I shouted.

Shortly I'd said farewell to the holy fathers and was under the shadows of the reaching beech trunks. Carefully I turned Thistle westward.

I crunched slowly and silently through the drifted snow. A wan sun broke the gray cloud cover and turned the world to a dull glisten cut by purple shadows. Then in the far distance I heard a familiar clink like a smithy at his task and knew 'twas the bell of Dunsmere. I forced myself to kneel and pray, took out a slab of bacon and bread to eat.

I followed the meandering wall over hills and through valleys, ever glancing ahead and to my left. What a long way we'd walked, me with my blistered feet. Then the wall turned to my right and I hesitated—hadn't we found it near here? I studied the landscape, trying to imagine it by moonlight in spring, saw the copse we'd used as guide. I turned away from the wall and forced my eyes upward to the horizon.

There it was—Wanthwaite.

Silent and still as a memory.

Towers, park, bridge hidden by trees. And somewhere in the sky above, the souls of my parents, waiting, hoping.

31

T WAS COMPLETELY DARK WHEN I REACHED Dunsmere village. Thistle stumbled again and again in the rutted paths, and I had to wait for the thin high moon to float from behind the clouds before I dared urge him ahead. Finally I dismounted to lead him. But lead him where? The huts looked as alike as overgrown toadstools in the night and I couldn't remember the exact location of Dame Margery's.

Then a bowlegged wight opened the door of his cot, stood silhouetted against the dim light and pissed into the street.

"Pardon me, sir," I called, "can you tell me where Dame Margery and Tom live?"

He leaned forward as if trying to see me. "They done nothing wrong," he snarled.

"Of course not," I replied, startled. "I'm an old friend, back from a long journey."

After another pause as he pondered, he pointed and said gruffly, "Three houses beyond the church, then second behind the pigsty." And he slammed the door.

Once I'd passed the church, the pigsty was easy to smell and soon I stood in front of a structure which I vaguely recalled as the hut where Maisry and I had hidden. It had no windows or firehole to show that it was occupied, but I knew Dame Margery must be there. I knocked on the door.

"Dame Margery!" I called loudly. "Dame Margery, open up! It's me, Alix, come home at last."

No answer.

Perplexed and apprehensive, I knocked harder. "Daughter to Lord William and Lady Catherine. For God's sake, let me in!"

The door opened a grudging crack. "Who are you? Who sent you?"

I tried to enter but she kept the door firmly in place with her foot. "Surely you haven't forgotten me, Nurse. I'm Alix, your own milk-daughter . . ."

"Alix be dead. I seen her buried myself, two years ago. Be ye from the Devil?"

I crossed myself fearfully to ward off the omen of death.

"I've been with King Richard on his Crusade—that's why it's taken me so long—but I'm alive, no ghost. Feel my hand."

She shrank back.

I became desperate. What a disconsolate homecoming! "Look you, I went with the Scot, Enoch Angus Boggs. Remember? And I took my wolf Lance. Soothly you couldn't have seen my actual body in the grave because here I am. Think, Margery."

"The face war mashed in." Her voice wobbled. "And the clothes war different, but Sir Roland said as how he seen the face and 'twar Alix. He found you in the Inn of the Gray Falcon."

Jimmy! I withdrew my hand and leaned on the doorpost, grieved beyond measure. A poor innocent boy had been my surrogate in death. Like Maisry. A black rage now made it difficult to speak: "'Twas Jimmy, the stableboy."

There was another long silence as Margery digested this, whereupon the door opened. She gripped me in powerful arms.

"Lady Alix, be it you? Alix, friend to my Maisry?"

"Aye, Nurse, I'm home!"

She pressed me so close and tight that I felt my ribs begin to pain and I couldn't breathe at all. Her chapped lips kissed my face all over, her hands ran through my tangled hair and she repeated again that I was home, thanks be to God, I was home. I, too, was toty with joy as her voice, her smell and feel brought back a host of memories from my infancy onward, joy and sadness as well. We stood mumbling and swaying so in almost pitch dark, for the only light came from the feeble glare of the firepit; even so, I gradually became aware that we were not alone. Margery's husband, Tom, the town tippler, lay curled on a fur close to the fire, his eyes closed, his slack lips twitching as he occasionally snorted. From the far wall, I heard the plaintive tremor of: "I . . . see . . . some . . . body!"

"Aye, Mam! 'Tis Lady Alix!" Margery shouted to the shadowy creature; then, to me, "Sit close by the fire, dear, and take off yer cape. Yer hands be like ice. Have ye et?"

I looked uneasily at a stringy rat boiling in a pot. "I brought some bacon."

"Bacon! We haven't had—" Her voice became restrained. "No, dear, this squirrel be good enow fer the likes of us. Tom just killt it fresh."

I put a firm hand on her arm. "Bacon for all, Nurse. How often do we have such a wondrous homecoming to celebrate? Now I must see to my horse."

"Aye, we'll put him in the cow-byre."

Together we led Thistle to the back of the cot where a lean-to was attached for cows. 'Twas sweeter and warmer than the hut, I trowe. Quickly I unsaddled my beast and removed the slab of bacon from my drafsack. Soon we were back by the fire and dipping crusts in good bacon fat. Tom snorted and worked his mouth at the odor, but didn't wake.

All the time we ate, Margery keened for the dead child who was buried beside my mother. What a heinous crime! What an ogre Sir Roland was.

"He war sent by Northumberland to look to Wanthwaite after the Scots left, but we'd be better off with Scots."

'Twas the most damning judgment Dame Margery could make.

I didn't recall how much of the true tale of the sacking I'd confided of yore, but now told it exactly as my father had related it to me. She listened intently, then nodded with satisfaction.

"I knowed it in my gullet, that I did. Ask Tom when he comes to if I didn't say over and over, that Roland no more 'rescued' this castle than a wolf rescues sheep."

"Rescued!" The revulsion of two years ago seemed like yesterday. "When he . . . he . . . killed my own mother."

The dame leaned close, clasped my hands so I winced. "And Maisry?" she asked hoarsely. "He murthered her as well?"

I nodded dumbly, then realizing she couldn't see in the dense smoky pall, muttered, "Aye, I witnessed it."

Her hands continued to squeeze mine painfully. Words were not necessary; anger and grief ran through our fingertips and we understood each other completely.

"I . . . smell . . . some . . . thing," came the querulous voice.

Dame Margery released my hand and sopped an oatcake in the bacon fat. "Come greet my mam. She'll rest easier when she knows who ye be."

We squatted beside the fragile supine figure. Her bones were twisted as grapevines, eyes and ears clouded, but there was nothing wrong with her mind. "You was here that last day with Maisry. You held my hand."

"That's right," I shouted, then told Dame Margery: "We were running away from Roland after he spotted us at the fair."

"He ran after ye?"

"Aye."

I answered her relentless questions as honestly as I could, until finally she left the subject of Maisry.

"Ye said you were in Jerusalem with the king. Did ye get yer writ then?"

"Yes and no," I hedged. "He granted me a writ for Wanthwaite, but said that I was too young to assume the barony. Therefore he made a writ assigning the Scot as my guardian."

"That Enoch Angus Boggs?" Her voice was properly horrified. "He must have lied like the Devil to get his favor."

I hurried on. "Aye, that he did, and he's determined to take the whole of Wanthwaite. He is on his way here now."

The ease we'd begun to enjoy vanished instantly. Dame Margery stiffened; her voice again took on the wobbly fear it had had at first. "The Scots be coming? Oh, my dear honey-pot, where can ye hide this time?"

"I'm not going to hide," and my voice was hard, "for I have a plan if you'll help me."

"Anything! Anything!"

The dame cautioned me to say no more by putting a finger to my lips, and she pointed to Tom's stirrings. She then led me to the cow-byre where our conversation continued.

"Now tell me, does Roland have knights in his service?" I asked when we'd settled on a bale of straw.

"If ye call such rogues *knights*, he has a few scruffy thieves that ride with him to pillage and rape as they list," she answered contemptuously.

My heart sank. "Thieves or no, they must be dealt with. Are there any good fighters among the villagers?"

"Depends on what ye mean by good." Her voice reminded me of Mercadier's: loyal, ruthless, intent. "They be not armed like yer fancy nobles, but they do the job when the heart moves them."

"Where do their hearts stand in this matter?"

She paused briefly. "The same as mine, if that answers."

It did.

I took a deep breath. "One other question and I'll tell you my plan. Does the moot court still meet at Crophill?"

It did.

"And who are the judges?"

"The priest of course—that be Father Gerald what was here in your time—and Ralph of Cogshill the forester, Archie Werwillie and Lord Roland as our lord."

"Archie Werwillie? Wasn't he betrothed to Maisry?"

"Aye, he wanted her."

And she him; poor Maisry.

"Well then, this is my plan . . ."

Our only disagreement was on when we should execute our scheme. I insisted on the morrow; Margery demanded more time for adequate preparation. I then attempted to explain my problem with Enoch, playing on her hatred of the Scots. Surely he would march in our direction within two days, three at the most. 'Twas imperative that Sir Roland be ousted before Enoch arrived.

Finally she agreed: tomorrow.

WHEN I ROSE from my straw at dawn, Dame Margery had already gone on her errands. I dressed carefully in Maid Marian's tunic, dipped bread with Tom and the old lady, then waited impatiently. Haute Tierce came and went; my head began to throb with anxiety. Twice I thought I heard Scottish pipes in the distance: once it was a goat's bleating, the second time a shepherd's fife.

Then she was back with a full sack. "Got everything, love, but the pigeon took time."

"Let's away," I said anxiously, "or it will be too late."

"You look wondrous pretty, Alix," she said adoringly. "Like Lady Catherine except that you have your father's coloring."

Her words heartened me more than she knew. Bemused, I recalled King Richard riding his gaudy poop into Messina, spangled cape waving defiantly in the wind, glorious smile turning this way and that. *As we are seen, so are we esteemed*, but he also meant that an imposing appearance gave the leader himself inner confidence. With my green and gold dress, I *felt* like a baroness, not a pretender. Aye, I would assume the mantle of greatness and let the rest follow.

I was aware of the villagers' curious looks as we walked the crooked paths of Dunsmere. A weak sun had pulled them from their cottages into the open air and they sat at tables counting and sifting seeds. Dame Margery greeted every one as we passed and again I became impatient.

"Do hurry, Dame," I urged. "I want the priest to be near when I call."

"Easy, love," she replied calmly. "Ye also want these folk as witness that ye were with me and in good health before ye left."

Finally we were walking beside the familiar curved furrows of black glistening fields, the withered thorn hedges and ditches. We were headed toward Wanthwaite and my heart hit my ribs painfully, whether from memory or anticipation I couldn't be sure.

"This be far enough," Margery said.

We were a few feet from where Maisry had died when Margery stopped.

"'Tis really Maisry who's going to court today," she said quietly.

I agreed. "Maisry and my mother. Well, Dame, let's not delay."

Together we beat our way through the thornbush to the narrow

verge by the shallow ditch where I'd lain long ago. This time I
stretched on hard frozen turf as Dame Margery knelt beside me.

"This won't hurt," she promised, "but 'twill seem strange. Be
patient, darling."

Her hands explored and I trembled, fought to stay still. "I'm
cold."

Twice she erred, but the third time she suceeded.

"Be careful how ye walk," Margery advised.

"Aye. Besmotter me a bit."

She dug mud from the ditch's bottom and smeared my face,
then pulled my bodice asunder.

"Go to, My Lady. I'll be close behind."

"But out of sight," I warned.

I left her and returned to Dunsmere alone, walking as fast as I
dared, feeling taut as a bowstring. Then I reached the village and
saw people ahead.

"Rape!" I screamed with all the power I could muster. "Help!
Help me, somebody! I've been raped!"

Two small boys ran from a bush and gaped.

"Go get your mother," I sobbed. "Rape!"

They didn't move but a man ogled me from his sill, gestured
wildly to someone in his hovel, then rushed to grab my arm.

"What happed, lass? Be ye hurt?"

"I've been raped! Take me to the church, please!"

Now a woman came, then another, who insisted that the man go
away, though he didn't.

"What happened, child? Who did the deed?" a heavy dame
demanded.

"Lord Roland!" I gasped. "Please give chase—I want to charge
him in court!"

"She's raising the hue and cry against *Roland*," an awed voice
said. "We mun help her!"

"Roland again. Scurvy cur."

By now an excited jabbering crowd had collected and several
hands tried to support and cover me.

"Bleeding like a sticked swine, she is. Can you walk, lass?"

Soothly 'twas difficult, for in order to keep the dame's work intact, I must take small mincing steps, hug my thighs tight. Fortunately, arms lifted me into the church. Thus wafted on a babble of horror, I watched the tonsured priest turn from his altar.

"Raped! She's raped!" a man shouted, then a woman, then everyone.

"By Roland!" added another. "Roland!"

"Not again!" the father cried. "He's possessed by the Devil!"

"Nay, Father Gerald, he be Old Clootie in the flesh," stammered a goodwife. "Remember what he done to my Wilma."

"Raped!" I repeated. "Oh, help me, Father! Lord Roland!"

I fell against the priest who hefted me onto the altar. Then I was surrounded by a blur of sympathetic faces, tried to bring tears to my eyes without success, nevertheless gazed imploringly at Father Gerald.

In a weak voice, but distinctly, I said, "Call the moot court, Father, at once, for it must be within twenty-four hours. I'll press charges against him."

"What do you mean?" His hound's face quivered, his liver spots seemed to darken, his brown eyes stared fixedly.

I raised my head and said more clearly, "I want you to summon Lord Roland to the moot court *at once*. He raped me and must pay the price."

My months with Zizka had taught me when I have my audience, and the group around me was now enthralled at the incipient high drama; therefore I played to them with all my heart.

"Surely this cannot be the first offense Roland has committed?" I asked them.

"Lor' no, lass. The gels in these parts be like so many pricked birds," a bitter voice replied.

"He pricks the gels, steals the pigs!"

There was an angry mutter.

"But he's the lord. What can we do? Us villeins got no rights."

"I'll tell you and show you if you stand by me," I said. I rose on my elbows. "I am Lady Alix of Wanthwaite."

The crowd heard without comprehending; nonetheless they fell silent.

Father Gerald trembled, his eyes glazed. "But—but I myself buried Lady Alix two years ago."

"You buried a boy in my place," I told him. "Look on me, Father Gerald. Didn't you once come to Wanthwaite at Christmas to aid Father Michael? And I played the angel?"

"God be praised!" he whispered, awed. "But how . . . ?"

"Later. It's your responsibility. As an orphaned minor, I am your ward—you are my legal guardian. I want to press charges."

He nodded, then shook his head violently. "'Tis no use, Lady Alix. Even from you. He'll never answer such charges."

"Tell him he's to *judge* a rape case," I instructed. "Tell him the man who's accused is willing to pay good money for an acquittal and show him these silver coins for surety, with more coming tomorrow."

"That's right—trap the weasel!" a delighted voice hooted.

"We're with thee, My Lady!"

There was a general rustle of excited approval.

The priest, torn between bewilderment and relief at my authority, took the money. "I'll go as soon as I know you're all right."

"Where is the poor gel?" an authoritative voice rang out. "Let me to her."

"'Tis Mistress Evote, the midwife," Father Gerald warned. "She'll have to be witness that you were really raped and that you were a virgin."

Pressing my lips tight, I nodded.

"You're the victim?" A deeply seamed face with currant eyes leaned close. "Someone mop her forehead or she'll get a chill. Thankee, Babs. Now, dear, I'll be gentle, but . . . Spread your legs, so, and bend your knees . . ."

I stared resolutely upward where disturbed bats fluttered on the church beams.

"Too much blood to see," Evote muttered. "Mercy, mercy."

I was clutched on both sides as cold greasy fingers moved up my thighs. Desperately I clenched my teeth, held my breath. Then exactly as planned, Dame Margery screamed from the doorway, rushed to the altar, hurled herself across me.

"My God, what did he do to you? Oh, my poor honey-pot."

"Careful, Margery," Evote said, "she's pretty bad tore. I hate to make her move, but if she wants to bring charges like she says, I have to see her piss."

My tears now flowed with ease and I was almost too weak to move. Dame Margery helped me to go behind the rood screen and held the jug.

When we presented it to the midwife, the thick, white, viscous scum of egg white floated on the bottom.

"Now look at that," she exclaimed with awe. "Best example I e'er saw of a man's seed."

"How dare he plant his vile seed in My Lady Alix!" Margery screamed hysterically. "You should all raise up agin him! He's despoilt our own rightful baroness! Can't ye see who she is? Have ye no eyes? Why do ye gawk like sheep? Do something!"

She frothed, and raged, shook her fist, cried for vengeance again and again. The crowd looked at me uncertainly.

Then one burly fellow stood forth. "Remember me, My Lady? Friend to Maisry?"

"Archie Werwillie," I said, holding out my hand.

He squeezed it hard. "I'm with ye. Tell me what ye want."

"And me." A red sweating wight came as well.

"Clac the Swineherd?" I knew his profession by his smell, his name from Dame Margery.

Soon I was surrounded by eager shouting villagers, each begging for instructions.

With Margery's help I stood on the altar, so all could hear. "As rightful heiress to Wanthwaite, I am ward of the King of England. King Richard himself gave me a writ restoring Wanthwaite and all its fiefs. When I presented this writ to Lord Roland a short time ago, he tore it from me, then threw me to the ground and attacked me most cruelly."

"Kill the monster!" a woman screamed.

I held up both hands. "He's broken God's and the king's law— we will enforce the law."

"How?"

"I'll charge him at the moot court. And with God's help I'll get the judgment. But *you* must administer justice. Can you do it?"

"Tell us how, My Lady!"

"What means 'administer justice'?"

"To punish the blackguard."

"Aye, that we can do." An angry mutter spread.

"We are an army . . ." I looked at their seamed worn faces, their emaciated bodies, milky eyes, diseased mouths, unset broken bones, and quailed at the task.

"Armies do not win by numbers alone, or King Richard could never have taken Acre." More truly, the Saracens could not have held it so long; but no matter, the principle was what counted, and they would need confidence.

"An army wins by strategy, and the best strategy is surprise. We will surprise Sir Roland."

"Kill him!" Archie screamed. "Cut him down! Butcher . . ."

The cry was picked up and echoed throughout the church.

I lifted both hands, as Richard would do. "Stop!" I shouted. "Stop this at once! *I'm* in command. You'll follow my orders or we move not at all."

Archie jumped onto the altar beside me. "Quiet!" he bellowed. "Listen to Lady Alix. Go on, My Lady."

I thought of King Richard, invoked his image for guidance. "First, you must have some understanding of the law, which will be read in Latin."

They listened courteously, but with a sinister waiting look.

"And now the enforcement, the punishment."

Their eyes sparked.

"How many of you are skilled with the hunting bow?"

Eight men and one woman stood forth eagerly.

"Daggers or knives?"

Everyone claimed to be gifted in that area. Feeling more and more like Richard, I divided them into ranks, told them how to follow my leadership. With cunning peasant eyes, they nodded and smiled. Aye, this was the day I used the king's training and example, with two exceptions: I had a rustic army with the paltry hunting bow as my Mategriffon; and I did not plan to have any *enfants perdus*.

FATHER GERALD returned from Wanthwaite in late afternoon.

"He took the bait," he said with satisfaction. "Especially when I told him there would be more silver at the mootpit."

"Thank you, Father. Until morning then."

After he left, I gazed at the northern horizon, stood very still to listen. No sign or sound of the Scots yet, which meant no danger till the morrow. But I didn't doubt they were camped just over the hills.

The following morning Father Gerald and all the villagers were already waiting, breaths steaming in the cold air, their faces nipped red when I stepped forth. They waved and one fellow raised a shiny dagger.

"Here's to Lady Alix, our new mistress!" Clac shouted.

"Hail, Lady Alix!"

I waved back, then gathered close about me the homespun cope Margery had provided and pulled its hood over most of my face.

"Shall we pray?" Father Gerald suggested.

We dropped to our knees on the frozen ground and listened solemnly as he intoned the familiar Latin phrases invoking God's help. Then we formed a line to begin our long walk up Crophill to the mootpit of our ancestors.

Archie Werwillie strode by my side. He carried a hunting bow and a quiver with two sharp arrows. His dark blond hair hung like bronze wires low on his forehead, and grew in an unruly crop on his eyebrows. His nose was red, a bit damp, and his hazel eyes were filled with hatred.

"This Roland got Maisry, didn't he?" he asked without preamble. "I heard her condition when she was brought in and I figured . . ."

I put my hand on his arm. "Don't think of it, Archie. Or if you must, remember that Roland was seeking me. She saved my life."

"And today we'll get his."

"I pray we do."

"His or mine," he said laconically.

Dame Margery shuddered.

When we turned off the path to march up Crophill, we faced an earth turned to fire, for the frosted gorse was scarlet on the hills. The rectangular mootpit was set in the midst of this flaming world, and we paused on its rim to study it before descending. 'Twas carved in six tiers of earthen seats with a flat space in the middle where a trestle had been placed.

"Do you want us archers to stand on the rim or the top tier?" Gordoc the Smith asked deferentially.

I considered. "The sixth. Don't expose your backs. Those with daggers farther down, toward the middle."

"And what's the middle? The third or fourth?" Clac wanted to know.

"The tiers are deep; best say the third. I doubt if you could hurl a knife with force any farther."

Those who carried clubs or axes chose their own places. I took careful note of where everyone sat and prayed that a combination of surprise and our superior number against Roland's single person would suffice. Finally, I sat on the first tier at the bottom of the pit, wedged between Dame Margery and Tom.

Father Gerald moved to behind the judges' table opposite me and put the relic box from the church on the table: St. Anne's right ear. Archie joined him, then Ralph of Cogshill, the third judge. We awaited the chief judge, Sir Roland.

"He's coming and he's not alone," Clac's wife Adelwisa called from the rim.

"How many are with him?" I shouted up to her.

"I can't see yet. Looks to be eight or nine."

"Armed?"

"Aye, I believe for hunting." She gestured that she couldn't say more.

Archie nodded to reassure me; the priest remained calm. There was a shuffle directly behind me and sharp knees pressed into my back. I glanced over my shoulder to see a taciturn Dane called Thorketil. He smiled grimly.

"Heigh, Lord Roland, is it true you're planning to hunt the boar?" Adelwisa cried from the rim in a penetrating nasal whine.

"Aye, immediately after the trial," the remembered voice rumbled. "Now you could keep me home if you liked, Mistress Fulltits."

We heard the stamp and snort of horses, the rattle of weapons, as the knights dismounted.

"I'd like to very much, but what would we do with your *six* friends?"

Six, I recorded her message. Too many but not as formidable as the eight she'd first mentioned.

"You're a talented wench, Wisa. Certainly you can accommodate six lusty knights."

"I'll make a pact: I'll take you and your company every one if you let me polish your swords during the court session, as I did last time. I could use a few pence," she replied archly.

"What say you, men? The wench is worth a copper."

With many bawdy japes and laughter, the men dropped their steel with a clatter for clever Adelwisa. But she didn't get all.

Not daring to turn my head, I could nonetheless hear the clink of metal as the first knight leaped down the tiers. He came all the way to the front and crowded between Tom and me. A fleeting glance showed that it was Magnus Barefoot.

I sat like a rock, petrified. Subtle twists of his torso revealed that he was staring at me, but he said naught. I hoped he was merely curious to see the girl who had brought the plaint.

Next came Sir Roland. He, too, had kept some weapon despite his promise to Adelwisa, for I knew well that faint rattle of hilt against belt. Certainly he had no suspicions, for he took a long time descending; he stopped frequently to exchange greetings with various villagers. I marveled at how deftly they returned his japes. Zizka's troupe could not have performed with more conviction. The loathsome knight edged behind the judges' table, and sat in the middle between Archie and Ralph of Cogshill. I adjusted my hood closer and stared through my fingers at his face: same predatory eyes, scarred cheek, bad teeth, patchy hair. I swore he'd not leave this pit alive.

Now the rest of the knights had found their places, all separated from one another because we had connived to leave only a few free places. I had no notion as to whether they were still armed in some way.

Father Gerald rose, spread his arms in blessing and said a prayer. Then he intoned in a loud clear voice: "The ward of Dunsmere Township is now in session. Let the plaintiff step forward."

My moment had come. I stepped to the table and stood opposite Sir Roland.

"Place your hand on the relic box and take your oath," the priest told me.

I laid my hand on the box.

"I entreat you as plaintiff through the Father, Son and Holy Ghost, that you do not in any manner attempt to lie or default in this court in any way whatsoever. Do you so swear?"

I thought of my mother and Maisry. "I do so swear."

"Will you then make your accusation in the full sight of the court and point to your assailant?" He removed the relic box.

I took a deep breath and looked squarely into Roland's eyes for the first time since the inn. "By the Lord to whom this relic is holy, so do I prosecute my suit with full folkright, without fraud, without deceit, without guile. I do swear that yesterday morning in the hours after Haute Tierce that I did meet my assailant on the path west of Dunsmere, that he did there throw me to the ground and thereby disturbed God's and the king's peace, that he did forcibly enter me and raft my maidenhead, thereby destroying my sacred member. After he was finished and had departed, I rose and ran to the village where I did make a hue and a cry that I had been foully raped. The villagers gave the chase, examined me to confirm the truth of my claim. This do I swear."

Roland's eyes were both puzzled and aroused. He seemed half-convinced by my tale, but had already forsworn justice by accepting silver from my "assailant." He glanced around to find his benefactor.

"Excellently expressed, poor maiden," he said. "Don't be afraid now—point to the assailant."

"You are my assailant."

He turned peevishly to the priest. "The girl's obviously been made lunatic by her experience. Explain that I'm her judge. I think she knows not the meaning of *assailant*."

Father Gerald looked to me.

I repeated firmly. "You raped me, Roland, you and you alone."

"Nonsense," he snapped. "I never laid eyes upon you. What is this, Father? Where's the man with silver you spoke of?"

Father Gerald was pale but firm. "Best listen, Lord Roland. You are now the defendant."

Roland was vexed, but still controlled. He bared his gray teeth in a travesty of a smile. "You surprise me, Father. I confess I would not have thought you capable of such a jest."

Father Gerald repeated, "Answer the charge, or prepare to be sentenced."

"What *charge*? From some wanton little hussy who's been coached? Bad timing, my dear, for I was in Cockermouth yesterday and have six knights to swear it. Can you come up with the necessary thirty-six of your common oathhelpers to balance that?"

"Yes, I can." I raised my hand.

Instantly an exultant chorus behind me shouted, "We swear!"

"Ignorant fools!" Roland blared, exasperated. "You've been beguiled by this wench and don't understand the consequences. By law I could demand your lives for perjury."

"We be telling the truth at last, *ignorant fool*!" a dame yelled back.

Roland turned to Father Gerald. "For God's sake, Father, stop this charade. In the first place, no female can sue in a court."

Father Gerald looked uncertain.

"Women can sue in cases of felony," I said. "That is, homicide or rape. And you're guilty of both."

The knight tried to lean closer to see under my hood. "Forget your schemes, little hussy. Settle on someone of your own class, for I assure you that you'll not snag me. You won't live to see another sunrise."

"One of us won't," I agreed. "Father Gerald, read him the law."

Roland sneered, and turned as if dismissing the whole affair.

Nothing happened. Father Gerald picked up the parchment I had prepared and glanced at the stiff arrogant back. 'Twas obvious that Roland could no more follow the sonorous Latin phrases than the meanest villein present, but everyone was awed by the solemn authority of the words:

"*Quod si impudice discooperuerit eam et se super eam posuerit, omnium possessionem suarum uncurrit damnum . . .*"

Vexed beyond endurance, Roland stopped the priest. "It can't apply, no matter how long you read, you oafish prelate! Whores have no rights!"

Evote croaked indignantly, "She war a virgin, you pisspot!"

For the first time, Roland seemed aware of the hostility facing him. His eyes raced from one of his knights to the other, but he shrugged brazenly and remained above the rabble.

"You have a taste for virgins, haven't you?" Archie asked, a sinister threat in his voice. "Read *that* law, Father."

"*Et est raptus virginum quoddam crimen quod femina imponit alicui . . .*"

"Save your breath, Father," Roland again interrupted. "Why read Latin to apes? Besides, I see the plot at last. What is this harlot to you, Archie? Your sister? Do you believe you can *marry* your way to Wanthwaite?"

"I'll never marry you, Roland," I said with force.

"Good," he snapped. "On that we agree."

"But I'll take Wanthwaite." My voice shook with passion. "And your life as well."

"You're the ape what can't understand Latin!" Archie hooted derisively "We want your eyes, your balls and your land!"

Sir Roland looked at the priest derisively. "Stop this mockery before I'm forced to harm you. 'Tis the last time I'll warn you. Whatever happened to this lass, she's still only a commoner and I'm her lord. What she's doing is insurrection! She can't bring suit!"

I threw back my hood. "I'm Lady Alix of Wanthwaite and I charge you with sacking my castle, slaughtering my parents, raping and murdering Maisry of Dunsmere, killing Jimmy of the Gray Falcon . . ."

There was a fleeting moment of stunned recognition—then he moved. Instantly Archie and Ralph grabbed him from each side.

"To arms!" Roland shouted. "Magnus, take the girl!"

I whirled and saw Thorketil crash an ax through Magnus's skull. "Alix!"

I heard Archie's warning too late. Roland had kicked the trestle and thrown his captors off balance; now he leaped to grab me. Behind me everyone screamed and struggled.

I fought against Roland like a demon for I saw he wanted to use me as a shield between him and the people. I used every trick I knew to no avail. He twisted me flat in front of him, wrenched my arms behind me with one of his hands, put a sharp dagger at my throat with the other. In that position, we faced a bloody spectacle: villagers clustered in tight circles around the flailing knights, as ears, hands and heads gave way to hacking blades.

"Swords! Swords!" Adelwisa passed the weapons to willing villagers.

"To arms! On your feet, men!" Roland shouted over the din. "What's wrong with you cowards?"

Two knights still fought like tigers. Poor Clac received a death-slash across his red face, and a small child fell in a gush of blood and screamed frantically. Then one knight fell to an arrow, the other to a series of club blows.

Roland was now alone—except that he held me as hostage.

"One move toward me and the girl's dead," he warned ominously.

Panting, bleeding men and women stopped, gazed on helplessly, as we moved back in deadly quiet. Then a whiz and thud—Archie had shot an arrow! I felt the impact travel through Roland's shoulder and knew at once that the thrust was not fatal. He tried to press his blade against me and I turned enough so that it didn't cut deep, reached in my skirt for my father's dagger. Pushed it hard into his chest-spoon.

Our faces were close, as if we were in embrace, and I watched the light of life fade from his eyes. Warm blood coursed down my hand and puddled at my feet. *Benedicite*, I had killed him! I watched him slide to the ground, horrified by my own act. Then I recalled

King Richard's words about his own father: "It was his life or mine and he ran to the point."

I turned to see a world gone mad. *Everyone* was killing the dead. Women pounded on inert pulpy knights with clubs and stones. Children joined the game with rocks. Men hacked at heads to rip them off their shoulders. Genitals and eyes were held high as grisly trophies. Blood spurted and ran down the tiers, turned the mud to red broth, and seven jagged draining heads finally rode aloft on long pikes.

"Up you go!" Archie and Margery lifted me together to the shoulders of waiting grinning men to be carried in triumph back to Dunsmere. I looked down on a pit of blood. Three villagers still crouched by their own dead or wounded. Dame Margery's face was streaked with gore like a savage's, her eyes filled with uncanny light. I turned away, frightened. The crowed chanted an incoherent screaming jabber in step to the eerie bouncing heads as I held on to the hair of my human carriers.

Even at this moment, however, I was thinking ahead. Swaying under the vacant leers of the beheaded men, I cast my own eyes anxiously over the barren horizon. Empty as the desert, not even a bird. But wait, was there a sound behind all these shrieks? I strained to hear, to no avail.

Screaming, keening, blabbering, laughing. On and on in woodly parade we created our trail of blood. In the lead hopped a frenzied Dame Margery. Dazed, I wondered if *she* had commanded the villagers and used me as an excuse for awesome revenge. Finally we reached Dunsmere and I saw a huge pile of faggots in the church square. Aye, this orgy was a celebration long awaited. Someone lighted the pyre and I was placed on the ground to be passed from hand to hand as I was hugged, kissed, pounded. Finally I thumped against the priest who quickly pulled me clear of the mob.

"With a *heave*, and a *ho*, off you *go* to Hell!" the villagers yelled as they flung the battered corpses into the fire. Then with Dame Margery at the head they formed a snake-chain around the blaze, chanting their chant, screaming in manic glee as the bodies puffed and burst, the smoke took on a sweetish stench of burning flesh.

I glanced up at the priest: his eyes were filled with reflected fire.

"I never dreamed . . ." I said. "Oh, Father . . ."

"What you'd unleash?" He grimaced. "Some spark was bound to catch, Lady, for the faggots were laid, the anger smoldering. 'Twas only a matter of time."

The blood made the flames hiss, then subside, and the dancers used liquid fire to tipple. I saw Dame Margery share a flask with Tom, her face twisted beyond recognition.

Then I looked back into the flames, and thought of Enoch. Fear rolled like a boulder in my stomach. What was I doing here wasting my time? Enoch could easily bypass Dunsmere, aye, and would too.

"I'm going up to Wanthwaite," I told Father Gerald.

He was shocked. "Not without some of the men, you can't. How do we know we slew all of Roland's knights? They come and go . . ."

"I'll take care, but I must leave. Now!" Urgency and panic made it hard to speak. "Come with me, Father. You're my guardian."

I turned and ran toward Dame Margery's to get Thistle and my things. The sun was directly overhead as I trotted past the frenzied, distracted dancers. Father Gerald swung up on Thistle's rump, his robes flying.

Out in the open fields, I spurred Thistle to a gallop straight toward the distant tower of Wanthwaite. I reined to a sudden stop at the river, wanting to savor my entry into the park. The water was crusted with ice along the edges, the spinney slick under the trees where snow had stayed frozen, yet a few red leaves clung to the beeches and the sky was a blinding blue. Each trunk, each limb, each rock held a memory for me and my chest was suffused with warmth. I was coming home.

Yet I heeded the priest's warning that there might be people about and listened as we went. No need: 'twas as silent as a grave-yard. Indeed, when we reached the bailey we found it exactly as I had left it on the dreadful day of the sacking. Stubs of burnt huts had begun to rot, but nothing had been rebuilt, nor were there any animals. Strange. What had Roland done for milk? For eggs? For pigeons? Or grain? Where were the villeins?

Thistle's hooves rang hollowly on the moat bridge and I forced myself not to look downward into the water. Dame Margery would tell me in good time what had happened to my father's corpse. Then we were inside the court and stared with wonder. Drifted leaves banked the old catapult which seemed like a scrawny bird with its long skinny neck thrust forward, its cradle gaping like a hungry beak. Piles of gear were scattered at random. I turned Thistle to the stables.

Here the situation at least showed life, for a pretty mare and her foal gazed at me with mild curiosity when we entered. I fed the pair as well as Thistle, stripped my steed of his bridle, then went to explore inside the castle. Father Gerald tactfully let me go alone.

Appalled, I stood at the entrance to the great hall. The wooden wall where my parents had sat in the window seat had been replaced by a massy stone structure with Norman fireplace and arrow-slits. Naturally the firepit was gone, likewise the smoke hole above it. But that wasn't the worst. The whole place appeared to be a campground used by waves of fleeing hordes after disaster had struck. Layers of discarded armor, bits of clothing, furs, scraps of furniture lay mixed with animal and human leavings. The odor was execrable. Horses had lived here, aye, but horses were clean compared to their masters. Nor was the filth without its own inhabitants. Rats climbed boldly over the heaps and glared with eager black eyes, noses twitching for new spoils. Above, bats stirred like the flying rats that they were and dropped their own crunchy ordure over the whole.

Sickened, I walked up the stairs. Kites shrieked from my laurel gourds when I entered my own chamber and something that I didn't wait to see twisted in the mangy furs on my bed. My parents' room was even worse, for the floor was covered with gray hairy mold which made my feet stick to the ground.

I ran back to the fresh air and sun, disappointed unto death. I hadn't come after all—there was no home! Except in my mind. Aye, memory and yearning were all that were left. I could have found Wanthwaite better by remaining forever away from this foul, fetid spot; at least then 'twould have stayed untainted, protected.

My head pounded with grief.

Pounded—with the beat of a drum!

I raised my eyes, pricked my ears and heard it close upon the river. The Scottish pipes! *Deus juva me*, Enoch!

I ran back into the hall. Came back and clutched the priest fiercely by the arms. Not knowing what to do.

32

HE OMINOUS BEAT OF THE DRUM, THE THIN raucous screech of the fife, the repetitious drone and skirl of the pipes grew steadily in volume as the army crossed the river below and began its slow ascent through the park. I pulled the nervous priest to my side and placed myself firmly at the entry. The terror was still there making every innard tremble, but I would be damned in Hell if I let Enoch see so much as a hair quiver on my head.

When at last he came in sight on the far side of the bridge, however, I felt such a rush of panic that it took the memory of my father and my mother to hold me in place. Only my expectation and the general outline of his body told me it was Enoch at all, for he appeared more like a garish oversized insect atop a courser. His skin was painted a glistening blue-black and his head was covered by a flat helmet with a long metal nose-guard and high plumes, for all the world evoking the feelers and proboscis of a giant wasp. He wore silver-studded wooden shields like hard shells before and aft, blood-red kilts and vest, a miniver cape, sporrans and spears bristling like wire hairs from his body.

Behind him in close ranks came his wasp-army in similar fearsome garb, with each man wrapped in plaid. The sight and sound of these infamous intruders rumbling and skirling across my bridge stiffened my resistance. By the time Enoch had reached me, I saw him as the usurper that he was, the ruthless viper who'd sold my body to the king. He'd been wise to arrive with an army behind him or I swear I would have killed him; let him ride the same pike as Sir Roland.

With an abrupt gesture, he stopped the din. The Scots came to a restless halt and waited as he dismounted. He walked toward me and stopped a few feet away. Dark eyes peered from the shelter of his visor.

"You arrive too late, Enoch. The castle is mine," I said coldly.

Slowly, deliberately, he removed his helmet and his eyes instantly turned a bright blue. He quickly surveyed my female form before he responded caustically:

"Aye, I saw the gore below. Ye've learned how to kill from Richard, it seems."

"I was defending myself," I protested. "Besides, Sir Roland raped me. 'Twas the sentence of the court."

"A convenient rape methinks, boot a waste of maidenhead."

He removed a scroll from his waist, the infamous writ at last, and handed it to the priest.

"Read her the writ, Father," Enoch ordered.

"No need; I know the contents," I said quickly. "And it's not valid."

The Scot's teeth bared. "Why nocht?"

"Many reasons—I possess Wanthwaite."

"Nocht legally, methinks."

"But you—student of Magister Malcolm—must agree that a judgment in a felony takes precedence o'er . . ."

"The king's command?" he pointed to the writ.

"Except that this writ cannot apply," I asserted in triumph, "because it was conceived under false premises! I am not Alex, not a boy, not a baron. 'Tis a worthless document."

Enoch leaned closer. "A *new* writ, Alix. I advise that ye listen."

Panic returned in an instant and I fought to control a telltale twitch in my eyelids. I nodded curtly to Father Gerald.

He cleared his throat and wet his lips. "It's a royal writ from King Richard with the usual flourishes. Shall I begin with the pertinent part? Yes? Well then."

As he fidgeted more, seeking the right light and distance for his

eyes, getting the vellum to lie flat where he wanted it, I turned back
to Enoch. Our eyes caught and held in a way which roused a vast
surge of foreboding unlike any I'd experienced with the Scot before.
I had no time to think on it, but I was aware that some great change
had taken place between us and my mind was able to grasp only the
central fact: Enoch now hated me, was sick with hatred in a con-
suming monumental spite such as I'd seen only once before, in the
eyes of King Philip when he looked on King Richard. Aye, and I
hated him as Richard did Philip. *Pimpreneau.* Then my attention
was caught by Father Gerald's words.

"'I, Richard, King of England by the grace of God, do hereby
assign the barony of Wanthwaite, its castle, buildings, all lands,
rentals and fiefdoms as described in our charter, to Lord Enoch
Angus of Dingle-Boggs, Scotland, in accordance with the agreement made between us in Acre, the twelfth day of August 1191,
with the aforesigned as witness to the act, and in accordance with
the spirit and letter of my contract with William, King of Scotland
by the grace of God, upon his release in September 1189.'"

Appalled, I whirled to the Scot whose face was set in an implac-
able mask of victory.

"'Said barony of Wanthwaite belongs to the crown by the laws
of the realm in which such lands and titles revert to the king when
the rightful owner dies without an adult heir. Therefore I assign the
hand of Lady Alix, Baroness of Wanthwaite, ward to the crown, in
marriage to Lord Enoch Boggs, such marriage to be consummated
with all due haste. *Teste me ipso. Ex mandato reggio*, Richard, *Rex
Anglicarum.*'"

"Never!" I screamed.

Heedless of witnesses, I lunged in fury at Enoch who clasped
my wrists and held me away.

"You have no right!" I cried. "Wanthwaite is mine, awarded by
the court; I was raped . . ."

"Did ye use the liver of a chicken or a pigeon?" Enoch queried
sarcastically. "And do ye still think a village moot court takes precedence o'er the king's order?"

Father Gerald joined the Scot. "He's right, Lady Alix, we must
obey the king. Besides, you can't run the estate alone, just a wisp of
a lass."

"A pox on all cowardly priests!" I howled. "King Richard was right! You're all deceitful traitors. How much did Enoch pay you to turn on me?"

"Alix! I never . . ." His hound's eyes moistened and turned red.

But my mind was already beyond him. A pox on all vengeful kings! Aye, betimes Fortune's Wheel runs backward, but betimes it also gets a hard push—and Richard had squashed me to a pulp with his thrust. Clever ruthless king, to concede my castle to Scotland, get rid of Enoch and punish me for not returning to his bed—all in a single move.

Enoch relished my writhings. "I canno' say I'm flattered by yer reaction, Alix, but mayhap ye're concealing yer enthusiasm fram modesty. Be as be may, prepare yerself fer the ceremony day after tomorrow."

"I'll never marry you."

His sarcasm became deadly. "In case ye have any misconceptions, *Lady* Alix, I have e'en less stomach fer the deed than you have. But by God, I'll do it and sae will ye." He turned to his army. "Dismount!"

The Scots clattered to the ground, led their horses to the stable, gabbled in their strange tongue and looked curiously about them. To my astonishment, a full third of their number were women, their skins also an oily blue, their weapons bristling, skirts hoisted to their waists with a long expanse of knotty hairy leg showing. Some of them had babes on cradleboards and there were a few half-grown children. Never would such barbarians get Wanthwaite! Never would I wed their scorpion leader!

I ran into the great hall. Enoch stood in the center kicking at the filth to see the rats scuttle.

"Take your army elsewhere to camp, Enoch," I demanded. "You'll not bed in my home." *Never in my bed.* I trembled in disgust at the thought.

"Nocht with the rats," he agreed. "Clean this pissmar."

"Let the Scots help me," I countered, seeing some advantage in their presence.

He raised his brows. "That I will, and see ye do a good job."

He left me and soon a hand touched my shoulder. 'Twas a hefty lass with a broad, flat face, pale shallow eyes and jutting teeth. "My name be Gruoth," she introduced herself shyly. "I be cousin to Enoch and he sayed as how ye needed us women to help clean."

"Women!" I cried so that she jumped. "We need men! Aye, and perhaps horses. This work is too much for a few women."

Now she was equally astonished. "These be knights, Lady. They hunt and fight, but doona grub on the floor."

"They'll work if they want to sleep here," I said sternly.

She was too astounded to reply, so I gave her instructions about where the water and pails might be found, if the latter still existed, and she called her women who volunteered their own spades and axes to the piles of filth. Together we lugged the battered rats into the court where several of the knights took their ease in the declining sun.

"With a heave and a ho," I imitated the villagers, and flung the slops where the viscous stuff accidentally stained a few boots.

After the first shock, the offended knights jumped up and attacked a few innocent women with fierce fury, hitting and smacking like savages. No pallid demoiselles, these brawny northern Amazons clawed back.

"Quhat do ye think ye're doing? I'll throw ye into the schit-gong!" Enoch bawled.

"Tell them to get off their toute-asses and *work*! I believe that's what you used to say to me! Aye, and what the Crusaders *did*!"

"Because we had no women along, you fool!" he shouted.

I know not how it would have ended if a sandy-haired wight hadn't come between us. "The lass has right, Enoch," he said. "My Gruoth tells me that we mun all bend our backs to the rats or we'll have no peace this nicht."

Enoch's spleen cooled somewhat, though he muttered an unintelligible curse at me as he turned to the scrapping Scots.

In short order, the men had joined us in the battle against rodents. We finished toward sundown and looked like executioners, but the great hall was somewhat restored. For a moment I forgot my unwelcome comrades and gazed around me, gripped in memory.

"Get yer fresh tunic, Alix," Gruoth said. "We mun dip and clean ourselves."

"Aye." I had no clean female tunic—only my boy's garb.

Carrying my clothes fastidiously at arm's length, I joined the roaring, laughing Scots as they ran toward the river. I thought we could collect water in pails and heat it for bathing, but no; the north-men plunged into the icy current like playful seals, men and women naked together.

"I can't do that," I said to Gruoth, horrified.

"It doesna feel cold if ye beat hard and doona stay too long. Cum, ye'll love it."

Well, I couldn't remain as I was, besmottered and stained, so I reluctantly peeled off my clothes.

Benedicite!

With a howl of laughter, Gruoth shoved me in! With equal speed, I shot right out again! I'd never been so shocked in my entire life, hot blades puncturing every pore.

"Stop shaking, Alix!" Gruoth yelled, still laughing so hard that she yexxed. "And I'll rub ye dry!"

I could see myself turning dark blue, hear my teeth rattle like castanets in my ears. Then my heart gave a twitch as if a giant needle turned on a saucer therein, and I looked over my shoulder. Enoch had just emerged, stood in a trance gazing on me. He was under the shadow of a thicket and may not have realized I could see him as well, or he was too hypnotized to care. He ogled my curved shape, my small breasts, and a spasm shook his face before he turned away. Hastily I slipped on my braies and tunic, but I was most confused by what I'd witnessed. Enoch's expression had been a mix of wonder—mayhap desire—and, aye, nostalgia, as if he hoped against hope that under my robes I was still Alex!

Every muscle ached; I didn't dare think of that odious writ or my own future—but 'twas the Scot's disturbing reaction that still clung to my consciousness as I rolled in my goatskin close to the others before the fire that night. Poor Enoch, mourning the loss of Alex. Poor Alix, competing with the Alex who'd never been, first with Richard, now with the Scot.

Except that I didn't want their affection on any terms. I was glad I was female and if Enoch pined for Alex, let him construct a false prick to carry, for that was the only part of Alex which hadn't been Alix forsooth.

• • •

I WOKE, desperate. For once I could think of no way to escape and still hold Wanthwaite.

"I cannot marry that thief," I announced to Dame Margery when she appeared that morning, her head splitting. "If you knew . . ." But I couldn't say that he'd sold my body. 'Twas too shameful.

"No, of course not," she concurred. "How will ye avoid it, lambkin?"

"I'll not participate in the vows, won't answer the questions." It seemed so weak. "Or if I have to, I'll never permit consummation."

She bit her lip. "Go see the king again; ask him to change his mind."

Her awesome ignorance was almost ludicrous. Go find Richard on the plains between Acre and Ascalon? Get him to change his mind?

"Or wait." The dame turned crafty. "Go through the ceremony to obey the law, and afterward I'll use the hemlock on him."

I thought of the mootpit. God knows I had good reason to hate the Scot but I would never permit her to slay him. Unlike Roland, Enoch had not raped or killed.

We sat in my parents' chamber in dismal silence. Below us, we could hear the Scots singing and japing as they decorated the hall for the occasion.

"What will ye wear?" Margery asked.

What a woodly question. "My pageboy garb." I laughed hollowly.

"Come," she said, and took my hand.

I followed her into my parents' garde-robe which had been only partly cleaned. In the corner was stacked a pile of armor mixed with tools. Margery tugged at the lot, peeling off layer after layer to reveal a flat wooden chest.

"My mother's?" I asked with wonder.

"Aye, I covered it the first day and kept adding as I could. Mayhap Roland never found it. Let's look."

We opened the heavy lid to the mixed scent of cedar and roses, and there lay my mother's gowns, the ruby tunic folded hastily on top. My throat tightened as I stroked the materials which had last caressed her body. It seemed a desecration to use her clothing for such a bitter occasion, but I yearned to put her robe next to my skin. Finally I selected a lavender and silver laced gown, amazed that it almost fit. There was even a small crown of amethysts.

The following morning Gruoth banged on the door and the reality of the occasion was upon me. Dame Margery smoothed my hair, pulled my bodice a little lower, licked her finger to rub my brows and told me how beautiful I appeared, while all the time I felt like a puppet being moved by an unseen hand. Dazed, I tried to think how to escape this manipulation, but was strangely compelled to take the next step, then the next as ordered, hoping something would occur to me at the last moment to make me my own mistress again.

"Waesucks, Alix," Gruoth gasped in admiration, "ye're the mast bonny winsing bride I never did see."

"You're lovely yourself, Gruoth," I answered courteously.

Soothly the lass was striking with three bold plaids doing war on the vast mound of her belly, chicken feathers bristling from her matted hair, leather jewelry studded with garnets hugging wrists and ankles, a heavy rank skin fastened to her shoulder. Indeed, she looked like the legendary orphan brought up by bears.

We walked through a hall laden with red gorse and holly, its fresh green rushes scented with laurel, and then mounted two gentle mares to ride to the church. We were followed by the Scottish women, my own personal gaudy escort, and as we rode from the court our bridles jingled with silver bells. At an unseen signal, the women burst into savage song. Their words were incomprehensible but even in my burning rage I was aware of a strange barbaric beauty.

Then we were across the river, across the fields, riding inexorably to Dunsmere church with its small spire hurtling into a lapis sky, met there by the villagers who raised an excited shout of welcome.

"Hail to Lady Alix!"

"Welcome to our baroness!"

"May you always be happy, Alix!"

I waved back and glowered. Yesterday they'd been my army;

today they willingly accepted the Scottish yoke. People don't appreciate freedom; aye, the Church was right to call us sheep.

We stopped at the door of the church where Father Gerald stood waiting. Helping hands lifted me to the ground, guided me to my place in the morning sun, for we were to be wed outside in the open. Children were pushed to the front to watch, as is the custom, so they can record in their long memories the truth of our marriage. A mangy border cur rushed forth, jumped up joyfully, then sat beside me, leaning his shedding coat against my knee. Fingers snapped and voices wheedled to no avail; the dog had elected to be part of the ceremony.

Now came the familiar drone of the pipes as the men approached. I strove to keep my eyes on the dog, but as the drone became louder, and the smell and sound of the horses were upon us, my lids quivered, my eyes rose against my own will, and through my lashes I gazed upon Enoch. Magnificent in scarlet and white, he was indeed a swan among ducks this day. Then my heart chilled at the comparison as I recalled my dream on Dere Street when the Scot had appeared as a swan. *Deus juva me*, that dream must never come true! Now he, too, had dismounted, had walked to the door and taken his place opposite me. He was heavily scented with sweet woodruff.

The service began. Father Gerald addressed Enoch first, asking if he would be my husband in the eyes of God, if he would be faithful all our days together, if he would honor and protect his chattel.

Honor and protect. I listened to Enoch's low assent with outrage, thought of his contracting me as a "weasel" for the royal bed, and bitter bile stung my lips.

Now the priest turned to me. I felt a soft pressure on my back and realized that Gruoth's stomach was pushed against me. *Lady Alix, do you take Lord Enoch as your wedded husband?*

"I do *not!*" I said in a loud clear voice.

A murmur ran through the crowd and a baby started to cry. I looked into Enoch's storm-blue eyes, caught his faint frown to the priest, felt the hard stomach press closer. Then something thin and cold moved under my ear. Enoch leaned forward and touched my neck. When he drew his hand away, he turned it so I could see the stain of my own blood! Startled, not believing my eyes, I gazed again into his angry orbs and believed.

Father Gerald gazed from one to the other, then stated again: "Lady Alix, do you take Lord Enoch to be your lawful wedded husband?"

I put my trembling hand on the dog's head. "I do take *the cur* as husband," I replied weakly.

'Twas a small gesture but all I had. Thus we were married.

DRUNKALEWE as a mouse, I swayed morosely that night on the improvised dais in Wanthwaite's great hall, rising and falling like a bucket in a well, going round and round like a whirlwind in chaff, bibulous on bile or ale, I know not which.

"Cum, my buxom burdie, lat's fling a foot!"

Strange red hands pulled me from my perch and set me to the floor, where I began to jiggle frantically to the piper's beat, still a puppet on a pole, as my partner skirted around me in a blur of gaudy feathers and sporrans.

"Ho-la, gae aft, lass! Gi'e a hap, stap and lowp, than a curchie!"

Toty as a beheaded hen, I tried to hop, skip and leap but fell forward when I dipped.

"Grab her hurdies!" cried the merry voice.

"She flies like a gonnet, Enoch! Best clip her wings!"

And I was thrown into my *husband*'s arms.

"Time to gi'e her the skean dhu!" screamed the Scots.

To my besotted horror, Enoch placed a small wicked dagger between his lips. "Dinna make blather," he growled. "'Tis anely a custom."

Whereupon he began a headlong scamper around me, twisting and kicking like a demon in smoke, crouching, pouncing, jigging in ever more fiendish pace as his audience of devils howled approval. Then he glowered over me and hissed, "Take it!"

I knew not what he meant, lifted my hand for the knife, but he struck it aside and put his mouth on mine, carefully transferring the ugly weapon to my teeth. I stood like a surprised dog who's caught a bone, not knowing if I would be struck or petted for my trick.

Enoch sprang back and whirled into the sulfurous mist as I slipped the sharp steel up my sleeve.

"Swill the yil-caup!" chanted the swarthy legions around me. "Bouse at the nappy."

Needing no further urging, I drank eagerly from a large cup of ale. Then the traitorous false-friend Gruoth grabbed my arm.

"Cum, lass, 'tis time to be wed."

I pushed her away and waved my skean dhu. "Don't dare touch me, Gruoth. I'll have no more weddings at the point of a knife!"

"'Tis Enoch's orders," quoth she, as if citing Scripture. "Ye mun be handfasted befar it has meaning."

Even in my jug-bitten state, I comprehended she was saying that in some manner I was not yet espoused.

"I'll not do it," I proclaimed loudly. "Kill me dead if you will, but I'll not be wed more."

I might escape my fate yet.

But I was scooped up in strong arms, hoisted atop a sea of knarry shoulders and rode my human raft toward the river. In front of me sizzling pine torches showed the outline of Enoch who rode his own litter down the steep spinney. Yellow smoke rose from the torches and wound around the fingery branches. Suddenly we were by the river, water dark as a black cat's blood. *Ah*, I thought, we'll wed under water like monsters of the deep. Better that than nuptial bed. I was placed on a wide flat rock that jutted into the river. On the opposite side, Enoch was put down on a comparable spit that almost closed the tide. Only a narrow rill separated us, though a gulf as wide as the sea was between us in spirit.

Enoch sucked his thumb and thrust it toward me.

"Put yer thumb to yer tongue and touch his," Gruoth ordered.

I did so. His thumb was as ice-cold as all demons' are.

"Alix of Wanthwaite, I noo do handfast thee as my wife as lang as both shall live," Enoch boomed in the stilly night.

"Now ye mun say the same," Gruoth whispered, her eyes dead oysters in the dark.

"Never," I said firmly and yexxed.

"Say it, Alix," she warned. Suddenly she pushed me and the oily current yawned up to take me, except that the wench held my tunic in her hand. *Deus juva me*, better a knife at my throat than a plunge into that icy grasp.

I said the words.

"Very good, Alix; now hald this in yer hand." She pressed a denier into my fingers. "Gi'e it to him."

I did so, not liking the symbolism at all.

Then I repeated the words as she instructed: "Catch the plack, dear husband, for what is mine be also thine."

However I felt somewhat better when Enoch said the same words and gave me a coin of his own.

Then we turned around thrice as the Scots chanted and waved the torches in eerie arcs over our heads. Owls hooted nervously in the void.

"Ah, 'tis a sign of the good witch Abunda when houlets croon," Gruoth sighed. Together we stared upward at a shadow on the moon and I remembered how I'd received my caul the last time.

"Spring o'er the gutter, groom," the men shouted at Enoch.

He did so, pulled to safety by Gruoth's strong hand. My heart pounded in fear as he towered close in the darkness.

Gruoth's husband, a sandy-topped wight with a turned-up snout, joined us on the rock.

"Time to eat the infar. Enoch gaes first, then the bride."

He produced a round of shortcake; Enoch ate half, and I finished it. There was frenzied applause, and we were once again hoisted, this time to ride close as the panting Scots carried us back up the hill. Into the hall we went and were deposited on the hearth. Enoch handed me a broom.

"This tong be the symbol of our home together, wife. Clean it fer me."

"Sweep," Gruoth whispered.

I took a few awkward swipes.

"Noo ye be truly wed," Donald cried. "Gi'e her a kiss, mon. She willna bite."

I set my teeth to do just that, but Enoch attacked me like a tiger, pressing his own fangs into my mouth so that only his strong arms kept me from tumbling backward. I couldn't breathe, couldn't move, thought I would be the first bride since the world began to be suffocated to death by her nuptial kiss. Dimly I heard shouts of laughter around us. Finally the Scot drew away, his eyes as black as the icy reams of the river.

"Awwww, dinna stop now, lad," Donald wheedled, "give her tither skelpin kiss."

Enoch turned away. "Push me too far, lads, and I willna be able to stop!" There was another roar of mirth, as my own heart froze.

Again the dancers twirled. Again I swilled from cogs and cups as fast as they were offered. The villagers were now sufficiently jug-bitten to jig and whirl with the skirted savages and I danced with Archie, Thorketil, Tom and I know not who else, everyone I trowe. Then finally the torches burned low, the sky showed a faint gray and the moment could be put off no longer. Once again Enoch and I were half-carried, half-pushed up the narrow steps to my parents' chamber.

"Blow the buck's horn fer a merry hunt!"

"Reach fer the finch, mon!"

"Dight the bridge and tomorrow 'twill gae easier!"

"Spend every drop of gold! 'Twill replenish faster!"

"'Tis best to croke bolt upright!"

"Suck the cud, stick the hole and ye'll kape happy cows!"

Faces leered into the dark chamber; voices chanted lewd japes. Enoch laughed, then waved his candle and kicked the door shut.

He stood with his back to me, listening to the noisy crew outside. The candle flickered in his hand, the smoke curled around the outline of his wavy locks, and I held the little skean dhu in my fist ready to defend my honor.

I counted two hundred and forty-nine heartbeats before he turned. 'Twas the length of time it took for me to become cold sober. Carefully he placed the candle on a small trestle and walked toward me. My stomach tightened; my fingers twitched. And he passed me by. Puzzled, I turned to see him grope atop the bed. Then he jerked off a fur mantle and threw it to the floor by the wall as rosehips and laurel rained in the air. He rolled himself in the fur and lay still as a stone.

After a very long silence, I sat on the bed.

"Are you going to sleep on the floor?" I asked.

"Dinna ask tinty questions."

I stared at the candle. "I suppose you don't care that you've taken the only pelt. I'll freeze."

"For Goddes sake, slape between the mattress and board. And blaw out the light."

Somewhat deflated by this anticlimax to the day, for I'd been preparing for a brawl, I killed the flame and climbed onto the hard splintery boards. I'd never intended for us to sleep together, but I'd wanted to reject *him*, looked forward to the moment as my only pleasure.

"You'll not get Wanthwaite by marrying me, you know," I said bravely, though our situation mocked my words.

His answer when it came showed that he was no more sleepy than I. "I paid King Richard a thousand silver livres for Wanthwaite."

Shocked and a little flattered, I gasped, "You paid the king a thousand livres for *me*?" Never mind that he'd earned the money by selling me, 'twas a handsome sum.

He snorted like dry husks rubbing. "Nay, Alix. I bought the apple, got the worm fer free."

"I think you forget that the worm *owns* the apple." Then I could have bit my tongue for accepting his comparison. "And I'm not a worm."

"Nay, I shouldna insult the wee slimy beasties, fer they're honest snakes fer all they havena much appeal. Boot ye live to lie!"

I sat up. "I lied to live! My father told me to lie about my sex if that's what you mean. He said I couldn't move a yard as a girl or I'd be killed or abducted by some greedy varlet who wanted my estate. And you've proved him right!"

"Filling me with false feinyeit words, making gekkis at me behind my back, pretending to be my brother! Ye're a fork-tongued asp!"

"Better your brother than your wife! You learn on one day that I'm female and the very next day you contrive to get a writ to marry me! You've ruined my life!"

He, too, sat up, now a dark gray silhouette in the predawn. "I promise ye on my honor as a MacPherson, Alix, that ye and I will ne'er be wed in fact. I war forced to gae through the public act, same as ye, but I'll not touch yer midding hole as long as I live."

He thumped to the floor again and disappeared under his fur. I, too, squirmed underneath my mat but was too angry to sleep. King Richard and now Enoch, both of them repulsed by my body.

I watched the sky lighten at the arched window where my mother had groaned aloud for my father that last night, and thought of them in a new way, as a happily married couple. I believed they might be unique in the history of mankind. How I envied them! How I missed them still!

I watched the dawn through the prism of my own tears, sighed, reviewed the chain of events since I'd returned to Wanthwaite. When I reached my present point, I sat up suddenly in my bed.

Benedicite! Where was my head? Enoch had just made the most stupid blunder he possibly could. By canon law, if we didn't consummate, we weren't married at all in the eyes of the Church. Annulment was the simple matter of telling the priest!

I would have to give it a little time, of course, to make my complaint credible, but I could wait. I was still free after all! I went to sleep finally with a smile on my lips.

33

 WOKE TO THE HEAVY RATTLE AND SLURP OF rainfall. A puddle spread under the window, the air was thick and chill. Then I remembered Enoch. I peeked over my mattress: the fur was in a tangle, the Scot gone. *Benedicite*, my fantastick cells had swollen to twice their normal size, my tongue seemd to grow hair as if I'd dined on raw persimmons. I tried to recall my euphoria at dawn and the reason for it, but my roiling innards took precedence.

A few moments later, I stood at the top at the stair gazing down on an army of Scots laboring to put the hall in order. Rain came unimpeded through the new roof where the smoke hole had once been, so that the men and women sloshed in water ankle-deep as they tried to dismantle the dais, push away the soaked rushes and damp ashes from the fireplace. Shivering, I went back to the chamber and pulled Enoch's sleeping fur over my shoulders before I descended to help.

"How did ye fare last nicht, Alix?" Gruoth greeted me boldly.

"How do you suppose?" I half-snarled. "Marriage at the point of a dagger is not conducive to love."

She bridled. "I anely followed orders. Enoch sayed as how ye was tinty and couldna be trusted."

Suddenly I recalled the reason for my early euphoria. *Deus juva me*, I could use this wench as my first witness.

Noting the avid eyes of two hussies squatted behind her, I leaned forward and whispered: "Nothing happened last night."

"Nothing?" she asked aloud.

Signaling for her to be discreet, I leaned again. "He wants only my estate, not me."

She tried to look surprised but her broad face was transparent and she knew I spoke the truth. "'Twill get better; it always do," she muttered, and squeezed my hand.

Well, I'd made a start. She was too Scottish to be a primary witness, but she would be able to corroborate my plaint.

Enoch and a half dozen men then returned to the hall. "Ah, there she be," he said curtly, nodding toward me. "Alix, gae to the chamber."

None of the men who'd danced so gaily with me yesterday deigned to greet me even that much. I stared at my "husband" and the group around him, at first not comprehending this unfriendliness. They were not hostile: 'twas more as if I didn't exist. I'd been a bride with an estate to covet: now I was a wife, chattel to the man who'd won my estate. Stunned to be so abruptly demeaned from baroness to drudge, I glanced at Gruoth and the women around her. Had they, too, gone through such a transformation? Aye, I believe they had.

"For what purpose should I go to the chamber?" I asked Enoch.

"Because I say so," he snapped, his brow twisting.

"For what *purpose?*" I repeated.

He flushed as he leaned to me. "We mun talk about money, wife. We mun spend or starve. Be that clear enow?"

"I'll meet you when the bell rings Sext," I said. My heart was quaking but I kept my eyes steady.

"At Sext," he conceded, and turned back to talk to the men.

THE SCOT carried a candle into the chamber, though 'twas the middle of the day, and placed it close to the bed. He then pulled two faldstools for us, using the bed as table, and spread three pages of water-streaked vellum on the mat.

"These be yer father's records," he began.

I pulled them close. Aye, 'twas my father's hand.

"'Tis an inventory of all the equipment ye own—rather, that ye shuld own yif the estate is to work. Read it."

I took the proffered sheet and saw a long list of animals and machines: two teams of six oxen each, fifty sheep to be herded by Ted, fifty by Bruce, a pigeoncroft with sixty birds, plows, saddles, chickens, pigs, horses and many other items where the writing grew small at the bottom. The Scot took the sheet and handed me another.

"This be services: baking, milling, cutting, planting, with a list of villeins and half-villeins. Those at the top in the second column be cottars."

This was not what I'd expected at all, but I read every word with great care so I couldn't be trapped.

"All animals and equipment hae been stolen. We have no pens for beasts, no shelter for workers, the mill wheel be rotted, the oven rusted. In short, My Lady, our condition be desperate."

"I see."

"Good, I hope ye do."

He took the vellum back and rolled it tight.

"Yer father says in one place that he hae bought oxen with silver fram the treasure."

Finally I saw his drift. My back stiffened and I stared at the slanted rainfall.

"Ye'll take me to that treasure," he said flatly.

I turned wide eyes. "I know of no treasure. If my father wrote that—and I didn't see it myself—he may have meant his silver scabbard, or maybe our silver nef which I vaguely recall."

The Scot ran his tongue over his teeth and then pressed his lips. "I didna expect this to be easy, knawing well how ye ate and took fram me on the road whan all the time ye carried a fortune between yer legs."

"Or what you thought could make a fortune," I interrupted, referring to my false prick and his selling me to Richard, but he was too dense to comprehend.

"'Twar a fortune!" he shouted. "I felt it myself in Messina whan ye were hit by the broadsword. Saw it when ye swam. Ye didna pluck it fram trees. Yer father tald ye where to dig it up, and ye dug before ye left."

"My father never told me a word about any fortune," I replied truthfully; 'twas my mother who'd shown me.

"Then mayhap yer mother," the Scot guessed with uncanny shrewdness. "Well, well, fer once ye look guilty, caught in a lie."

He leaned back, triumphant.

"Stop grucching about the money you spent on me," I retorted, thinking it better to lead the subject away from the treasure. "I always meant to pay."

I fumbled in my tunic, found a notched stick and threw it on the bed; took a drafsack from my waist and threw that as well.

"That's a record of your expenditures and a bag of silver with the exact amount."

Quickly he produced a notched stick of his own and held the two sticks side by side. "Why do ye not have this dent?" he asked, pointing to a notch on his stick.

I studied it. "That's the period when you were with your hussy, Poll, by the Rhône River. I was with Richard and Ambroise."

He turned choleric red.

"However," I continued, "you'll note that I am willing to pay for crumbs you gave me even when I served the king and supped most often with him."

He flung the sticks down and pounded the bed so the silver jumped. "I doona want yer paltry payment! I canna run Wanthwaite on buckets—I mun go to the well!"

"Go to the well where you drew a thousand livres to purchase my estate!" I shouted, jumping to my feet.

He jumped as well, inadvertently pulling the silver so it spilled on the floor. "And it's now mine! I'll permit ye to live here and grub, but ye'll pay yer way, by God!"

"I have!" I cried. "Haven't I just offered you a small fortune?"

"I won't take it!"

"Fine. I'll take it back then, but never accuse me of stealing from you again."

I bent to collect the coins; just as quickly Enoch stooped as well and we bumped our heads with a mighty thump.

The next thing I knew, I was lying cradled in Gruoth's lap and was surrounded by a circle of faces, Enoch's in the middle.

"Where is . . . ?" I tried to raise my head. The silver had disappeared. One look at Enoch's bland innocent face told me where it had gone. He grinned like a cat licking cream from his whiskers, but the predatory gleam in his eye told me that he wouldn't be satisfied till he'd eaten the pet bird as well.

Three days later thirty-eight men and women departed for Scotland in order to avoid the winter snows, leaving Gruoth, an older woman called Matilda, their husbands Donald and Dugan as well as six other knights, Enoch and me to contend with the elements here in Wanthwaite. Now the work began in earnest.

Our foremost problem was food. We all hunted every day. Gruoth and Matilda rode with bunched skirts, arrows over their shoulders, and both brought home at least a squirrel every time out. The men used Scottish deerhounds to go after the hart and managed to bring down three in as many weeks. For expedience, I donned my Plantagenet boy's outfit to hunt and often went alone for wild goose and duck, plover, curlew, crane and dottrel. Oft I thought of burying my mother's vial and father's sword, but dared not go to the silver trove for my father's sword, lest Enoch see me.

I took a certain wry satisfaction in noting Enoch's eyes flicker after my boy's garb. Twice he was so surprised that he called me "bairn" before he caught himself. Yet in the privacy of our chamber where I slept on the bed, he on the floor, he spoke not at all. I mused on the discrepancy in his behavior. He might jangle all he pleased about my deception and selfishness along the road, but the hard fact was that he forgave the boy, condemned the girl. 'Twas passing strange. I knew Enoch didn't suffer from Richard's malady, nor was he overly respectful of the Church, but he seemed subtly influenced by both: like Richard, he put brotherhood and chivalry among men far above the relationship between the sexes; like the Church fathers, he acted as if I carried the obscene Gateway to Hell whereby men lose their virtue. He even reflected Andreas Capellanus who claimed in his *Tractus de Amore* that women are sullied by greed, are slaves to their bellies. I was willing to admit that I would do most anything to eat, but so would the men about me.

Twice Enoch and I rode forth to meet with our villeins. I said little but lent my presence to give the Scot authority. Such forays were tense to the extreme. We learned the dreadful condition of the renters firsthand which depressed us both. Most of the tension, however, came from Enoch's hostility toward me.

When I felt a twinge of guilt for not digging into my wealth to purchase whatever was needed—not that there was much to be had from a ravaged countryside—Enoch stopped me by his churlish attitude. Formerly I'd mourned because people, including the Scot, loved me only because of my estate. How naive I had been! They'd never *loved* me, only curried favor because I had something they wanted. Now Enoch controlled Wanthwaite and I was hardly more than a serf to my own soil. If my plan of annulment should fail, the treasure was my escape of last resort: I would buy my way into a nunnery.

One night Enoch and I were suddenly wakened from a deep sleep by a pounding on the door and Father Gerald rushed in, a wax lantern held high.

"Did you call for me, Lord Enoch?"

Enoch pulled himself upward and stared at the priest. "Yif I had, surely ye could wait till marnin'."

"I thought you were ill unto death," Father Gerald answered, a faint note of defense in his voice. He glanced quickly at me, back to Enoch on the floor, grasped our bedding arrangement. "I see that— er—I was mistaken. Do forgive me. Unless—are you all right, Alix?"

"Aye, Father, thank you."

"Who tald ye I war sick?" Enoch asked bluntly.

"He was mistaken. Well, good night."

"Wait, Father Gerald," I said. "Please sleep by our fire for the rest of the night. The way is too dangerous."

"Thank you, dear, I believe I shall."

Mumbling apologies, he left.

Enoch spoke from the dark floor. "Who war his informant, Alix?"

"How should I know?"

"Mayhap he got wind that ye war gang to put poison in my broth."

"Don't be daft."

I pulled my pelt high, much pleased. I had a witness of undeniable repute; it had gone just as Dame Margery and I had planned.

DAME MARGERY urged me to act while the event was still fresh, for if we waited Enoch might claim that that particular night had been an exception in our sleeping habits. I hedged, saying I needed one more witness. Unexpectedly, the winter gales came to my aid.

"'Tis time to bundle," Gruoth informed me. "Privacy mun give way."

'Twas said in front of Enoch and the others; no one demurred.

I'd heard of bundling oft on the road, but had never done it to my knowledge and wasn't sure exactly what it meant. 'Twas very simple: we would lie in a close human heap for warmth. Human flesh is very hot and many lives have been saved by bundling. Unfortunately lusts are also hot and not likely to abate under such conditions.

"'Tis why most babes be born in September and October," Matilda told Gruoth and me. "I'm hopin' Dugan comes through this time."

"'Twill help you as well," Gruoth informed me, for despite my balking on my wedding day, she thought I yearned for Enoch.

It would, but not in the way she meant. A circle of furs was placed near the fire and we all lay down close as pups in a litter. Naturally husbands and wives were next to each other, though hardly alone. Enoch was too proud by far not to stay by me, though a wight called Charles was just as close on the other side. Soothly I was grateful for the custom on many counts: now all the Scots would be witness to my chastity; for the first time in weeks, I was warm enough to sleep.

During the first night of bundling everyone was discreet, but thereafter Dugan and Donald exercised their conjugal rights regularly within sight and sound of the whole group. Their activity didn't rouse comment, but Enoch's lack of interest in me certainly did. I caught the furtive looks, the occasional pitying or wondering words that a lusty groom would neglect his duties.

After two weeks of this situation, Gruoth took me aside one day. "Alix, do ye see any change?"

"In what way?"

"In Enoch's—his interest."

"You're with us every night, so you know."

"Do he never invite ye up to yer chamber? I thought mayhap . . ."

"Never." I was pleased at her noticing. "Why?"

Her red face got redder. "Well, I been putting a love philter into yer slops."

Enoch and I had been sharing a bowl and I'd thought the last batch of stew tasted like toads boiled in witches' brew.

"What's in it, Gruoth?"

"'Tis a staunch recipe, has never failed: entrails of bulls, fish scales, nail parings, human blood and mandragory. Think you it could be because I'm somewhat lacking in ground loadstone?"

I didn't answer, for soothly it had worked all too well—but on the wrong person. Lying close against Enoch, I'd been kept wide awake all night because of my treacherous liver which zoomed like Greek fire through my body.

Be as be may, there was no longer any reason to tarry. I had all the witnesses I was likely to have, and Gruoth's use of the philter substantiated that Enoch was at fault, not I. Dame Margery assured me that the villagers would move in with me for protection if the Scots left, so I had no excuse whatsoever. Nevertheless, 'twas almost the day of the Nativity before I broached the subject. By some miracle the Scots were out seeking holly for the hall, leaving Enoch and me alone.

"Enoch, we must talk," I began.

Just as he raised his lugubrious face from watching the fire, there was a sharp rap on the door.

"I'll see who's there." I ran to the entry, relieved at the interruption. "Hello, Archie. Who's this?"

Archie Werwillie stood with a fat wolf pup in his arms. He handed me the woolly babe and stepped inside.

"'Tis a present for ye, Alix. Maisry once said as how ye like them."

"How thoughtful! Aye, I love their wild eyes. Don't you?" I traced the pup's silver mask with my finger, stared into his tilted topaz eyes, as innocent as honey.

"We doona need another mouth to feed," Enoch growled ungraciously.

Archie flushed and shifted his weight awkwardly. "Well, I don't want to bother ye. I'd best be going."

I stood at the open door and chatted a bit to ease his leavetaking, thanked him again, and when I returned to the hall I was in the choleric humor necessary for my discussion.

Enoch, too, was choleric. "Doona ask me for bones, whan ye're too selfish to support yer own home wi' the treasure."

"I'll feed him from my bowl," I answered. "But I'm glad you admit Wanthwaite is my home, for that's what I want to talk about."

"*My* home!" he shouted. "Mine! Paid for by money! Paid for by suffering yer presence all these years! Fram the time I took ye and the ferst Lance on the road, I've had no peace. I've *earned* this cursed hall."

I put the pup down. "This one will not be called Lance."

"Whatever ye call him, mayhap I doona want him in *my house!*"

"You want an appropriate name? Very well then, insofar as Wanthwaite is about to revert to the crown, I'll call him King Richard."

I saw Enoch's foot swing back but I moved too slowly to save the pup. In an instant the babe was hurled against the stone wall, fell to the floor, a lifeless pile of fur.

"Oh my God, my God!" Enoch cried in a frenzy as he rushed to the beast. "Alix, I didna mean to . . . forgive me!"

And I lost my sanity!

"Forgive? Aye!" I lunged at his middle with my fist forward to knock breath from his chest, but missed. "I'll kill you, you demon!"

"Stop it! Stop it, I say!"

He grabbed my wrists and I bit his thumb near to the bone.

"Damnatioun! Ye fanged tiger! Stop, or I'll beft ye!"

I attacked his knees, toppled him like a horse, jumped on his shoulders, sought a poker to finish the job, was thrown off and he was on top.

"Aye," I hissed. "Get prepared to live tangled like snakes forever—for if I get one finger free, you're dead!"

"Alix, I'm sorry. I'll get ye another wolf, I swear. Shall we make truce?"

"Truce! Truce! So you can find some other way to steal from me? Deprive me of every coin so that I couldn't even enter a convent!"

"Ye in a *convent*?" He howled with derision. "*Sister* Alix! Be there a convent fer heilie harlots?"

"Let me up, you *pimpreneau*."

"You won't try to murther me?"

I promised and soon we were facing each other, both of us torn and bruised. The Scot was glowering, his face perplexed.

"Why did ye call me *pimpreneau*?"

"You know very well—but that's not what I want to discuss." I took a deep breath, tried to recall my plan but was much shaken. "You remember when Father Gerald came?"

"I remember, boot yif ye want to talk aboot that, ye mun tell me why *pimpreneau*, or I'm mum as an oyster."

Our eyes locked, his demanding, mine refusing. Then I shrugged.

"If you insist, though 'tis a subject I'd think you would want to avoid."

"Nay, I want to hear all yer fantastick mind can invent. 'Tis becoming my hobby. Gae on: *pimpreneau*."

"Very well. Ambroise told me on my last day in Acre." Then I reconsidered. "Actually King Richard hinted as well, and Sir Gilbert said the same. So you see, I have three sources."

"Sir Gilbert? What died?"

"He may be dead now, but he was very much alive when he put poison in our meat."

Recognition crossed his face. "Very well, the varlet sayed that I war a *pimpreneau*. For whom?"

"For me," I replied with deadly quiet. "You made a contract to sell me to Zizka. You procured."

He turned a greenish pallor. "I—*quhat*?"

"With Fat Giselle and Zizka, you agreed to sell me to Ambroise."

He looked sick. "But ye war there, heard it all, sae much fer each performance . . ."

"Except that I was too *innocent* to understand what you meant by *performance*. I was to be the king's pretty boy! To . . . do . . . you know."

"Ye dare say that aboot me?" Now his face was purple and I hoped someone would come in at once. Why had I been so foolish as to talk of this dangerous topic?

"That's not—not all," I stuttered on despite myself. "Richard paid you even more when he wanted me in his tent. Aye, gave you the earldom of Northumberland . . . and other favors as well. And you concealed it all from me. Kept me ignorant. Speak not to me of deception!"

"Lies! Lies! All lies!" he bellowed. "Made up by Sodomites to save their own skins! I tried to protect ye!"

"Protect!" I shrieked back. "You occupy my land like a conquering army! Kill my wolf! But you outwitted yourself by refusing my body. The priest is now witness to the fact that our marriage is not consummated. That we sleep separately! I'm going to get an annulment as fast as I can!"

And I leaped up the stairs to my chamber, slammed the door shut.

Almost immediately I heard him follow me, and he knocked.

"Go away!"

He opened the door and silently handed me the wolf. "He war only stunned."

He stepped in and closed the door behind him.

His chest was heaving and his blue eyes were wild. Soothly I feared for my life. I held the trembling cub up as a shield.

"Ye have insulted me most grossly and while that reflects on yer character more than mine, for soothly ye mun know better, I'll not be leavin' such remarks stand without refutation," he said as formally as he could in his distress. "Ferst, ye talked of how I gave ye a bit of cocky-leeky along the road."

"Venison as well, and fish when it could be had," I conceded quickly.

"Aye, but yer stomach would not have traveled far if Magnus and Roland had caught ye in the inn, or yif I hadn't taken ye safely through the woods."

"That's true. Aye, I should have mentioned that—and that was before you knew I was wealthy."

"Ye lied to me every way possible in London-town, made me yer slubberdegullian afore the innkeeper, Gladys, everybody, but I still accepted ye as my brother and took ye to France, paid fer yer room fer a year."

"I paid you back! Have you forgotten?"

"I signed to crusade. Think ye that I yearned to see the wonders of Jerusalem? That I wanted to serve yer English King? No, I wanted to protect ye! Cared for thee—loved thee, God help me. Didn't I shaw it every day we were together?"

"You left me at the Rhône River," I said stubbornly.

He groaned and beat his head. "I wouldn't have yif I'd knawn ye were female. I thought ye were a pretty winsing boy, and in Marseilles I got wind of the scheme to catch ye fer the king. Fram that time on, I risked my life to protect ye. Have ye forgot the fight on the Far?"

I blanched. Somehow I had. One event wiped out another and all I could seem to remember were those last two days in Acre.

"Even in Jerusalem, I stuck like a Scottish thistle, even whan ye tried hard to pluck me off ye, My Lady. By now, I knew ye war moon-eyed for the king and that I'd lost the battle. *He* understood well enow that I was fighting his schemes. Why do ye think he sent me into the tunnel to sap his wall? Because I war his 'best engineer'? I war his worst obstacle to takin' ye."

"Thank you, Enoch," I said weakly. My face grew hot.

"As for Northumberland, Richard offered me the title yif I would leave the Crusade. Otherwise he would give me every woodly assignment to have me dead. That is the truth, Alix." There was a long pause and his voice shook with intensity. "I never received a farthing for yer 'services,' whate'er they were, nor any thanks fram ye either. King Richard lied to ye outright. As for Ambroise or Gilbert, they either lied or they didna knaw the truth."

His eyes blazed with outrage. I started to speak but he cut me short. "The thing that hurts most is that ye knaw every word of this already, aye, and mar besides. Either yer mind be twisted or ye have the meanest, mast ungrateful disposition since Lilith and I doona knaw why I waste my time on ye!"

He slammed out of the room, and a few moments later I heard the muted beats of his horse as he crossed the snow-covered bridge.

ENOCH DIDN'T RETURN till after dark. There was a general sigh of relief when he entered as no one is safe when the sun is down. We had a thick rabbit stew to eat, but I wasn't very hungry. As soon as we were finished, Enoch held out his hand to me.

"Shall we retire upstairs tonight, wife?"

Gruoth shot a triumphant look at me.

Silently I followed the Scot up the steps, my heart pounding. Perhaps I shouldn't have told him of my scheme for annulment; perhaps he was going to consummate just to thwart me.

He put the candle down in our cold chamber, as he had on our wedding night.

"Alix, I been thinkin'; I, too, want an annulment."

I felt I'd been pushing a gate which had suddenly opened and I was off balance.

"There's no hurry . . ."

"I be leavin' fer Scotland tomorrow."

Soothly dazed, I sat on the bed.

"And leave me all alone? How will I get through the winter?"

His shadowed face twisted bitterly. "I knaw how concerned ye are fer yer ane stomach and comfort. I talked to Archie, Gordoc and some others. They'll cum in the morning."

A throatball lodged in my neck. "Is Father Gerald willing?"

"Yif ye and I both admit we doona care fer each other, there's no difficulty."

"I see." I took a deep breath. "I guess I should thank you. I mean, I realize you're doing this for me—after you've spent a thousand livres of your own money . . ."

He laughed in that dry husky way that makes me nervous.

"Which gives ye measure of how desperate I am. Frankly, I'd pay mar than a thousand livres to escape this boggy pissmar."

"It's better in spring," I said defensively, not knowing why I suddenly felt so wretched. I'd won, hadn't I? I should be dancing in circles.

"I wasna referrin' to the weather, Alix," he answered in that same odious dry manner. "The fumes and fens lie within. All's gang awry, but in Scotland I'll begin to heal."

More and more uneasy, I thought it only fair to appease the oaf somewhat. "I don't know what you're talking about."

"I thought not."

"But I want to—to apologize for believing that you took money for . . . that you sold me."

"Slavery be nocht my trade."

I was beginning to sweat. "And I know 'tis belated, but . . . thank you for all you did for me. In the inn and . . . you know, everything."

"Ye're welcome. Now, since I'm leavin' early, I'll bed wi' the others downstairs." He stood silently. "Goodbye, Alix."

Abruptly, he turned and left. I threw myself across the bed.

What had I done? He hadn't tried to consummate—didn't want me any more than I wanted him. We were getting along fine, restoring Wanthwaite, until I stirred the Scot's latent hatred with my accusations. I was sorely confused at my feelings, at his, and pushed my brain to its limits trying to sort it all out.

My conclusion: I couldn't abide being here without him. When all the winnowing was done, that remained. He *must* stay. I was weak with pain at the thought of his leaving. The rest could be resolved if he'd remain at Wanthwaite. Somehow we'd get back on our old footing and all would be well. Just how, I'd work out day by day.

I reviewed every moment since he'd returned to Wanthwaite, balanced this item against that like my notched stick and finally logic rewarded me.

Benedicite, I knew what ailed the oaf!

'Twas so simple to fix! I'd talk to him first thing in the morning.

WHEN I WOKE, Enoch was gone.

"When did he leave?" I shouted furiously at Donald.

"Befar Prime, My Lady."

"Go after him then! He can't have gone far and I must talk with him."

Donald stared curiously. "I'm sorry, Alix, boot have ye looked at the weather? There be a blizzard cumin' on."

Indeed snow fell aslant before a heavy wind.

·"But he can't travel in this!" I cried, anguished. "He'll freeze to death!"

Gruoth signaled to Donald to leave, then put her arms around me. "Don't fret, darlin', Enoch's nocht a fool and he rides wi' three other brawny highlanders. Yif it's truly too dangerous, they'll turn back."

"I must get him, Gruoth. If no one else will go, I'll ride alone."

She pulled me close and stroked my back. "I take it that the philter worked then."

"No!" I jerked away. "That wasn't what was needed at all. I see what's bothering him—have a plan. Oh, Gruoth, I must talk with Enoch. Everything will be all right once he understands."

At Sext, I donned a fur hood and cape, high boots and gloves, and went to saddle Thistle. Donald came with me, over Gruoth's objections. But she needn't have carried on so, for we didn't even get as far as the Wanthwaite River. If I hadn't known every tree and shrub of the park, we would have been lost the instant we crossed the bridge, so fierce was the blizzard, so blinding the snow.

Through the long dreary afternoon we sat huddled by the fire and I sensed the Scots' unvoiced criticism. What had I done to drive Enoch to give up his life in a storm? As for me, I suffered bereavement and guilt in equal parts. 'Twas worse than when he'd fallen into the Rhône, for I could bear no responsibility for the bridge's breaking. In this case, I knew well that he was running from me.

Then the door flew open in late afternoon and they were back! Like snow-covered bears they stumbled in carrying Dugan in their arms. His toes, perhaps his feet as well, had been taken by frost and they'd had to turn back to try to save him.

"Ye've killed him wi' yer woodly journey!" Matilda accused Enoch. "I hope now ye'll stay home."

"I'm leavin' in the morning," he said stoically. "Boot I'll gae alone."

Gruoth and I joined Matilda in heating water and ale, my heart galloping in my chest. For long hours we labored over poor Dugan. Enoch thought he might lose three toes, but the others could be saved. Meantime, the wind growled around the castle and my heart sang counterpoint: be as be may, he couldn't leave in this gale.

Then I took my bold step. "Husband, 'tis time we retired." I held out my hand, defying him to refuse in front of the others.

But he did.

Raising gruff brows, he ignored my hand. "I'll sleep next to the fire."

Placing my rejected hand to my hair in a pretense of arranging a wisp, I repeated. "Nonetheless, you'll not refuse me a few moments of your time before retiring. 'Tis a matter of life and death."

Everyone was watching. Enoch pressed his lips and gazed at me wearily, as if 'twere a common tug between us.

Then he rose and walked heavily up the stair. Gruoth quickly thrust a candle in my hand and I followed.

The Scot sat on the bed, his head buried in his hands. I placed the candle on the trestle and leaned against the door so he couldn't escape without hearing me.

"I'm very glad you returned, Enoch. It gives me a chance to tell you something now."

He didn't move. I wondered if he'd gone to sleep in that position.

"You see, I've changed my mind. Now that I know . . . of course we need not seek an annulment. You understand that naturally as long as I thought you a *pimpreneau* . . ."

He raised a face haggard and sober in the dim light. "*I* want the annulment. And I'll get it."

"I know very well you don't want to be wed to me. Didn't you tell me the very first night? And of course you haven't . . ."

"And won't."

"But you went through the ceremony and so did I. And there are certain advantages so long as we understand each other. Therefore . . ."

He moved to rise and I rushed forward to stop him. Grabbed his blouse.

"I know why you don't want to be wed to me!" I cried.

"Do ye soothly?" There was a note of detached curiosity in his voice. He disentangled my hands and politely pushed me back.

"Aye, 'tis clear as water. You don't want to be wed to me because I'm a female!"

"*Quhat?*" His face showed I was right. He was interested again.

"You see, I *do* know. All I had to do was to look back. In Acre when you said: 'Betimes I'd rather have a schitten kite for a brother but I do love thee.' And in Messina when . . ."

"I remember," he said sharply. "Air ye suggestin' I'd like to be married to Alex?"

"Aye, Alex but not Alix." I almost laughed in triumph. "You want a *brother*. I might not understand if I hadn't been on Crusade but I believe most men prefer brothers to wives. The oath of chivalry and . . ."

He raised his hand. "Alix, I doona want to be wed with a boy. Alex and Alix be as alike as a pea and a pearl in my mind . . ."

"In mine too! I'll dress like a boy! Act like a boy! In time you'll forget."

Now he stood and walked into the dark. I picked up the candle to follow and found him leaning against the wall. I placed the candle on the trestle, wondered if I dare touch him now. Then he turned and his face reminded me oddly of Richard's in the depth of his despair.

"Well, I wanted to avoid this fer both our sakes, but yif you insist, and only yif ye'll speak the truth . . ."

"I promise!" My heart leaped with hope despite his tone. He must love me still.

"I doona want ye as wife because ye have changed, but I'm not referrin' to yer sex. I tried to keep ye innocent and I loved ye innocent. But when ye fell—'twas over."

"Fell? From the quintain?"

"Dinna play stupid, Alix, I warned ye. Ye knaw well what I mean."

There was a profound silence between us. From the hall below, Gruoth's voice rose in a plaintive song. I knew she was trying to help me, but I needed quiet to think.

"No, Enoch, I don't. You'll have to explain. I'm sorry."

"Very well. I doona know exactly when the foul act took place, but I learned about it the day after ye left Acre."

"Go on: 'foul act.'" My heart sank. His very tone made me feel guilty of some heinous crime, though I knew not what.

He had difficulty. "When ye became the king's mistress." He strode to the window and pretended to gaze out into the black blizzard. The wind's shriek mixed with Gruoth's wail.

"*The king's mistress!*" I laughed hysterically.

"'Tis nocht comical to me!" He turned back. His voice shook and rose in pitch. "Aye, I knaw that the two of ye mun have laughed to think how ye were foolin' the poor slubberdegullian Scot, makin' him gae into the tunnel, fight in the field and all the time ye were slaverin' and kissin' in the king's pavilion."

"You fool! Oaf! Dullard!" I screamed. "How could I be mistress to a man who loves boys? How could I have suspected that you'd sold me as a boy if I'd been making love as a girl?"

"The king himself told me! Begged me to relieve him of yer puling caresses! Sayed how he was sick of yer childish passion whan he had work to do!"

Rage at Richard overwhelmed my immediate concern. "*He* said that of *me*? How dare he! If you could have seen him weeping when he discovered the truth! Seen how he almost killed me! He thought you put me up to fooling him! Did he tell you that as well?"

"Boot I didna knaw . . ."

Now I was so angry that I no longer cared what happened. "Even so, suppose I had been the king's lover. You took doxies night and day, aye, right under my nose so that at times I had no place to bed. But did I ever accuse you?"

"Boot I'm a man!"

"We were brothers! Took an oath to let the other do as he pleased in love."

"We couldna be brothers whan ye were a girl."

"Why not? So I lost one bulge and gained two others, my character is the same! My mind! My heart! Alex is Alix, I am I!"

"And both Alex and Alix be a fool, say I, yif ye think the placement of bulges doesna matter. Men air not the same and therefore our behavior canna be the same. I have such desires ye canna dream of." He almost choked, leaned his forehead to the wall.

I recalled my boiling liver in Paris but thought it best not to argue the point.

"So because I'm female, I'm besmirched by love. Is that what you mean?"

For a moment he was struck dumb, then tried to reply in his strangled voice. "Yif ye *loved* King Richard, I canna make complaint, I grant ye."

I turned away from him, agitated. Gruoth's plaintive song rose and I sought a message in its throbbing notes.

Then, behind me, Enoch spoke again, his question tinged with dread. "Tell me soothly, Alix. *Did ye love Richard?*"

I took a long deep breath.

"Not in *that* way," I answered with absolute conviction. There was no time now to explain exactly what I'd felt, but I kenned that my future happiness depended upon persuading Enoch of my innocence. "He wore sweet woodruff as my father did, even looked like my father, and after the Rhône he said he was willing to be my parent. I clung to him because I couldn't bear to lose another father."

"Boot ye could bear to lose a brother. When ye did lose the king, ye didna cum to me; ye tried to escape me forever."

"Only because I knew you were following me," came words deep from inner recesses. "I knew you'd sought passage on Philip's ship."

"Ye knew I followed, aye, but ye ran wi' all yer might." His inexorable logic followed.

More and more affrighted by his power of argument, I became foolhardy. "You blithering idiot, I would never try to get away permanently. We fought a game of bones between us from the first hour we met, as you well know, but underneath I never wanted to win the roll. Why do you think I almost died when I thought you drowned? Why did I seek you in panic if I woke and found you gone? You know I never want to lose you! Haven't I just offered to be a boy forever if you'll stay? Please!"

There was a long silence. Gruoth no longer sang; only wind snarled in the courtyard below.

"Ye're mast cunning when ye need me, Alix. Ye have a strong bent fer survival. How do I knaw that ye want me fer myself and not fer my skills in running Wanthwaite?"

"I want you for yourself, Enoch." I took a deep breath and prepared to use my last weapon. "I swear on our treasure buried in the fruit cellar."

He stood still as a stone. Hadn't he heard me? Or understood? My heart thumped in panic.

"Nay, Alix," he said at last, his voice muffled. "That no longer be the treasure I crave."

Now I was suffocated by fear.

"I have nothing more to give. Except myself."

I saw his teeth gleam in a sudden smile.

"Air ye still offering yerself as a boy?"

My lips trembled so it was hard to answer. "Boy or girl, it doesn't matter. Whichever you prefer."

His hand reached forth, caught a strand of my hair and wound it on his finger. "Don't ye knaw?"

"Mmmm, no." I could barely speak.

"Did ye ne'er notice how oft I suggested we bed doon early in Acre? I couldna wait to put my arms around ye."

"I didn't think . . ."

"Or how I found excuse to kiss yer bonny face when we greeted, when we said farewell, when angry or glad?"

"Maybe I did . . ."

"Waesucks, I was worriet sick that I might have caught the king's complaint." His hand went to my shoulder, pulled me forward a step. "Alix, yif I stay, ye mun be my wife. Do ye ken my meaning?"

Don't think too hard, just do it. "Aye, aye," I breathed.

"And I willna sleep on the floor again." His voice was thick as velvet, and close.

My heart pounded in panic, victory, I know not what. Everything was moving so fast. Was this what I'd planned?

"I under—stand . . ."

"Alix, I love thee."

The words hung like jewels.

"*I love thee!*"

He snuffed out the candle and I fell or was pulled into his arms.

"Would never leave thee, never. Or my heart would breist."

I felt his heart drum against my cheek.

"Have yearned for thee night and day, canna bear one more instant . . ."

"Love," I echoed faintly.

He pulled at himself and great shadowy birds flew in the rafters.

"Want you, love you . . ."

"Love," I repeated giddily.

Then his lips were on mine, strange in their devouring passion, and 'twas hard to remember how well I knew him. Everything throbbed and thrummed around us and I couldn't think at all. Then he picked me up in strong possessive arms, so like and unlike former times, and I tried to recall other instances so I wouldn't be frightened but somehow couldn't for this moment was too strong, and I thought I must swoon.

He laid me on the bed where I quaked with cold and fear. Now I learned that the flying birds had been his clothes and, gently, he began to remove mine.

"Don't tremble, little love, for I adore thee soothly, would never hurt thee. Ah, my dearworth gem, wi' lips swater than any spice, swater than dews that donk the dunes . . ."

And I was warmed by his body which fit mine so perfectly and his kisses grew deeper, deeper, and an inner glow warmed me as well and all I knew was the contact between us, the center of everything.

"Oh, Alix, Alix, *there* . . ."

We were locked together, riding on Dere Street again, galloping harder and harder as the tangled trees whizzed above us and we panted in the effort to get where we were going, pounding, and I was suffused with wondrous joy as we came closer, closer and closer . . .

Fermented honey bubbles exploded all through me and I lay suspended in spreading sweetness.

I LOST ALL TRACK of the world. Our bodies wearied, quickly revived, felt exhilaration after exhilaration such as I'd never imagined. We were cooing doves, busy bees, curious cats; we mixed sweet confession with bawdy laughter and seering ecstasy. And I was happy, aye, so happy I couldn't bear my own joy. To think that we were wed! That this would go on forever! Why had no one ever told me? Fortune's Wheel whirled like a dervish.

Once, in a quiet moment while Enoch slept, I thought on Richard. I had denied him to Enoch, even as Judas had his Lord, and I sent a quiet prayer for forgiveness around the hostile globe to the king, wherever he might be. I pictured him lying under the flapping canvas of his pavilion in the winter rains, his body wrapped in cold steel instead of flesh-and-blood arms, and I pitied him with all my heart. 'Twas vain and toty for an insignificant lass to feel compassion for a great king, I knew, but for one brief period I had been privy to his heart and in some odd manner knew him better than anyone. Soothly he was the *enfant perdu par excellence*, lost from the cradle onward in a grim world of hatred, venomous rivalries and chilling rejection. By comparison, how fortunate I had been. Although I had lost those dearest to me, my father, mother, Maisry, their love still resided here as long as I drew breath. And I saw in a great awesome revelation that even my present glorious love with Enoch had built on all those former loves, including my first intense passion for Richard. No, no love should ever be denied, nor could it die even if it were not to be consummated; *therefore, Richard, forgive me*.

No sooner had I thought the words than the fur robe at the arched window billowed inward, bringing with it a breeze warm as springtime, redolent of blossoms, and a shimmering silver miasma floated across the room, then hovered directly over me. In awe, I recognized a stirring and knew that my soul had been restored. I was encapsulated in total silence, lost all sense of time or space, caught in a sweet peace I'd not felt since my father rode forth many years ago. Instantly I understood that my parents were now ready to depart for Heaven, had come to bid me final farewell, but without sadness, for we were connected by a cord of love which stretched forward and backward to all eternity.

I burrowed my face close to Enoch's strong beating heart: and I was home at last.

ACKNOWLEDGMENTS

My first published work was a short essay called "Why I Like to Read," submitted by my third-grade teacher to *Scholastic* magazine. Since that time I have read so much, absorbed so many tales, legends and histories that I cannot, with any authority, separate what is original in my work and what is a pastiche of digested lore. So to all those fantasies that became a part of me, and to the people who recounted them, I am deeply grateful.

At a more conscious level, I would like to give special recognition to a selected few of the many works that stimulated and informed my imagination during the writing of *Shield of Three Lions*. In the first chapter of Susan Brownmiller's *Against Our Will* there was a brief description of the medieval rape laws. I pursued her references, read further on my own and finally discovered the seminal work for me: *Tractabus de legibus* by Ranulf de Glanvill, written in the twelfth century for Henry II. Of the many useful biographies, I should mention *Richard the Lion Heart* by Kate Norgate, *Eleanor of Aquitaine and the Four Kings* by Amy Kelly and *England Without Richard* by J. T. Appleby. Histories of the Third Crusade were kept by the royal historians and commentaries were written by their Arab counterparts; I was particularly influenced by *The Crusade of Richard Lion-Heart* by Ambroise and translated from the Old French by Merton Jerome Herbert. The fine books on the medieval background are endless in number but the most important is *Daily Living in the Twelfth Century* by Urban Tigner Holmes, Jr. The author loosely translates one of the most informative works written during the period, *De nominibus utensilium* by Alexander Neckham. Neckham, milk-brother to Richard I, had a vigorous curiosity which he applied to every aspect of life. He traveled from Oxford to Paris where he studied, then returned to serve in the Plantagenet Court. Even writers of his own day quote him extensively. Ultimately, of course, literature itself was my best source. The period comes to life in the poignant lyrics, bawdy drinking songs, troubadour poetry and the works of Chaucer and William Dunbar.

I also visited the locations of the novel. I lived in Northern England, made rambling forays across the border, talked to Cumberland "roughs" to learn their folklore; I went to Paris, Chinon, Poitiers, Marseilles, Italy and Greece, where the old Norman Empire has left its traces.

Many of my friends, colleagues and family contributed to the book both directly and indirectly: My departments at Californian Lutheran College and

473

Santa Monica College granted me leave of absence to get the work under way; Dr. Alfred E. Longuiel, Professor of English at U.C.L.A., guided me through Chaucerian literature; then Dr. C. Warren Hollister, Professor of Medieval History at the University of California at Santa Barbara, suggested portions of the Northumberland sequence; Historian Bruce Coy read the military sections; Dorothy Seligman, Gabriel Coy, and Damiana Chavez made further valuable contributions. When the manuscript was almost finished, my agents, Richard Curtis and Susan Cohen, supplied the necessary enthusiasm and expertise to get it a proper reading. Finally, I had the great good fortune to work with a perceptive, sensitive editor in Lisa Healy.

However, it was my husband Charles A. Kaufman who provided indispensable assistance. Not only did he urge me to write and make it possible for me to do so, but he gave generously of his own professional skills to guide me through the inchoate world of writing. An author himself, he knew when to support, when to criticize, when to tell me to risk. For his patience, his intelligence, his loving tenacity, there are no words to express my gratitude to Charlie.

SCOTLAND

IRELAND

Wanthwaite Castle

NORTH SEA

SWEDEN

DENMARK

BALTIC SE

ENGLAND

London

Dover

ENGLISH CHANNEL

Boulogne

POLAND

VEXIN

Paris

SEINE RIVER

HOLY ROMAN

EMPIRE

Tours

FRANCE

Chinon

LOIRE RIVER

Vézelay

ATLANTIC OCEAN

ANGEVIN EMPIRE

ENOCH'S BRIDGE

BURGUNDY

Lyons

RHÔNE RIVER

VENICE

Venice

Genoa

Portofino

NAVARRE

Nice

ITALY

Marseilles

Rome

CASTILE

ARAGON

Salerno

N

KINGDOM OF THE TWO SICILIES

Córdoba

DOMINIONS OF THE ALMOHADS

W   E

S

Messina

SICILY

Algiers

Tunis

ALIX'S JOURNEY

palacios

0   MILES   300

Tripoli